名译选读丛书

丛书主编　华先发　熊兵

中华词曲英译名篇选读

主编　华满元　华先发

编者　华满元　华丹丹　华先发　刘　瑾　张　玲

Selected English Translations of Classical Chinese Lyrics and Arias

WUHAN UNIVERSITY PRESS

武汉大学出版社

图书在版编目(CIP)数据

中华词曲英译名篇选读/华满元,华先发主编.—武汉:武汉大学出版社,2018.8

名译选读丛书/华先发,熊兵主编

ISBN 978-7-307-20388-4

Ⅰ.中…　Ⅱ.①华…　②华…　Ⅲ.①宋词—英语—翻译理论—高等学校—教材　②元曲—英语—翻译理论—高等学校—教材　Ⅳ.①I207.23　②I207.37　③H315.9

中国版本图书馆CIP数据核字(2018)第162603号

责任编辑:罗晓华　　责任校对:汪欣怡　　版式设计:马　佳

出版发行:**武汉大学出版社**　(430072　武昌　珞珈山)

(电子邮件:cbs22@whu.edu.cn 网址:www.wdp.com.cn)

印刷:湖北金海印务有限公司

开本:787×1092　1/16　印张:30.5　字数:720千字　插页:1

版次:2018年8月第1版　　2018年8月第1次印刷

ISBN 978-7-307-20388-4　　定价:58.00元

总　序

自从国内部分高校的外语院系兴办本科和硕士翻译专业以来，我们在此领域取得了长足的进步，培养方案的制定、课程设置、教材编写及教学研究等均呈现出一派欣欣向荣的景象。然而这只是万里长征发轫之始，要想让翻译专业发展得更好，目前需做的工作还很多，编写新教材就是其一。

应该说，国内数家出版社在过去的几年中出版了许多内容丰富的翻译教材，其中也不乏在教学实践中得到好评的教本，但从教学实际的需求来看，学生更需要一些能有助于他们提升翻译能力的新教材。这种新翻译教材的设计应具有创新理念，应集名家之译作于一体，聚译笔之精华于一身，旨在通过样例的张力来启示读者，让其在阅读中体悟大家译笔之奥妙、传神之灵气，以便发现自身之不足，从而达到增强个人翻译实践能力之目的。换言之，这种教材应为学生提供模仿(imitation)的学习机会。古希腊学者亚里士多德认为，“人和动物的一个区别就在于人最善模仿，并通过模仿获得了最初的知识”(亚里士多德《诗学》)。这种模仿实质上就是“博观而约取，厚积而薄发”(苏轼《稼说“送张琥”》)，“它山之石，可以攻玉”(《诗经·小雅·鹤鸣》)。我们深信，以此思维来设计翻译教材是符合目前我国翻译专业教学实际的。本着这一理念，我们组织了以本校翻译研究中心老师为主的人员编写了这套《名译选读丛书》；全套教材共11本，分别涵盖了一些著名文学作品和非文学作品的名译。教材中每一原文后面所选一个或数个译文皆出自名家之手，希望读者阅后能够“操千曲而后晓声，观千剑而后识器”(刘勰《文心雕龙·知音》)，最终实现在翻译专业上“铁杵磨成针”之夙愿！

汉代学者王冲在《论衡·超奇篇》中曾就学问档次评论道，“故夫能说一经者为儒生，博览古今者为通人，采掇传书以上书奏记者为文人，能精思着文联结篇章者为鸿儒。故儒生过俗人，通人胜儒生，文人逾通人，鸿儒超文人。故夫鸿儒，所谓超而又超者也”。要想在翻译领域做一个鸿儒，进取之途并非平坦通畅。让我们虚心学习名家，先当通人，后做文人，继为鸿儒，终成国家建设需要的合格翻译人才！这也正是我们编写本套教材的初衷所在！

华先发

二零一四年秋于华中师范大学

前　言

宋词和元曲是我国五千年璀璨文明中的两颗璀璨明珠，其丰富的乳汁和耀眼的光芒不仅惠及代代华夏儿女，更是福泽西方文学艺术。在过去三百多年的中西文化互动过程中，大量中华词曲被翻译成外文特别是英文。其译者既有西方学者，也有中国学者。其译艺之高明，令人钦佩不已；其译笔之精彩，让人回味无穷。这些译文不仅向西方世界介绍了中华词曲的艺术风采，而且也为我们思考中国古典诗歌如何翻译成外文提供了极佳的范例。目前，我国不少高等院校的英语专业开办了翻译硕士专业。鉴于该专业培养高层次专业化的翻译人才，特别强调学生的英汉双语语言基础和翻译理论与实践方面的基础知识和技能，因此在学生学习期间为其提供高质量的译文供其模仿、学习和批评，无疑对其提高自身的翻译实践能力能起到十分积极的作用。正是出于这一考量，我们精选了部分中华词曲的英译，将之编辑成册，希望能为学习翻译的广大学生和从事翻译教学工作的教师提供一部优质教材！

本书共收集了265首中华词曲，每首均选配1至多篇英语译文，供读者学习、分析和批评。希望广大读者能从这些精选的英语译文中体悟到高雅文学作品翻译的不易、诀窍和快乐。尽管本书是为我国高校外语院校的翻译硕士而设计的，但它也适合高校翻译专业的本科生、研究生使用，同样也适合从事翻译专业教学工作的教师以及爱好翻译及从事翻译研究的人士使用。

本书由华满元、华先发二人负责总体设计，华先发负责第一章，华满元负责第二章，华丹丹负责第三章，刘瑾负责第四章，张玲负责第五章。全书编辑完稿后由华满元和华先发二人负责初审和终审定稿。华中师范大学外国语学院英语专业的硕士研究生邹风霞、李佳欣等同学均参与资料的收集和抄写工作，武汉大学出版社的谢群英老师为此书的设计、编辑和出版提供了无私的帮助。在此，我们对他们的热心帮助和无私付出表示衷心的感谢！同时，我们更应感谢的是国内外翻译家们的大力支持，特别是龚景浩先生、许渊冲教授和辜正坤教授等翻译家的热情支持，才使得本书如愿付梓。签于编辑的时间和编者的水平所限，本书难免存在瑕疵，敬请广大读者提出宝贵的批评意见。

编　者

二零一七年一月二十八日于武昌桂子山

目录

CONTENTS

第一章
宋以前

1.1　清平调词三首(李白)

一

云想衣裳花想容，春风拂槛露华浓。

若非群玉山头见，会向瑶台月下逢。

二

一枝红艳露凝香，云雨巫山枉断肠。

借问汉宫谁得似？可怜飞燕倚新妆。

三

名花倾国两相欢，长得君王带笑看。

解释春风无限恨，沉香亭北倚阑干。

〖作品简介〗

据晚唐五代人的记载，这三首词为李白在长安供奉翰林时所作。相传唐玄宗天宝二年(743年)或天宝三年(744年)春天的一日，唐玄宗和杨贵妃在宫中沉香亭观赏牡丹花时，召翰林待诏李白进宫写此三首新乐章，用来替换伶人们表演歌舞以助兴吟唱的旧日乐词。第一首，以牡丹花比贵妃的美艳；第二首，写贵妃的受宠幸；第三首，总承一、二两首，将牡丹和杨贵妃与君王融为一体：人倚阑干、花在栏外，多么优雅风流！全诗语言艳丽，句句金玉，字字流葩，人花交映，迷离恍惚，深得玄宗及贵妃的喜爱。

〖注　释〗

清平调：一种歌的曲调，“平调、清调、瑟调”皆周房中之遗声。**槛**：有格子的门窗。**华**：通花。**群玉山**：神话中的仙山，传说是西王母住的地方。**瑶台**：传说中仙子住的地方。

【译 文】

Elling Eide 译

A Suite in the Ch'ing-p'ing Mode ①

Part One

As clouds think of her clothing, as blossoms think of her face,
Spring wind caresses the railings
and dew is thick on the flowers.
If you do not find her by the Mountain of Numerous Jewels,②
You may head for the Jasper Terrace③
to meet her beneath the moon.

Part Two

A branch of red voluptuousness, the dew congealed perfume,
For clouds and rain on Sorceress Mountain,④
Why go breaking your heart?
I wonder who could be compared in the palaces of the Han?
Would it be dear Flying Swallow⑤
trying new powder and rouge?

Part Three

Beauty to topple a nation in the company of famous flowers,
They always succeed with His Majesty
Making him turn with a smile.
Knowing that the spring wind may bring regrets unending,
North of the Aloeswood Pavilion
they lean on the balustrade.

① These lyrics are believed to have been written at imperial command on an occasion in 743 or 744 when Emperor Hsüan Tsung and Precious Consort Yang (Yang Kuei-fei) were enjoying the tree peonies in the imperial gardens.

② In the wonderful realm of the mythical Queen Mother of the West, who is attended by beautiful immortals.

③ The palace of the Queen Mother of the West.

④ "Clouds and rain" are the usual figures for delicately suggesting sexual intimacy. The original dalliance that resulted in sex being associated with clouds and rain took place on Sorceress

Mountain（Wu Shan）in southwest China.

⑤ Chao Fei-yen. A beautiful Han Dynasty dancer who caught the eye of Emperor Ch'eng and ultimately became his empress in 16 B. C. E. It is said that Li Po was banished from court when the eunuch Kao Li-shih called it slanderous to compare Precious Consort Yang with Flying Swallow.

1.2 菩萨蛮（李白）

平林漠漠烟如织，寒山一带伤心碧。暝色入高楼，有人楼上愁。
玉阶空伫立，宿鸟归飞急。何处是归程？长亭更短亭。

【作品简介】

此词乃描写深秋暮色景象之作，充满离情愁绪。有人视为一首怀人之作，写思妇盼望远方行人久候而不归的心情，也有人认为它是羁旅行役者的思归之辞。宋僧文莹《湘山野录》卷上：此词不知何人写在鼎州沧水驿楼，复不知何人所撰。魏道辅泰见而爱之。后至长沙，得古集于子宣（曾布）内翰家，乃知李白所作。

【注　释】

平林：平展的树林。**漠漠**：迷蒙貌。**伤心碧**：使人伤心的碧绿色。一说"伤心"表示程度，与"极"同义。**伤心**：蜀语，要命、要死之意。**暝色**：夜色。**玉阶**：阶之美称。一作"玉梯"。**伫立**：久立。**归程**：归途。**长亭更短亭**：古代设在路边供行人休歇的亭舍。庾信《哀江南赋》云："十里五里，长亭短亭。"说明当时每隔十里设一长亭，五里设一短亭。亭，《释名》卷五：亭，停也，人所停集也。"更"一作"连"。

【译　文】

(1) Wai-lim Yip 译

Tune："BEAUTIFUL BARBARIANS"

Trees shading trees，mist-smoke weaves.
Cold mountains，a belt，of heartbreaking green.
Dusk enters a high tower；
In it someone grieves.

All alone upon the jade terrace;
Homing birds return in haste.
Where is the way to return?
Long rest, short rest, bower after bower.

(2) 许渊冲 译

Tune: "Buddhist Dancers" by Li Bai①

O'er far-flung wooded plain wreaths of smoke weave a screen,
Cold mountains stretch into a belt of sorrowful green.
    The dusk invades the tower high
    Where someone sighs a longing sigh.

    On marble steps she waits in vain,
    But to see birds fly back amain.
    Where should she gaze to find her dear?
    She sees but stations far and near.

① This poem describes the sorrow of a young woman who mounts a high tower at dusk, looking far into the wooded plain and the belt-like mountains, but fails to find her husband on his way home.

(3) Cyril Birch 译

Tune: "Strangers in Saint's Coif" (*P'u-sa man*)

Silent planes of woods woven in mist,
Cold hills a tinted thread to knot the heart.
    Dusk ascends the tall tower,
    On the tower, someone grieving.

    Aimless on this moonlit terrace
    Watching the birds' swift homing;
    Try to make out the road back—
    Halt after halt diminishing.

1.3 忆秦娥(李白)

箫声咽，秦娥梦断秦楼月。秦楼月，年年柳色，灞陵伤别。
乐游原上清秋节，咸阳古道音尘绝。音尘绝，西风残照，汉家陵阙。

【作品简介】

此词作双片四十六字，伤今怀古，托兴深远。上片以月下箫声凄咽引起，已见当年繁华梦断不堪回首。次三句，更自月色外，添出柳色，添出别情，将情景融为一片，想见惨淡迷离之叹。下片揭响云汉，摹写当年极盛之时与地。而“咸阳古道”一句，骤落千丈，凄动心目。再续“音尘绝”一句，悲感愈深。“西风”八字，只写境界，兴衰之感都寓其中。其气魄之雄伟，实冠今古。古人曾将此词誉为“百代词曲之祖”。

【注　释】

箫：一种竹制的管乐器。**咽**：呜咽，形容箫管吹出的曲调低沉而悲凉，呜呜咽咽如泣如诉。**梦断**：梦被打断，即梦醒。**灞[bà]陵**：位于今陕西省西安市东，乃汉文帝的陵墓所在地。当地有一座桥，为通往华北、东北和东南各地必经之处。《三辅黄图》卷六：“文帝灞陵，在长安城东七十里。……跨水作桥。汉人送客至此桥，折柳送别。”**伤别**：因别离而伤心。**乐游原**：又叫“乐游园”，位于长安东南郊，乃汉宣帝乐游苑之故址，因其地势较高，可俯视长安城，故是唐代游览之地。**清秋节**：指农历九月九日的重阳节，是当时人们重阳登高的节日。**咸阳古道**：咸阳，秦都，在长安西北数百里，是汉唐时期由京城往西北从军、经商的要道。古咸阳在今陕西省咸阳市东二十里。唐人常以咸阳代指长安，“咸阳古道”就是长安道。**音尘**：一般指消息，此处是指车行走时发出的声音和扬起的尘土。**残照**：落日的光辉。**汉家**：汉朝。**陵阙[què]**：皇帝的坟墓和宫殿。

【译　文】

(1) Alan Ayling and Duncan Mackintosh 译

A flute's sad notes
Break the dream of a girl in a moonlit tower of Ch'in,
A moonlit tower of Ch'in.
Yearly changing willows quicken
Parting's anguish at Pa Ling.

At Autumn Festival time on the heights of Lê-yu-yüan
The ancient road to the capital shows no sign of him,
    Shows no sign of him.
    A bleak wind: sunset paints
    In flame the imperial tombs of Han.

(2) 许渊冲 译

Tune: "Dream of a Maid of Honor" by Li Bai[①]

    The flute plays a sobbing tune,
She wakes from dreams when o'er her bower wanes the moon.
    When o'er her bower wanes the moon,
    Year after year green willows grieve
    As from the Bridge the people leave.

All's merry on Clear Autumn Day,
But she receives no word from ancient northwest way.
    And now o'er ancient northwest way
    The sun declines, the west wind falls
    O'er royal tombs and palace walls.

① This lyric depicts the solitude of a young woman who wakes from a dream of her husband on the eve of Clear Autumn Day or Mountain-climbing Day, that is, the 9th day of the 9th lunar month. It recalls her parting with him at the Bridge east of the capital. She then goes to the Merry-making Plain where she waits until sunset without seeing a messenger coming from her husband. Another commentator says that the people taking leave were those who were going to the war against the rebels in 755, so this lyric predicted the decline and fall of the Tang Empire.

1.4 渔歌子(张志和)

西塞山前白鹭飞，桃花流水鳜鱼肥。青箬笠，绿蓑衣，斜风细雨不须归。

【作品简介】

此词乃唐代词人兼画家张志和所作。作品通过描写山、水、白鹭和肥鱼、斜风细雨及悠哉自在的渔父，在秀丽的水乡风光和理想化的渔人生活中，寄托自己爱自由、爱自然的情怀。

〖注 释〗

渔歌子：词牌名。此调原为唐教坊名曲。分单调、双调二体。单调二十七字，平韵，以张氏此调最为著名。双调，五十字，仄韵。《渔歌子》又名《渔父》或《渔父乐》，大概是民间的渔歌。据《词林纪事》转引的记载说，张志和曾谒见湖州刺史颜真卿，因为船破旧了，请颜真卿帮助更换，并作《渔歌子》。词牌《渔歌子》即始于张志和写的《渔歌子》而得名。“子”即“曲子”的简称。**西塞山**：浙江湖州。**白鹭**：一种白色的水鸟。**桃花流水**：桃花盛开的季节正是春水盛涨的时候，俗称桃花汛或桃花水。**鳜[guì]鱼**：淡水鱼，江南又称桂鱼，肉质鲜美。**箬[ruò]笠**：竹叶或竹篾做的斗笠。**蓑[suō]衣**：用草或棕编制成的雨衣。**不须**：不一定要。

〖译 文〗

(1) 许渊冲 译

Tune: "A Fisherman's Song" by Zhang Zhi-he①

In front of western hills white egrets fly up and down,
In peach-mirrored stream mandarin fish are full grown.
　　In my blue bamboo hat
　　And green straw cloak, I'd fain
Go fishing careless of slanting wind and fine rain.

① Zhang Zhi-he (730-782) served in the court as a petty official and then retired to the riverside and lived in seclusion. This poem describing the happiness of a fisherman was wide spread and soon reached Japan. Even the Japanese Emperor (reigned 804-823) wrote five lyrics following the rhyme of his poem.

(2) 龚景浩 译

"Yu Ge Zi (Tang)" by Zhang Zhi He

In front of Sise Mountains① egrets fly.
Peach blossoms, running brooks and delicious trout.

A blue straw hat and green raincape② I don.
When there's slanting wind and drizzling rain,
I need not go home.

① Mountains near Suzhou(Soochow), Jiangsu Province.
② Blue straw hat and green raincape—fishermen's garb.

(3) 张炳星 译

"A Fisherman"
Zhang Zhihe

In front of the Western Hill are flying egrets.
In the peach blossom-covered stream mandarin fish are fat.
A fisherman in a green balm-bark raincoat
and a green bamboo hat is fishing in a small boat.
He needn't go home,
although he in the rain and wind is caught.

1.5　忆江南(其一)(刘禹锡)

春去也，多谢洛城人。弱柳从风疑举袂，丛兰裛露似沾巾。独坐亦含颦。

【作品简介】

此词作乃《忆江南》全两首中的一首。作者以太子宾客分司东都(洛阳)时于开成三年(838年)所作。题下原有作者自注："和乐天(即白居易)春词，依《忆江南》曲拍为句。"该词抒发了一位洛阳少女的惜春、伤春之情：她一边惋惜春天的归去，一边又觉得春天对她也有无限依恋之情。全词通过拟人化手法，不写人惜春，却从春恋人着笔，增添了全词惜春、伤春的抒情色彩。

【注　释】

多谢：殷勤致谢之意。**洛城人**：洛阳人。**袂**[mèi]：衣袖。**裛**(yì)：沾湿。**颦**[pín]：皱眉。

〖译 文〗

Jiaosheng Wang 译

Tune: "Memories of the South"
A Spring Lyric After Po Chü-yi

Spring is going, gone!
Having thankfully bid adieu
To the people of Loyang.
Willow tendrils quivering in the breeze
Wave good-bye;
Clustered orchids drip dew
To wet their handkerchiefs.
And she sits alone,
Knitting her moth-eyebrows.

1.6 竹枝词九首(其二)(刘禹锡)

山桃红花满上头，蜀江春水拍山流。花红易衰似郎意，水流无限似侬愁。

〖作品简介〗

此词描写一个失恋女子心中的痛苦。头两句写眼前景色：满山桃花红艳艳，江水拍山而流，描写了水恋山的情景。此景虽美，但恰恰勾起了失恋女的无限痛苦："花红易衰似郎意，水流无限似侬愁。"这两句用两个比喻对景抒情：花红易衰，正像郎君的爱情虽甜，但不久便衰落；而流水滔滔不绝，正好像自己的无尽愁苦。

〖注 释〗

竹枝词：巴渝民歌的一种，唱时以笛、鼓伴奏，同时起舞，乃人们于劳作之余抒发感情，去除疲惫之娱乐形式。刘禹锡在夔州，看到后极为欣赏，所以向当地人们请教，填写了很多竹枝词，这首只是其中之一。**山桃**：野桃。**上头**：山头，山顶上。

【译　文】

(1) Burton Watson 译

"BAMBOO BRANCH SONG" by LIU YÜ-HSI(772-842)

(Patterned after a folk song of the region of Shu, present-day Szechwan.)

Red blossoms of mountain peach crowd the uplands,
spring waters of Shu rivers buffet the mountains as they flow.
Crimson blossoms so quickly fading, like my lover's ardor;
flowing water so endless, like the sorrow I feel.

(2) 许渊冲 译

Tune: "Bamboo Branch Song" by Liu Yu-xi①

The mountain's red with peach blossoms above;
　　The shore is washed by spring water below.
Red blossoms will fade as my gallant's love;
　　The river as my sorrow will e'er flow.

① Liu Yu-xi(772-842) was well-known for his popular songs which depict the life and love of the common people. This song displays a happy combination of natural scenery and inner feeling of the persona.

1.7　忆江南(白居易)

江南好，风景旧曾谙。日出江花红胜火，春来江水绿如蓝。能不忆江南？

【作品简介】

此词描写江南春色，抒发了作者对江南春色的无限赞叹与怀念。

【注　释】

忆江南：词牌名，又名《望江南》《梦江南》等。据《乐府杂录》，此词又名《谢秋娘》，系唐李德裕为亡姬谢秋娘所作。分单调、双调两体。单调二十七字，双调五十四字，皆平韵。**忆**：怀念。**谙**：熟悉。**江花**：江边的花朵。一说指江中的浪花。**蓝**：一种植物，叶蓝绿色，可以用来制作染料。

〖译 文〗

(1) 龚景浩 译

"Yi Jiang Nan (Tang)"
Bo Ju Yi

Kiangnan① is an alluring land.
Oh, the sights and sounds I knew so well:
At sunrise the flowers on river banks
Were suffused with a flame-like red.
In springtime, the river water turned turquoise blue.
How can I help remembering?

① Kiangnan—Literally, south of the River, referring generally to the fertile lower Yangtze River valley just south of the River, and specifically to the more prosperous areas in Jiangsu and Zhejiang Provinces.

(2) 张炳星 译

"Recalling the South of the Yangtze River"

How beautiful are the scenes in the South
which I experienced in my youth!
At sunrise flowers by the riverside are as red as fire.
In the spring, river water is greener than emerald by far.
How can I refrain from thinking of the South?

1.8 长相思(白居易)

汴水流，泗水流，流到瓜洲古渡头。吴山点点愁。
思悠悠，恨悠悠，恨到归时方始休。月明人倚楼。

【作品简介】

此词描写一位女子倚楼怀人：上片写景，暗寓恋情；下片直抒胸臆，写女子久盼丈夫不归的怨恨。前三句用三个“流”字，写出水的蜿蜒曲折，也酿造成低徊缠绵的情韵；下面用 两个“悠悠”，更增添了愁思的绵长。全词以“恨”写“爱”，用浅易流畅的语言、和谐的音律，表现人物的相思之痛、离别之苦；特别是那一派流泻的月光，更烘托出哀怨忧伤的气氛，增强了艺术感染力，显示出这首小词言简意富、词浅味深的特点。

【注　释】

长相思：词牌名，调名取自南朝乐府“上言长相思，下言久离别”句，多写男女相思之情。**汴水**：源于河南，东南流入安徽宿县、泗县，与泗水合流，入淮河。**泗水**：源于山东曲阜，经徐州后，与汴水合流入淮河。**瓜洲古渡**：在江苏省扬州市南长江北岸。瓜洲本为江中沙洲，沙渐长，状如瓜字，故名。一作“瓜州”。**吴山**：在浙江杭州，春秋时为吴国南界，故名。此处泛指江南群山。**悠悠**：深长的意思。

【译　文】

(1) 许渊冲 译

Tune: “Everlasting Longing” by Bai Ju-yi①

　　See the Bian River flow
　　And the Si River flow!
By Ancient Ferry, mingling waves, they go,
　　The Southern hills reflect my woe.

　　My thought stretches endlessly,
　　My grief wretches endlessly,
So thus until my husband comes to me,
　　Alone on moon-lit balcony.

① Bai Ju-yi(772-846) was a popular realistic poet who served as an official in the south of the Yangzi River. This lyric depicts the longing of a young woman for the return of her husband. Leaning on the railings of a balcony on a moon-lit night, she sees the two rivers meet at the ancient ferry where people used to bid farewell, but where she cannot find her husband home-coming, so she feels the hills there saddened by her grief.

(2) 龚景浩 译

"Chang Xiang Si"

The River Pian① flows,
The River Si② flows,
They flow to the ancient ferry at Melon Shoal,
With the Wu Mountains③ dotted with gall.

The thought of you lingers,
My regret meanders.
They will only cease when you return.
In a bright moon I lean up high against the window.

①② The Pian River originates in Henan. It flows into the Si River in Jiangsu Province, at an ancient ferry crossing.

③ Wu Mountains—i. e. , the mountains of Wu, which refers generally to the region around Suzhou.

1.9 梦江南(皇甫松)

兰烬落，屏上暗红蕉。闲梦江南梅熟日，夜船吹笛雨萧萧。人语驿边桥。

【作品简介】

此词乃描写旅客思乡之作。作者先写旅邸的夜景，然后转入梦境，通过对梦中江南暮春夜景绘声绘色的描写，词人把自己的情绪全部隐藏到具体的景物背后，诗情含而不露，情景交融。落笔之处，尽显词人对故乡的深深思念之情。

【注　释】

兰烬：烛火的灰烬，因烛光似兰，故称。烬乃物体燃烧后剩下的部分。**暗红蕉**：谓更深烛尽，画屏上的美人蕉模糊莫辨。**梅熟日**：指江南夏初黄梅时节，阴雨连绵。**萧萧**：同潇潇，形容雨声。**驿**：馆驿。古代官吏住宿、换马之处。驿边有桥称驿桥。

〖译　文〗

(1) Stephen Owen 译

Tune: "Dream of the Southland" (*Meng Jiang-nan*) by Huang-fu Song (Early 9th Century)

Oil, scented with orchid, burns down in the lamp,
And on my folding screen the red
　　Banana flowers grow dark:
I peacefully dream of the Southland,
　　Of the day when plums are ripe,
Of a flute played in a boat by night,
　　As the rain pelts down,
Of someone speaking on the bridge
　　By the way station.

(2) 许渊冲 译

Tune: "The South Recalled" by Huang-fu Song①

　　Candle-wick burned,
Red cannas painted on the screen dark turned.
I dreamed of mume-fruit rip'ning on the Southern shore,
Of flute-songs played adrift one rainy night of yore,
　　Of whispers lost
In running stream below the bridge beside the post.

① Huang-fu Song was one of the precursors of the lyric poets of the "School among Flowers". This lyric describes one of his dreams on a night when the candle-wick was burned out. It reveals his nostalgia for the Southern country.

1.10　望江南(温庭筠)

梳洗罢，独倚望江楼。过尽千帆皆不是，斜晖脉脉水悠悠。肠断白蘋洲。

〖作品简介〗

这是一首闺怨词，写的是思妇楼头，望人不归。全词表现了女主人公从希望到失望以致最后“肠断”的感情。

〖注 释〗

独：独自，单一。**望江楼**：楼名，因临江而得名。**斜晖**：日落前的阳光。**晖**：阳光。**脉脉**：本作“眽眽”，凝视貌。《古诗十九首》有“盈盈一水间，脉脉不得语”。后多用以表示含情欲吐之意。**肠断**：形容极度悲伤愁苦。**白蘋**[pín]：水中浮草，色白。古时男女常采蘋花赠别。**洲**：水边陆地。

〖译 文〗

(1) Burton Watson 译

Tune: “Dreaming of the South” by WEN T’ING-YÜN (812-872)

She stops combing her hair,
lean alone from the upstairs window that looks out over the river:
a thousand sails pass by, but none of them are his.
She stares and stares at the slanting sunshine, the water flowing far away,
brokenhearted by white-weed shoals.

(2) 龚景浩 译

“Wang Jiang Nan (Tang)”
Wen Ting Yun

Her toilet over,
Alone, looking down from River View Tower:
A thousand sails glide by
But without the one she’s expecting.
A slanting sunset lingers, the river leisurely flowing.
On the Islet of Snow-White Fern her heart’s breaking.

(3) Xu Zhongjie 译

"Yijiangnan"

Washed and combed, she watches the river from above.
Many sails pass; she sees no signs of her love.
The slanting sun-rays cast a lingering glow;
The broad river in its continuous flow;
The islet with its plots of white flowers in bloom;
Each and all contribute to her utter gloom.

(4) 许渊冲 译

Tune: "Dreaming of the South"

After dressing my hair,
Alone I climb the stair.
On the railings I lean
To view the river scene.
A thousand sails pass by,
But not the one for which wait I.
The slanting sun sheds sympathetic ray;
The carefree river carries it away.
My heart breaks at the sight
Of the islet with duckweed white.

1.11　菩萨蛮(温庭筠)

小山重叠金明灭,
鬓云欲度香腮雪。
懒起画蛾眉,
弄妆梳洗迟。

照花前后镜,

花面交相映。
新帖绣罗襦,
双双金鹧鸪。

〖作品简介〗

此词写女子起床梳洗时的娇慵姿态,以及妆成后的情态,暗示了人物孤独寂寞的心境。全词把妇女的容貌写得很美丽,服饰写得很华贵,体态也写得十分娇柔,仿佛描绘了一幅唐代仕女图。词中委婉含蓄地揭示了人物的内心世界,并成功地运用反衬手法。鹧鸪双双,反衬人物的孤独;容貌服饰的描写,反衬人物内心的寂寞空虚。

〖注　释〗

小山:眉妆的名目,指小山眉,弯弯的眉毛。另外一种理解为:小山是指屏风上的图案,由于屏风是折叠的,所以说小山重叠。**金**:指唐时妇女眉际妆饰之“额黄”。**明灭**:隐现明灭的样子。**金明灭**:形容阳光照在屏风上金光闪闪的样子。一说描写女子头上插戴的饰金小梳子重叠闪烁的情形,或指女子额上涂成梅花图案的额黄有所脱落而或明或暗。**鬓云**:像云朵似的鬓发。形容发髻蓬松如云。**度**:覆盖,过掩,形容鬓角延伸向脸颊,逐渐轻淡,像云影轻度。**欲度**:将掩未掩的样子。**香腮雪**:香雪腮,雪白的面颊。**蛾眉**:女子的眉毛细长弯曲像蚕蛾的触须,故称蛾眉。一说指元和以后叫浓阔的时新眉式“蛾翅眉”。**弄妆**:梳妆打扮,修饰仪容。**罗襦**:丝绸短袄。**鹧鸪**[zhè gū]:贴绣上去的鹧鸪图,这说的是当时的衣饰,就是用金线绣好花样,再绣贴在衣服上,谓之“贴金”。

〖译　文〗

(1) Wai-lim Yip 译

“Beautiful Barbarians”

Small hills upon small hills: sungold sheen comes and goes.
Locks of hair to cross fragrant cheeks of snow.
She gets up late, carefully does her eye-lining,
And washes and combs and powders, taking her time.

To reflect a flower, front mirrors again rear mirrors.
Flower and face, each to each, shines.

Newly ironed, a petticoat of embroidered silk:
In pairs, gold partridges, going side by side.

(2) Alan Ayling and Duncan Mackintosh 译

Hills fold on fold; of shining gold, then shadow.
Hair billowing up to break on cheeks of scented snow.
Laggard to rise, she paints a moth-eyebrow,
Dallying over all she has to do.

Her mirror shows a mirrored flower behind her;
Flower and face each other's grace declare.
On silk embroidered jacket, newly pressed,
Are golden partridges, pair by pair.

(3) Zong-qi Cai 译

Layer on layer of little hills, golds shimmer and fade,
Cloud locks hover over the fragrant snow of a cheek.
Lazily rising to paint on moth eyebrows,
Dallying with makeup and hair.

Blossoms are mirrored behind and before,
Flower faces reflect one another.
Newly embroidered on a jacket of silk
Are pair after pair of golden partridges.

(4) James Liu 译

The manifold hills look golden and dark upon the panelled screen,
Her cloudy hair droops over the snow of her fragrant cheeks.
Too lazy to rise and paint her eyebrows,
Over her make-up she dallies and delays.

Mirrors before and behind reflect a flower;
The flower and her face on each other shine.

Her newly made silk jacket is embroidered,
With golden partridges flying two by two.

(5) Lois Fusek 译

Tune: "Deva-Like Barbarian"

The mountains on the screen shimmer in the golden dawn;
A cloud of hair brushes the fragrant snow of her cheek.
Lazily, she rises and paints mothlike brows;
Slowly, tardily, she gets ready for the day.

Mirrors, front and behind, reflect a flower,
Face and flower shining each upon the other.
Stitched in the silk of her bright new coat,
Golden-threaded partridges fly pair by pair.

(6) Burton Watson 译

Tune: "Deva-like Barbarian"

WEN T'ING-YUN (**812-872**)

On the many-leafed bedscreens, gold flickers and fades. ①
Her cloudy locks threaten to shroud the fragrant snow of her cheeks.
Lazily she rises, paints her moth eyebrows,
fiddles over her makeup, endlessly combing and washing.

She catches her flowery form in mirrors front and back,
reflecting her flowery face now in one, now in the other.
On her newly donned embroidered gauze jacket
are pairs and pairs of golden partridges.

① The "gold" may be the morning sun shining in on the lazy sleeper.

(7) Cyril Birch 译

Tune: "Strangers in Saint's Coif" by Wen T'ing-yun

On the bedscreen's folding panels, gold glimmers and fades.
Clouds of hair verge upon the fragrant snow of cheeks.
Languorous she rises, pencils the moth-eyebrows,
Dawdles over her toilet, slowly washing, combing.

Mirrors front and back reflect her flowers;
Face and blossoms illumine one the other.
Upon her new-embroidered silken jacket
Pairs and pairs of partridges in gold.

1.12　菩萨蛮(温庭筠)

水精帘里颇黎枕。暖香惹梦鸳鸯锦。江上柳如烟。雁飞残月天。
藕丝秋色浅。人胜参差剪。双鬓隔香红。玉钗头上风。

『作品简介』

此词是作者组词《菩萨蛮》(共十四首)的第二首，表现思妇在玉楼苦于思忆而梦魂颠倒的情景。全词上阕写她居处的环境，借助景物的烘托委婉地透露出人物的心理状态；下阕描述她的穿戴打扮，通过几个细节勾勒了人物的形貌，合起来是一幅玲珑明丽的女子怀春图。

『注　释』

颇黎：李白《玉阶怨》"却下水精帘"，李商隐《偶题》"水纹簟上琥珀枕"，表示光明洁净的境界，和这句相类。"颇黎"即玻瓈、玻璃。**"江上"两句**：张惠言《词选》评注："江上以下，略叙梦境。"后来说此篇者亦多采用张说。说实了梦境似亦太呆，不妨看作远景。详见《读词偶得》。**藕丝秋色浅**：当断句，不与下"人胜参差剪"连。藕合色近乎白，故说"秋色浅"，不当是戴在头上花胜的颜色。这里"藕丝"是借代用法，把所指的本名略去，古词常见。如温庭筠另首《菩萨蛮》"画罗金翡翠"不言帷帐；李璟《山花子》"手卷真珠上玉钩"不言帘。这里所省名词，当是衣裳。作者另篇《归国谣》："舞衣无力风敛，藕丝秋色染"，可知。李贺《天上谣》："粉霞红绶藕丝裙。"**胜**：花胜，以人日为之，亦称"人胜"。《荆楚岁时记》："正月七日为人日……剪彩为人，或镂金簿(箔)为人以贴屏风，亦戴之头鬓；又造华胜以相遗。”华胜男女都可以戴；有时亦戴小幡，合称幡胜。到宋时这风俗犹存，见《梦粱录》《武林旧事》“立春”条。**香红**：指花，即以之代花。此处“隔”字用得颇为讲究，因为双鬓正是隔开在脸庞两边，形象鲜明如见，而且仿佛“双鬓”有了某种主动性，还似有若无地流露出一丝遗憾不足的意味。**玉钗头上风**：幡胜摇曳，“花气”摇荡，都在春风中。作者《咏春幡》诗“玉钗风不定，香步独徘徊”意境相近。

〖译　文〗

Stephen Owen 译

Tune: “Boddhisattva Barbarian” by Wen Ting-yun (d. 870)

Inside a curtain of crystal,
　　on a pillow of lapis lazuli,
warm incense coaxes a dream,
　　bedspread embroidered with lovebirds:
beside the river, willows like mist,
wild geese flying and a sky
　　of dying moonlight.

Threads of lotus root, fall colors pale,
cloth figures cut in various forms,
two long tresses blocked by scented red,
and the jade hairpin: wind on her head.

1.13　菩萨蛮(温庭筠)

玉楼明月长相忆，柳丝袅娜春无力。门外草萋萋，送君闻马嘶。
画罗金翡翠，香烛销成泪。花落子规啼，绿窗残梦迷。

〖作品简介〗

此词是作者组词《菩萨蛮》(共十四首)的第六首，表现思妇在玉楼苦于思忆而梦魂颠倒的情景。全词起两句为入梦，结两句为梦醒，“门外”两句为梦中幻景，“画罗”两句为梦时衬景，从室外写到室内，由梦前写到梦后，层次分明，脉络清晰，兼有幽深、精绝之美。

『注　释』

玉楼：楼的美称。**袅娜**[niǎo nuó]：细长柔美貌。**春无力**：即春风无力，用以形容春风柔软。**萋萋**：草茂盛貌。

『译　文』

(1) Cyril Birch 译

Tune: "Strangers in Saint's Coif" by Wen T'ing-yun

There in her moonlit chamber she is dreaming of him still
How delicate the willows, how languorous the spring!
In the grasses growing thick outside the gate
She hears his horse neigh as she waves goodbye....

By her colored quilt with kingfishers worked in gold
The scented candle has melted into tears.
Among the falling blossoms a nightjar cries
And behind her green-gauze window the dream dissolves.

(2) James Liu 译

"P'u-sa Man"
Wen T'ing-yun

In the moonlit bower of jade memory of you for ever dwells.
The silk willow twigs are swinging, soft and weak as spring.
The grass was growing thick beyond our gate;
Seeing you off, I heard the horse's neigh.

Behind the curtain gilt with kingfishers,
The perfumed candle has dissolved in tears.
Amid the fading flowers and the cuckoo's cries,
A broken dream still haunts my window green.

1.14 菩萨蛮(温庭筠)

翠翘金缕双鸂鶒，水纹细起春池碧。池上海棠梨，雨晴红满枝。
绣衫遮笑靥，烟草粘飞蝶。青琐对芳菲，玉关音信稀。

〖作品简介〗

此词的上阕写鸂鶒鸟在春池中掀起粼粼水纹，两情欢洽，树上棠梨花开，雨后新晴，红花满枝，景色幽美，气象清新；下阕先以真实的描绘直写女主人公的欢愉之情，后转写音信稀，表现她的孤寂之情。前六句写美景是为后两句写哀情作反衬。

〖注　释〗

翠翘：翠绿色的尾羽。**金缕**：金色羽毛。**鸂鶒**[xī chì]：水鸟，似鸳鸯而比鸳鸯略大，多紫色，喜雌雄并游，又名紫鸳鸯。**海棠梨**：又名海红、甘棠，二月开红花，八月果熟。一说就是海棠花，又一说即棠梨。**靥**[yè]：笑时面颊上的酒窝。**青琐**：刷青漆且雕镂有连琐纹的窗户，泛指华美的窗户。此处借指华贵之家。周祈《名义考》云："青琐，即今之门有壳隔者，刻镂为连琐纹也。以青涂之，故曰青琐。"**芳菲**：泛指花草树木，谓美好时节。**玉关**：即玉门关，在今甘肃敦煌西北，隋唐时的遗址，大约在今甘肃安西县城东50公里处的疏勒河岸双塔堡附近。

〖译　文〗

Cyril Birch 译

Tune："Strangers in Saint's Coif" by Wen T'ing-yun

Blue tail-feathers and markings of gold on a pair of mandarin ducks,
And tiny ripples of water stirring the blue of a pond in spring;
Beside the pond there stands a crabapple tree,
Its branches filled with pink after the rain.

Her figured sleeve covers a dimpled smile
As a flying butterfly lights on the mistlike grass.

Her window gives on all this loveliness—
And news so seldom comes from the Jade Pass![1]

① Frontier garrison west of Tun-huang.

1.15 菩萨蛮(温庭筠)

其十一

南园满地堆轻絮，愁闻一霎清明雨。雨后却斜阳，杏花零落香。
无言匀睡脸，枕上屏山掩。时节欲黄昏，无聊独倚门。

其十二

夜来皓月才当午，重帘悄悄无人语。深处麝烟长，卧时留薄妆。
当年还自惜，往事那堪忆。花落月明残，锦衾知晓寒。

〖作品简介〗

此两首词是作者组词《菩萨蛮》(共十四首)中的两首。前一首写的是一独处闺中女子在春暮时节昼睡醒来时的形态。其上阙点明了时节：春暮飞柳絮，杏花残留香；同时也点明了人情，惜杏花落，闻雨而愁，“愁”“闻”二字将其展露无疑。下阙点明主人公是刚刚睡醒，睡脸依旧。后一首被视为是温词十四首《菩萨蛮》中的上乘之作。此词写思妇长夜难眠的情态，通过由室外而室内、由环境而人情、由往昔回忆而眼前现实的布景转换，写透了思妇心境，刻画了思妇的无限哀怨。词首写美人半夜独眠，写景如画。“皓月当午”写出了时分，“重帘悄悄”则说明地点是闺房深处，同时写出了院落的幽静。在这种幽静的气氛之下相思之情悠然而生。三四句描写周围的情景，将一二句所营造的气氛进一步表现出来。五六句写追忆往事，流年似水，不堪回首。“花落月明残”一句虚写，系美人所感受之景，恰是露残月明，更引起人物的伤春之感。“锦衾知晓寒”之“知”字尤为巧妙，不写人但将人的感受十分逼真地刻画出来。陈廷焯《词则·大雅集》中评曰：“知”字凄警，与“愁人知夜长”同妙。

〖注 释〗

一霎：一阵子。**却**：再，又。“**无言匀睡脸，枕上屏山掩**”句：这两句说的就是独处闺中女子醒来时的寂寥形态。“无言”意即无人来说话，说明孤独之意。“屏山”意即画着山水的屏风。“匀”此处作动词，是说把胭脂匀抹在脸上。“**无聊独倚门**”句：倚门看黄昏结束。黄昏鸟兽均归巢团聚，而自己只能独处闺中，可见悲伤孤独之意。**当午**：指月亮悬于正中天。**帘**：疆村本《尊前集》作“门”。**麝烟**：火燃麝香所散发的香烟。唐人成彦雄

《夕》:“台榭沉沉禁漏初。麝烟红烛透虾须。”“烟”,本作“香”。**卧时**:本作“梦魂”。**薄妆**:淡妆。薄妆者与浓妆相对,谓浓妆既卸,犹稍留梳裹,脂粉匀面。古代妇女浓妆高髻,梳裹不易,睡时稍留薄妆,支枕以睡,使髻发不致散乱。**“花落”**句:谓拂晓前残月尚明。**锦衾**[qīn]:锦制的被子。《诗经·唐风·葛生》:“角枕粲兮,锦衾烂兮。”

【译 文】

Cyril Birch 译

Tune: “Strangers in Saint’s Coif” by Wen T’ing-yun

In the southern courtyard everywhere willow floss covers the ground.
Sadly she listens to the sound of a sudden spring’s-end shower;
After the rain, the slanting rays of sunset
And scent of almond blossoms fallen and scattered.
She silently makes up her sleepy face
And sets the folding screen about her pillow.
The time of day is nearing yellow twilight
As languorous and alone she leans by the gate.

A brilliant moon has just now reached the zenith of the night.
Behind the lowered blind all’s still, no one to say a word.
Secluded there amid perpetual incense
She goes to bed in her same old careless make-up.
Sufficient are her sorrows of this year—
How could she bear to think about the past?
Flowers lie fallen as the moonlight pales,
And under her quilt she knows the chill of dawn.

1.16 更漏子(温庭筠)

玉炉香,红蜡泪,偏照画堂秋思。眉翠薄,鬓云残,夜长衾枕寒。
梧桐树,三更雨,不道离情正苦。一叶叶,一声声,空阶滴到明。

【作品简介】

此词抒写思妇之离愁:上阕写室内物象,虽是温暖祥和的场景,但孤独的思妇辗转难眠而容颜不整，鬓发散乱，忍受着枕衾间的寒冷与痛苦；下阕通过写思妇在室内听到室外的雨声来描摹人物的心情。全词从室内到室外，从视觉到听觉，从实到虚，构成一种浓郁的愁境。上阕辞采密丽，下阕疏淡流畅，一密一疏，一浓一淡，情感变化发展自然。

【注　释】

更漏子：词牌名。《尊前集》入“大石调”，又入“商调”。《金奁集》入“林钟商调”。四十六字，前片两仄韵，两平韵，后片三仄韵，两平韵。该词牌类似渊源于欧洲中世纪骑士文学的《小夜曲》，歌唱的是午夜情事。**更漏**：古人用铜壶滴漏来计时，将一夜分为五更。**子**：曲子的简称。**鬓云**：鬓发如云。**梧桐**：落叶乔木，古人以为是凤凰栖止之木。**不道**：不管、不理会的意思。**空阶滴到明**：语出南朝何逊《临行与故游夜别》：“夜雨滴空阶。”

【译　文】

(1) Zong-qi Cai 译

To the Tune of "On the Water Clock at Night"

Incense in the jade burner,
Red wax tears
Unbidden, reflect an autumn mood in the painted hall.
Blackened brows fade,
Cloud locks are tousled,
The night is long, quilt and pillow cold.

Wutong trees and
Third-watch rain are
Unaware of separation throes.
Leaf after leaf,
Sound by sound
Drips on the empty steps 'til dawn.

(2) James Liu 译

An incense-burner of jade,
A red candle in tears:
Why do they reflect autumn thoughts in the painted room?
Her eyebrowns losing their colour,

Her cloudy hair disheveled,
Her pillow and quilt grow cold in the lengthy night.

Upon the wu-t'ung trees
The midnight rain is beating,
Indifferent to the bitter sorrow of parted lovers.
Leaf after leaf,
Drop after drop—
They fall on the empty steps till break of day.

(3) Robert Kotewall and Norman L. Smith 译

To the tune of *The Waterclock*

Jade incense-burner's fragrance,
Red candle's tears,
Unevenly light the decorated chamber's sadness.
Eyebrows' black thin,
Tresses' clouds fallen:
Night long, coverlet and pillow cold.

Wu-t'ung trees,
Third watch rain,
Care not for separation's sorrow's utter bitterness.
Single leaf by leaf,
Single sound by sound,
On the empty steps dripping until dawn.

1. 17　更漏子(温庭筠)

柳丝长，春雨细，花外漏声迢递。惊塞雁，起城乌，画屏金鹧鸪。
香雾薄，透帘幕，惆怅谢家池阁。红烛背，绣帘垂，梦长君不知。

【作品简介】

此词描写一位女子长夜闻更漏声而触发的相思与惆怅。上阕围绕“漏声”写相思中的女子对外界的种种感受和印象，下阕承上，转写主人公的居处环境。

【注　释】

漏声：指报更报点之声。**迢递**[tiáo dì]：遥远。**塞雁**：北雁，春来北飞。**城乌**：城头上的乌鸦。**画屏**：有图饰品的屏风，为女主人公居室中的摆设。**金鹧鸪**[zhè gū]：金线绣成的鹧鸪，可能绣在屏风上，也可能是绣在衣服上的。**薄**：通"迫"，逼来。**惆怅**[chóu chàng]：失意、烦恼。**谢家池阁**：豪华的宅院，这里即指女主人公的住处。谢氏为南朝望族，居处多有池阁之胜，后来便成为一共名。韦庄《归国遥》词中有"日落谢家池阁"句。**红烛背**：背向红烛；一说以物遮住红烛，使其光线不向人直射。

【译　文】

(1) James Liu 译

"Keng Lou Tz'u(Song of the Water-clock at Night)"

　　The willow twigs are long,
　　The spring rain is drizzling,
While endless runs the water-clock beyond the flowers.
　　Rousing the crows on the citadel,
　　The wind geese on the frontier,
And the golden partridges on the painted screen.

　　A light fragrant mist
　　Drifts in through the curtain:
The ponds and pavilions of the Hsiehs are full sorrow.
　　Sheltered from the candle,
　　Behind the embroidered curtain,
　　Long I dream, but you are unaware!

(2) Cyril Birch 译

Tune: "Water-clock" (*Keng-lou tzu*)

Willows boughs long,
Spring rain thin;
Faint beyond the blossoms sounds the night-watch.
Startling migrant geese,

Rousing the crows on the walls…
Here on the painted screen, the partridges are gilt.

Tenuous wisps of fragrance
Seep through layered curtains
Where languishes a Lady Hsieh amid her pools and courts.
Shading the crimson candle
She lowers the patterned blind;
Her dreams endure, but he will never know.

1. 18 酒泉子(司空图)

买得杏花，十载归来方始坼。假山西畔药阑东，满枝红。
旋开旋落旋成空，白发多情人更惜。黄昏把酒祝东风，且从容。

〖作品简介〗

此词感时伤世，借花抒怀，由种花、赏花、惜花，进而祝告东风，乞驻春光护花，寄寓了忧国之思。

〖注　释〗

坼[chè]：裂开。**旋**：片刻之间。**从容**：舒缓，不急进。

〖译　文〗

龚景浩 译

"Jiu Quan Zi (Tang)"
Sikong Tu

I bought apricot trees.
Ten years later they bloomed: not until I returned home.
Planted west of the garden rockeries,
East of the herbal plot,
The apricot blossoms opened a lovely pink.

The flowers opened, then fell, as if they'd never been.
The deep emotions of a hoary man
Are to be cherished all the more.
At dusk I raised a wine cup to the east wind and prayed:
Prithee, go easy with the world.

1.19　如梦令(李存勖)

曾宴桃源深洞，一曲清歌舞凤。长记别伊时，和泪出门相送。如梦，如梦，残月落花烟重。

『作品简介』

此词为忆旧抒感的小令，写得缠绵悱恻、意蕴深沉。

『注　释』

如梦令：词牌名。胡仔《苕溪渔隐丛话》："东坡言《如梦令》曲名，本唐庄宗制。一名《忆仙姿》。嫌其不雅，改名《如梦令》。庄宗作此词，卒章云'如梦，如梦，和泪出门相送。'取之以为词名。"**清歌舞凤**：亦作"舞鸾歌凤"，鸾凤，鸾鸟和凤凰，古代传说中吉祥美丽的鸟。

『译　文』

(1) C. H. Kwôck and Vincent McHugh 译

Tune: "Memories of Fairy Grace" (*Yi hsin-tzu*)

Feasted once
　　in deep peach glades
One song
　　phoenix to phoenix
　　danced and sang
I recall
　　—how long!
　　Saying goodbye to her

Tears mingled together
　　hand on arm to the door
　　like a dream
　　like a dream
faded moon
fallen blossoms
　　thick mist
　　over all

(2) 龚景浩 译

"Ru Meng Ling"① by Li Cun Xu

I've feasted in a deep cave in Peach Blossom Land,
A lovely song accompanying the Phoenix Dance.
I shall long remember the hour we part:
With tears in her eyes
She sees me off to the gate.
All this is like a dream, a dream:
A waning moon; falling petals; and heavy mist.

1.20 山花子(其二)(和凝)

银字笙寒调正长，水纹簟冷画屏凉。玉腕重金扼臂，淡梳妆。
几度试香纤手暖，一回尝酒绛唇光。佯弄红丝蝇拂子，打檀郎。

【作品简介】

此词描写闺房中一对情侣饮酒吹笙的逗趣之乐。上片描写的是秋夜的寒凉天气，词人饮着酒，听一位女子吹笙奏乐。那女子手中的笙管幽寒而音调悠长，身下的竹席清冷而屏风冰凉。吹笙女子雪白的手腕上戴着金圈，手臂上戴金钏，因而使手腕显得沉重。她薄施脂粉，淡扫娥眉，衣着素净，风韵宛然。下片刻画的是女子的行动：一曲吹奏完了，几次将那纤纤素手伸向香炉试探取暖，又端起酒杯尝一口酒，红唇泛起了湿润的光泽。词人调笑了她几句，她嫣然一笑，随手拿起红丝蝇拂子，娇嗔地打向情郎。全词表现了一个风情万种、艺色双全的撒娇女子情态。

〖注　释〗

银字笙：一种笙管乐器，银字是笙管上音阶的标记之类。《古今词话·词品》："银字制笙，以银作字，饰其音节。'银字笙调'，蒋捷句也；'银字吹笙'，毛滂句也。"**水纹簟**：水纹竹席。**"簟"**[diàn]：本义为竹席，古诗词中总是与美人、秋夜、梦境、孤独等一起构成一种清寒寂寞的意境。如李商隐《细雨》一诗："帷飘白玉堂，簟卷碧牙床。楚女当时意，萧萧发彩凉。"**玉腕重金扼臂，淡梳妆**：女子手腕上戴着金圈，手臂上戴金钏，使手腕显得沉重。这表明衣着不多，才能见到玉腕。所以梳妆也是薄施脂粉，淡扫娥眉。**金扼臂**：古代女性缠绕于臂的一种装饰，用金银带条盘绕成螺旋圈状，其盘圈数一般三至八圈，也有多到十二三圈的，两端另用金银丝编制成环套，通过它与钏体衔接后调节松紧。又叫做"缠臂金"(苏东坡《寒具》诗中有"夜来春睡浓于酒，压褊佳人缠臂金")，或曰"臂钏"，别名叫"跳脱"。**纤手**：纤纤素手。**蝇拂子**：一种扑打蝇蚊的器物，用丝或马尾制成。**檀郎**：代称美男子。西晋的潘岳(即潘安)姿仪秀美超群，其小字为檀奴，后被人称为檀郎。到了唐代，人们常以檀郎称婿。罗隐《七夕》诗："应倾谢女珠玑箧，尽写檀郎锦绣篇。"这里是对意中情郎的爱称。

〖译　文〗

Stephen Owen 译

Tune: "Mountain Flower" (*Shan-hua-zi*) by He Ning (898-955)

Cold notes from silver-inlay pipes,
　　a melody held long.
Chill is the ripple-patterned mat,
　　cool the painted screen.
Her alabaster wrist weighed down
　　with bracelets of gold,
hair combed, and lightly made up.

Again and again she adds incense,
　　her ruby lips gleam.
Feigning to play with the red strands
　　of the fly-whisk,
she swats her true love.

1.21 长命女(冯延巳)

春日宴，绿酒一杯歌一遍。再拜陈三愿：一愿郎君千岁，二愿妾身常健，三愿如同梁上燕，岁岁长相见。

〖作品简介〗

此词写春日开宴，夫妇双方祝酒陈愿。词以妇人口吻陈愿，用语浅近而又含蓄，带有民歌情调。末两句以梁燕双栖喻夫妻团圆，天长地久。

〖注　释〗

长命女：词牌名。**绿酒**：古时米酒酿成未滤时，面浮米渣，呈淡绿色，故名。**陈**：陈述。

〖译　文〗

Robert Kotewall and Norman L. Smith 译

To "The Long-lived Woman"

A spring day's feast,
One cup of green wine, one catch of song.
I bow again and utter three wishes;
First, I wish my good man long life;
Second, I wish for myself ever good health;
Third, I wish that we be like the swallows in the rafters,
Yearly meeting without a break.

1.22 清平乐(冯延巳)

雨晴烟晚，绿水新池满。双燕飞来垂柳院，小阁画帘高卷。
黄昏独倚朱阑，西南新月眉弯。砌下落花风起，罗衣特地春寒。

【作品简介】

这首词描写的是女子独居伤怀、望夫归来的情景。上片描写了一派绿意盎然的春色，下片“独倚”二字点出女主人公等待归人的淡淡哀怨与怅恨。

【注　释】

独倚：独自倚靠。**砌**：台阶。**特地**：特别。

【译　文】

龚景浩 译

“Qing Ping Yue：(Five Dynasties)

Feng Yan Si

Sunshine after rain; then a misty evening,
Blue water newly filled the pond.
Two swallows flew into a garden of weeping willows,
With painted curtains rolled up high
In the snug penthouse.

Alone at dusk, leaning on the vermilion railing,
In the southwest the eyebrow of a new moon rising.
A wind whipped up fallen petals beneath the steps.
Wearing satin, I was suddenly chilled
By the onslaught of spring.

1.23　蝶恋花(冯延巳)

谁道闲情抛弃久？每到春来，惆怅还依旧。
日日花前常病酒，不辞镜里朱颜瘦。
河畔青芜堤上柳，为问新愁，何事年年有？
独立小桥风满袖，平林新月人归后。

【作品简介】

此词抒写了一片难以指实的、浓重的感伤之情，大有“春花秋月何时了，往事知多少”的那种对于整个人生的迷惘和无法解脱的苦闷，同时包含着主人公对美好事物的无限眷恋，以及他甘心为此憔悴的执著感情。“独立小桥风满袖，平林新月人归后”两句，表现了主人公如有所待，又若有所失的情状，语淡而意远。

【注　释】

蝶恋花：词牌名。清王鹏运《半塘丁稿·鹜翁集》云：“冯正中《鹤踏枝》十四首，郁伊倘况，义兼比兴。”调名即《蝶恋花》。“**谁道**”句：近人梁启超云：“稼轩《摸鱼儿》起处从此脱胎。文前有文，如黄河液流，莫穷其源。”(《阳春集笺》引)。**闲情**：即闲愁、春愁。**病酒**：饮酒过量引起身体不适。**不辞**：不避，不怕。**朱颜**：青春红润的面色，这里指红润的脸色。

【译　文】

(1) James Liu 译

“Tieh Lüan Hua”

Who says that this idle feeling has long been left aside?
Whenever spring comes, my melancholy returns as before.
Every day, before the flowers, I'm ill with too much drinking,
Yet dare I refuse to let my image in the mirror grow thin?

O you green grass by the river and willows on the dam,
Pray tell me: why does new sorrow arise with each year?
Alone on a little bridge I stand, my sleeves filled with wind;
The new moon rises above the woods and everyone else is gone.

(2) Alan Ayling and Duncan Mackintosh 译

Who can say his listless moods
Were thrown off long ago?
Each time spring comes in
It's the old heart-ache still.

Blossom has always led to wine
　　leaving me so ill
How can I avoid my mirrored face
　　grown worn and thin?

River path and river bank,
　　green of grass and willow,
　　What is it freshly grieves
　　Each year, what brings it on?
I stand on the little bridge alone,
　　the wind filling my sleeves
　　At tree-top level a new moon.
　　Now everyone is gone.

1.24　渔歌子(李煜)

浪花有意千重雪，桃李无言一队春。
一壶酒，一竿纶，世上如侬有几人?
一棹春风一叶舟，一纶茧缕一轻钩。
花满渚，酒满瓯，万顷波中得自由。

〖作品简介〗

此词调名亦作《渔父》，《历代诗余》中作《渔歌子》。据宋阮阅《诗话总龟》载：“予尝于富商高氏家，观贤画《盘车水磨图》，及故大丞相文懿张公弟，有《春江钓叟图》，上有南唐李煜金索书《渔父词》二首。其一曰：‘浪花有意千里雪……’其二曰：‘一棹春风一叶舟……’。”词中所写皆反映后主为情势所迫，沈潜避祸，隐遁世尘并写词表露自己的遁世之心，以释文献太子的疑嫉。

〖注　释〗

浪花：《词谱》《花草粹编》中均作“阆[làng]苑”。阆苑，传说中神仙居住的地方。**有意**：本作“有情”。**千重雪**：《词谱》《花草粹编》《历代诗余》中均作“千里雪”。千重，千层，层层叠叠。**桃李**：《历代诗余》《全唐诗》《诗话总龟》中均作“桃花”。**一队春**：指桃李盛开，由近及远，好像队列一样有序排列着，实言春色正浓，春意盎然。**一竿纶**：一根钓竿。**侬[nóng]**：指我，江南口语。**纶**：《五代名画补遗》中作“轮”。纶，钓鱼用的粗丝线。**棹[zhào]**：划船的一种工具，形状和桨差不多。**缕[lǚ]**：线。**渚[zhǔ]**：水中小块陆地。瓯[ōu]：指中国古代酒器，形为敞口小碗式。

【译 文】

(1) Burton Watson 译

Tune: "The Fisherman"

(*From early times in Chinese literature the solitary fisherman has been idealized as a symbol of perfect freedom.*)

1.
Wave blossoms for my delight, a thousand sheets of snow;
peach blossoms wordless, the regiments of spring:
one pot of brew,
one pole and line—
in this world we live in, how many men like me?

2.
One scull in the spring wind, one leaf of a boat;
one thread of silk line, one light hook:
blossoms fill the shore,
wine fills the jug—
ten-thousand-acre waves—I roam them as I please!

(2) Robert Kotewall and Norman L. Smith 译

To "The Fisherman"
(Two Poems)

SPRAYS of wave purpose to make a thousand layers of snow;
Peach and plum trees, wordless, make Spring's cluster.
A bottle wine,
A rod and reel—
In all the world how few are so well off as I?

A PADDLE in spring's breeze, a leaf-like boat,

A silken line, a slender hook,
Flower-filled islet,
Wine-filled flask—
In the myriad ripples I attain freedom.

1.25　菩萨蛮(李煜)

花明月暗笼轻雾，今宵好向郎边去。
刬袜步香阶，手提金缕鞋。
画堂南畔见，一向偎人颤。
奴为出来难，教君恣意怜。

『作品简介』

此词描写小周后与作者欢爱之事：一个繁花盛开、月光淡淡的夜晚，一个少女与情人幽会的情形。

『注　释』

月暗：月光淡淡。**笼轻雾**：笼罩着薄薄的晨雾。笼，一作“飞”；一作“水”。**今宵**：今夜。**郎边**：一作“侬边”。**刬**[chǎn]：《全唐诗》及《南唐书》中均作“衩”。刬，只，仅，犹言“光着”。刬袜，只穿着袜子着地。唐《醉公子》词中有：“刬袜下香阶，冤家今夜醉。”**步**：这里作动词用，意为走过。**香阶**：台阶的美称，即飘散香气的台阶。**手提**：一作“手携”。**金缕鞋**：指鞋面用金线绣成的鞋。缕，线。**画堂**：古代宫中绘饰华丽的殿堂，这里也泛指华丽的堂屋。**南畔**：南边。**一向**：同一晌，即一时，刹时间。**偎**：紧紧地贴着，紧挨着。一作“畏”。**颤**：由于心情激动而身体发抖。**奴**：一作“好”。奴，古代妇女自称的谦词，也作奴家。**出来**：一作“去来”。**教君**：让君，让你。一作“教郎”；一作“从君”。**恣**[zì]**意**：任意，放纵。恣，放纵，无拘束。**怜**：爱怜，疼爱。

『译　文』

(1) Burton Watson 译

Tune: “Deva-like Barbarian”

Blossoms bright, the moon dark, shadowed in thin mist,
tonight’s just right for making my way to you—

In stocking feet she goes out by the scented stairs,
holding in her hand her gold-threaded slippers.

On the south side of the painted hall she sees him,
clings to him for a time, trembling—
It's so hard for me to slip away,
tonight you may love me any way you please!

(2) Stephen Owen 译

Tune: "Boddhisattva Barbarian" (*Pu-sa man*)

The flowers are bright, the moon is dark,
  veiled beneath light fog:
tonight would be the perfect time
  to go and see her love.
She treads the stairs in stocking feet,
holding in hand
  slippers with golden threads.

To the south of the painted hall they meet,
she trembles a moment in his arms.
"It's so hard to get out now—
let's grab all the pleasure we can."

1.26 清平乐(李煜)

别来春半，触目柔肠断。砌下落梅如雪乱，拂了一身还满。
雁来音信无凭，路遥归梦难成。离恨恰如春草，更行更远还生。

【作品简介】

此词表现了作者在恼人的春色中，触景生情，思念离家在外的亲人的情景。

【注　释】

别来春半：意思是，自分别以来，春天已过去一半，说明时光过得很快。“春半”即半春，春天的一半。唐代柳宗元《柳州二日》诗中有句：“宦情羁思共凄凄，春半如秋意转迷。”**柔**：吕本二主词、吴本二主词、侯本二主词、《尊前集》《全唐诗》《词综》等本中均作“愁”。柔肠，原指温柔的心肠，此指绵软情怀。**砌[qì]下**：台阶下。砌，台阶。**落梅**：指白梅花，开放较晚。全句意思是，台阶下飘落的白梅花犹如雪片纷飞。**拂了一身还满**：指把满身的落梅拂去了又落了满身。**雁来音信无凭**：这句话是说鸿雁虽然来了，却没将书信传来。古代有凭借雁足传递书信的故事。《汉书·苏武传》中记载：“天子射上林中，得雁，足有系帛书。”故见雁就联想到了所思之人的音信。“无凭”意为无凭证，指没有书信。**遥**：远。**归梦难成**：指有家难回。**恰如**：《全唐诗》《古今词统》《古今诗余醉》等本中均作“却如”；毛本《尊前集》中作“怯如”。**更行更远还生**：更行更远，指行程越远。更，越。还生，还是生得很多。还，仍然，还是。

『译 文』

(1) Burton Watson 译

Tune："Pure Serene Music"

Since we parted, spring half over.
everywhere I look, grief overwhelms me.
Below the steps, fallen plum petals like tumbles of snow—
I brush them off only to be covered with them again.

Wild geese arrive but bring no letters.
The road's so long, even in dreams it's hard to go home.
This pain of separation is like the spring grass—
the farther away I journey, the ranker it grows.

(2) Jiaosheng Wang 译

Tune："Pure Serene Music"

Spring is half gone since we parted.
My heart breaks when I see
Snowy plum petals at the foot of the stairs in disarray
That all but cover my body
For all my brushing.

Wild geese come back—can I trust the message they bring?
The way so long—no use to dream of returning.
The pain of separation is just like the spring grass:
The more it grows, the farther away you are.

(3) Alan Ayling and Duncan Mackintosh 译

Since I left spring's half gone by.
All I look at feeds my misery.
Down garden steps plum blossom petals fall, in snow-drifts lie;
You brush them off and still its snow you're covered by.

The wild geese have flown in yet there's no trace of news.
The journey is too long even in dreams to dare.
The bitter grief of leaving is like the spring grass;
However far you go you find it growing there.

1.27 子夜歌(李煜)

人生愁恨何能免,
销魂独我情何限。
故国梦重归,
觉来双泪垂。

高楼谁与上,
长记秋晴望。
往事已成空,
还如一梦中。

【作品简介】

此词作全称为《子夜歌·人生愁恨何能免》,是后主入宋后的作品,表达了亡国之君的悲痛及其对故国的无限思念。

【注 释】

独我:只有我。**何限**:无限。**重归**:别作“初归”。**谁与**:与谁。**秋情**:晴朗的秋天。

【译　文】

Burton Watson 译

Tune："Song of Tzu-yeh"

Life's sorrows and regrets—who can escape them?
But I alone waste away my soul in thoughts that have no end.
To my old kingdom in dreams I return once more,
and when I wake, tears stream down in pairs.

The high tower—who's to climb it with me?
Autumn's clear vista as I've known it for so long,
but past events have turned to emptiness,
become like things in a dream.

1.28　望江南（李煜）

多少恨，昨夜梦魂中。还似旧日游上苑，车如流水马如龙，花月正春风。

【作品简介】

此词为作者亡国入宋后所作。全词写梦忆江南，以反写正，以乐写悲，以欢情写凄苦，昔与今的对比形成了极大的反差，抒发了作者的故国之思和亡国之痛。

【注　释】

此词调名于《花草粹编》中注云："一名《梦游仙》《梦江南》《江南好》。"《全唐诗》《词谱》等均作《忆江南》。**梦魂**：古人认为在睡梦中人的灵魂会离开肉体，故称"梦魂"。唐代刘希夷《巫山怀古》中有句："颓想卧瑶席，梦魂何翩翩。"**还似**：《花间集补》中作"还是"。**上苑**：封建时代供帝王玩赏、打猎的园林。**车如流水马如龙**：意思是车子接连不断像流水一样驰过，马匹络绎不绝像一条龙一样走动。形容车马络绎不绝，十分繁华热闹。语出袁宏《后汉纪·孝章皇帝纪》："建初二年(马)太后诏曰：'吾万乘主，身服大练，食不求甘，左右旁人无香熏之饰，衣但布皇，如是者欲以身率服众也……前过濯龙门，见外家车如流水马如龙。吾亦不谴怒之，但绝其岁用，冀以默愧其心……'"**花月正春风**：春天鲜花怒放，春夜月光明朗，春风微拂的情景，描绘春光的明媚。“花月”的字面意思是“花和月”，这里泛指美好的景色。

〖译　文〗

(1) Jiaosheng Wang 译

Tune: “Memories of the South”
A Reminiscence

Regrets untold!
In a dream last night
I was again out touring High Park
As in days of old:
Luxurious coaches in streams,
Fine steeds soaring like dragons—
A blaze of moonlight and flowers
In the balmy breezes of spring.

(2) Alan Ayling and Duncan Mackintosh 译

No end to pain!
Last night in dreams—where still I reign—
My spirit wandered, as in old times, over my domain.
Carriages flowed like water and horses like a dragon.
Flowers and the moon greeted spring winds again.

(3) Jerome Ch'en and Michael Bullock 译

HOW MUCH REGRET?

How much regret,
In a dream last night?
I wandered back to my hunting lodge,
　　as in the past:

The chariots ran on like a stream
And the horses galloped like flying dragons.
The blossoms, the moonlight and the gentle wind
　　were the joy of spring.

(4) Burton Watson 译

Tune: "Gazing at the South"

Unspeakable sorrow!
Last night my soul went dreaming
and I thought I was once again wandering in the royal gardens I knew,
the carriages like flowing water, their horses fine as dragons,
blossoms by moonlight, and just then a spring breeze—

(5) Arthur Waley 译

Tune: "Gazing to the South" [*Wang Chiang-nan*]

Immeasurable pain!
My dreaming soul last night was king again.
As in past days
I wandered through the Palace of Delight,
And in my dream
Down grassy garden ways
Glided my chariot, smoother than a summer stream;
There was moonlight,
The trees were blossoming,
And a faint wind softened the air of night,
For it was spring.

1.29　虞美人(李煜)

春花秋月何时了？往事知多少。小楼昨夜又东风，故国不堪回首月明中。
雕栏玉砌应犹在，只是朱颜改。问君能有几多愁？恰似一江春水向东流。

〖作品简介〗

这首词以问起，以答结；由问天、问人而到自问，通过今昔交错对比，表现了一个亡国之君的无穷哀怨。

〖注 释〗

虞美人：此调原为唐教坊曲，初咏项羽宠姬虞美人死后地下开出一朵鲜花，因以为名。又名《一江春水》《玉壶水》《巫山十二峰》等。双调，五十六字，上下片各四句，皆为两仄韵转两平韵。**了**：了结，完结。**雕栏玉砌**：指远在金陵的南唐故宫。“砌”指“台阶”。**应犹**：一作“依然”。**朱颜改**：指所怀念的人已衰老。**君**：作者自称。**能**：或作“都”“那”“还”“却”。

〖译 文〗

(1) Wai-lim Yip 译

“Beauty Yu”

Spring flowers, autumn moon: when to end?
The past: how much is known?
Upon the tower last night, east winds blow again.
Native country: unbearable to look back amidst the bright moon.

Carved railings, jade inlays should still be there,
Only faces are changed.
How much sorrow do you have?
The way a spring river eastward flows.

(2) Zong-qi Cai 译

To the Tune of “Beautiful Lady Yu”

Spring flowers, autumn moon—when will they end?
Past affairs—who knows how many?

Last night in the small pavilion the east wind came again.
I dare not turn my head toward my homeland in the moonlight.

The inlaid balustrade and jade stairs must still be there
—It's only the youthful faces that have changed.
I ask you, how much sorrow can there be?
Just as much as a river full of spring waters, flowing east.

(3) Hans H. Frankel 译

Tune Pattern: "The Beautiful Lady Yu"

Spring blossoms and autumn moon—when will they end?
How much has happened in the past!
On the balcony last night, again an east wind,
The moon was so bright, I couldn't bear to look toward the old land.

The carved galleries and jade steps must still be there,
Only the rosy cheeks have changed.
I ask you, how much sorrow can there be?
It's just like a whole river full of eastward flow in spring.

(4) 许渊冲 译

Tune: The Beautiful Lady Yu

When will there be no more autumn moon and spring flowers,
For me who had so many memorable hours?
My attic which last night in vernal wind did stand,
Reminds me cruelly of the lost moonlit land.

Carved balustrades and marble steps must still be there,
But rosy faces cannot be as fair.
If you ask me how much my sorrow has increased,
Just see the overbrimming river flowing east!

(5) Jerome Ch'en and Michael Bullock 译

BIRTHDAY

Spring flowers and autumn leaves,
    will they never end?
How many things have happened?
In this little tower, last night,
    the east wind blew once more.
Can I bear to look back at the old country
    in the bright moon?

The carved hand-rails and marble steps
    must still be there,
But not my youthful cheeks.
How much sadness can I bear?
As much as an eastward-flowing river filled with
    spring water.

(6) Stephen Owen 译

Tune: "Pleasure in the Lovely Woman" (*Yu mei-ren*)

Flowers in spring, moonlight in fall,
    when will they ever end?
and how much can we know
    of what is past and gone?
Upstairs in my room last night
    the east wind came again;
I cannot bear to turn and look home
    in the light of the moon.

Its carved railings and marble pavements
    are, I'm sure, still there—
all that changes is the flush
    on the face of youth.

Tell me then of sorrow—how much can there be?
It is exactly like：
　　a whole river of springtime waters
　　flowing off to the east.

(7) Cyril Birch 译

Tune：“The Beautiful Lady Yü”（*Yü mei-jen*）by Li Yü

When will the last flower fall, the last moon fade?
So many sorrows lie behind.
Again last night the east wind filled my room—
O gaze not on the lost kingdom under this bright moon.

Still in her light my palace gleams as jade
Only from bright cheeks beauty dies.
To know the sum of human suffering
Look at this river rolling eastward in the spring.

1.30　乌夜啼(李煜)

林花谢了春红，太匆匆，无奈朝来寒雨晚来风。
胭脂泪，相留醉，几时重，自是人生长恨水长东。

〖作品简介〗

此词描写作者亡国后被囚禁于开封的苦闷心情。作者不敢在词里直抒胸臆，只好借助这首词描写春残花谢的自然景象，借以喻指国破家亡和人生失意的无限仇恨。人生就如东逝的长江水，流去了就再也回不来了！

〖注　释〗

乌夜啼：此调原为唐教坊曲，又名《相见欢》《秋夜月》《上西楼》。三十六字，上片平韵，下片两仄韵两平韵。**谢**：凋谢。**胭脂泪**：指女子的眼泪。女子脸上搽有胭脂，泪水流经脸颊时沾上胭脂的红色，故云。**几时重**：何时再度相会。

【译 文】

(1) Burton Watson 译

Tune: "Crows Crying at Night"

Blossoms of the wood have scattered their spring crimson—
it came too suddenly! —
powerless before the dawn-borne rains, the night-borne winds.

Rouge-stained tears
detaining a lover, making him drunk—
will such times ever come again?
These are life's endless regrets, a river flowing endlessly east.

(2) 许渊冲 译

Tune: "Crows Crying at Night" by Li Yu

Spring's rosy color fades from forest flowers
    Too soon, too soon.
How can they bear cold morning showers
    And winds at noon!

    Your rouged tears like crimson rain
    Intoxicate my heart.
    When shall we meet again?
As water eastward flows, so shall we part.

(3) Cyril Birch 译

Tune: "Night Crow Calling" (*Wu yeh t'i*) by Li Yü

The flowered woods have dropped their springtime rose festoon,

So soon, so soon.
But night-blowing winds and the cold dawn rain were bound
to be.

Your tear-stained rouge will keep me
Drinking here beside you.
Then—who knows when again?
Our lives are sad like rivers turning always toward the sea.

1.31 相见欢(李煜)

无言独上西楼，月如钩。寂寞梧桐深院锁清秋。
剪不断，理还乱，是离愁。别是一般滋味在心头。

【作品简介】

此词为作者亡国做囚后所作。该词上片选取典型的景物为感情的抒发渲染铺垫，下片借用形象的比喻委婉含蓄地抒发真挚的感情。

【注 释】

西楼：指西边的楼。**锁清秋**：深深被秋色所笼罩。**离愁**：指去国之愁。**别是一般**：也作“别是一番”，另有一种意味。

【译 文】

(1) Stephen Owen 译

Tune: "The Pleasures of Meeting" (*Xiang-jian huan*)

Without a word I climbed the western tower—
the moon was like a hook.
The silent yard stretched deep
through chestnut trees,
enclosing autumn, cool and clear.

You can cut it, but never cut it through,
get it set,
    then it's a mess again—
that's the sadness of being apart.
It has a flavor all its own
    in the human heart.

(2) 许渊冲 译

Tune: "Joy at Meeting" by Li Yu

Silent, I climb the Western Tower alone
And see the hook-like moon.
Parasol-trees lonesome and drear
Lock in the courtyard autumn clear.

    Cut, it won't sever;
    Be ruled, 'twill never.
    What sorrow 'tis to part!
It's an unspeakable taste in the heart.

(3) Cyril Birch 译

Tune: "Happiness of Meeting" (*Hsiang chien huan*) by Li Yü

Wordless, alone, I go upstairs to the western chamber.
The moon is like a sickle.
The lonely trees in the courtyard are locked up there with
    the autumn night.

Scissors do not sever,
Nor reason unravel,
The pain of separation.
It lodges in the heart with a taste of its own.

(4) Zong-qi Cai 译

To the Tune of "Crows Call at Night"
(or "Pleasure at Meeting"[*Xiang jian huan*])

Without a word, alone I climb the West Pavilion.
The moon is like a hook.
In the lonely inner garden of *wutong* trees is locked late autumn.①

Cut, it doesn't break,
Tidied, a mess again—
This separation grief.
It's altogether a different kind of flavor in the heart.

① The *wutong* is the Chinese parasol tree (Firmiana simplex).

1.32　浪淘沙(李煜)

帘外雨潺潺，春意阑珊，罗衾不耐五更寒。梦里不知身是客，一晌贪欢。

独自莫凭栏，无限江山，别时容易见时难。流水落花春去也，天上人间。

【作品简介】

此词抒发了词人的亡国之痛和囚徒之悲，生动地刻画了一个亡国之君的艺术形象。

【注　释】

此词原为唐教坊曲，又名《浪淘沙令》《卖花声》等。唐人多用七言绝句入曲，南唐李煜始演为长短句。双调，五十四字(宋人有稍作增减者)，平韵，此调又由柳永、周邦彦演为长调《浪淘沙漫》，是别格。**潺潺**：形容雨声。**阑珊**：衰残。一作"将阑"。**罗衾**[qīn]：绸被子。**不耐**：受不了。一作"不暖"。**身是客**：指被拘汴京，形同囚徒。**一晌**[shǎng]：一会儿，片刻。一作"饷"[xiǎng]。**贪欢**：指贪恋梦境中的欢乐。**凭栏**：靠着栏杆。**江山**：指南唐河山。

【译 文】

(1) Burton Watson 译

Tune: "Ripples Sifting Sand: A Song"

Beyond the blind, the rain rattles down,
spring moods fading away,
yet the gauze coverlet can't keep off the fifth watch cold.
In dreams I forget I'm a stranger here,
clutching at happiness for a moment—

Don't lean on the railing all alone,
before these endless rivers and mountains.
Times of parting are easy to come by, times of meeting hard.
Flowing water, fallen blossoms—spring has gone away now,
as far as heaven from the land of men.

(2) Lin Tongji 译

To the Tune of "Waves Washing Sands"

Beyond the curtain,
Rain trickles on—
Lingering now Spring's last spell.
Silken quilts yielding
To the chill-at-dawn:
A dream it was—
With all the merriments of yore,
As if captive no longer.

Gaze not alone from the balcony,
For the landscape infinite extends.
How ever easier parted than met.
The river flows—
The blossoms fall—

Spring going—gone：
In Heaven as on earth！

(3) 许渊冲 译

Tune："Ripples Sifting Sand" by Li Yu

The curtain cannot keep out the patter of rain；
Springtime is on the wane.
In the deep of the night my quilt is not cold-proof.
Forgetting I am under hospitable roof,
Still in my dream I seek for pleasure vain.

Don't lean alone on railings and
Yearn for the boundless land！
To bid farewell is easier than to meet again.
With flowers fallen on the waves spring's gone away,
So has the paradise of yesterday！

(4) Jerome Ch'en and Michael Bullock 译

SPRING SHOWER

Outside the curtains the rain is pattering
As the season draws to its end.
My satin bed-cover cannot keep out
　　the chill at dawn.
In the dream, I forgot
　　that I was in exile,
And for a time there was joy.

Never lean against the balustrade in solitude.
O, my mountains and rivers—
It was so easy to part,
But the return proves to be so hard.
Spring, will you go with the falling petals
　　and the drifting currents

To paradise? Let me remain a while.

(5) 杨宪益、戴乃迭 译

To the Tune of "Lang Tao Sha"

Without the blind the rain is pattering,
Last intimation of spring.
These gauzy coverlets too little warmth at midnight bring
To one who in his dreams fancied he was his own once more,
Once fed and avid for the thing.

I'd lean upon the rail, but what's the worth?
Of hills to across there is not dearth.
Visions of what I left so lightly bring me no more mirth
That fallen flowers faring home upon a running stream.
Heaven is high, and man is on earth.

1.33 菩萨蛮(韦庄)

人人尽说江南好,游人只合江南老。春水碧于天,画船听雨眠。
垆边人似月,皓腕凝霜雪。未老莫还乡,还乡须断肠。

【作品简介】

此词描绘了江南水乡秀丽的景色和曼妙的人物,既表达了诗人对江南山水的依恋、陶醉,又突出了"春日游子"的"思乡怀人"之情。

【注　释】

游人只合江南老:这里指飘泊江南的人,即作者自谓。**只合**:只应。**碧于天**:一片碧绿,胜过天色。**垆边**:指酒家。垆,旧时酒店用土砌成酒瓮卖酒的地方。《史记·司马相如列传》记载,司马相如妻卓文君长得很美,曾当垆卖酒:"买一酒舍沽就,而令文君当垆。"**皓腕凝霜雪**:形容双臂洁白如雪。凝霜雪,像霜雪凝聚那样洁白。**须**:必定,肯定。

【译 文】

(1) James Liu 译

Everyone is full of praise of the beauty of the South:
What can I do but end my days an exile in the South?
    The spring river is bluer than the sky;
As it rains, in a painted barge I lie.

    Bright as the moon is she who serves the wine;
Like frost or frozen snow her white wrists shine.
    I'm not old as yet: let me not depart!
    For going home will surely break my heart!

(2) Burton Watson 译

Tune: "Deva-like Barbarian" by WEI CHUANG (836-910)

People all say the southland's better—
for a traveler, the southland's the place to grow old,
springtime waters bluer than the sky,
painted boats where you listen to the rain and doze—

Beside the wine-warmer, someone like the moon,
pale arms two drifts of frozen snow.
"You're not that old—don't go home—
go home and your heart is bound to break!"

(3) Stephen Owen 译

Tune: "Boddhisattva Barbarian" (*Pu-sa man*) by Wei Zhuang (ca. 836-910)

Everyone says that the Southland's fine,

in the South the traveler should remain
    till old and gray.
Springtime waters are bluer than sky,
in a pained boat lie,
    listening to the rain.

Beside the bar, a woman like moon,
her gleaming wrists both of compacted snow.
Never go home until you are old,
for if you go home, it will break your heart.

(4) 许渊冲 译

Tune: "Buddhist Dancers" by Wei Zhuang

All men will say the Southern land is fair,
A wanderer is willing to spend his whole life there.
He's like to see spring water bluer than the sky
And, listening to rain, in painted ship to lie.

The wine-shop waitress looks like the moon bright,
Like snow or frost congealed her arms are white.
Till he grows old, from South lands he won't part,
To leave this land for home would break his heart.

(5) Cyril Birch 译

Tune: "Strangers in Saint's Coif" (*P'u-sa man*)

Every one's always saying how fine it is in the south,
How the best thing for the wanderer is to stay the rest of his days.
In spring the waters are bluer than the skies;
You drowse in your painted boat to the rain's murmur.

The wine-shop girls are lovely as the moon,
Their gleaming arms like paired drifts of snow.

Don't go back to your home until you're old—
Go home and it will surely break your heart.

1.34 荷叶杯(韦庄)

记得那年花下，深夜，初识谢娘时。水堂西面画帘垂，携手暗相期。
惆怅晓莺残月，相别，从此隔音尘。如今俱是异乡人，相见更无因。

〖作品简介〗

此词写男子对女子的忆念：上片追叙男子与情人初次相见倾心的情景，下片写男子与女子分别的痛苦画面及离恨。

〖注 释〗

谢娘：晋王凝之妻谢道韫有文才，后人因称才女为"谢娘"。唐·韩翃《送李舍人携家归江东觐省》诗："承颜陆郎去，携手谢娘归。"**水堂**：临近水池的堂屋。**相期**：相约会。李白《月下独酌》："永结无情游，相期邈云汉。"**残月**：谓将落的月亮。白居易《客中月》诗："晓随残月行，夕与新月宿。""宋·柳永《雨霖铃》词："今宵酒醒何处？杨柳岸、晓风残月。"**隔音尘**：音信断绝。"音尘"意即"消息"。**因**：缘由，这里指机会。

〖译 文〗

(1) Burton Watson 译

Tune: "Lotus-leaf Cup"

I remember that year, under the blossoms,
late at night
when I met her the first time,
a lakeside room, painted blinds on the west side lowered,
and I held her hand, making secret promises—

Dismayed at dawn orioles, the leftover moon,
we said good-bye—
and since that time, all word cut off,
the two of us live now in different lands,

with no way at all to meet!

(2) 张炳星 译

A Rendezvous

Wei Zhuang

I remember that year deep in the night under flowers
I made the first acquaintance with you, my lover.
It was to the west of a waterside pavilion
that we had a happy union.
I held your hand, warm and tender,
and arranged a secret rendezvous for you to consider.

We parted full of melancholy early in the morning,
when orioles were warbling and the moon was waning.
Ever since, we have heard no more from each other.
Now, both of us are strangers in a foreign zone,
we have no reason to see each other.

1.35 谒金门(韦庄)

空相忆，无计得传消息。天上嫦娥人不识，寄书何处觅。
新睡觉来无力，不忍看伊书迹。满院落花春寂寂，断肠芳草碧。

〖作品简介〗

此词通过刻画主人公的心态，由人去楼空，往事不堪回首，而转入一种欲寄书寻觅的痴情，表达了作者的悲伤之感。词作描写了爱姬的才貌：她既有“天上嫦娥”之美貌，又有才情，工文善书，字迹娟秀。

〖注　释〗

《谒金门》：原为唐教坊曲，后用为词牌，双调，仄韵四十五字。代表作有冯延巳的《谒金门·风乍起》、李好古的《谒金门·花过雨》等。**无计**：没有办法。**“寄书”**句：意思是本想请嫦娥代为传书，但因不相识，而无处寻找她。**书**：信。**觉**：醒。**伊**：她。**书迹**：指过去的来信。

〖译　文〗

(1) Zong-qi Cai 译

To the Tune of "Audience at Golden Gate"

Vain to remember him,
No way to get news through.
Chang'e in the heavens doesn't recognize me.
Where shall I seek him, to send him a letter?

Waking, languid, from new sleep,
Can't bear to take up the remains of his letter.
A courtyard full of fallen blossoms—spring is lonely, lonely
—Heartbreaking, the fragrant grasses green.

(2) Cyril Birch 译

Tune: "A Visit to Golden Gate" (*Yeh Chin-men*)

Useless, thinking of him;
No way to get word to each other.
The Lady in the Moon is beyond men's reach—
If you sent her a letter, where would it find her?

I've just awakened, and I feel so helpless.
I couldn't bear to take up his old letters.
All over the garden the flowers have fallen—
A lonely, lonely spring—
The sweet grass is so green it breaks my heart.

1.36　女冠子(韦庄)

昨夜夜半，
枕上分明梦见，

语多时。
依旧桃花面,
频低柳叶眉。

半羞还半喜,
欲去又依依。
觉来知是梦,
不胜悲。

〖作品简介〗

此词记述了一对恋人离别之后在梦中相见的情景。二人把臂欷歔,说不尽的离愁别绪。“语多时,依旧桃花面”,特别是“频低柳叶眉”“欲去又依依”的神态音容,宛在眼前。然而,夜长梦短,梦醒之后,更令人不胜伤悲。此词不似多数花间词之浓艳,而是在清淡中意味深远,耐得咀嚼。所谓“意婉词直”“似直而纤”,别具风味。

〖注　释〗

柳叶眉:如柳叶之细眉,这里以“眉”借代为“面”,亦是“低面”的意思。**依依**:恋恋不舍的样子。**胜**:尽。

〖译　文〗

(1) Burton Watson 译

Tune:“The Taoist Priestess” by WEI CHUANG(836-910)

Last night at midnight
by my pillow in a dream distinctly I saw her,
and in all the talk that followed,
her peach blossom face, just as it used to be,
repeatedly lowered eyes under willow leaf eyebrows—

Half ashamed, half delighted,

she made as though to go, yet kept on lingering—
And when I woke up and knew it was a dream,
the pain was more than I could bear!

(2) 张炳星 译

A Dream
Wei Zhuang

Last night, at midnight,
obviously I dreamed of her on the pillow light.
We talked a lot during the night.
She still had a peach blossom face in my sight.
She frequently lowered her slender eye brows
which look like the leaves of willows.

She was half shy and with half joy.
She wanted to go,
but was reluctant to go.
Upon waking up, I knew it was a dream,
I was overwhelmed by gloom.

1.37　天仙子·其二(韦庄)

深夜归来长酩酊，扶入流苏犹未醒。醺醺酒气麝兰和。惊睡觉，笑呵呵，长笑人生能几何。

〖作品简介〗

此词描写贵公子酒后的状态，流露出对人生的消极思想，也影射了时代的混乱。

〖注　释〗

酩酊[mǐng dǐng]：形容大醉。《晋书·山简传》：时有童儿歌曰："山公出何许？往至高阳池。日夕倒载归，酩酊无所知。"**苏**：帐上下垂的彩须或彩穗之类，这里借代为帐子。**醺醺**：醉酒者的酒气。**麝兰**：麝香与兰香。

【译　文】

(1) Stephen Owen 译

Tune: "Immortal in Heaven" by Wei Zhuang(834? -910)

He comes home late always staggering drunk
to be hoisted through tassels onto the bed,
　　still not sober.
The smell of alcohol on his breath
　　blends with musk and orchid scent. ①
He wakes from his stupor with a start,
laughs out loud and always says,
"How long does a man's life last?" ②

① The "musk and orchid scent" suggests that he has been with courtesans.
② "How long does a man's life last" was a venerable cliché in drinking songs.

(2) Cyril Birch 译

Tune: "The T'ien-t'ai Fairy" (*T'ien hsien-tzu*)

I came back in the dead of night, sodden drunk as usual.
They helped me in through the curtains—I still didn't sober up.
The reek of liquor mingled with the scent of musky perfumes.
When they woke me up
I laughed out loud:
As the saying goes—how long does a man's life last!

1.38　小重山(韦庄)

一闭昭阳春又春。夜寒宫漏永，梦君恩。卧思陈事暗销魂，罗衣湿，红袂有啼痕。

歌吹隔重阍。绕庭芳草绿，倚长门。万般惆怅向谁论？凝情立，宫殿欲黄昏。

【作品简介】

此词传说也是为宠姬而作，是代姬人写的一首宫怨词。上片首言一入深宫，与世隔绝，幽禁得愈久愈严，心则愈渴望自由与幸福。"梦君恩"以下是对过去爱情的怀恋。下片再转一层，以他人隔重门的歌舞欢乐，反衬自己的凄苦，并以景托情，把人物的心理活动与环境的描写统一起来，把主人公深闭宫中、旧怀难忘、空倚长门的无限怅望之情，化入芳草碧萋、宫殿黄昏的苍茫景色之中，含蓄不尽，韵味无穷。

【注　释】

《小重山》：词牌名，又名《小重山令》。《金奁集》入"双调"。唐人例用以写"宫怨"，故其调悲。五十八字，前后片各四平韵。**昭阳**：本汉代宫名，此借指王建之宫。**春又春**：过了一春又一春。**宫漏**：古时宫中的铜壶滴漏计时。**陈事**：往事。**红袂**：红袖。**歌吹**：歌唱弹吹，泛指音乐之声 。**重阍**[hūn]：宫门。**长门**：汉代宫名，汉武帝陈皇后失宠之后，退居长门。**情**：情意专注。

【译　文】

Cyril Birch 译

Tune: "Little Ch'ung-shan" (*Hsiao Ch'ung-shan*)

Shut out of Chao-yang Palace while springs come and go,[①]
Through endless watches of chilly nights
She dreams of his royal love.
She lies there thinking over the past, her soul all but dissolved,
Till her gown of gauze is wet,
Its red sleeves stained with tears.

To the sound of song and flute through door past door,
She walks the courtyard among the sweet green grasses
And leans at the Long Gate.
Her many, many sorrows—to whom can she tell them?
She stands there with her feelings knotted within
As the palaces grow dim in the yellow twilight.

① Han Emperor Ch'eng-ti built this palace for a new favorite, displacing Pan Chieh-yü to whom is attributed the first of the innumerable laments on her fate.

1.39 醉公子(薛昭蕴)

慢绾青丝发，光研吴绫袜。床上小熏笼，韶州新退红。
巨耐无端处，捻得从头污。恼得眼慵开，问人闲事来。

作品简介

此词一名《四换头》，写出了贵族公子醉生梦死的无聊生活。

注 释

绾[wǎn]：绕束成结。**青丝发**：如青丝般的头发，言其黑细而光润。**研**[yà]：用石块磨光其他物品，称为"研光"，唐代口语，此处为动词。据《开元天宝遗事》载：汝阳王琎戴研光帽打曲，明皇自摘槿花，置之帽上，帽极滑，久而方安。《花间集》汤显祖注："昔西王母宴群仙，戴研光帽，簪花舞，'研光'，二字本此。"《玉篇》："今之布匹及纸，用石碾研光滑者，俗名研光布、研光纸。"**熏笼**：熏香取暖的小烘笼。**"韶州"**句：意为床上的物品为韶红所染，色彩新鲜。**韶州**：今广东省曲江一带，此地所产红色染料著名，称为"韶红"。**退红**：粉红色。王建《牡丹》诗："肉色退红娇。"**"巨耐"**二句：可恶的是没有原因，就弄脏了全身。**巨**[pǒ]**耐**：无可奈何，引申为"可恶""讨厌"。"巨"意为"不可"。"耐"通"奈"。敦煌曲子词《鹊踏枝》："巨耐灵鹊多谩语，送喜何曾有凭据?"**无端**：无故，说不出原因。**捻**[niǎn]：用手搓转。**从头污**：到处都弄脏。

译 文

Stephen Owen 译

To "The Drunken Lord" (*Zui gong-zi*)

Languidly binding her dark strands of hair,
her Wu mesh stockings are ironed smooth.
On the bed a small hamper for scenting clothes,
with a new piece of fabric,
    Shao-zhou's "faded red."

Oh no!
　　Out of nowhere
he comes sneaking in,
　　Stained with wine from head to toe.
He pesters me until
　　I groggily open my eyes
and ask me all sorts of silly things.

1.40　女冠子(薛昭蕴)

求仙去也，翠钿金篦尽舍。入岩峦，雾卷黄罗帔，云雕白玉冠。
野烟溪洞冷，林月石桥寒。静夜松风下，礼天坛。

〖作品简介〗

此词的全名为《女冠子·求仙去也》。全词上片二十三字，下片一十八字，写女道士求仙，思想意义不大。前三句写女道士"尽舍"人间烟火，"入崖"求仙。接着描绘她求仙的服饰以及"入岩峦"的景象和天坛礼拜的情形，表现了不同人世的冷寂"仙气"。

〖注　释〗

翠钿金篦：首饰。**尽舍**：全都抛弃。**"雾卷"**二句：意思是黄罗绸的披肩如雾飞卷，白玉冠帽如云彩所饰，将其衣着与云雾配合描写。**黄罗帔**：黄色丝罗披肩。**礼天坛**：登坛拜天，道家的礼仪。

〖译　文〗

Cyril Birch 译

Tune: "The Taoist Priestess" (*Nu-kuan tzu*) by Hsieh Chao-yun

She has gone to seek the immortals,
Leaving behind her kingfisher pins, leaving her golden combs—
Gone to the cliffs and peaks
Curling the vapors round her for scarf of yellow gauze,
Shaping a cloud for nun's coif of white jade.

Cold the wild mists and the caves of mountain streams,
Chill the forest moon and the bridge of stones
Where in the still of night beneath the wind in the pines
She serves at Heaven's altar.

1.41 生查子(牛希济)

春山烟欲收，天淡星稀小。残月脸边明，别泪临清晓。
语已多，情未了，回首犹重道：记得绿罗裙，处处怜芳草。

【作品简介】

此词上片写别景，下片写别情，由景入情，构思巧妙，所蕴涵的感情细腻而真挚。

【注释】

烟：此指春晨弥漫于山前的薄雾。**残月**：弯月。**了**：完结。末两句可能出自南朝江总妻《赋亭草》："雨过草芊芊，连云锁南陌。门前君试看，是妾罗裙色。"颇见诗人构思之巧、寓意之挚。

【译文】

龚景浩 译

"Sheng Zha Zi (Five Dynasties)"
Niu Xi Ji

Over spring hills the mist is dispersing,
In a pale sky stars are sparse and shrinking.
A waning moon is bright on your face;
And tears of farewell at the coming of dawn.

Many things said,
But loving-feelings have not all been expressed.
Looking back, she urged again:
Remember my green skirt of silk gauze,
And hold dear fragrant grasses, everywhere.

1.42　醉公子（尹鹗）

暮烟笼藓砌，戟门犹未闭。尽日醉寻春，归来月满身。
离鞍偎绣袂，坠巾花乱缀。何处恼佳人，檀痕衣上新。

【作品简介】

此词从一个女子迎接醉公子的角度描写了贵公子日暮醉归的情景。

【注　释】

戟[jǐ]门：显贵人家的门。唐代制度规定：官、阶、勋俱三品得立戟于门。白居易《裴五》诗："莫怪相逢无笑语，感今思旧戴门前。"戟是古时的一种武器，合戈矛为一体，可以直穿横击。**"离鞍"**二句：意思是，他下马后，醉态恍惚，紧靠搀扶者的绣腕，垂下的头巾上花片散乱地点缀着。**"何处"**二句：意思是他不知在何处，又引逗过美貌的姑娘？看那衣衫之上，还留印着脂粉的痕迹。**恼**：逗引，撩拨。杜甫《奉陪郑驸马韦曲》诗之一："韦曲花无赖，家家恼杀人。"又宋王安石《夜直》诗："春色恼人眠不得，月移花影上栏干。"唐人常用"恼"字，有戏谑的意思。

【译　文】

Stephen Owen 译

Tune: "The Drunken Lord" (*Zui gong-zi*) by Yin E (Early 10th Century)

Evening mist veils the mossy pavements,
　　the gate of the mansion, still not shut tight.
All the day long he's been drunk,
　　off seeking springtime pleasures,
and as he returns
　　his body is swathed in the moonlight.

He left his saddle with arms around
　　some girl with embroidered sleeves,
and on his kerchief that fell to the ground
　　a tangle of petals stuck.

But what thing in particular
    upsets the lovely lady most? —
it is the marks of lipstick,
    fresh upon his clothes.

1.43 醉花间(毛文锡)

休相问，怕相问，相问还添恨。春水满塘生，㶉鶒还相趁。
昨夜雨霏霏，临明寒一阵。偏忆戍楼人，久绝边庭信。

〖作品简介〗

此词是一首女主人公对征人思念的闺怨词。前三句连用三个“相问”，并以“休”“怕”“添恨”加深其感情色彩，将思妇怨情写浓了。“春水”二句，以眼前之景烘托心情；换头二句，从环境烘写心境。这四句隐隐传出了主人公对征人的思念之情，烘托出了她的孤寂、清冷。末二句，写己忆深，写彼信绝，相思怨情充溢字里行间；十个字，画龙点睛，道出全篇主旨。全词语浅情真，情致缠绵。

〖注　释〗

醉花间：唐教坊曲，《词谱》引《宋史·乐志》入“双调”。四十一字，前片三仄韵，一叠韵，后片三仄韵。**㶉鶒**(xī chì)：一种水鸟，头有缨，尾羽上矗如舵，羽毛五彩而多紫色，似鸳鸯稍大，故又名紫鸳鸯。**趁**：趁便，乘机。**夜**：一作“日”。**霏霏**(fēi)：雨雪盛貌。**临明**：即将天明。**寒一阵**：犹言阵阵寒气。**戍楼**：边防驻军的瞭望楼。**绝**：无，没有。**边庭**：边地，边塞。

〖译　文〗

Burton Watson 译

Tune: “Drunk Among the Flowers”

I mustn’t ask about him—
I’m afraid to ask—
Asking would only add to my heartache—
Spring waters swell and flood the pond,
The crested ducks follow each other around.

Last night the rain came pouring down,
Toward dawn a cold spell set in,
And all I do is think of that man in his lookout tower—
How long since I've had news from the border!

1.44 诉衷情(顾敻)

永夜抛人何处去?绝来音。香阁掩,眉敛,月将沉。争忍不相寻?怨孤衾。换我心,为你心,始知相忆深。

【作品简介】

此词是一首闺怨词,通过女主人公口语式的内心独白,揭示了作为一个闺中弱女子被负心人所折磨而带来的心灵创伤,表现了旧社会情爱悲剧的一个方面。主人公怨中有爱,爱怨兼发,心情复杂。作品在艺术构思与表现手法上甚见匠心,深得后代词评家的赞赏。

【注 释】

诉衷情:唐教坊曲名。因毛文锡词句有"桃花流水漾纵横",又名《桃花水》;因顾敻本词,又名《怨孤衾》。**永夜**:长夜。**眉敛**:指皱眉愁苦之状。**争忍**:怎忍。**孤衾**:喻独宿。

【译 文】

(1) Burton Watson 译

Tune: "Telling of Innermost Feelings" by Ku Hsiung (fl. 928)

Long nights when he neglects me—where's he gone?
No word at all,
my scented room shut tight,
eyebrows pluckered,
the moon about to set—
How can he do this, not come to see me!
I loathe this lonely coverlet!
If I could exchange my heart,

Somehow make it your heart,
Maybe then you'd know how much I care!

(2) Robert Kotewall and Norman L. Smith 译

"Declaring My Inner Feelings"
KU HSIUNG

All night long you have deserted me, whither gone?
No news has come;
My scented chamber is closed.
Brows knitted, moon just setting,
How can I bear not to grope for you,
Weeping under my lonely coverlet?
Change your heart into my heart,
And learn the depth of my pining.

1.45 杨柳枝(顾夐)

秋夜香闺思寂寥，漏迢迢。鸳帷罗幌麝烟销，烛光摇。
正忆玉郎游荡去，无寻处。更闻帘外雨潇潇，滴芭蕉。

〖作品简介〗

此词写女主人公的闺中情思。上片写她秋夜深闺独处，十分寂寞的情怀。首句"思寂寥"三字，将情怀点出。以下是环境的描写，意在渲染孤凄的气氛，烘托寂寥的心情。下片写她对丈夫的不尽思念。前两句直接抒情，"正忆"而"无寻处"，痛苦之状宛在眼前。后两句言室外萧瑟凄凉的声音，愁苦之情自在不言中。

〖注　释〗

寂寥：寂寞空虚。**漏迢迢**[tiáo]：更漏之声悠长。古时以漏壶滴水计时。**鸳帷**：绣着鸳鸯的帷帐。**罗幌**：丝罗床帐。**麝烟**：焚麝香发出的烟。烟，一作"香"。**玉郎**：古代女子对丈夫的爱称。**潇潇**：风雨声，一作"萧萧"。《诗经·郑风·风雨》："风雨潇潇，鸡鸣胶胶。既见君子，云胡不瘳。"

【译 文】

Cyril Birch 译

Tune: "The Willow Branch" (*Yang-liu chih*) by Ku Hsiung

On an autumn night in her scented room she broods in the lonely
stillness.
The night wears on and on.
Incense fades among the hangings embroidered with ducks
and drakes;
The gleam of the candle flickers.

Her thoughts are of her lover, off roaming far and wide—
No telling where he is,
As she listens to the murmur of the rain outside the blind
Where it drips on the plantain leaves.

1.46 临江仙(鹿虔扆)

金锁重门荒苑静，绮窗愁对秋空。翠华一去寂无踪。玉楼歌吹，声断已随风。

烟月不知人事改，夜阑还照深宫。藕花相向野塘中。暗伤亡国，清露泣香红。

【作品简介】

此词乃暗伤后蜀亡国之作。全篇摹写亡国后境界：通过描写重门紧锁、绮窗紧闭、月照深宫、残荷泣露的旧苑，作者营造了静寂凄清、荒凉悲怆的意境，表达了词人的盛衰之感、亡国之痛。

【注 释】

鹿虔扆：生于五代十国时期，曾在后蜀任职，蜀亡后没有出仕新朝。**翠华**：皇帝的仪仗。

【译 文】

Cyril Birch 译

Tune: "The Fairy by the River" (*Lin-chiang hsien*) by Lu Ch'ien-yi

Far behind gate on fretted gate the weedgrown court is still;
Curtained windows forlornly face the autumn emptiness.
The feathered banners all are gone, no footfall breaks the silence,
The sound of song and flute from marble pavilions
Long broken off and scattered with the wind.

The misty moon, all unaware of change in men's affairs,
Still shines in the dead of night on the inner palace.
Lotuses huddle in a forgotten pool;
Mutely mourning the fallen kingdom
The pure dew weeps upon the fragrant petals.

1.47 河传(阎选)

秋雨，秋雨，无昼无夜，滴滴霏霏。
暗灯凉簟怨分离，妖姬，不胜悲。
西风稍急喧窗竹，停又续，腻脸悬双玉。
几回邀约雁来时，违期，雁归，人不归。

【作品简介】

此词描写了女子的秋雨闺怨。起首四句中三句重叠，笔势劲急，透出怨情，结尾语气舒缓而情更急切。

【注 释】

无昼无夜：不分昼夜的意思。**霏**：飘扬。**簟**[diàn]：竹席，席垫。**妖姬**：美丽的姑娘。姬，美女。《吴越春秋》卷三："于是庄王弃其秦姬越女，罢钟鼓之乐。"**稍**：逐渐，渐渐。**喧窗竹**：使窗前竹枝发响。**腻脸**：指敷着脂粉的脸。腻[nì]，光滑。**双玉**：两行泪。

〖译　文〗

Cyril Birch 译

Tune: "River Tales" (*Ho-ch'uan*) by Yen Hsüan

Autumn rain,
Autumn rain!
No moon, no night.
Drip, drip! Pour, pour!
Lamp gone out, pallet cold, hating loneliness—
Pretty witch,
Unbearably sad!

West wind rustles faintly in the bamboo by the window,
Stops and begins again.
On her cold-creamed cheeks two teardrops hang like jade.
How many times he promised, "When the wild geese come—"
He broke the date;
The geese came back, he didn't.

1.48　定西番(毛熙震)

苍翠浓阴满院，莺对语，蝶交飞，戏蔷薇。
斜日倚阑风好，余香出绣衣。未得玉郎消息，几时归。

〖作品简介〗

此词作共三十五字，描写妻子对丈夫的怀念之情。词的上片写时写景：“莺对语，蝶交飞，戏蔷薇”，借景生情。下片头二句写女主人公的娇好，最后二句总结出对丈夫的怀念。

〖注　释〗

蔷薇：花名。落叶灌木，茎细长，花白色或淡红色，有芳香。**玉郎**：对丈夫的爱称。

【译 文】

Glen W. Baxter 译

Tune: "Conquering Tibet" (*Ting His-fan*) by Mao His-chen

Bright green, dark shade mottle the garden;
Orioles chirp to each other,
Butterflies dart in pairs
Sporting with the rose.

By the rail in the slant late sunlight, gentle breezes
Draw out the fragrance of a damask dress,
But bring no breath of news about a lover
Or when he's coming back.

1.49 浣溪沙(欧阳炯)

相见休言有泪珠，酒阑重得叙欢娱，凤屏鸳枕宿金铺。
兰麝细香闻喘息，绮罗纤缕见肌肤，此时还恨薄情无。

【作品简介】

此词纯写男女欢合之事。上片写别后重逢的欢欣，下片写其欢合。

【注 释】

酒阑：酒意已深。**金铺**：门上的装饰物，制成龙蛇兽头之形，用以衔门环，其色金，故曰“金铺”。这里以“金铺”借代“门”，意思是宿于屋里的凤屏之内、鸳枕之上。**无**：表示疑问。唐人诗中，“无”字用于句末时，多表疑问语气。如朱庆余《近试上张水部》：“妆罢低声问夫婿，画眉深浅入时无?”“入时无”即“合时宜吗”。又：王驾《古意》：“一行书信千行泪，寒到君边衣到无?”“衣到无”即“衣到了吗”。

【译　文】

Stephen Owen 译

Tune: "Washing Creek Sands" (*Huan xi sha*) by Ou-yang Jiong (896-971)

Speak no more when we meet
　　of tears that filled your eyes,
when the wine is done we can again
　　speak our pleasure and delight,
behind phoenix screens on lovebird pillows
　　a night spent in golden bedding.

A delicate scent of orchid and musk,
　　I hear her breathing hard,
and the fine threads of lace she wears
　　reveal flesh—
at such a time does she still resent
　　that her lover was untrue?

1.50　贺明朝(欧阳炯)

忆昔花间初识面，红袖半遮，妆脸轻转。石榴裙带，故将纤纤，玉指偷捻。双凤金线。

碧梧桐锁深深院。谁料得两情，何日教缱绻？羡春来双燕，飞到玉楼，朝暮相见。

【作品简介】

此词描写男子对情人的怀念。上片追忆与女子初次见面的情景，由“忆昔”领起，“花间初识面”，含义有二：一是所见之地在花下；二是所见之人，面亦如花。“红袖”二句正面写女子的娇羞之态；“石榴裙带”三句写其细微动作，侧面表现她的柔媚之情。下片则是现实的怀想，分两层写出：“碧梧”三句，念及情人深闺难出，缱绻无期；“羡春来双燕”三句，就眼前景，人与物比，羡双燕朝暮双飞，衬托自己的孤独；同时也含有双燕自由而多情，朝暮能与自己相会，而所爱之人却难相见。作品充分表现了词人的孤独与寂寞。

【注 释】

石榴裙带：石榴花色的裙带，即鲜红色。**缱绻**[qiǎn quǎn]：感情融洽，难分难舍。韩愈《赠别元十八协律》诗："临当背面时，裁诗示缱绻。"

【译 文】

Lois Fusek 译

Tune: "Offering Congratulations to the Enlightened Reign" by Ou-yang Chiung

I remember the day when we first met among the flowers.
I lifted my red sleeve to hide my face,
And so frivolously turned my head away.
I played with the sash on my red skirt,
And quite deliberately with my slender,
Jadelike fingers, I began to pick away,
A pair of phoenixes stitched with gold.

The green *wu-t'ung*① trees are locked deep in the garden.
Who could know how much we would love one another?
Will there be a time when we can be forever close?
I envy the mated swallows that come in the spring.
Flying, they descend to the jade tower,
Where day and night, they are together!

① The scientific name for the *wu-t'ung* is *Sterculia platanifolia* or *Firmiana platanifolia*. In English, it is called the kolanut or Chinese parasol tree. An ornamental tree frequently found growing in the courtyards of Chinese temples and houses, it has large leaves that afford excellent shade. As a literary trope, it occurs constantly in poems and is used to evoke feelings of sadness experienced by someone who hears raindrops lugubriously falling upon its broad leaves. Here, we may also interpret its name as a homophone for "we-together".

1.51 风流子(其二)(孙光宪)

楼倚长衢欲暮，瞥见神仙伴侣。微傅粉，拢梳头，隐映画帘开处。无语，无绪，慢曳罗裙归去。

【作品简介】

此词是一首小令，共三十四字，词中抒发了男子对姑娘的倾慕之情。首二句写在长街暮色之中，瞥见如仙女般的漂亮姑娘。“微傅粉”三句，写姑娘隐约映现在画帘揭开之处，素淡的妆束，宛如画中人。“无语，无绪”四字生动地刻画了姑娘沉静的神态。结尾句更妙，姑娘飘然而去，神态自若；而少年倾慕，流连忘返，久久难舍。

【注　释】

衢[qú]：大道。**傅粉**：搽粉。**拢**：收束。“**隐映**”句：姑娘隐约出现在画帘揭开的地方。

【译　文】

Cyril Birch 译

Tune: "Free and Easy" [*Feng-liu tzu*]

At a house on the avenue, toward sundown,
I caught a glimpse of a mate for an immortal!
Daintily touched with powder,
Hair combed loose,
She gleamed in the shadow beneath the painted blind;
Then without word
Or sign,
Slowly trailing her silken sleeves, withdrew.

1.52　长相思三首(敦煌曲子词)

旅客在江西，富贵世间稀。终日红楼上，□□舞着棋。频频满酌醉如泥，轻轻更换金卮。尽日贪欢逐乐，此是富不归。

哀客在江西，寂寞自家知。尘土满面上，终日被人欺。照照立在市门西，风吹泪□双垂。遥望家乡长短，此是贫不归。

作客在江西，得病卧毫厘。还往观消息，看看似别离。村人曳在道傍西，耶娘父母不知。身上劄牌书字，此是死不归。

〖作品简介〗

此作品属联章体《长相思》，因在敦煌莫高窟内被发现，编入《敦煌歌辞总编》卷三，故又称唐无名氏联章词(三不归)，是中原内地西去商贾等人在敦煌停留时吟诵所留，叙述了吟诵人怀着对未来捉摸不定的期待与恐惧，来到敦煌追求其黄金美梦的复杂心情。

〖注　释〗

□：首一和首二中表示原文残缺部分。**金卮**[jīn zhī]：金制酒器。**作客**：寄居在别处。**毫厘**：毡毯之类毛织物。**村人曳在道傍西**：村人将他的尸体拖到西头大路边。**耶娘**[yē rɑ́ng]：意为"父母"，后多作"爷娘"。**剟**[duō]：刺。

〖译　文〗

Burton Watson 译

Tune: "Eternal Longing"
ANONYMOUS

I.
He was a traveler west of the river,
with wealth and eminence rare in this world.
All day long in vermilion towers
… dancing and singing songs.

The cup filled again and again, till he's drunk as mud;
lightly, lightly trading golden goblets,
wearing out the day tasting joys, pursuing pleasures—
Some people are rich and never go home.

II.
He was a traveler west of the river;
only he knew how lonely he was,
dust and dirt covering his face,
all day long being cheated by others.

Morning after morning standing by the west gate of the market,
the wind blowing the tears that came down in two streams,
gazing toward his native land so many roads away—
Some people are poor and never go home.

III.
He was a traveler west of the river,
then he took sick, lay an inch away from death.
Still he stayed on, looking for news,
though as time went by it seemed he'd have to depart.

The villagers dragged him to the west side of the road—
his father and mother knew nothing about it—
tied a tag on his body with his name written on it—
Some people die and never go home.

1.53　鹊踏枝(敦煌曲子词)

叵耐灵鹊多谩语。送喜何曾有凭据。几度飞来活捉取。锁上金笼休共语。

比拟好心来送喜。谁知锁我在金笼里。欲他征夫早归来。腾身却放我向青云里。

〖作品简介〗

本作品为敦煌曲词即蝶恋花。词中通过埋怨灵鹊虚报喜讯来表现女主人渴望征人早日返家的急切心情。全词运用拟人化和对话等手法，语言活泼生动而又含义丰富。上片是写少妇埋怨灵鹊报喜不准，捉来锁进金笼。下片是写灵鹊答话。说我好心好意打算送喜信给你，就被你捉住；并要求快快打开金笼，以便直上青云，前去探听征夫消息。

〖注　释〗

叵耐灵鹊多谩语：古代有“灵鹊报喜”的说法。敦煌亦词义说：“正见庭前双鹊喜，君在塞外远征回。”“谩语”意为“言过其实”。“谩”一作“漫”。“叵耐”[pǒ nài]意为“不可能，可恶”。**灵鹊**：民间以闻鹊声为喜兆，称之为“灵鹊报喜”。**金笼**：坚固而又精美的鸟笼。**休共语**：不要和他说话。**比拟**：打算，准备。**征夫**：出远门的人，这里是指关锁灵鹊的人的丈夫。**腾身**：跃身而起。

〖译 文〗

(1) Burton Watson 译

A Lyric from Tun-huang Anonymous(8th-9th Century)
Tune: "Magpie on the Branch"

I can't stand the wily magpie and all his extravagant stories!
He brings me good news, but what proof does he ever have?
One of these times when he flies by, I'll grab him, capture him live,
shut him up in a golden cage to put a stop to his chatter!

With the best of intentions I went to her, delivered my good news—
who'd have thought she'd shut me up in a golden cage?
I only hope her soldiering husband comes home soon
so she'll lift me up, turn me loose to head for the blue clouds!

(2) Stephen Owen 译

Anonymous (Dun-huang), to "The Magpie Steps on the Branch" (*Que ta zhi*)

"I can't stand that 'lucky' magpie—
its words are full of lies;
it brings good news, but never
news of something true.
Several times it's flown here,
now I've captured it alive
and locked it in a cage of gold
to stop it talking to me."

"I simply wanted to be nice
and bring her some good news,
I never thought she'd lock me up

inside this cage of gold.
I really hope her soldier man
comes home very soon—
she'll set me free to fly away
off into blue clouds."

(3) 许渊冲 译

Tune: "The Magpie on a Branch" (Anonymous)

How can I bear to hear the chattering magpie
Announce the happy news on which I can't rely?
So thus I catch it alive when it flies to me again
And shut it in a cage where lonely 'twill remain.

—With good intent I brought her a happy message.
Who would expect she'd shut me in a golden cage?
I wish her husband would come back soon so that I
Might be set free and take my flight to the blue sky.

1.54　醉公子(敦煌曲子词)

门外猧儿吠，知是萧郎至。刬袜下香阶，冤家今夜醉。
扶得入罗帏，不肯脱罗衣。醉则从他醉，还胜独睡时。

『作品简介』

此词收入《全唐诗·附词》，出于民间作者之手。词牌为《醉公子》，意即咏醉公子。诗人着意于"醉"，刻画人物内心活动，极有层次，写得辗转多姿、曲折有致。此词于朴素自然中体现了深厚的情味。

『注　释』

猧[wō]：一种供玩赏的小狗。**萧郎**：泛指女子所爱恋的男子。**刬**[chǎn]：光着。**冤家**：女子对男子的爱称。

【译 文】

(1) Stephen Owen 译

Anonymous (8th Century?), to "The Drunken Lord" (*Zui gong-zi*)

The hound is barking at the gate,
I know that my man has come.
I go down scented stairs in stocking feet—
my darling's drunk tonight.

I lift him through the bed's gauze curtains;
he won't take off these robes of gauze.
If he's drunk, well let him be drunk then—
it's still better than sleeping alone.

(2) Cyril Birch 译

Tune: "The Drunken Young Lord" (*Tsui kung-tzu*)

Outside my door
    the dog barking
I know what it is
    My lover's here
Off with my stockings
    down
    perfumed stairs
My good-for-nothing lover
    is drunk tonight

I help him into
    my silk-curtained bed
Will he take off the silk gown?
    O! O! not he
Milord is drunk
    and drunk let him be

Better that
    than sleeping alone

1.55 渔歌子（敦煌曲子词）

绣帘前，美人睡，庭前猧子频频吠。雅奴白，玉郎至，扶下骅骝沉醉。

出屏帏，整云鬓，莺啼湿尽相思泪。共别人好，说我不是，得莫辜天负地。

【作品简介】

此词描写了夫妻之情。上片写夜等丈夫醉归，下片写男子的浮薄轻狂和女子的抱怨责备，言外可见她的真挚情意，却是借助一个细节式生活小场面体现出来。

【注释】

雅奴：丫环。**猧子**[wō zǐ]：小狗。**骅骝**[huá liú]：赤红色的骏马，周穆王的“八骏”之一。这里指代骏马。**屏帏**[píng wéi]：犹内室。

【译文】

Stephen Owen 译

Anonymous (Dun-huang), to “Fisherman’s Lyrics” (*Yu ge ci*)

Behind the embroidered curtains
a lovely woman lies asleep,
when the hound in the yard barks frantically.
And the maidservant says:
“The master’s back.”
He’s helped off his splendid steed,
    dead drunk.

She comes from behind the screen,
straightening hair like piles of cloud,
and sheds tears of love as orioles sing.
“You’ve been messing around with someone else!”

He says, "I have not!"
"It's obvious you have betrayed me."

1.56 拜新月(敦煌曲子词)

荡子他州去。已经新岁未还归。堪恨情如水。到处辄狂迷。不思家国。花下遥指祝神祇。直至于今。抛妾独守空闺。

上有穹苍在。三光也合遥知。倚幈帏坐。泪流点滴。金粟罗衣。自嗟薄命。缘业至于斯。乞求待见面。誓不辜伊。

【作品简介】

此词作源出《云谣集杂曲子》，为当时流行于三陇一带的民间曲子词，形式为长调。作品描写了妻子思念外出未归的丈夫的愁苦之情。

【注　释】

荡子［dàng zi］：指辞家远出、羁旅忘返的男子。**辄**［zhé］：总是。**狂迷**：狂妄昏乱。

【译　文】

Stephen Owen 译

Tune: "Bowing to the New Moon" (*Bai xin yue*) (Before 850)

My traveling man's off in another land,
already now it's the new year, and
　　he still has not returned.
I am galled by his loves, so like water:
wherever he roams he strays recklessly
and takes no thought of his home.
Beneath the flowers I point far away,
　　and to gods of Heaven and Earth I pray—
up to this very day
he has left me alone to stay in my empty room.

Above me Heaven's blue arch remains,
there sun, moon, and stars surely know,
    though far away.
I sit against the curtain screen,
in drops my tears stream
on my gauze gown with golden beads.
I sigh at my unlucky destiny;
bad karma has brought me to this.
But still I wish to see his face
and swear never to betray him.

第二章
北　宋

2.1　点绛唇(王禹偁)

雨恨云愁，江南依旧称佳丽。水村渔市，一缕孤烟细。
天际征鸿，遥认行如缀。平生事，此时凝睇，谁会凭栏意。

〖作品简介〗

此词被认为是作者传世的唯一作品。全词以清丽的笔触描绘了江南水乡的风物景色，并通过描绘江南雨景，寄寓了作者积极用世、渴望有所作为的政治理想和怀才不遇的苦闷情怀。全词寓情于景，因情绘景，风格清丽，感情质朴。此词还有一个版本：雨恨云愁，江南依旧称佳丽。水村渔市，一缕孤烟细。天际征鸿，遥认行如缀。平生事，此时凝睇，谁会阑意。

〖注　释〗

点绛[jiàng]唇：词牌名。杨慎《词品》曰：“点绛唇”取梁时江淹诗‘白雪凝琼貌，明珠点绛唇’以为名。”此词牌又名“点樱桃”“十八香”“沙头雨”“万年青”等。**雨恨云愁**：谓江南一带烟雨迷漾，容易使人感到愁闷。**佳丽**：景色秀丽。**孤烟**：炊烟。**征鸿**：大雁。因雁秋天南徙，春天北归，故称。**行[háng]如缀**：排成行的大雁，一只接一只，如同缀在一起。**凝睇[dì]**：凝视。“睇”意为“斜视的样子”。**会**：理解。**凭栏**：倚靠栏杆。

〖译　文〗

许渊冲 译

Tune: “Rouged Lips”
Reflection by Wang Yu-cheng

Laden with frowning cloud and steeped in tearful rain, the southern shores still beautiful remain. In riverside village flanked with fishermen's fair, a lonely wreath of slender smoke wafts in the air.

Afar a row of wild geese fly, weaving a letter in the sky. What have I done in days gone by? Gazing from the balustrade, could I weave my way as far as they?

2.2 踏莎行(寇準)

春色将阑，莺声渐老。红英落尽青梅小。画堂人静雨蒙蒙，屏山半掩余香袅。

密约沉沉，离情杳杳。菱花尘满慵将照。倚楼无语欲销魂，长空黯淡连芳草。

【作品简介】

此词乃即景写闺情的小令，情致缠绵，属伤时惜别之作。作品上片重在写景，暮春季节，微雨濛濛，自然界的春天呈现一派寂寥无人的景象；下片主要抒写离情：两人别后没有音讯，引起思念之情。全词以细腻而优美的笔触刻画暮色景物的衰残、画堂风光的孤寂，进而透露人物内心的惆怅和迷惘，外在与内在交汇，情怀与物象相通，激荡回旋，错综交织，谱写成一首伤春念远的闺怨心曲，委婉有致，真切动人，活画出这位独守空闺的女性对于羁旅天涯、久客不归的心上人的无限思念和一片深情。其风格之清新、语言之晓畅，足显婉约派高度的词艺技巧。

【注　释】

踏莎[suō]**行**：词牌名。又名"柳长春""喜朝天"等。双调五十八字，仄韵。**阑**[lán]：残，尽，晚。**红英**：红花。南唐李煜《采桑子》词："亭前春逐红英尽。"**屏山**：指屏风。唐温庭筠《南歌子》词："扑蕊添黄子，呵花满翠鬟，鸳枕映屏山。"**密约**：指男女之间互诉衷情，暗约佳期。**沉沉**：深沉。此指重大之事，即终身之事。**杳**[yǎo]**杳**：深远，无边际。**菱花**：指菱花镜，亦泛指镜子。**慵**[yōng]**将照**：懒得拿起镜子来照。"慵"意为"懒散"；"将"意为"拿"。**销魂**：形容极度伤心。

【译　文】

许渊冲 译

Tune: "Treading on Grass" by Kou Zhun

Springtime is on the wane; the oriole's song grows old, all red flowers fallen and green mume fruit still small. Quiet is painted hall despite the drizzling rain, half-hidden by the screen a wreath of incense cold.

Our vow deep, deep in the heart, we're sad to be far, far apart. I will not look into my brass mirror dust-grey. Silent, I lean on rails, my soul pining away; my longing like green grass would join the vast dim sky, alas!

2.3 酒泉子(潘阆)

长忆观潮，满郭人争江上望。
来疑沧海尽成空，万面鼓声中。
弄潮儿向涛头立，手把红旗旗不湿。
别来几向梦中看，梦觉尚心寒。

【作品简介】

此词上片回忆观潮，表现了钱塘江的宏伟壮观；下片回忆弄潮，表现人定胜天的奇迹。全词以豪迈的气势和劲健的笔触，描绘了钱塘江潮涌的壮美风光以及弄潮儿的英勇无畏精神，具有很强的艺术感染力。

【注　释】

长：通假字，通“常”，常常、经常。**郭**：外城，这里指外城以内的范围。**万面鼓声中**：潮来时，潮声像万面金鼓，一时齐发，声势震人。**弄潮儿**：指朝夕与潮水周旋的水手或在潮中戏水的少年人。周密《武林旧事》曰：八月十五钱塘大潮，吴地少年善游水者数百人，都披散着头发，身上刺满花纹，手持大旗，争先恐后，迎着潮头，在万丈波涛中出没腾飞，做出各种姿势，旗帜却一点没有沾湿。此词现多用来比喻有勇敢进取精神之人。**觉**：睡醒。**心寒**：心里感觉很惊心动魄。

【译　文】

(1) Alan Ayling and Duncan Mackintosh 译

I often remember watching the tidal bore;
Riverside crowds from all around the district
　　jostled to see.
As it came, I imagined the mighty ocean
　　would empty itself on me,

Thronged with the clamour of tens of thousands of
　　Drums.

The tidal-riders poised upright
　　on the lip of the giant wave.
Scarlet banners in their hands
　　and never a banner wet.
Since I left, how often the sight
　　returns in my dreams
And I wake with the cold thrill of it on me yet.

(2) 许渊冲 译

Tune: "Fountain of Wine" by Pan Lang

I still remember watching tidal bore,
The city poured out people on the shore.
It seemed the sea had emptied all its water here,
And thousands of drums were beating far and near.

At the crest of huge billows the swimmers did stand,
Yet dry remained red flags they held in hand.
Come back, I saw in dreams the tide o'erflow the river;
Awake, I feel my heart with cold still shiver.

2.4 长相思(林逋)

吴山青，越山青，两岸青山相对迎，谁知离别情？
君泪盈，妾泪盈，罗带同心结未成，江边潮已平。

【作品简介】

此词描写了一女子与情人诀别的情景。全词运用《诗经》中回环咏唱即民歌中常见的复沓形式，以回旋往复、一唱三叹的节奏和清新优美的语言，以一个女子的声音，抒写了她因爱情生活受到破坏，被迫与心上人在江边诀别的悲怀。全词上片起兴，点明送别，下片写情，寄托离恨，语言直白，蓄意深沉，令人回味无穷。

〖注 释〗

长相思：词牌名，调名取自南朝乐府“上言长相思，下言久离别”句，多写男女相思之情。**吴山**：泛指钱塘江北岸的群山，古属吴国。**越山**：泛指钱塘江南岸的群山，古属越国。

谁知离别情：一作“争忍有离情”。**泪盈**：含泪欲滴。**同心结**：将罗带系成连环回文样式的结子，象征定情。**潮已平**：指江水已涨到与岸相齐。

〖译 文〗

(1) 许渊冲 译

Tune: “Everlasting Longing” by Lin Bu

The northern hills so green,
The southern hills so green,
They greet your ship which sails the river between.
My grief at parting is so keen.

Tears streaming from your eyes,
Tears streaming from my eyes,
In vain we tried to join by marriage ties.
I see the silent river rise.

(2) 许渊冲 译

Tune: “Everlasting Longing” by Lin Bu

Northern hills green, southern hills green, the green hills greet your ship sailing between. Who knows my parting sorrow keen?

Tears from your eyes, tears from my eyes, could silken girdle strengthen our heart-to-heart ties? O see the river rise!

2.5 苏幕遮(范仲淹)

碧云天，黄叶地。秋色连波，波上寒烟翠。山映斜阳天接水。芳草无情，更在斜阳外。

黯乡魂，追旅思。夜夜除非，好梦留人睡。明月楼高休独倚。酒入愁肠，化作相思泪。

【作品简介】

此词抒写了羁旅思乡之情，题材基本上不脱离传统的离愁别恨的范围，但意境却十分阔大。

【注 释】

苏幕遮：词牌名，又名《云雾敛》《鬓云松令》。其调为西域传入的唐教坊曲，宋代词家用之是另度新曲。**碧云天，黄叶地**：大意是蓝天白云映衬下的金秋大地，一片金黄。**黄叶**：落叶。**秋色连波**：秋色仿佛与波涛连在一起。**波上寒烟翠**：远远望去，水波映着蓝天翠云青烟。**山映斜阳天接水**：夕阳的余晖映射在山上，仿佛与远处的水天相接。**芳草无情，更在斜阳外**：草地延伸到天涯，所到之处比斜阳更遥远。**黯乡魂**：心神因怀念故乡而悲伤。**黯**：黯然，形容心情忧郁、悲伤。**追旅思**：撇不开羁旅的愁思。**追**：紧随，可引申为纠缠。**旅思**：旅途中的愁苦。**夜夜除非，好梦留人睡**：每天夜里，只有做返回故乡的好梦才得以安睡。**夜夜除非**：即"除非夜夜"的倒装。按本文意应作"除非夜夜好梦留人睡"。

【译 文】

(1) James Robert Hightower 译

Tune："Sumuche Dancers"

Fan Chung-yen (*989-1052*)

Blue cloud sky
Yellow leaf ground
Autumn waves
Under cold blue mist.
Hills catch the setting sun, sky and water merge.
Unfeeling, fragrant grasses grow
On and on past the setting sun.

Unhappy homesick soul
Obsessed with travel cares—

Night bring no relief
Except when pleasant dreams prolong the sleep.
Don't look out the high window when the noon shines—
The wine in your melancholy heart
Will turn to tears of longing.

(2) 许渊冲 译

Tune: "Screened by Southern Curtain" by Fan Zhong-yan

Emerald clouds above
And yellow leaves below,
O'er autumn-tinted waves, cold, green mists grow.
The sun slants o'er the hills, the waves blend with the sky,
Unfeeling grass grows sweet beyond the mountains high.

A homesick heart
Lost in thoughts deep,
Only sweet dreams each night can retain me in sleep.
Don't lean alone on rails when the bright moon appears!
Wine in sad bowels would turn into nostalgic tears.

(3) 龚景浩 译

"Su Mu Zhe (Song)"
Fan Zhong Yan

Blue skies,
Ground strewn with yellow leaves,
The colors of autumn going down to the waves,
Over which a chilly bluish mist pervades.
Slanting sunrays shine among the hills,
The sky joins the water.
Sweet grasses, unfeeling, have grown beyond the sunset.

Ah, missing my native place,
Recalling my travels each night

Unless sweet dreams keep me in their land, tight.
A bright moon shining on a many-storeyed building—
Do not stay up there alone!
Any wine that pours into a sad person
Turns immediately into tears of lovesick pining.

(4) 张炳星 译

Sorrow of Separation
Fan Zhongyan

White clouds float in the blue sky grand,
Yellow leaves spread over the ground.
Autumn tint extends to the riverside.
A layer of chilly green mist hangs over the pond,
the setting sun kisses the mountain high
while the distant water touches the sky.
The fragrant grass, so relentless,
expands beyond the setting sun, no less.

What makes the traveler deeply grieved: homesickness.
Every night only sweet dreams bring me comfort and ease.
Under bright moon, don't lean alone against the railings
to look at the distant view.
Wine drops entering my sad heart
have become tear drops, not a few.

2.6 渔家傲(范仲淹)

塞下秋来风景异，衡阳雁去无留意。四面边声连角起，千嶂里，长烟落日孤城闭。

浊酒一杯家万里，燕然未勒归无计。羌管悠悠霜满地，人不寐，将军白发征夫泪。

〖作品简介〗

此词上片写景，下片抒情。词中反映了边塞生活的艰苦和词人巩固边防的决心和意愿，同时还表现出外患未除、功业未建、久戍边地、士兵思乡等复杂的心情。

〖注 释〗

渔家傲：词牌名，双调六十二字，仄韵，上下片各四个七字句，一个三字句，每句用韵，声律谐婉。**塞下**：边界要塞之地，这里指西北边疆。**风景异**：指景物与江南一带不同。**衡阳雁去**："雁去衡阳"的倒语，指大雁离开这里飞往衡阳。相传北雁南飞，到湖南的衡阳为止。**边声**：指各种带有边境特色的声响，如大风、号角、羌笛、马啸的声音。**角**：古代军中的一种乐器。**千嶂**：像屏障一般的群山。**长烟**：荒漠上的烟。**燕然未勒**：指边患未平、功业未成。**燕然**：山名，即今蒙古境内的杭爱山。**勒**：刻石记功。据《后汉书·窦宪传》记载，汉和帝永元元年(89年)，东汉窦宪追击北匈奴，出塞三千余里，至燕然山刻石记功而还。**羌[qiāng]管**：羌笛。出自古代西部羌族的一种乐器。

〖译 文〗

(1) 龚景浩 译

"Yu Jia Ao (Song)"

Fan Zhong Yan

Outside the border fortress the autumn scene was strange.
Wild geese flew past with no sign of course change.
Called up by the bugle, border sounds came alive far and near.
Among numerous mountain tops
A pall of smoke hung straight against the sunset
In the tight-shut fortified town.

Holding up a cup of cheap wine
To my home thousands of miles away:
Before the enemies are checked
There is no way of returning.
Music from the aliens' flute floated around,
The ground hoary with frost.
No sleep!
The general's white hair, the men's sobs.

(2) Chu Dagao 译

On the Frontier

All aspects change on the frontier when autumn comes:
Wild geese fly southward without faltering;
Shouts echo on all sides along the border when the bugle blows;
Amid a thousand mountains,
In the spreading mists and the westering sun, the lonely citadel is closed.

A cup of poor wine, —my native land is ten thousand miles away;
The Huns have not yet been conquered, I have no power to go home.
The Tartar flute comes wailing over a land frost-bound;
One can hardly sleep—
The general's white hair and the soldiers' tears.

(3) 许渊冲 译

Tune: "Pride of Fishermen"

When autumn comes to the frontier, the scene looks drear;
South-bound wild geese won't stay
E'en for a day.
An uproar rises with horns blowing far and near.
Walled in by peaks, smoke rises straight
At sunset over isolate town with fastened gate.

I hold a cup of wine, yet home is far away;
The Northwest is not won; I'm obliged to stay.
At the flutes' doleful sound
Over frost-covered ground
None fall asleep;
The general's hair turns white and the soldiers weep.

2.7 御街行(范仲淹)

纷纷坠叶飘香砌,

夜寂静，寒声碎。
真珠帘卷玉楼空，
天淡银河垂地。
年年今夜，
月华如练，
长是人千里。

愁肠已断无由醉，
酒未到，先成泪。
残灯明灭枕头攲，
谙尽孤眠滋味。
都来此事，
眉间心上，
无计相回避。

〖作品简介〗

此词层深曲折，愁意、愁态、愁容步步逼近，层层翻出，将词人怀人的愁思表现得淋漓尽致。其上阕着重描写秋叶，开头一个“碎”字，不但写出秋叶纷纷坠地的无奈，更渲染出寂夜中悲凉寥寞的心情；紧接着从视觉来写，视线越过珠帘投向楼外，看见垂地般的银河，皓月当空，将词人的思绪引向千里之外的故人，景中透情，引起下阕。下阕抒写离恨，“愁肠已断”作情极之语，已不能自持，潸然泪下，在辗转难眠之中饱尝了愁苦滋味。最后三句用白描手法写愁思，很是真切生动。

〖注 释〗

香砌：有落花的台阶。**寒声碎**：寒风吹动落叶发出的轻微细碎的声音。**真珠**：珍珠。**天淡**：天空清澈无云。**月华**：月光。**练**：白色的丝绸。**无由**：无法。**明灭**：忽明忽暗。**攲**[qī]：倾斜，斜靠。**谙**[ān]**尽**：尝尽。**都来**：算来。

〖译 文〗

Wai-lim Yip 译

Tune: “Walk on the Imperial Street”

Fan Chung-yen (989-1052)

Confused leaves fall, fluttering fragrant steps.

Night stills.
Cold cracks.
Bead-blinds rolled up: jade chamber is empty.
Sky thins: Milky Way touches the ground.
This night each year
Moonlight shines like silk.
Always the loved one a thousand miles away!

Guts cut by grief, no way to get drunk.
Before wine gets there
Tears form.
Dying lamp flicker, pillow aslant,
Darkens the taste of solitary bed.
This matter as always
Between brows, in the heart,
No trick to escape.

2.8 雨霖铃(柳永)

寒蝉凄切，对长亭晚，骤雨初歇。都门帐饮无绪，留恋处，兰舟催发。执手相看泪眼，竟无语凝噎。念去去，千里烟波，暮霭沉沉楚天阔。

多情自古伤离别，更那堪冷落清秋节！今宵酒醒何处？杨柳岸，晓风残月。此去经年，应是良辰好景虚设。便纵有千种风情，更与何人说？

【作品简介】

此词乃作者从汴京南下时与一位恋人的惜别之作。全词遣词造句不着痕迹，描景直白自然，场面栩栩如生，起承转合优雅从容，情景交融，蕴藉深沉，将情人惜别时的真情实感表达得缠绵悱恻、凄婉动人，堪称抒写别情的千古名篇。

【注 释】

长亭：古代在交通要道边每隔十里修建一座长亭供行人休息，又称“十里长亭”。靠近城市的长亭往往是古人送别的地方。**凄切**：凄凉急促。**骤雨**：急猛的阵雨。**都门**：指汴京。**帐饮**：设帐置酒宴送行。**无绪**：没有情绪。**兰舟**：鲁班曾刻木兰树为舟，后用作船的美称。**凝噎**：喉咙哽塞，欲语不出的样子。**去去**：重复言之，表路途之远。**暮霭沉沉**：傍晚云雾很浓，天气阴沉沉的。**经年**：经过一年又一年。**风情**：男女相爱之情，深情蜜意。

【译 文】

(1) Wai-lim Yip 译

Tune: "Bells in the Rains"

Liu Yung (fl. 1045)

Cold-day cicada's cutting creak.
Last evening before the tall pavilion
Sudden rains freshly still.
Farewell drinking outside the city: no good mood.
While hankering after all this,
The magnolia boat is pressed to go.
Hold hands, face to face, eyes in tears
Speechless, words blocked and locked.
This departure:
A thousand miles of smoke-waves
Mist in dust sinks, sinks: Southland sky widens.

All ancient men of emotion grieved over separation.
Now this cold, deserted, clear autumn!
Today: sober from wine? how and where?
Willowed banks, morning winds, leftover moon.
This departure: many years.
Good times, great scenes, all there in vain.
A thousand styles of sentiment I may have
To whom can I spell them?

(2) 龚景浩 译

"Yu Lin Ling (Song)"

Liu Yong

The chilled cicadas were shrill,
We sat facing a roadside pavilion in the failing light,
A sudden shower having just passed.

In no mood to drink in the city-gateside tent,
We'd like to dawdle around a while,
But the orchid boat must go.
Holding hands and looking into each other's teary eyes,
We choked, unable to utter words from the heart.
A thousand miles of misty waves would now keep us apart,
With the evening haze heavy under southern skies.

For emotional people paring has always been difficult,
Not to mention the season—a lonely Harvest Moon Festival!
Where would I wake up tonight to my hangover?
A grassy bank of willows,
The breeze at dawn, and a vanishing moon.
This parting would last for years,
Rendering good times and pleasurable moments to
    nought!
Even though I had many delicate feelings to share,
Who can I speak to?

(3) Jiaosheng Wang 译

Tune: "BELLS IN THE RAINS"
Sadness of Parting

Liu Yung (*987? -1053*)

It was at the roadside pavilion that we were to bid adieu.
A sudden evening rain had just come to a lull,
Lugubrious the chirp of cicadas in the chill air.
At the farewell dinner outside the city gate,
We drank in low spirits,
Unable to tear ourselves away at the boatman's summons.
Hand in hand we gazed at each other's tear-stained eyes,
Words choked on the verge of utterance,
As we brooded over the misty waves
That swept a thousand tricents away,
And a dusky haze silhouetted against
A wide southern sky.

Parting with a loved one has ever been painful since days of old,
Let alone in the season of bleak autumn.
Where shall I be this evening when I sober up?
On a bank o'ergrown with willow—
The moon waning, the wind of dawn blowing.[①]
Once parted, year after year must elapse
When to relive pleasant hours and gay scenes
Will be but an illusion,
And even thou I have a thousand delicate sentiments,
To whom can I bare my aching heart?

① In the original Chinese, this line is traditionally considered famous for its poignant picturesqueness.

(4) Rewi Alley 译

Tune: "Yu Lin Ling"

Now comes the note of the cicada
mournfully; at our place for parting
evening falls; the rainstorm that broke
has cleared away; we drink to each other
and I cannot say what is in my heart,
cannot forget; the boatman urges
departure; we clasp hands, faces wet
with tears; unable to say anything
because of the emotion of the moment;
and I know that soon I shall be far
from here, over the hills;
at night a mist will come
down from heavens, and soon
I'll be in Hupeh, where
skies are high, and ground low;

ever have people hated
leaving their friends, and now
the cold autumn with its sadness
on top of it all; maybe I have

drunk too much, but when I awake
where shall I be? Perhaps
by the willows and populars
in the morning wind under the setting
moon; I shall be away for long
and even if the weather is fair,
the scenery glorious,
I'll not care much; what use
to have such good things
and no friend to speak of them to?

(5) 许渊冲 译

Tune: "Bells Ringing in the Rain"

Cicadas chill
Drearily shrill.
We stand face to face at an evening hour
Before the pavilion, after a sudden shower.
Can we care for drinking before we part?
At the city gate
We are lingering late,
But the boat is waiting for you to depart.
Hand in hand, we gaze at each other's tearful eyes
And burst into sobs with words congealed on our lips.
You'll go your way
Far, far away
On miles and miles of misty waves where sail the ships
And evening clouds hang low in boundless Southern skies.

Lovers would grieve at parting as of old.
How could you stand this clear autumn day so cold!
Where will you be found at daybreak
From wine awake?
Moored by a riverbank planted with willow trees
Beneath the waning moon and in the morning breeze.
You'll be gone for a year.

What could I do with all bright days and fine scenes here!
Howe'er coquettish I am on my part,
To whom can I lay bare my heart?

2.9 八声甘州(柳永)

对潇潇暮雨洒江天，一番洗清秋。渐霜风凄紧，关河冷落，残照当楼。是处红衰翠减，苒苒物华休。唯有长江水，无语东流。

不忍登高临远，望故乡渺邈，归思难收。叹年来踪迹，何事苦淹留？想佳人，妆楼颙望，误几回、天际识归舟。争知我，倚栏杆处，正恁凝愁！

〖作品简介〗

此词表达了作者常年宦游在外，于清秋薄暑时分，感叹漂泊的生涯和思念情人的心情。

〖注　释〗

潇潇：风雨之声。**一番洗清秋**：一番风雨，洗出一个凄清的秋天。**霜风凄紧**：秋风凄凉紧迫。**霜风**：秋风。**凄紧**：一作“凄惨”。**是处红衰翠减**：到处花草凋零。**是处**：到处。**红，翠**：指代花草树木。语出李商隐《赠荷花》：“翠减红衰愁杀人。”**苒**[rǎn]**苒**：渐渐。**渺邈**：遥远。**淹留**：久留。**颙**[yóng]**望**：抬头远望。**误几回、天际识归舟**：多少次错把远处驶来的船当作心上人回家的船。语出谢朓《之宣城郡出新林浦向板桥》：“天际识归舟，云中辨江树。”**争**：怎。**恁**[nèn]：如此。**凝愁**：忧愁凝结不解。

〖译　文〗

(1) Alan Ayling and Duncan Mackintosh 译

Sudden and violent rain in the evening
　　has drenched the river scene,
　　Washing away the cool autumn air;
And now, frost in the wind, a deepening cold, severe
　　On desolate mountain, deserted river:
　　A feeble sunlight touches the tower.
Here is a scene of wasting petals, withering leaves;

Slowly nature's glory is being cut down-
Only the waters of the Great River
Flow on eastwards without a sound.

I cannot bear that distant view from the height,
Facing my own country far away.
Racked by thoughts of returning home
I lament my past years' coming and goings;
What led me to accept that sad delay?
I think of my loved one up in her bedroom
gazing out to the distant
Horizon; how often she must have mistaken
for mine other boats returning!
And how can she know I am leaning now
Over the balcony here
Filled with same deep yearning?

(2) Zong-qi Cai 译

To the Tune of "Eight Beats of a Ganzhou Song"

I face the splashing evening shower sprinkling from the sky over the river
And washing clean the cool autumn.
Gradually the pressing frosty wind gets more and more chilly,
The mountain passes and rivers turn bleak,
While the last ray of the sun lingers on the balcony.
Here and there the red withers and the green decays—
Slowly nature's blossoms fade.
Only the water of the Yangtze
Silently flows east.

I cannot bear to ascend the height and look into the distance.
I look toward my homeland afar, not to be seen;
Thoughts of returning home just would not stop.
I sigh over my wanderings these years;
What is it that keeps me here?

I imagine my fair one is now gazing earnestly out of her window,
Mistaking again and again some returning boat on the horizon for mine.
How could she know that I, leaning against the balustrade here,
Am lost in sorrow?

(3) 许渊冲 译

Tune: "Eight Beats of a Ganzhou Song" by Liu Yong

Shower by shower
Besprinkles evening rain the sky
Over the river,
Washing cool the autumn air both far and nigh.
Gradually frost falls and blows the wind so chill
That few people pass by hill or rill,
In fading sunlight drowned is my bower.
Everywhere the red and the green wither away,
There's no more splendor of a sunny day.
Only the waves of River Long
Silently eastward flow along.

I cannot bear
To climb high and look far, for to gaze where
My native land is lost in mists so thick
Would make my lonely heart homesick.
I sigh to see my rovings year by year.
Why should I linger hopelessly now there, now here?
From her bower my lady fair
Must gaze with longing eye.
How oft has she mistaken homebound sails
On the horizon for those sails of mine?
How could she know that I,
Leaning upon the rails,
With sorrow frozen my face, for her I pine!

(4) Robert Kotewall and Norman L. Smith 译

To the Tune of "Kan-chou with Eight Rhymes"

Before me the dreary, dreary evening rain spatters
river and sky,
Wholly washing the Autumn clean.
Slowly comes the frost, and the bleak wind presses;
The frontier-pass and the river are cold and desolate;
And the dying sun fronts the tower.
Here the red grows sere and the green fades;
Slowly, slowly the glory of Nature departs.
Only there is the Long River's water
Silently flowing eastward.

I dare not climb on high to gaze afar,
For fear that my village is out of sight,
And the longing for home too hard to quell.
I sigh to think of these years of wandering;
What tarries me here to lament my lagging?
Methinks my fair wife has long watched from her tiring-
room.
Oft beguiled as she marks a homeward ship on the
horizon.
Little knowing that I am here leaning on this balustrade.
At this moment what heaped-up sorrow!

2.10 看花回(柳永)

屈指劳生百岁期。荣瘁相随。利牵名惹逡巡过，奈两轮、玉走金飞。
红颜成白发，极品何为。
尘事常多雅会稀。忍不开眉。画堂歌管深深处，难忘酒盏花枝。
醉乡风景好，携手同归。

【作品简介】

此词是作者创作的一组词中的上首。全词咏人生短暂，认为功名利禄、尘世荣辱不过都是过眼云烟，只有抛却烦恼及时行乐，在音乐、美女的陪伴下沉入醉乡，才能弥补人生的缺憾，对抗生命的短暂。这首词反映了词人超脱世俗的思想感情。词中他看破了现实生活中的名和利，以“醉乡深处，温柔乡里”作为人生最终的归宿，表现了词人复杂的心情。

〖注　释〗

屈指：掐指计算。**劳生**：辛劳奔波的一生。**百岁期**：百年时间，这里代指人的一生。**荣瘁**：荣辱，这里指政治生涯中的穷达，或得志或失意。**利牵名惹**：为名利所羁绊。**逡巡**：迟疑不决而徘徊或不敢前进。**两轮**：指日轮与月轮，即日月。**玉走金飞**：玉指玉兔，代称月亮。**金**：指金乌，代指太阳。玉走金飞，日月运行迅速，即说光阴流逝很快。**极品**：最高的官位。《宋史·职官志六》中记载：“凡内侍初补曰小黄门……次迁都都知，遂为内臣极品。”**尘事**：即尘世俗事。**雅会**：美好的相会。**忍不**：怎忍不。**开眉**：展开眉头，即心情愉快。**画堂**：指华美的房屋。**歌管**：唱歌奏乐。**花枝**：代指艳丽的女子。**醉乡**：指沉湎于醉酒之中。

〖译　文〗

Stephen Owen 译

Tune: “Turning Back After Seeing the Flowers” (*Kan-hua hui*) by Liu Yong (987-1053)

When I reckon up these hundred years
　　burdened with life,
high times and wretchedness follow each other.
The tug of advantage, the lure of renown—
　　both go by in a flash,
and nothing stops the two orbs,
　　a jade moon rushing,
　　a golden sun in flight.
The bloom on your cheeks becomes white hair,
and what good does having the highest rank?

Worldly troubles are always too many,
　　fine parties are always too rare.
So how can you help breaking into a smile?
In the deepest spot of the painted hall

songs are sung to flutes,
and never forget the cup of wine
and the woman, a spray of flowers.
The scenes are sweet in the land of drunkenness—
Take my hand and we'll go there together.

2.11 夜半乐(柳永)

冻云黯淡天气，扁舟一叶，乘兴离江渚。渡万壑千岩，越溪深处。怒涛渐息，樵风乍起，更闻商旅相呼；片帆高举。泛画鹢、翩翩过南浦。

望中酒旆闪闪，一簇烟村，数行霜树。残日下、渔人鸣榔归去。败荷零落，衰柳掩映，岸边两两三三、浣纱游女。避行客、含羞笑相语。

到此因念，绣阁轻抛，浪萍难驻。叹后约、丁宁竟何据！惨离怀、空恨岁晚归期阻。凝泪眼、杳杳神京路，断鸿声远长天暮。

〖作品简介〗

此词乃作者用旧曲名创制的新声乐府之一。全词共分三片。这也是作者首创，在其以前的敦煌曲子词中，尚未发现有此类作品。全词三片之间有着明显的分工。第一片写途中的经历；第二片写途中之所见；第三片抒发去国离乡的感叹。

〖注　释〗

夜半乐：唐教坊曲，后用为词牌。**冻云**：冬天浓重聚积的云。**扁舟**：小船。**乘兴离江渚**：自己乘兴离开了江边。**江渚**：江边。**渚**：水中沙洲，此指水边。**万壑千岩**：出自《世说新语·言语》：顾恺之自会稽归来，盛赞那里的山川之美，说："千岩竞秀，万壑争流。"这里指千山万水。**越溪**：泛指越地的溪流。**樵风**：指顺风。**乍起**：指山风突然地吹起来。**商旅**：行商之旅客，这里泛指旅客。**画鹢**[yì]：船其首画鹢鸟者，以图吉利。鹢是古书上说的一种水鸟，不怕风暴，善于飞翔。这里以"画鹢"代指舟船。**翩翩**：形容穿行轻快的样子。**南浦**：南岸的水边，泛指水滨。**望中**：在视野里。**酒旆**：酒店用来招引顾客的旗幌。**一簇烟村**：一处冒着炊烟的村庄。**鸣榔**：用木长棒敲击船舷。渔人有时用来敲船，使鱼受惊入网；有时用它敲船以为唱歌的节拍，这里用后者，即渔人唱着渔歌回家。**浣纱游女**：水边洗衣劳作的农家女子。**因**：这里是"于是""就"的意思。**绣阁轻抛**：轻易抛弃了偎红倚翠的生活。**浪萍难驻**：漂泊漫游如浪中浮萍一样行踪无定。**后约**：约定以后相见的日期。**丁宁**：同"叮咛"，临别郑重嘱咐。**何据**：有什么根据，是说临别时相互的约定、嘱咐都不可靠，都无法实现。**空恨**：徒恨。**杳杳**：遥远之意。**神京**：指都城汴京。**断鸿**：失群的孤雁。**长天暮**：远天出现茫茫暮色。

『译 文』

Stephen Owen 译

Tune: "Joy at Midnight" (*Ye-ban le*) by Liu Yong (987-1053)

A solid mass of cloud,
    dark and gloomy weather,
in a tiny boat
riding my whim
    I left the river isles;
and passed through thousands of canyons and cliffs
to the deepest spots in the creeks of Yue.
There raging waves gradually calmed,
and a breeze of woodsmen suddenly rose,
when I heard merchant travelers
    shouting back and forth.
With sails raised high
painted prows glided,
    they bent swiftly past the southern shores.

Tavern signs flashed in my gaze,
a village lay clumped in the fog,
and several lines of frosty trees.
As the fading sun set, the fishermen
    made their way home, knocking clappers.
Broken lotus shed petal shreds,
dying willows appeared in bits;
by the bank in twos and threes
girls washing gauze
fled the traveler,
    bashful and giggling to one another.

Coming here, my thoughts turn
to splendid chambers too lightly left,
and myself, wave-borne duckweed that cannot rest.
Too bad that our pact to meet, made earnestly,
    will finally be hard to keep.

Depressed at being apart, helplessly upset
that I can't make the date
to return to you late in the year.
Tears well in my eyes,
the road to the capital stretches faint and far.
Far off the voice of a wild goose,
lost from the flock,
in the long skies of evening.

2.12 凤栖梧(柳永)

伫倚危楼风细细，望极春愁，黯黯生天际。草色烟光残照里，无言谁会凭阑意。

拟把疏狂图一醉，对酒当歌，强乐还无味。衣带渐宽终不悔，为伊消得人憔悴。

〖作品简介〗

此词上片写登高望远所引起的无尽离愁，以迷离的景物描写渲染出凄楚悲凉的气氛；下片写主人公为消释离愁决意痛饮狂歌，但强颜为欢终觉无味，最后以健笔写柔情，自誓甘愿为思念伊人而日渐消瘦憔悴。全词巧妙地把漂泊异乡的落魄感受，同怀恋意中人的缠绵情思融为一体，表现了主人公坚毅的性格与执著的态度。

〖注 释〗

伫[zhù]倚危楼：长时间倚靠在高楼的栏杆上。**伫**：久立。**危楼**：高楼。**望极**：极目远望。**黯黯[ànàn]**：心情沮丧忧愁。**生天际**：从遥远无边的天际升起。**烟光**：飘忽缭绕的云霭雾气。**会**：理解。**阑**：同"栏"。**拟把**：打算。**疏狂**：狂放不羁。**强[qiǎng]乐**：勉强欢笑。**强**：勉强。**衣带渐宽**：指人逐渐消瘦。语本《古诗十九首》："相去日已远，衣带日已缓。"**消得**：值得。

〖译 文〗

许渊冲 译

Tune: "Phoenix Perching on Plane Tree" by Liu Yong

I lean alone on balcony in light, light breeze; as far as the eye sees, on the horizon dark parting grief grows unseen. In fading sunlight rises smoke over grass green. Who understands why mutely on the rails I lean?

I'd drown in wine my parting grief; chanting before the cup, strained mirth brings no relief. I find my gown too large, but I will not regret; its worth while growing languid for my coquette.

2.13 菩萨蛮(张先)

忆郎还上层楼曲，楼前芳草年年绿。绿似去时袍，回头风袖飘。

郎袍应已旧，颜色非长久。惜恐镜中春，不如花草新。

【作品简介】

这是一首以感春怀人为内容的闺怨词。它在运思、谋篇方面自出机杼，别具一格，推陈出新。

【注　释】

菩萨蛮：原为唐教坊曲，后用为词牌。亦作“菩萨鬘”，又名“子夜歌”“重叠金”等。

镜中春：指镜中女子的容颜如春光般姣好。

【译　文】

龚景浩 译

“Pu Sa Man (Song)”

Zhang Xian

Remembering you, I mounted the winding stairway.
Each year, the grasses before our lodge turn green:
The color of your robe when you left.
Turning back to wave, how your sleeves ballooned deft.

The robe now must be worn,
Colors cannot last long.

I am afraid that mirrored spring
Cannot compete with blossoms newly sprung.

2.14 天仙子(张先)

水调数声持酒听，午醉醒来愁未醒。送春春去几时回？临晚镜，伤流景，往事后期空记省。

沙上并禽池上暝，云破月来花弄影。重重帘幕密遮灯，风不定，人初静，明日落红应满径。

【作品简介】

此词为临老伤春之作，全词将作者概叹年老位卑、前途渺茫之情与暮春之景有机地交融一起，工于锻炼字句，体现了张词的主要艺术特色。

【注　释】

水调：曲调名。**流景**：像水一样的年华，逝去的光阴。**景**：日光。**后期**：以后的约会。**记**：思念。**省**[xǐng]：省悟。**并禽**：成对的鸟儿，这里指鸳鸯。**暝**：天黑，暮色笼罩。**弄**：摆弄。

【译　文】

(1) 许渊冲 译

Tune: "Song of the Immortal" by Zhang Xian

Wine cup in hand, I listen to Water Melody, awake from wine at noon, but not from melancholy. When will spring come back now it is going away? In the mirror, alas! I see happy time pass. In vain may I recall the old days gone for aye.

Night falls on poolside sand where pairs of love-birds stay; the moon breaks through the clouds, with shadows flowers play. Lamplights veiled by screen on screen can't be seen. The fickle wind still blows; the night so silent grows. Tomorrow fallen reds should cover the pathway.

（2）龚景浩 译

"Tian Xian Zi (Song)"

Zhang Xian

Wine cup in hand, I listened to snatches of rippling song.
Waking up from a wine stupor, my sadness was not gone.
I sent spring away, but when will it return?
Touching up before the mirror at dusk,
I grieved over the scene fleeting by:
The past and the future—what use to remember?

Two waterfowl from the sands dozed off on the pond.
Clouds broke, the moon emerged,
And flowers flirted with their own shadows.
Layers of heavy door-curtains sealed off the lamps,
The winds were erratic,
The bustle of human activity had quieted down.
Tomorrow, fallen petals shall cover the footpaths all around.

2.15 更漏子（张先）

锦筵红，罗幕翠。侍宴美人姝丽。十五六，解怜才。劝人深酒杯。
黛眉长，檀口小。耳畔向人轻道。柳阴曲，是儿家。门前红杏花。

【作品简介】

此词以才子佳人的爱为主题，颇有戏剧性地叙写了才子佳人歌筵酒席之间的邂逅。全词以紧凑之笔墨对场面、人物、动作及对话作了极为精彩的描述，风格清新、明秀而又含蓄，情感热烈、轻倩而不流于浅薄，读来引人入胜、回味无穷。

【注 释】

锦筵：美盛的筵席。**罗幕**：丝罗帐幕。**侍宴**：宴享时陪从或侍候于旁。**姝[shū]丽**：美丽。**解**：了解，懂得。**怜才**：爱慕有才华的人。**黛[dài]眉**：黛画之眉，特指女子之眉。**檀[tán]口**：红艳的嘴唇，多形容女性嘴唇之美。**檀**：浅绛色，即浅红色。**柳阴**：亦作"柳荫"，柳下的阴影。**儿家**：古代年轻女子对其家的自称。

【译　文】

Ronald C. Egan 译

To the Tune of "The Waterclock"

The brocade mat is red,
The gauze curtain is green.
The girl in attendance is beautiful.
Fifteen or sixteen,
She knows to love the talented one
And urges him to fill his winecup.

Her black eyebrows are long.
Her pink mouth is small.
She whispers in his ear:
'At the willow-shaded corner,
That's my house.
With red apricot blossoms by the gate.'

2.16　破阵子(晏殊)

燕子来时新社，梨花落后清明。
池上碧苔三四点，叶底黄鹂一两声。日长飞絮轻。
巧笑东邻女伴，采桑径里逢迎。
疑怪昨宵春梦好，元是今朝斗草赢。笑从双脸生。

【作品简介】

此词通过描写清明时节的一个生活片断来表现节日的气氛和少女身上的青春活力及纯洁心灵。全词纯用白描，笔调活泼，风格朴实，形象生动。

【注　释】

破阵子：词牌名，原为唐教坊曲名。又名《十拍子》。双调六十二字，平韵。**新社**：社日是古代祭土地神的日子，以祈丰收，有春秋两社。新社即春社，时间在立春后、清明前。**碧苔**：碧绿色的苔草。**飞絮**：飘荡着的柳絮。**巧笑**：形容少女美好的笑容。**逢迎**：碰头，相逢。**疑怪**：诧异，奇怪。这里是“怪不得”的意思。**斗草**：古代妇女的一种游戏，也叫“斗百草”。**双脸**：指脸颊。

〖译 文〗

许渊冲 译

Tune:“Dance of the Cavalry” by Yan Shu

When swallows come, we worship gods of spring;
Then flowers fall, we mourn for the dear dead.
We hear, amid the leaves, the orioles sing;
Beside the pool we see the green moss spread.
The willow catkins fly as the day's lengthening.

My neighbor's daughter and her friends are sweet,
Mulberry leaves to gather now they meet.
Last night, she wonders, why such happy dreams?
They foretell that she wins the game of grass, it seems.
A sparkling smile upon her fair face beams.

2.17 破阵子(晏殊)

燕子欲归时节，高楼昨夜西风。求得人间成小会，试把金尊傍菊丛。歌长粉面红。

斜日更穿帘幕，微凉渐入梧桐。多少襟情言不尽，写向蛮笺曲调中。此情千万重。

〖作品简介〗

此词是作者的一首感怀词作。全词描写虽然是寻常景物，但经诗人的点染，却成了一幅郁郁悲凉、惜别、思念之作。季节本无形，词中用燕子这一意象代替写出来，具体生动，画面感徒增。蕴涵了诗人的忧伤情怀。

〖注 释〗

归：归去。**西风**：秋风。**小会**：短暂的聚会。**金尊**：金色的酒器。**尊**：亦作“樽”，中国古代的盛酒器具。**歌**：作动词，唱。**面**：脸。**斜日**：夕阳。**更**：正。**襟情**：情怀。南朝宋·刘义庆《世说新语·赏誉》：“许掾尝诣简文，尔夜风恬月朗，乃共作曲室中语，襟情之咏，偏是许之所长，辞寄清婉，有逾平日。”唐代权德舆《送信安刘少府自常州参军选授》诗曰：“襟情无俗虑，谈笑成逸躅。”**蛮笺**[mán jiān]：谓蜀笺，唐时指四川地区所造彩色花纸。

〖译 文〗

Stephen Owen 译

Tune: "Breaking Through the Ranks" (*Po zhen-zi*) by Yan Shu (991-1055)

That time of year when swallows are set to go,
And in high rooms last night, west wind.
I sought a small party in
    This mortal world,
We held our golden cups beside
    Clumps of chrysanthemums.
The songs lasted long, and faces
    Powdered white flushed red.

Then sinking sunlight again
    Pierced the curtains,
Light chill progressively touched the beech.
So much in the heart I could not say—
On slips of fine paper
    I wrote into melody
these feelings, in thousands, one after another.

2.18 浣溪沙(晏殊)

一曲新词酒一杯，去年天气旧亭台。夕阳西下几时回？
无可奈何花落去，似曾相识燕归来。小园香径独徘徊。

〖作品简介〗

此词虽含伤春惜时之意，却实为感慨抒怀之情。词之上片绾合今昔，叠印时空，重在思昔；下片则巧借眼前景物，重在伤今。词中对宇宙人生的深思，给人以哲理性的启迪和美的艺术享受。

【注 释】

一曲新词酒一杯：此句化用白居易《长安道》意："花枝缺入青楼开，艳歌一曲酒一杯。""一曲"乃"一首"之意。因为词是配合音乐唱的，故称"曲"。"新词"指刚填好的词，意指新歌。**去年天气旧亭台**：是说天气、亭台都和去年一样。此句化用五代郑谷《和知已秋日伤感》诗："流水歌声共不回，去年天气旧池台。"晏词"亭台"一词本作"池台"。去年天气，是说跟去年此日相同的天气。旧亭台，曾经到过的或熟悉的亭台楼阁。**夕阳**：落日。**西下**：向西方地平线落下。**几时回**：什么时候回来。**无可奈何**：不得已，没有办法。**似曾相识**：好像曾经认识。形容见过的事物再度出现。后用作成语，即出自晏殊此句。**燕归来**：燕子从南方飞回来。燕归来，春中常景，在有意无意之间。**小园香径**：花草芳香的小径，或指落花散香的小径。因落花满径、幽香四溢，故云香径。**独**：副词，用于谓语前，表示"独自"的意思。**徘徊**：来回走。

【译 文】

(1) 龚景浩 译

"Huan Xi Sha (Song)"
Yan Shu

A new poem set to music, a cup of wine,
Last year's weather, the same terrace and pavilion,
A setting sun in the western sky—
But when will you return?

Flower petals, helpless, are falling.
Swallows I seem to have seen before, are returning.
Among the perfumed paths in the little garden,
I loiter, alone.

(2) Zong-qi Cai 译

To the Tune of "Sand in Silk-Washing Stream"

A new song, a cup of wine;
Last year's weather at the old pond terrace.
The setting sun sinks in the west—when to return?

Do what one may, blossoms will fall;
As if we knew each other, the swallows come back.
In the little garden I pace a fragrant path alone.

(3) John A. Turner 译

Mutability

A new song, and another cup of wine!
An air of yesteryear is haunting still
This ancient lodge. But will that twilight day
That's sinking in the West come back again?

And ineluctably the blossoms fall.
And swallows, like the ones I knew, return.
And mournfully I tread the scented ways
Of this small pleasure-garden, to and fro.

(4) 许渊冲 译

Tune: "Silk-Washing Stream"

I compose a new song and drink a cup of wine
In the bower of last year when weather is as fine.
When will you come back like the sun on the decline.

Deeply I sigh for faded flowers' fall in vain;
Vaguely I seem to know the swallows come again.
Loitering on the garden path, I alone remain.

(5) Ronald C. Egan 译

To the Tune of "Sands of the Washing Stream"

A new song, a single cup of wine,
Last year's weather, the same pavilions and balconies.

The sun sets in the west, when will it return?

The flowers will fall for all you can do.
And the swallows that look familiar return.
On the scented garden path I pace to and fro.

2.19 浣溪沙(晏殊)

一向年光有限身。等闲离别易消魂。酒筵歌席莫辞频。
满目山河空念远，落花风雨更伤春。不如怜取眼前人。

【作品简介】

此词是一首伤别之作，叹人生有限，抒写离情别绪，所表现的及时行乐的思想，反映出词人的无奈与洒脱。全词在章法结构方面上下关合：下片“满目”句照应上片次句，因离别而念远；“落花”句照应上片首句，因慨叹人生短暂而伤春。结句借用《会真记》中的诗句，即转即收。

【注　释】

一向：一晌，片刻，一会儿。**年光**：时光。**有限身**：有限的生命。**等闲**：平常，随便，无端。**销魂**：极度悲伤，极度快乐。**莫辞频**：频，频繁。不要因为次数多而推辞。**怜取眼前人**：元稹《会真记》载崔莺莺诗：“还将旧来意，怜取眼前人。”**怜**：珍惜，怜爱。**取**：语气助词。

【译　文】

(1) Stephen Owen 译

Tune: “Washing Creek Sands” (*Huan xi sha*) by Yan Shu (991-1055)

Only a moment, this season’s splendor,
　　this body, a bounded thing;
to part now as if it didn’t matter
　　easily breaks the heart;
so don’t be hasty, refusing

the party's wine, the banquet's song.

Mountains and rivers fill our eyes, but care
is wasted on things too far;
besides which, this grief at spring passing,
at wind and rain that bring down flowers;
it is better by far to take as your love
the person before your eyes.

(2) 许渊冲 译

What can a short-lived man do with the fleeting year and soul-consuming separations from his dear? Refuse no banquet when fair singing girls appear!

With hills and rills in sight, I miss the far-off in vain. How can I bear the fallen blooms in wind and rain! Why not enjoy the fleeting pleasure now again?

2.20 蝶恋花(晏殊)

槛菊愁烟兰泣露。罗幕轻寒，燕子双飞去。明月不谙离恨苦。斜光到晓穿朱户。

昨夜西风凋碧树。独上高楼，望尽天涯路。欲寄彩笺兼尺素。山长水阔知何处。

【作品简介】

这是一首写闺思的词，词之上片运用移情于景的手法，选取眼前的景物，注入主人公的感情，点出离恨；下片承离恨而来，通过高楼独望把主人公望眼欲穿的神态生动地表现出来。

【注释】

槛[jiàn]：栏杆。**罗幕**：丝罗的帷幕，为富贵人家所用。**朱户**：犹言朱门，指大户人家。**不谙**[ān]：不了解，没有经验。**谙**：熟悉，精通。**碧树**：绿树。**彩笺**：彩色的信笺。**尺素**：书信的代称。古人写信用素绢，通常长约一尺，故称尺素，语出《古诗十九首》："客从远方来，遗我双鲤鱼。呼儿烹鲤鱼，中有尺素书。"

『译 文』

(1) 龚景浩 译

"Die Lian Hua (Song)" by Yan Shu

Outside the railings chrysanthemums are sad
And orchids are shedding tears of dew.
The silk curtains hang light and cool,
A pair of swallows flying off.
The bright moon knows not the sorrow
Of departure and solitude,
Its slanting rays piercing the vermilion portals
Till dawn breaks.

Last night the west wind withered the emerald leaves.
Alone, I mounted the stairs
To look down the endless road.
I'm ready to send reams of letters and elegant notes.
But the rivers are wide, the mountains so high,
I do not know where to locate you.

(2) 张炳星 译

The Sorrow of Parting

Yan Shu

The chrysanthemums by the balustrade were covered with
sorrowful smoke,
while orchids shed tears of dew.
Gauze curtains looked slightly cold.
Swallows flew away by pairs as of old.
The bright moon unable to know the bitterness of separation,
peeped slantwise into the red chamber until dawn.

Last night the west wind withered the green trees,

causing leaves all fall down.
I mounted the high tower alone and
gazed into the corners of the earth for long.
I wish to send poems and letters to my lover,
but with such long mountains and wide rivers,
I don't know where to find her forever.

2.21 玉楼春（晏殊）

绿杨芳草长亭路，年少抛人容易去。楼头残梦五更钟，花底离愁三月雨。
无情不似多情苦，一寸还成千万缕。天涯地角有穷时，只有相思无尽处。

〖作品简介〗

此词写闺怨，表现思妇刻骨相思之情，刻画出一位对爱情忠贞不渝的女子形象。其主题歌咏了凄凄的哀怨与静静的相思。

〖注 释〗

长亭：秦汉时每隔十里建一亭，故称十里长亭，即供行人休憩饯别之处。**容易**：轻易，随便。**一寸**：指心、心绪。**穷**：穷尽，终了。

〖译 文〗

(1) James Robert Hightower 译

Tune: "Spring in the Jade House" by Yen Shu

Green willows and fragrant grass by the posthouse road
Where the young man left me without a pang.
An unfinished dream at the fifth watch bell
The sorrow of parting under the blossoms in a third month rain.

Insensitive misses susceptible's bitterness,
Whose every inch turns into a thousand myriad strands.
The sky's edge, earth's corner—sometime they come to an end;
It's just this longing that is never done.

(2) 许渊冲 译

Tune: "Spring in Jade Pavilion" by Yan Shu

Farewell Pavilion green with grass and willow trees! How could my gallant young lord have left me with ease! I'm woke by midnight bell from dim dream in my bower; parting grief won't part with flowers falling in shower.

My beloved feels not the grief my loving heart sheds: each string as woven with thousands of painful threads. However far and wide the sky and earth may be, they can't measure the lovesickness o'erwhelming me.

2.22 木兰花(宋祁)

东城渐觉风光好，縠皱波纹迎客棹。绿杨烟外晓寒轻，红杏枝头春意闹。
浮生长恨欢娱少，肯爱千金轻一笑。为君持酒劝斜阳，且向花间留晚照。

【作品简介】

此词赞颂明媚的春光，表达了及时行乐的情趣。上阕描绘春日绚丽的景色，下阕直抒惜春寻乐的情怀。全词收放自如、井井有条，用语华丽而不轻佻，言情直率而不扭捏，把对时光的留恋、对美好人生的珍惜写得韵味十足。

【注　释】

木兰花：原唐教坊曲名，后用为词牌名，调同“玉楼春”。《金奁集》入“林钟商调”。此词为双调五十六字，前后片各三仄韵。**縠**[hú]**皱波纹**：形容波纹细如皱纹。**縠皱**：即皱纱，有褶皱的纱。**棹**[zhào]：船桨，此指船。**春意**：春天的气象。**闹**：浓盛。**浮生**：指漂浮无定的短暂人生。语本《庄子·刻意》：“其生若浮，其死若休。”**肯爱**：岂肯吝惜，即不吝惜。**一笑**：特指美人之笑。**持酒**：端起酒杯。《新唐书·庶人祐传》：“王毋忧，右手持酒啖，左手刀拂之。”**晚照**：夕阳的余晖。南朝宋武帝《七夕》诗之一：“白日倾晚照，弦月升初光。”

【译　文】

(1) 许渊冲 译

The scenery is getting fine east of the town; the rippling water greets boats rowing up and down. Beyond green willows morning chill is growing mild; on pink apricot branches spring is running wild.

In our floating life scarce are pleasures we seek after. How can we value gold above a hearty laughter? I raise wine cup to ask the slanting sun to stay and leave among the flowers its departing ray.

(2) 龚景浩 译

"Mu Lan Hua (Song)" by Song Qi

From the east side of the city, spring beckons.
To all visitors' boats the wavelets on the lake say: Welcome!
From the green mist atop the willows.
The morning chill lifts
Among the red-apricot branches spring runs riot!

'Tis often a regret life holds so little joy.
We love gold more, than we do a winning smile.
So I hold up a wine cup for you to the sinking sun:
Leave your afterglow in the flowering bushes!

2.23 醉蓬莱(欧阳修)

见羞容敛翠，嫩脸匀红，素腰袅娜。红药阑边，恼不教伊过。半掩娇羞，语声低颤，问道有人知么。强整罗裙，偷回波眼，佯行佯坐。

更问假如，事还成后，乱了云鬟，被娘猜破。我且归家，你而今休呵。更为娘行，有些针线，诮未曾收啰。却待更阑，庭花影下，重来则个。

〖作品简介〗

此词被人视为欧阳修所作俗词。俗词有别雅词，多叙事，注意情节结构的自然发展和心理动作的细腻描写。这首《醉蓬莱》叙写了一对男女私会的情景，并商量如何骗过女子的母亲，以便更阑之际，重来欢会。其内容充满俗情，甚至还带有色情色彩。但作者对女子既羞涩又向往、既担心母亲发现又宽慰对方勿躁的心理，描写得形象传神。

〖注 释〗

素腰袅娜：形容女子细腰袅娜、亭亭玉立的苗条身材。**红药阑边**：在芍药栏边见面。

却待更阑，庭花影下，重来则个：等到夜深更阑人静，我们再来庭花影下这里吧。

〖译 文〗

(1) James Robert Hightower 译

Tune: "Drunk in Fairyland"

By Ou-yang Hsiu (*1007-1072*)

Shyly she knits her brows
And shows a face delicately rouged:
Supple waist in white silk
Beside the peony balustrade.
Vexed, she won't let him approach—
Half hiding her coy face,
Her voice low and shaking,
She asks, "Does anyone know?"
Smoothing her silk skirt,
She steals an upward glance
And takes a step or two away.

Then she asks,
"If I do it and then
My hair comes all undone
And mother guesses what's up?
No, I am going home—
You leave me alone for now.
Besides, I've needlework to do for mother;
She'll scold me if I don't get it done.
Wait until late tonight,
And come again
Under the shadows of the courtyard trees, okay?"

(2) Ronald C. Egan 译

To the Tune of "Drunk in Paradise"

Shy, she knits her eyebrows in a frown,

Her tender face evenly rouged,
Her slender waist swaying.
Beside the red safflower railing
Annoyed, she won't let him come near.
Then, half hiding her bashfulness,
In a low quivering voice
She asks, 'Does anyone know? '
Struggling to straighten her silk gown,
She steals a look back with limpid eyes,
Pretending now to walk away, now to sit.

Again, she asks, 'What if,
Afterwards,
My hair is mussed
And Mother guesses the truth?
I'll go home.
Will you stop for now?
Besides, I'm on an errand for Mother.
There's some embroidery
I've been scolded for not finishing.
Wait until later tonight.
The shadows of the courtyard blossoms—
I'll meet you there! '

2.24 玉楼春(欧阳修)

别后不知君远近，触目凄凉多少闷。渐行渐远渐无书，水阔鱼沉何处问。
夜深风竹敲秋韵，万叶千声皆是恨。故欹单枕梦中寻，梦又不成灯又烬。

〖作品简介〗

此词是一首别后相思愁绪之作，乃作者的早期作品。它受五代花间词的影响，以代言体(即女性第一人称方式)形式表达了闺中思妇深沉凄婉的离愁别绪。全词以景寓情，情景交融，词境委婉曲折、深沉精细而又温柔敦厚。发端句“别后不知君远近”是恨的缘由。因不知亲人行踪，故触景皆生出凄凉、郁闷，亦即无时无处不如此。

〖注 释〗

远近：不知道相距有多远，不知道在哪里的意思。**触目**：眼睛接触到的，指看到的。

多少："不知多少"之意。

【译 文】

Robert Kotewall and Norman L. Smith 译

After the parting I know not if he is far or near.
What meets the eye is bleak and doleful.
Slowly he journeys, slowly he goes farther, slowly his
letters grow fewer.
Broad are the waters, deep swim the fish, where can I
ask for him?

In depth of night the wind and bamboos tap out the
music of Autumn;
Myriad leaves give a thousand sounds—all are
lamentation.
So I choose the solitary pillow in search of dreams,
But dreams come not, and the lamp is guttering out.

2.25 阮郎归(欧阳修)

南园春半踏青时，风和闻马嘶。青梅如豆柳如眉，日长蝴蝶飞。
花露重，草烟低，人家帘幕垂。秋千慵困解罗衣，画堂双燕归。

【作品简介】

此词描写的是一位女子于仲春时节踏青时的见闻以及由此而产生的相思之情。词分上下两片，上片主要写春日郊外的秀丽景色和女子的见闻；下片由写景转入抒情，抒发了女子的相思之苦。全词清秀典雅、迤逦飘逸，借景抒情，情景交融，回环委婉，是极为典型的一首小词。

【注 释】

踏青：春日郊游。唐宋踏青日期因地而异。有正月初八者，也有二月二日或三月三日者。后世多以清明出游为踏青。**风和**：春风暖和。**马嘶**：指游人车马的声音。**嘶**：叫。**青**

梅如豆柳如眉：青梅结得像豆子那么大，柳叶长得像美人的眉毛。后世多以此句描绘明媚的春日风景。**日长**：过了春分的节令，白天渐渐长了。这里还有整个白天的意思。**草烟**：形容春草稠密。**帘幕**：帘子和帷幕。**慵**[yōng]**困**：困倦。**罗衣**：香罗衫。**画堂**：彩画装饰的堂屋。

【译　文】

Alan Ayling and Duncan Mackintosh 译

Spring in the South

Early spring in the southern gardens, a time to tread the grass
　　With a favouring wind you can hear the horse neigh.
Green plums the size of beans, willow-shoots like eyebrows.
　　Days lengthen, butterflies quiver.

　　Dew lies heavy on the flowers,
　　Mist hangs low on the grasses,
　　In houses blinds are hanging down.
Indolent girls on swings loosen their silken dresses.
　　On a painted beam a pair of swallows settle.

2.26　生查子(欧阳修)

去年元夜时，花市灯如昼。月上柳梢头，人约黄昏后。
今年元夜时，月与灯依旧。不见去年人，泪湿春衫袖。

【作品简介】

此词乃一首相思词，描写了主人公昔日一段缠绵悱恻、难以忘怀的爱情，抒发了旧日恋情破灭后的失落感与孤独感，揭示了物是人非、旧情难续的伤感心理。

【注　释】

元夜：农历正月十五夜，即元宵节，也称上元节。唐代以来有元夜观灯的风俗。**花市**：指元夜花灯照耀的灯市。**春衫**：年少时穿的衣服，可指代年轻时的自己。

〖译 文〗

(1) 许渊冲 译

Tune: "Mountain Hawthorn" by Ou-yang Xiu

Last year on this moonlit spring night,
Lanterns in Flower Fair were bright.
The moon rose above the willow tree,
At dusk he had a tryst with me.

This year on the same moonlit night,
The moon and lanterns are as bright.
Where is my beloved of last year?
My sleeves are wet with tear on tear.

(2) 龚景浩 译

"Sheng Zha Zi (Song)" by Ouyang Xiu

Last year on Lantern Festival① night,
The lanterns in Flower Market shone bright.
The moon rose above the willows' crown,
And men and women met after sundown.

This year the festive day again came round,
The lanterns and the moon were as bright and fair.
But my loved one of last year was not there,
And tears soaked the sleeves of my spring gown.

① Lantern Festival—January the 15th by the lunar calendar, also known as the Night of the First Moon.

(3) Robert Kotewall and Norman L. Smith 译

To a "Fresh Berries" by OU-YANG HSIU

Last year at the Lantern Festival
The flower-market lights were bright as day;
When the moon mounted to the tops of the willows,
Two lovers kept their tryst after the yellow dusk.

This year at the Lantern Festival
The moon and the lights are the same as then;
Only I see not my lover of yesteryear,
And tears drench the sleeves of my blue gown.

(4) Ronald C. Egan 译

To the Tune of "The Ripe Quince"

Last year on First Night
Lanterns made the flower market bright as day.
The moon rose to the tip of the willows,
My lover met me after dusk.

This year on First Night
The moon and the lanterns are as before.
But last year's lover is nowhere in sight,
My spring dress is moist with tears.

2.27 临江仙(欧阳修)

柳外轻雷池上雨，雨声滴碎荷声。小楼西角断虹明。阑干倚处，待得月华生。
燕子飞来窥画栋，玉钩垂下帘旌。凉波不动簟纹平。水精双枕，傍有堕钗横。

〖作品简介〗

此词写夏日傍晚,阵雨已过、月亮升起后楼外楼内的景象,几乎句句写景,而情尽寓其中。

〖注 释〗

月华：月光、月色之美丽。这里指月亮。**帘旌**[jīng]：帘幕。**簟**[diàn]：竹席。**水精**：即水晶。

〖译 文〗

(1) Stephen Owen 译

Tune: "Immortal by the River" (*Lin-jiang xian*) by Ou-yang Xiu (1007-1072)

Beyond the willows soft thunder,
  rain upon the pond,
and the sound of rain as it splatters
  lotuses to shreds.
By the small tower's west corner
  a broken rainbow bright,
where we lean upon the railing
waiting for moonlight.

The swallows come in flying,
  peer from rafters and beams,
from a jade hook dangles the curtain sash.
Motionless ripples of coolness,
  the bedmat's patterns flat.
There a pair of crystal pillows
and beside them, a fallen hairpin.

(2) 龚景浩 译

"Lin Jiang Xian (Song)"
Ouyang Xiu

Light thunder beyond the willow trees

Brought rain on the pond;
The patter of rain rived the lotus sound.
A slashed rainbow was kaleidoscopic
On the west corner of the lodge.
Leaning on the railings,
We awaited the rising moon.

The returning swallows were peering from the painted beam.
The jade hooks had let down the curtains green.
The cool wavelets looked still and the water smooth.
By the twin crystal pillows
Lay, aslant, a woman's hairpins.

(3) Teresa Yee-wha Yu 译

To the Tune of "Lin-Chiang Hsien"

A light peal of thunder
From beyond the willow trees.
Rain on the pond,
Falling,
Scatters and patters,
Upon the lotus leaves.
Across the western corner of the
Small house, a broken rainbow hangs
Brightly, as I rest on the balcony,
Awaiting moonrise.

A swallow comes flying,
Taking a peek under the painted beam.
Jade hooks let the curtain hang loose.
The cool waves remain still,
A bamboo mat spreads unruffled.
Beside the twin crystal pillows
Lies a fallen hairpin.

(4) 许渊冲 译

Tune: "Immortal at the River"

The thunder faints away beyond the willows green;
The raindrops drip from lotus leaves after the shower.
An imperfect rainbow is seen,
Shut out of view by Western Tower.
We lean on rails alone
To watch the rising moon.

A pair of swallows flies back to the painted eave;
Through fallen curtain they peep and perceive
The wavy mat still spread
Cold on the bed
As if none had slept in,
But by the crystal pillow twin
There is left a hairpin.

(5) Ronald C. Egan 译

To the Tune of "Immortal by the River"

Faint thunder beyond the willows, rain in the pool.
Rain, the sound of it hitting and shattering lotus.
Over the western corner of the building a fragment of rainbow glows.
They lean against the banister.
And wait for the moon to rise.

Swallows come to spy under painted beams,
The curtain hangs down from its jade hook.
The cool waves subside and the bamboo mat is still.
Beside the two crystal pillows
A fallen hairpin lies.

2.28 踏莎行(欧阳修)

候馆梅残，溪桥柳细。草薰风暖摇征辔。离愁渐远渐无穷，迢迢不断如春水。

寸寸柔肠，盈盈粉泪。楼高莫近危阑倚。平芜尽处是春山，行人更在春山外。

【作品简介】

此词描写早春的离情相思之情，上片写行人在旅途的离愁，下片写妇在家室的离愁。两地相思，一种情怀，全篇的主题即表现离愁。

【注 释】

候馆：迎宾候客之馆舍。《周礼·地官·遗人》："五十里有市，市有候馆。"注云："候馆，楼可观望者也。"**梅残**：意指寒梅日渐凋谢，只剩细细碎碎几片残瓣儿。**细**：细嫩，指溪桥边的柳树萌出的浅绿嫩芽。**草薰风暖**：江淹《别赋》："闺中风暖，陌上草薰。"**薰**：指草香。**征辔**[pèi]：行人坐骑的缰绳。**辔**：缰绳。**盈盈**：泪水充溢貌。**粉泪**：泪水流到脸上，与粉妆和在一起。**平芜**：平坦开阔的草原。**行人**：此指心上人。

【译 文】

(1) Burton Watson 译

Tune: "Treading on Grass"

At the post house lodge, plum flowers scattering,
by the valley bridge, willows coming out,
fragrant grass, warm wind that sways the traveler's reins:
parting grief—the farther apart, the more endless it grows,
long and unbroken like a river in spring.

Inch on inch of gentle heart,
brimming, brimming, her rouge-stained tears:
the tower so tall—don't go near, don't lean on the high railing!
At the very end of the level plain—spring hills are there,

but the traveler's even farther, beyond spring hills.

(2) Ronald C. Egan 译

To the Tune of "Treading the Sedge"

Plum blossoms have faded by the roadside inn.
Willow branches are slender at the river bridge.
Amidst fragrant grasses and warm breezes the reins sway.
Parting sorrow grows as the distance increases,
Stretching on interminably like a river in spring.

Inch after inch of a shattered heart,
Drop after drop of powdery tears,
Do not lean on the railing outside the high chamber.
The grassy plain reaches to distant spring hills.
The traveler is beyond those spring hills.

2. 29 采桑子(欧阳修)

十年前是尊前客，月白风清，忧患凋零。老去光阴速可惊。
鬓华虽改心无改，试把金觥。旧曲重听。犹似当年醉里声。

【作品简介】

此词是作者于宋神宗熙宁四年退居颍州后所作，词中以慷慨悲壮的感情发身世之慨，读来沉郁顿挫、荡气回肠，极一唱三叹之致，在《六一词》中属豪放一路。全词以情语胜，写情疏隽深婉、自然真切。全词抒发了词人对往日生活的怀念，仕途坎坷的悲凉，年华已逝、壮心不已的豪情。

【注　释】

凋零：本意为花草树木凋落。此处比喻为人事衰败。**鬓华**：两鬓头发斑白。**把**：手持。**金觥**[gōng]：大酒杯。《诗·周南·卷耳》："我姑酌彼兕觥，维以不永伤。"**觥**：古代酒器，腹椭圆，上有提梁，底有圆足，兽头形盖，亦有整个酒器作兽形的，并附有小勺。

〖译　文〗

Burton Watson 译

Tune:"Song of Picking Mulberry"

Ten years ago I was a visitor at the wine jar,
the moonlight white, the wind clear.
Then care and worry whittled me away,
time went by with astounding swiftness, and I grew old.

But though my hair has changed, my heart never changes.
Let me lift the golden flagon,
listen again to the old song,
like drunken voices from those years long past.

2.30　渔家傲(欧阳修)

近日门前溪水涨。郎船几度偷相访。船小难开红斗帐。无计向。合欢影里空惆怅。

愿妾身为红菡萏。年年生在秋江上。重愿郎为花底浪。无隔障。随风逐雨长来往。

〖作品简介〗

此词即景取譬，托物寓情，融写景、抒情、比兴于一体，以新颖活泼的民歌风味，以莲塘秋江为背景，歌咏水乡女子对爱情的追求与向往。

〖注　释〗

红斗帐：红色斗形小帐。**无计向**：没奈何，没办法。**合欢**：并蒂而开的莲花。**菡萏**[hàn dàn]：荷花。

【译 文】

Ronald C. Egan 译

To the Tune of "The Fisherman Is Proud"

Recently the stream before my gate has swollen.
My lover's boat had made several secret visits.
The boat is so small it's hard to spread the red dome-curtain.
With nowhere to turn
We grieve in vain amid the love-plant's shadow.

I wish I were a red lotus
Growing year after year on the autumn stream.
And I wish you were a wave beneath the flowers.
With no obstacle between us,
You could come and go freely with the wind and rain.

2.31 渔家傲(欧阳修)

花底忽闻敲两桨。逡巡女伴来寻访。酒盏旋将荷叶当。莲舟荡。时时盏里生红浪。

花气酒香清厮酿。花腮酒面红相向。醉倚绿阴眠一饷。惊起望。船头阁在沙滩上。

【作品简介】

此词以清新可爱而又富有生活情趣的语言，描写一群采莲姑娘荡舟采莲时喝酒逗乐的情景，塑造出活泼、大胆、清纯的水乡姑娘形象。上阕描绘了一幅采莲姑娘荡舟采莲时喝酒逗乐的夏日图景，下阙运用动静结合、融情于景的表现手法，紧扣秋江红莲的现境设喻写情。

【注 释】

渔家傲：词牌名。此调原为北宋年间流行歌曲，始见于北宋晏殊，因词中有“神仙一曲渔家傲”句，便取“渔家傲”三字作词名。双调六十二字，上下片各四个七字句，一个三字句，每句用韵，声律谐婉。南北曲均有。**逡**[qūn]**巡**：宋元俗语，犹指顷刻、一会儿。指时间极短。**旋**[xuàn]：随时，就地。**当**[dàng]：当做，代替。**“时时”句**：谓莲花映入酒杯，随舟荡漾，显出红色波纹。**红浪**：指人面莲花映在酒杯中显出的红色波纹。**清斯酿**[niàng]：清香之气混成一片。**斯酿**：相互融合。**花腮**[sāi]：指荷花。形容荷花像美人面颊的花容。**酒面**：饮酒后的面色。宋梅尧臣《牡丹》：“时结游朋去寻玩，香吹酒面生红波。”**一饷**[xiǎng]：即一晌、片刻。《敦煌变文集·王昭君变文》：“若道一时一饷，犹可安排；岁久月深，如何可度。”蒋礼鸿通释：“一饷，就是吃一餐饭的时间。”**阁**[gē]：同“搁”，放置，此处指搁浅。一作“搁”。

〖译 文〗

Ronald C. Egan 译

To the Tune of “The Fisherman Is Proud”

Beneath blossoms all at once I hear the knocking of oars,
Soon my girlfriend comes to join me.
Carefree, we turn our lily leaves into winecups.
Our lotus boat rolls
Red ripples appear in the cups.

The scents of the flowers and wine mingle sweetly,
Petals and wine-flushed faces both are red.
Drunk, we doze off in the green shade
Then awake with a start:
Our boat has run up on a sandspit.

2.32 南歌子(欧阳修)

凤髻金泥带，龙纹玉掌梳。走来窗下笑相扶，爱道画眉深浅入时无？
弄笔偎人久，描花试手初。等闲妨了绣功夫，笑问鸳鸯两字怎生书？

〖作品简介〗

此词的全称为《南歌子·凤髻金泥带》，它通过描写新娘子的举止神态，表现一对青年夫妇的新婚生活。上片写新娘上妆，为了博得夫婿的欢心，她细心打扮自己，还故意问眉毛画得是否合时宜；下片写新娘刺绣的情形，细腻地刻画了她对夫婿的依恋之情和撒娇之态。全词采用民间小词习见的口语和白描手法，塑造出女主人公活泼轻灵的形象，反映了夫妻情意之深厚。

〖注 释〗

南歌子：唐教坊曲名，后用为词牌名。又名“南柯子”“风蝶令”。《金奁集》入“仙吕宫”，上下片各二十六字，三平韵。例用对句起。宋人多用同一格式重填一片，谓之“双调”。**凤髻**：状如凤凰的发型。**金泥带**：金色的彩带。**龙纹玉掌梳**：图案作龙形如掌大小的玉梳。**画眉深浅入时无**：语出唐·朱庆馀《近试上张水部》：“洞房昨夜停红烛，待晓堂前拜舅姑。妆罢低声问夫婿，画眉深浅入时无?”**入时无**：赶得上时兴式样吗？时髦吗？**等闲**：轻易，随便。**怎生**：怎样。**书**：写。

〖译 文〗

Ronald C. Egan 译

To the Tune of “Southern Song”

A phoenix hairbun tied with gold-speckled ribbon.
A jade comb carved with dragons.
She runs giggling to the window and hangs on him
Asking eagerly, ‘Have I drawn my eyebrows
Stylishly? ’

Taking up her brush, she snuggles against him
And tentatively sketches flowers
Carelessly postponing her embroidery.
With a smile she asks, ‘How do you write
“Mandarin duck and drake”? ’

2.33 诉衷情·眉意(欧阳修)

清晨帘幕卷轻霜。呵手试梅妆。都缘自有离恨，故画作远山长。
思往事，惜流芳。易成伤。拟歌先敛，欲笑还颦，最断人肠。

〖作品简介〗

此词抒写女子的离愁别恨。作品以形传神，从人物的外貌转而深入其内心世界，通过描写一位歌女在冬日的清晨起床梳妆时的生活情景，展现了其苦闷的内心世界。

〖注 释〗

轻霜：气候只微寒。**试梅妆**：谓试着描画梅花妆。**远山**：形容把眉毛画得又细又长，有如水墨画的远山形状。比喻离恨的深长。**流芳**：流逝的年华。

〖译 文〗

Ronald C. Egan 译

To the Tune of "Telling How I feel"
On Eyebrows

A clear morning, the blind rolls up to disclose the frost,
She blows her hands warm and applies plum blossom rouge.
Because she feels parting sadness
She draws her eyebrows to resemble the distant hills.

Thinking of the past
She regrets her vanished youth
And is easily overcome with grief.
Ready to sing, she tries to compose herself.
About to smile, she frowns instead.
Most heartrending!

2.34 减字木兰花(欧阳修)

伤怀离抱。天若有情天亦老。此意如何。细似轻丝渺似波。
扁舟岸侧。枫叶荻花秋索索。细想前欢。须著人间比梦间。

〖作品简介〗

这首词描写与女子的伤别之情。上阕缠绵悱恻，情深意长；下阕用"人间"与"梦间"的对照，与上阕"天若有情天亦老"相呼应，回忆情感，表达了作者的感伤离别之情。

〖注 释〗

减字木兰花：词牌名，原唐教坊曲，双调四十四字，与“木兰花”相比，前后片第一、三句各减三字，改为平仄韵互换格，每片两仄韵，两平韵。**伤怀**：伤心，悲痛，出自《诗·小雅·白华》：“啸歌伤怀，念彼硕人。”**天若有情天亦老**：倘若上天也有感情，也会随着岁月蹉跎而老去的，形容强烈的伤感情绪，也指自然法则是无情的。出自唐·李贺《金铜仙人辞汉歌》：“衰兰送客咸阳道，天若有情天亦老。”**扁舟**：小船。**枫叶荻花**：“枫树”乃枫树叶，亦泛指秋令变红的其他植物的叶子；“荻花”乃荻的花，荻，多年生草本植物，生在水边，叶子长形，似芦苇，秋天开紫花。其出处为唐·白居易《琵琶行(并序)》：“浔阳江头夜送客，枫叶荻花秋瑟瑟。”**须著人间比梦间**：本句是说过去的事纵然真实，如今也形同梦寐，须用梦间的事来比照过去人间发生的事。

〖译 文〗

Ronald C. Egan 译

To the Tune of “Shortened Magnolia Flower”

Heartbroken, parted from your embrace.
If Heaven knew love Heaven too would grow old.
What are my feelings like?
As delicate as silken thread, as wide as the waves.

A single boat beside the bank.
Maple leaves and reed flowers sough in the autumn wind.
When I think back to former pleasures
I can only say that life is a dream.

2.35 采桑子(欧阳修)

荷花开后西湖好，载酒来时。不用旌旗。前后红幢绿盖随。
画船撑入花深处，香泛金卮。烟雨微微。一片笙歌醉里归。

天容水色西湖好，云物俱鲜。鸥鹭闲眠。应惯寻常听管弦。
风清月白偏宜夜，一片琼田。谁羡骖鸾。人在舟中便是仙。

残霞夕照西湖好，花坞苹汀，十顷波平，野岸无人舟自横。
西南月上浮云散，轩槛凉生。莲芰香清。水面风来酒面醒。

〖作品简介〗

此三首词选自作者所作《采桑子十首》中的第七、八、九首。作者晚年退居颍州，极喜爱当地西湖的景色，在此写下了十首词，其中前九首写景，最后一首抒情。和前六首一样，这三首词借鉴了民间鼓子词联章体的形式，创造性地运用了化整为零的构思方式，同时运用动静结合的手法描绘景物、创造意境，描绘颍州西湖的自然之美，写得恬静、澄澈，富有情韵，宛如一幅幅淡雅的山水画，从内容、手法和风格上都实现了对传统的突破，展现出平淡清新的风格特点，具有独特的审美价值和较强的词史意义。

〖注 释〗

幢[chuáng]：古代的帐幔。**琼田**：神话传说中的种玉之田。此处指月光照映下莹碧如玉的湖水。**骖**[cān]**鸾**：谓仙人驾驭鸾鸟云游登仙。**骖**：驾，乘。**莲芰**[jì]：即莲花。芰，菱。

〖译 文〗

Ronald C. Egan 译

To the Tune of "Plucking Mulberry Leaves"

With lotus in bloom, West Lake is lovely.
Embarking with wine aboard,
There's no need for flags or banners:
Red pennants and green canopies escort us ahead and astern.

We pole our painted boat into a thick patch of flowers.
Fragrance floats over the golden cups,
Mist and rain fall lightly.
With pipes and song we return drunkenly home.

The sky's hue and water's color make West Lake lovely.
Clouds and plants fresh,
Gulls and egrets idly nap.
They must be used to hearing flutes and strings.

When the wind is cool and the moon bright, night is especially fine:
A vast field of jade.
Who envies those who ride the phoenix?
Anyone on a boat here is an immortal.

Under sunset's fading mists West Lake is lovely,
Flowered dikes and duckweed islets,
A thousand acres of calm waves.
The bank is deserted, a boat swings in this current.

The moon rises in the southwest, clouds drift away.
At the railing the air turns chill.
Lotus and water-chestnut are fragrant,
Wind over the lake's face sobers my drunken face.

2.36 蝶恋花(欧阳修)

庭院深深深几许，杨柳堆烟，帘幕无重数。玉勒雕鞍游冶处，楼高不见章台路。

雨横风狂三月暮，门掩黄昏，无计留春住。泪眼问花花不语，乱红飞过秋千去。

【作品简介】

此词描写闺中少妇的伤春之情。上片写少妇深闺寂寞，阻隔重重，想见意中人而不得；下片写美人迟暮，盼意中人回归而不得，幽恨怨愤之情自现。全词写景状物，疏俊委曲，虚实相融，用语自然，辞意深婉，尤对少妇心理画写意传神，堪称欧词之典范。

【注　释】

几许：多少。**许**：估计数量之词。**堆烟**：形容杨柳浓密。**玉勒雕鞍**：极言车马的豪华。**玉勒**：玉制的马衔。**雕鞍**：精雕的马鞍。**游冶处**：指歌楼妓院。**章台**：汉长安街名。

《汉书·张敞传》有"走马章台街"语。唐许尧佐《章台柳传》记妓女柳氏事。后因以章台为歌妓聚居之地。**雨横**：指急雨、骤雨。**乱红**：这里形容各种花片纷纷飘落的样子。

【译 文】

(1) Zong-qi Cai 译

To the Tune of "Butterflies Lingering over Flowers"
(or "Magpie Perching on a Branch"[*Que ta zhi*])

Deep in the walled garden, deep-how deep?
Mist stacks on willows,
Uncountable layers of screens and blinds.
The jade bridle and ornate saddle are in the brothel district—
Though the tower is tall, one can't see Zhangtai Road.①

A driving rain, a mad wind, late in the third month.
A door keeps out the twilight,
But there's no way to keep spring from going.
With tear-filled eyes I ask the blossoms,
    but the blossoms do not answer—
In a swirl of red they fly into the swings.

① Zhangtai was a street in Han Dynasty Chang'an that became a euphemism for the brothel district.

(2) 许渊冲 译

Tune: "Butterflies Lingering over Flowers" ①

Deep, deep the courtyard where he is, so deep
It's veiled by smoke-like willows heap on heap.
By curtain on curtain and screen on screen.
Leaving his saddle and bridle, there he has been
Merry-making. From my tower he can't be seen.

The third month now, the wind and rain are raging late,
    At dusk I bar the gate,

But I can't bar in spring.
My tearful eyes ask flowers but they fail to bring
An answer. I see blossoms fall beyond the swing.

① The persona in this poem is a young wife complaining that her husband leads a free life in the brothel and leaves her alone at home in view of the raging rain and the falling flowers which can bring her no consolation but pass away with the departing spring. This poem is also included in *The Poetic Works of Feng Yan-yi*.

2.37 桂枝香(王安石)

登临送目。正故国晚秋，天气初肃。千里澄江似练，翠峰如簇。归帆去棹残阳里，背西风、酒旗斜矗。彩舟云淡，星河鹭起，画图难足。

念往昔、繁华竞逐。叹门外楼头，悲恨相续。千古凭高，对此谩嗟荣辱。六朝旧事随流水，但寒烟、芳草凝绿。至今商女，时时犹唱后庭遗曲。

〖作品简介〗

这是一首金陵怀古之词。上片写金陵之景，下片写怀古之情。寄托了作者对当时朝政的担忧和对国家政治大事的关心。

〖注　释〗

登临送目：登山临水，举目望远。**故国**：旧时的都城，指金陵。**千里澄江似练**：形容长江像一匹长长的白绢。语出谢朓《晚登三山还望京邑》："余霞散成绮，澄江静如练。"**澄江**：清澈的长江。**练**：白色的绢。**如簇**：这里指群峰好像丛聚在一起。**簇**：丛聚。**去棹(zhào)**：往来的船只。**棹**：划船的一种工具，形似桨，也可引申为船。**星河鹭(lù)起**：白鹭从水中沙洲上飞起。长江中有白鹭洲(在今南京水西门外)。**星河**：银河，这里指长江。**画图难足**：用图画也难以完美地表现它。**繁华竞逐**：(六朝的达官贵人)争着过豪华的生活。**竞逐**：竞相仿效追逐。**门外楼头**：指南朝陈亡国惨剧。语出杜牧《台城曲》："门外韩擒虎，楼头张丽华。"韩擒虎是隋朝开国大将，他已带兵来到金陵朱雀门(南门)外，陈后主尚与他的宠妃张丽华于结绮阁上寻欢作乐。**悲恨相续**：指亡国悲剧连续发生。**凭高**：登高。这是说作者登上高处远望。**漫嗟荣辱**：空叹什么荣耀耻辱。这是作者的感叹。**六朝**：指三国吴、东晋、南朝宋、齐、梁、陈六个朝代。它们都建都金陵。**商女**：歌女。**《后庭》遗曲**：指歌曲《玉树后庭花》，传为陈后主所作。杜牧《泊秦淮》："商女不知亡国恨，隔江犹唱《后庭花》"，后人认为是亡国之音。

【译　文】

(1) 龚景浩 译

"Gui Zhi Xiang (Song)"

Wang An Shi

Ascending the stairway to scan the horizon,
It would be late autumn in the old country:
The weather has just turned hoary.
The river transparent, a thousand miles long,
Is like a giant silk ribbon.
The emerald mountain tops are clustered.
A boat set sail into the dying sunset,
With the west wind at its back and wine shop signs aflutter:
The painted boat, the pale clouds,
The Milky Way, the herons flapping their wings:
Pictures fail to paint the scene.

Remembering the past,
The bustling world chasing itself fast.
A pity that outside gateways and up in grand houses,
Sorrow and regret follow hard upon one another.
Staying up high to view all this over a millennium,
Sighing over glory or disgrace is almost pointless.
Past events from the Six Dynasties① have flown by like water,
Only the cold mist and yellowing grass have some frozen green.
Even now, the Shang women
Frequently sing
The Inner Court Tunes left from old.②

① Six Dynasties: 222-589A. D. See Note to Sa Du La's *Bai Zi Ling* (Hundred-Word Poem).

② The Shang women / Frequently sing / The Inner Court Tunes left from old: Shang women—girls who sang in a chorus at the king's court. Inner Court Tunes—songs composed by the first ruler of the House of Chen during the Northern and Southern Dynasties period (420-586A. D.). This ruler had a brief reign (583-586A. D.). After his downfall a popular ditty at the time made its round: "Jade trees and Inner Court flowers / They last but a few hours." Du Mu, the Tang poet, has the following famous lines:

"The Shang women suffer no trauma
Over the loss of country;
Fleeing to the other side of the river,
They're still singing the Inner Court Tunes."

(2) Hans H. Frankel 译

Tune Pattern: "The Cassia Twigs Are Fragrant"

I climb up and look down, letting my eyes wander.
Just now it's late autumn in the old capital,
The weather is turning severe.
For a thousand miles, the clear river is like silk
And the green peaks are like bamboo shoots.
The homebound sailboat rests its oars in the setting sun
And turns its back to the west wind.
The wineshop flag slants high;
Above the painted boat the clouds are pale;
On the River of Stars an egret rises.
It would be hard to do justice to this in a painting.

I think of the past,
Successive dynasties vying for glory.
I lament what happened outside the gate and upstairs,
Continuous sorrows and pain.
For a thousand years, leaning on lofty railings,
Facing this scene, people have sighed over glory and shame.
Past events of the Six Dynasties have flowed away with the river,
There's only chilly mist
And fragrant grasses stiff with frost.
Even now, singing girls
From time to time still sing
The old song of blossoms in the rear court.

(3) 许渊冲 译

Tune: "Fragrance of Laurel Branch"

I climb a height
And strain my sight;
Of autumn late it is the coldest time;
The ancient capital looks sublime.
The limpid River, beltlike, flows a thousand miles;
Emerald peaks on peaks tower in piles.
In the declining sun sails come and go;
In the west wind wineshop flags flutter high and low.
The painted boat
In clouds afloat,
Like stars in Silver River[①] egrets fly.
What a picture before the eye!

The days gone by
For people in opulence vie.
Alas! Shame came on shame under the walls,[②]
In palace halls.
Leaning on rails, in vain I utter sighs
O'er ancient kingdoms' fall and rise.
The running water saw the Six Dynasties pass,
But I see only chilly mist and withered grass.
E'en now the songstresses still sing
The songs composed by captive king.

① The Chinese name for the Milky Way.
② Rulers capitulated under the walls of their capital during the Six Dynasties(221-280; 317-589).

(4) 张炳星 译

Nostalgic Musing Over the Past

Wang Anshi

I ascended a mountain to enjoy a distant view.

It was just late autumn in the ancient capital covered with dew.
The weather began to turn bleak anew.
Looked like a white ribbon, the extensive Yangtze River.
Green peaks were as sharp as arrows,
while sail boats under the setting sun shuttled to and for.
Facing the west wind, before a wine shop,
a streamer fluttered aloud.
A colored boat floated slantwise as if from the cloud.
An egret took off as if from a Milky Way.
Scenes were so beautiful and gay!
You can hardly describe them with your pen anyway.

I think of past events so weary,
people there used to vie with each other for luxury.
When enemy troops reached the city,
Prince Chen and his concubines were still seeking pleasure
throughout the night.
At last his country was conquered by a foreign tribe with might.
Such tragedies have continued generation after generation,
and were regretted by people in succession.
Since ancient times, people have ascended height,
lamenting in vain past glories and disgraces.
Past events of the Six Dynasties have gone like flowing water.
What remained were only cold mist and withered grass.
Up to now, singing girls still often sing such elegies
as "Back Court Flower", alas!

2.38 南乡子(王安石)

自古帝王州，郁郁葱葱佳气浮。四百年来成一梦，堪愁，晋代衣冠成古丘。
绕水恣行游。上尽层楼更上楼。往事悠悠君莫问，回头。槛外长江空自流。

〖作品简介〗

此词为王安石晚年罢居金陵时所作。因政治上受到压抑，作者似乎把情怀寄寓于世外的江河湖海，闲淡之中实际上有一股难以排遣的郁闷孤愤之情。

〖注　释〗

帝王州：指金陵(今江苏省南京市)。因三国的吴、东晋、南北朝的宋、齐、梁、陈等朝代在此建都，故称为“帝王州”。**郁郁葱葱**：草木茂盛。**佳气**：指产生帝王的一种气，这是一种迷信的说法。**四百年**：金陵作为历代帝都将近四百年。**晋代衣冠成古丘**：引自李白《登金陵凤凰台》诗中的名句：“吴宫花草埋幽径，晋代衣冠成古丘。”把晋代与吴宫并举，明确地显示出后代诗人对晋朝的向往。**冠**[guān]：古代士以上的穿戴，衣冠连称，是古代士以上的服装，后引申为世族、绅士。**古丘**：坟墓。**恣**[zì]**行游**：尽情地绕着江边闲行游赏。**恣**：任意地，自由自在地。**更**：再，又，不止一次地。**悠悠**：长久。遥远的样子。**回头**：指透彻醒悟。佛家语：“苦海无边，回头是岸。”**槛**：栏杆。语出唐代诗人王勃《滕王阁诗》中的名句：“阁中帝子今何在，槛外长江空自流。”

〖译　文〗

许渊冲 译

Tune：“Song of a Southern Country”

The capital was ruled by Kings since days gone by.
There rich green and lush gloom breathe a majestic sigh.
Like dreams has passed the reign of four hundred long years,
　　Which calls forth tears：
Modern laureates are buried like their ancient peers.

Along the river I go where I will,
Up city-walls and watch-towers I gaze my fill.
Do not ask what has passed without leaving a trail!
　　To what avail?
The endless river rolls in vain beyond the rail.

2.39　鹧鸪天(晏几道)

彩袖殷勤捧玉钟，当年拚却醉颜红。舞低杨柳楼心月，歌尽桃花扇底风。从别后，忆相逢，几回魂梦与君同。今宵剩把银釭照，犹恐相逢是梦中。

【作品简介】

此词描写词人与一个女子久别重逢的情景，以相逢抒别恨。上片利用彩色字面，描摹当年欢聚情况，似实却虚，当前一现，倏归乌有；下片抒写久别相思不期而遇的惊喜之情，似梦却真，利用声韵的配合，宛如一首乐曲，使听者也仿佛进入梦境。全词虽五十余字，却能造成两种境界，互相补充配合，或实或虚，既有彩色的绚烂，又有声音的谐美，故而使得此词成为作者脍炙人口的名作。

【注　释】

鹧鸪天：词牌名，又名“思佳客”，五十五字。此词黄升《花庵词选》题作《佳会》。**彩袖**：代指穿彩衣的歌女。**玉钟**：古时指珍贵的酒杯，是对酒杯的美称。**拚**[pàn]**却**：甘愿，不顾惜。**却**：语气助词。“**舞低**”二句：歌女舞姿曼妙，直舞到挂在杨柳树梢照到楼心的一轮明月低沉下去；歌女清歌婉转，直唱到扇底儿风消歇(累了停下来)，极言歌舞时间之久。**桃花扇**：歌舞时用作道具的扇子，绘有桃花。歌扇风尽，形容不停地挥舞歌扇。这两句是《小山词》中的名句。“低”字为使动用法，使……低。**同**：聚在一起。**剩**：通“尽”，只管。**把**：持，握。**银釭**[gāng]：银质的灯台，代指灯。

【译　文】

(1) Stephen Owen 译

Tune: “Partridge Weather” (*Zhe-gu tian*) by Yan Ji-dao (Mid-11th—Early 12th Century)

With such feeling your brightly colored sleeves
　　held up the goblet of jade to me,
　　but in those days we didn’t care
　　if faces flushed red with the wine,
when you danced the moon low in the willows
　　and sang out the breeze in the peach blossom fan.

Then,
　　after we each went our way,
　　I thought back on when we first met
　　and have joined you so often in dreams,

That perhaps tonight I overdo it,
taking the silver lamp in hand
to shine on you, still afraid
that this meeting too is a dream.

(2) 许渊冲 译

Tune: "Partridge in the Sky" by Yan Jidao

Time and again with rainbow sleeves you tried to fill my cup with wine that, drunk, I kept on drinking still. You danced till the moon hung low over the willow trees; you sang until amid peach blossoms blushed the breeze.

Then came the time to part, but you're deep in my heart. How many times have I met you in dreams at night! Now left to gaze at you in silver candlelight, I fear it is not you, but a sweet dream untrue.

(3) Robert Kotewall and Norman L. Smith 译

To "Partridge Sky"

My many-colored sleeves cordially held up the jade-
goblet,
At the feast I feared not to flush my cheeks with wine;
I danced until the moon over the tower came down to
the willows,
I sang until the peach-blossom fan had exhausted its
breeze.

After our parting
I thought of reunion.
Oft-times my spirit was with him in dreams.
At this remnant of night I shine the silver lamp on him,
Still in fear that our reunion is only in a dream.

2.40 蝶恋花(晏几道)

醉别西楼醒不记。春梦秋云，聚散真容易。斜月半窗还少睡。画屏闲展吴山翠。

衣上酒痕诗里字。点点行行，总是凄凉意。红烛自怜无好计。夜寒空替人垂泪。

〖作品简介〗

此词为离别感忆之作，但却更广泛地慨叹于过去欢情之易逝、此时孤怀之难遣、将来重会之无期，所以情调较之其他一些伤别之作，更加低徊往复、沉郁悲凉。词境含蓄蕴藉、情意深长。

〖注　释〗

西楼：泛指欢宴之所。**春梦秋云**：喻美好而又虚幻短暂、聚散无常的事物。白居易《花非花》诗："来如春梦几多时？去似朝云无觅处。"晏殊《木兰花》："长于春梦几多时，散似秋云无觅处。"**吴山**：画屏上的江南山水。"**红烛**"二句：化用唐杜牧《赠别二首》之二："蜡烛有心还惜别，替人垂泪到天明。"将蜡烛拟人化。

〖译　文〗

(1) Stephen Owen 译

Tune: "Butterflies Love Flowers" (*Die lian hua*) by Yan Ji-dao (Mid-11th—Early 12th Century)

I was drunk as I felt the western hall;
then sober, I couldn't recall.
A springtime dream, clouds of fall,
join and scatter all too easily.
My window half-filled with the moon descending—
small sleep again.
Peacefully spread on a painted screen
are the green hills of the South.

On my clothes the stains of wine
and in my poems the words—
a lot of dots and lines which mean,
taken on the whole, despondency.

My red candle is moved
　　but sees no resolution;
and wastes its tears on my behalf
　　in night's cold.

(2) 龚景浩 译

"Die Lian Hua (Song)"

Yan Ji Dao

Leaving the West Lodge, drunk;
Nothing is remembered, awake.
Dreams in springtime, clouds of autumn—
So easy to meet, and part.
A slanting moon half-fills the casement—
Oh, sleepless night!
A painted screen sits idly,
Displaying the Wu Mountains① blue.

Wine-stained clothes, words in a poem—
So many lines, so many dots,
Pensiveness always!
The red candles have regrets there are no good schemes,
Shedding tears in vain for people in the chilly night.

① Wu Mountains—See Note to Bo Ju Yi's *Chang Xiang Si* ("Missing You Long and Dearly").

2.41 玉楼春(晏几道)

东风又作无情计，艳粉娇红吹满地。碧楼帘影不遮愁，还似去年今日意。
谁知错管春残事，到处登临曾费泪。此时金盏直须深，看尽落花能几醉！

〖作品简介〗

此词被收录于晚清学者朱孝臧所编《宋词三百首》，写于汴京，是重阳佳节宴饮之作，饱含备尝坎坷沧桑之意，表达凄凉的人生感怀。全词为两句一意的蝉联布局，笔笔顿挫，层层叠进，写情波澜起伏，步步深化，由空灵而入厚重，音节从和婉到悠扬，适应感情的变化，整首词的意境悲凉凄冷，是一首伤春惜花遗恨之作。

【注　释】

艳粉娇红：指娇艳的花。**金盏**：酒杯的美称。**直须**：只管，尽管。

【译　文】

Stephen Owen 译

Tune: "The Springtime of Marble Halls" (*Yu-lou chun*) by Yan Ji-dao

The east wind did it again, unsentimental
　　In its designs; it blew the land full of petals,
　　passionate red and fetching white.
High in green mansions curtain shadows won't block away
　　melancholy—same mood as last year
　　on the same day.

You'd never know how I've always botched
　　spring's last moments so badly, with wasted tears
　　climbing high places everywhere.
But this time I'll have my golden flagon
　　filled to the rim. How often drunk hereafter
　　will I watch the blossoms all fall away?

2.42　阮郎归(晏几道)

天边金掌露成霜，云随雁字长。绿杯红袖趁重阳，人情似故乡。
兰佩紫，菊簪黄，殷勤理旧狂。欲将沉醉换悲凉，清歌莫断肠！

【作品简介】

此词写于汴京，是重阳佳节宴饮之作。词中感喟身世，抒发了作者客居思乡的悲凉心情。虽写抑郁之情，但并无绝望之意。

〖注 释〗

阮郎归：词牌名，又名《碧桃春》《醉桃源》等。《神仙记》载刘晨、阮肇入天台山采药，遇二仙女。留住半年，思归甚苦。既归则乡邑零落，经已十世。曲名本此，故作凄音。四十七字，前后片各四平韵。**金掌**：汉武帝时在长安建章宫筑柏梁台，上有铜制仙人以手掌托盘，承接露水。此处以“金掌”借指国都，即汴京。即谓汴京已入深秋。**雁字**：雁群飞行时排列成人字，有时排列成一字，故称雁字。**绿杯红袖**：代指美酒佳人。**人情**：风土人情。**“兰佩紫”**两句：佩戴紫色兰花，头上插黄菊。屈原《离骚》中有“纫秋兰以为佩”。**理旧狂**：重又显出从前狂放不羁的情态。

〖译 文〗

Stephen Owen 译

Tune：“Young Ruan Returns”（*Ruan lang gui*）by Yan Ji-dao

Here at the world’s edge dew turns to frost
　　on the statues’ golden palms，while clouds pursue
　　long lines in the sky，geese-drawn.
I make the most
　　of the Double Ninth-red sleeves
　　and glasses of green wine. The human heart
　　works here much as it does at home：
　　purple orchids in sashes
　　and yellow chrysanthemums stuck in hair.
I really try to govern that old wildness.
And I want to make a trade：deep drunkenness
　　for this dreariness，so stop that clear singing
　　which tears at the heart.

2.43 卜算子(王观)

水是眼波横，山是眉峰聚。欲问行人去那边？眉眼盈盈处。
才始送春归，又送君归去。若到江南赶上春，千万和春住。

【作品简介】

此词上片写友人一路山水行程，含蓄地表达了惜别深情；下片则直抒胸臆，兼写离愁别绪和对友人的深情祝愿。

【注 释】

卜算子：词牌名。**水是眼波横**：水像美人流动的眼波。**山是眉峰聚**：山如美人蹙起的眉毛。**欲**：要，想要。**行人**：指作者(王观)的朋友(鲍浩然)。**眉眼盈盈处**：山水交汇的地方。

【译 文】

(1) 许渊冲 译

Tune: "Song Divination"
Parting with Bao Hao-ran by Wang Guan

A stretch of rippling water is the beaming eye;
The arched brows around are mountains high.
If you ask where the wayfarer is bound,
Just see where beaming eyes and arched brows are found.

I've just seen spring depart.
And now again with you I'll part.
If you o'ertake in the South the spring day,
Be sure not to let it slip away.

(2) 龚景浩 译

"Bu Suan Zi (Song)"
Wang Guan

The water is the light in her eyes,
The hills are the knitting of her brows.

I asked the passer-by: Where are you heading?
To where those eyes and brows are beck'ning.

I have just sent spring away.
Now I'm seeing you off, my friend.
When you reach Kiangnan[1] and catch up with spring,
Be certain you keep it there.

① Kiangnan—See Note to Bo Ju Yi's *Yi Jiang Nan* ("Memories of Kiangnan").

2.44 庆清朝慢(王观)

调雨为酥，催冰做水，东君分付春还。何人便将轻暖，点破残寒。结伴踏青去好，平头鞋子小双鸾。烟郊外，望中秀色，如有无间。

晴则个，阴则个，饾饤得天气，有许多般。须教镂花拨柳，争要先看。不道吴绫绣袜，香泥斜沁几行斑。东风巧，尽收翠绿，吹在眉山。

〖作品简介〗

此词咏踏青，以工丽、尖新的笔触，从春日里天气的变化和姑娘们的踏青活动两方面入手来描绘春景，将两者和谐地组合成一幅生趣盎然的春景图。

〖注 释〗

东君：司春之神。古亦称太阳为东君。**小双鸾**：鞋面所绣之双鸾图案。**则个**：表示动作进行时之语助词，近于“着”或“者”。全句意思相当于“有时晴，有时阴”。**饾饤**[dòu dìng]：堆砌辞藻。此处亦作堆砌解，含幽默语气。**镂花**：一作“撩花”。**吴绫**：吴地所产绫罗丝绸。

〖译 文〗

龚景浩 译

"Qing Qing Zhao Man(Song)"
Wang Guan

Mixing rain into crumpet dough,

Inculcating ice to melt,
The East Wind has ordered the return of spring.
Who has expelled the remaining chill
With a light touch of tentative warmth?
'Tis the time to go outing with companions:
Dainty square-toed shoes covering dainty feet.
In the misty outskirts,
One sees the delicate colors:
Now they are there, now they are not.

Suddenly it's sunlight,
Suddenly it's overcast—
So changeable.
How the weather presents many faces.
To enjoy flowers and play with the willows,
All vie to be the first to view spring.
The embroidered satin hosiery from Wu①
Is splashed with streaks of fragrant mud.
The East Wind is skillful:
It gathers together all the dark emerald green
And blows it onto fair ladies' arched brows.

① Wu—Suzhou (Soochow) and surrounding areas.

2.45 蝶恋花(苏轼)

花褪残红青杏小。燕子飞时，绿水人家绕。枝上柳绵吹又少。天涯何处无芳草。

墙里秋千墙外道。墙外行人，墙里佳人笑。笑渐不闻声渐悄。多情却被无情恼。

〖作品简介〗

此词通过对残红退尽、春意阑珊的暮春景色的描写和远行途中的失意心境的描绘，借惜春伤情之名，表达出对韶光流逝的惋惜、宦海沉浮的悲叹和浮生颠沛的无可奈何。

【注 释】

褪：脱去。小：毛本作“子”。“子”，毛本误作“小”。飞：《二妙集》、毛本注“一作来”。**绕**：元本注“一作晓”。**柳绵**：即柳絮。韩偓《寒食日重游李氏园亭有怀》诗：“往年同在莺桥上，见依朱阑咏柳绵。”**“何处无芳草”**句：谓春光已晚，芳草长遍天涯。《离骚》：“何所独无芳草兮，尔何怀乎故宇？”**“墙里秋千”**五句：张相《诗词曲语辞汇释》卷五：“恼，犹撩也。……言墙里佳人之笑，本出于无心情，而墙外行人闻之，枉自多情，却如被其撩拨也。”又卷一：“却，犹倒也；谨也。”**却被**：反被。唐・胡曾《汉宫》诗：“何事将军封万户，却令红粉为和戎。”

【译 文】

(1) 许渊冲 译

Tune: “Butterflies Lingering over Flowers” by Su Shi

Red flowers fade, green apricots still small
　　When swallows pass
Over blue water which surrounds the garden wall.
Most willow catkins have been blown away, alas!
But there is no place where grows not the sweet green grass.

Without the wall there's a road; within there's a swing.
　　A passer-by
Hears a fair maiden's laughter in the garden ring.
As the ringing laughter dies away by and by,
For the enchantress the enchant'd can only sigh.

(2) 龚景浩 译

“Die Lian Hua (Song)”

Su Shi

The flowers are a faded red
And green apricots are small.
The returning swallows

Circle the houses girt by blue water.
The willow catkins have mostly blown away in the wind.
Fragrant patches of grass can be found everywhere like mint.

Swings within the garden wall and footpaths without.
Passers-by taking the footpaths
Hear laughter from fair ladies on the other side.
But the laughter dies away and voices are still.
Too much feeling be bothered by the unfeeling will.

(3) 张炳星 译

A Late Spring Scene

The red flower is fading low,
while the green apricot is still small.
Swallows dart to and fro.
A green brook encircles a mansion of the lord.
Willow catkins are blown fewer and fewer on the road.
Fragrant grasses can be found everywhere in the world.

Within the wall there is a swing,
and without the wall there is a road.
Without the wall passengers loiter,
while within the wall can be heard beauties' laughter.
Gradually laughter could hardly be heard
and voices gradually disappeared.
The affectionate passengers were vexed
at the apathy of the girls who disappeared.

2.46 江城子(苏轼)

十年生死两茫茫，不思量，自难忘。千里孤坟，无处话凄凉。纵使相逢应不识，尘满面，鬓如霜。

夜来幽梦忽还乡，小轩窗，正梳妆。相顾无言，惟有泪千行。料得年年肠断处，明月夜，短松冈。

【作品简介】

此词运用分合顿挫、虚实结合以及叙述白描等多种艺术表现方法，来表达作者怀念亡妻的思想感情，在对亡妻的哀思中又糅进自己的身世感慨，因而将夫妻之间的情感表达得深婉而真挚，使人读后无不为之动情而感叹哀婉。

【注 释】

十年：指结发妻子王弗去世已十年。**思量**[sī liɑnɡ]：想念。“量”按格律应念平声。**千里**：王弗葬地四川眉山与苏轼任所山东密州相隔遥远，故称“千里”。**孤坟**：孟启《本事诗·徵异第五》载张姓妻孔氏赠夫诗：“欲知肠断处，明月照孤坟。”这里指其妻王氏之墓。**纵使**：即使。**“尘满面”两句**，形容年老憔悴。**幽梦**：梦境隐约，故云幽梦。**小轩窗**：指小室的窗前。**轩**：门窗。**顾**：看。**料得**：料想，想来。**肠断处**：一作“断肠处”。**明月夜，短松冈**：苏轼葬妻之地。**短松**：矮松。

【译 文】

(1) Charles Hartman 译

Ten Years Living and Dead Have Drawn Apart
To the Tune of “Jiang Cheng Zi” by Su Shi

I do nothing to remember
But I can not forget
Your lonely grave a thousand miles away...
Nowhere can I talk of my sorrow—
Even if we met, how would you know me
My face full of dust
My hair like snow?

In the dark of night, a dream: suddenly, I am home
You by the window
Doing your hair
I look at you and can not speak
Your face is streaked by endless tears
Year after year must they break my heart
These moonlit nights?

That low pine grave

(2) Alan Ayling and Duncan Mackintosh 译

To His Dead Wife

Ten years ago; one living, one long dead; what gulfs apart!
Though heedless of her, yet
I could not well forget
Those thousand miles to her lonely grave;
Too far to talk to her from a lonely heart.
But even could we meet each other, would she recognize
This face engraved with care,
The hoar-frost in my hair?

One night, sleeping alone, I dreamed I was suddenly home again
At her little window; there
She was, combing her hair.
We looked at each other; we brought no words,
Only the many furrows of our tears.
Year after year I know my heart will visit that pitiful place
At night when the bright moon shines
On the hill with its stunted pines.

(3) 许渊冲 译

Tune: "A Riverside Town"

Dreaming of My Deceased Wife on the Night of the 20th Day of the 1st Moon.

For ten long years the living of the dead knows nought.
    Though to my mind not brought,
    Could the dead be forgot?
Her lonely grave is far, a thousand miles away.
    To whom can I my grief convey?
Revived, e'en if she be, oh, could she still know me?

My face is worn with care
And frosted is my hair.

Last night I dreamed of coming to our native place;
She's making up her face
Before her mirror with grace.
Each saw the other hushed,
But from our eyes tears gushed.
When I am woken, oh, I know I'll be heart-broken
Each night when the moon shines
O'er her grave clad with pines.

(4) Burton Watson 译

Tune: "Song of River City"

The year i-mao, 1st month, 20th day: recording a dream I had last night.

(*Written in 1075. The dream was of the poet's first wife, Wang Fu, whom he married in 1054, when she was fifteen. She died in 1065, and the following year he carried her remains back to his old home in Szechwan and buried her in the family plot, planting a number of little pines around the grave mound.*)

Ten years—dead and living dim and draw apart.
I don't try to remember
but forgetting is hard.
Lonely grave a thousand miles off,
cold thoughts—where can I talk them out?
Even if we met you wouldn't know me,
dust on my face,
hair like frost—

In a dream last night suddenly I was home.
By the window of the little room
you were combing your hair and making up.
You turned and looked, not speaking,
only lines of tears coursing down—

Year after year will it break my heart?
The moonlit grave,
its stubby pines—

(5) Lin Yutang 译

A Dream,
To the Tune of "Chiangch'engtse"

Ten years have we been parted:
The living and the dead—
    Hearing no news,
    Not thinking
    And yet forgetting nothing!
I cannot come to your grave a thousand miles away
To converse with you and whisper my longing;
And even if we did meet
    How would you greet
    My weathered face, my hair a frosty white?

    Last night
I dream I had suddenly returned to our old home
And saw you sitting there before the familiar dressing table,
We looked at each other in silence,
With misty eyes beneath the candle light.
May we year after year
    In heartbreak meet,
    On the pine-crest,
    In the moonlight!

(6) Cyril Birch 译

Tune: "The Charms of Nien-nu" (*Nien-nu chiao*)[①]

For ten years the living and the dead have been far severed;
Though not thinking of you,

Naturally I cannot forget.
Your lonely grave is a thousand miles away,
Nowhere to tell my grief.
Even if we could meet, you would not recognize me;
My face is all covered with dust,
The hair at my temples shows frosty.

Last night in a dream I returned home
And at the chamber window
Saw you at your toilet;
We looked at each other in silence and melted into tears.
I cherish in my memory year by year the place of heartbreaking,
In the moonlit night
The knoll of short pines.

① Written in memory of his wife, who died before either she or Su had reached the age of thirty.
编者注：译者在这里译为“The Charms of Nien-nu” [Nien-nu chiao]，是弄错了词牌，应为“江城子”之英译。

(7) 杨宪益 译

Tune: “Jiang Cheng Zi”

Recording my dream on the night of the twentieth of the first month of the year Yimao.

Ten years separated, one living, one dead;
Not thinking
Yet never forgetting;
A thousand li from her lonely grave
I have nowhere to tell my grief;
Yet should we meet again she would hardly know
These temples tinged with gray.

At night in a dream I am suddenly home again:
By my small study window
She sits at her dressing-table;
We look at each other and find no words.
But the tears course down our cheeks.
Year after year heart-broken I fancy her
On moonlit nights

By the hill covered with young pines.

2.47 满庭芳(苏轼)

蜗角虚名，蝇头微利，算来着甚干忙。事皆前定，谁弱又谁强。且趁闲身未老，须放我、些子疏狂。百年里，浑教是醉，三万六千场。

思量，能几许？忧愁风雨，一半相妨。又何须抵死，说短论长。幸对清风皓月，苔茵展、云幕高张。江南好，千钟美酒，一曲《满庭芳》。

〖作品简介〗

此词上片由讽世到愤世，下片从自叹到自适，尽情地展示了作者人生道路上受到重大挫折之后既愤世嫉俗又飘逸旷达的内心世界，表现了词人宠辱皆忘、超然物外的人生态度。全词以议论为主，夹以抒情，情理交融，肆意不羁，用语率真自然，风格奔放舒卷。

〖注　释〗

满庭芳：词牌名。又名《锁阳台》，《清真集》入"中吕调"。双调九十五字，前片四平韵，后片五平韵。过片二字，亦有不叶韵连下为五言句者。**蜗角**：蜗牛角。比喻极其微小。《庄子·则阳》谓在蜗之左角的触氏与右角的蛮氏，两簇常为争地而战。**蝇头**：本指"小"字，此取"微小"之义。**些子**：一点儿。**"百年里"三句**：语本李白《襄阳歌》："百年三万六千日，一日须倾三百杯。"**浑**：整个儿，全部。**"能几许"三句**：意谓计算下来，一生中日子有一半是被忧愁风雨干扰。**"苔茵"两句**：以青苔为褥席铺展，把白云当帐幕高张。

〖译　文〗

(1) 许渊冲 译

Tune: "Courtyard Full of Fragrance" by Su Shi

For fame as vain as a snail's horn
And profit as slight as a fly's head,
Should I be busy and forlorn?
　　Fate rules for long.
Who is weak? Who is strong?
Not yet grown old and having leisure,
Let me be free to enjoy pleasure!

Could I be drunk in a hundred years,
Thirty-six hundred times without shedding tears?

Think how long life can last,
Though sad and harmful storms I've passed.
Why should I waste my breath
    Until my death,
To say the short and long
    Or right and wrong?
I am happy to enjoy clear breeze and the moon bright,
    Green grass outspread
And a canopy of cloud white.
    The Southern shore is fine
    With a thousand cups of wine
And the courtyard fragrant with song.

(2) James Robert Hightower 译

Tune: "Fragrance Fills the Courtyard" by Su Shih

Vainglory in Snailhorn,
Petty profit on Flyshead:
It all adds up to effort wasted.
If everything is determined in advance,
Then who is weak, who is strong?
With what time I have left before I am old,
Let me be irresponsible for a little bit.
In my hundred years,
I'd still like to be drunk
Thirty-six thousand times.

Reckon it up—
How much can you have,
With worry and grief, wind and rain
Taking away a good half?
But why

Go on till you die, talking about the short end and the big deal?
Here we have a fresh breeze and a bright moon,
The moss-mat spread,
The cloud-curtain drawn—
It's good here in the south:
A thousand measures of fine wine
And "Fragrance Fills the Courtyard"① for a song.

① The tune title of this lyric.

2.48 水调歌头(苏轼)

(丙辰中秋，欢饮达旦，大醉，作此篇，兼怀子由。)

明月几时有？把酒问青天。不知天上宫阙，今夕是何年。我欲乘风归去，又恐琼楼玉宇，高处不胜寒。起舞弄清影，何似在人间？

转朱阁，低绮户，照无眠。不应有恨，何事长向别时圆？人有悲欢离合，月有阴晴圆缺，此事古难全。但愿人长久，千里共婵娟。

〖作品简介〗

此词是中秋望月怀人之作，表达了对胞弟苏辙的无限怀念。词人运用形象描绘手法，勾勒出一种皓月当空、亲人千里、孤高旷远的氛围，反衬自己遗世独立的意绪和往昔的神话传说融合一处，在月的阴晴圆缺当中，渗进浓厚的哲学意味，可以说是一首将自然和社会高度契合的感喟作品。

〖注　释〗

把酒：端起酒杯。**把**：执，持。**天上宫阙**[què]：指月中宫殿。**阙**：古代城墙后的石台。**归去**：回到天上去。**琼**[qióng]**楼玉宇**：美玉砌成的楼宇，指想象中的仙宫。**不胜**[shèng]：经受不住。**胜**：(旧读[shēng]，意为"承担、承受"。**弄清影**：意思是月光下的身影也跟着做出各种舞姿。**弄**：赏玩。**何似**：哪里比得上。**转朱阁，低绮**[qǐ]**户，照无眠**：月儿转过朱红色的楼阁，低低地挂在雕花的窗户上，照着没有睡意的人(指词人自己)。**朱阁**：朱红的华丽楼阁。**绮户**：雕饰华丽的门窗。**不应有恨，何事长**[cháng]**向别时圆**：(月儿)不该(对人们)有什么怨恨吧，为什么偏在人们分离时圆呢？**何事**：为什么。**此事**：指人的"欢""合"和月的"晴""圆"。**但**：只。**千里共婵**[chán]**娟**[juān]：虽然相隔千里，也能一起欣赏这美好的月光。**婵娟**：指月亮。

『译　文』

(1) Burton Watson 译

Tune: "Prelude to Water Music" by Su Shi

(*On mid-autumn night of the year ping-ch'en(1076) I drank merrily until dawn, got very drunk and wrote this poem, all the while thinking longingly of Tzu-yu.*)

Bright moon, when did you appear?
Lifting my wine, I question the blue sky.
Tonight in the palaces and halls of heaven
what year is it, I wonder?
I would like to ride the wind, make my home there,
only I fear in porphyry towers, under jade eaves,
in those high places the cold would be more than I could bear.
So I rise and dance and play with your pure beams,
Though this human world—how can it compare with yours?

Circling my red chamber,
low in the curtained door,
you light my sleeplessness.
Surely you bear us no ill will—
why then must you be so round at times when we humans are partied?
People have their griefs and joys, their joinings and separations,
the moon its dark and clear times, its roundings and wanings.
As ever in such matters, things are hardly the way we wish.
I only hope we may have long long lives,
may share the moon's beauty, though a thousand miles apart.

(2) Zong-qi Cai 译

To the Tune "Prelude to the River Tune"

(*On the night of the Mid-Autumn Festival of bingchen[1076], I enjoyed drinking until dawn—I got completely drunk. This piece was composed for the occasion and also to express my thoughts for my brother Ziyou.)*

For how long has the bright moon been there?
I hold up the wine cup and ask the blue sky.
I wonder in the palaces in heaven
What year tonight is.
I wish to ride the wind and return there,
But fear the crystal towers and jade galleries
So high up there would be too cold for me.
I rise to dance with my solitary clear shadow,
How does this compare to the human world!

Going round the crimson hall,
Creeping in through the decorated doorway
It shines on the sleepless me.
I should not owe it any grudge
Then why would it always turn full when we are separated?
Men are sad now, joyous then, because of parting and reunion;
Moon cannot but wane and wax, wax and wane.
Things can never be perfect.
I only hope we will both live long,
And, while a thousand miles apart, share the same moon's beauty.

(3) John A. Turner 译

Remembrance in Mid-Autumn
To the Tune of "Barcarole Prelude"

"When did this glorious moon begin to be?"
Cup in hand, I asked of the azure sky:
And wondered in the palaces of the air
What calendar this night do they go by.
Yes, I would wish to mount the winds and wander there
At home; but dread those onyx towers and halls of jade
Set so immeasurably cold and high.
To tread a measure, to sport with fleshless shade,
How alien to our frail mortality!

Her light round scarlet pavilion, 'neath broidered screen, down streams
On me that sleepless lie.
Ah, vain indeed is my complaining:
But why must she beam at the full on those that sundered sigh?
As men have their weal and woe, their parting and meeting, it seems
The moon has her dark and light, her phases of fullness and waning.
Never is seen perfection in things that die.
Yet would I crave one solitary boon:
Long be we linked with light of the fair moon
Over large leagues of distance, thou and I.

(4) 许渊冲 译

Tune: "Prelude to Water Melody"

(*On the night of the Mid-Autumn Festival of 1076, I drank happily till dawn and wrote this in my cups while thinking of my brother.*)

How long will the full moon appear?
    Winecup in hand, I ask the sky.
I do not know what time of year
    It would be tonight in the palace on high.
    Riding the wind, there I would fly,
Yet I'm afraid the crystalline palace would be
Too high and cold for me.
I rise and dance; with my shadow I play.
On high as on earth, would it be as gay?

    The moon goes round the mansions red
    Through gauze-draped windows soft to shed
    Her light upon the sleepless bed.
Against man she should have no spite.
Why, then, when people part, is she oft full and bright?
Men have sorrow and joy; they part or meet again;
The moon is bright or dim and she may wax or wane.
There has been nothing perfect since the olden days.
    So let us wish that man

Will live long as he can!
Though miles apart, we'll share the beauty she displays.

(5) Stephen Owen 译

Tune: "Song for the River Tune" (*Shui-diao ge-tou*) by Su Shi (1037-1101)

(1076, mid-autumn, drinking till dawn I wrote this. Also thinking of my brother Su Che.)

How long has the moon been up there? —
I ask blue Heaven, wine in hand.
And I wonder
    in those palaces of sky
what year this evening is?
I would ride the wind up there,
but fear
    those marble domes and onyx galleries
are up so high I couldn't bear the cold.
I rise and dance, clear shadow capering—
What can compare
    To this world of mortal men!

Curving past crimson towers,
then lower past grillwork doors,
it shines upon the sleepless.
It should not trouble me,
but why, when people part,
    is it always full and whole?
For mortals there is grief and joy,
    coming together and going apart;
the moon has bright and shadowed phases,
    wholeness and then something gone—
things never stay at perfection.
So I wish that we continue long
to share across a thousand miles

its lovely graces.

(6) Lin Yutang 译

How rare the moon, so round and clear!
With cup in hand, I ask of the blue sky,
"I do not know in the celestial sphere
What name this festive night goes by?"
I want to fly home, riding the air,
But fear the ethereal cold up there,
The jade and crystal mansions are so high!
Dancing to my shadow,
I feel no longer the mortal tie.

She rounds the vermilion tower,
Stoops to silk-pad doors,
Shines on those who sleepless lie.
Why does she, bearing us no grudge,
Shine upon our paring, reunion deny?
But rare is perfect happiness—
The moon does wax, the moon does wane,
And so men meet and say goodbye.
I only pray our life be long,
And our souls together heavenward fly!

(7) Charles Hartman 译

Title: "Shui Diao Ge Tou"
When Will the Moon Be Clear and Bright? by Su Shi

When will the moon be clear and bright?
With a cup of wine in my hand, I ask the blue sky
What season it would be up the heaven for tonight.
Oh Moon, how I wish to get closer
By riding on the breeze.
Yet I fear your crystal and jade chateau,
Are much too high and cold.

So, let me just dance here with my moonlight shadow.

Rounds and rounds, my red mansion, till you shine on my silk
pillow,
Sleepless, but bearing no regrets
Blame not the full moon when people has to apart
Sorrow or joy, be near or far,
Things happen like that, and we still believe in fate.
Toast to you, we are all blessed
Though distant away, we look at the same moon
And in that way, we have never been apart.

(8) Robert Kotewall and Noman L. Smith 译

To "Water Song"

(At the Mid-autumn festival in the year ping-ch'ên (1076) I enjoyed myself by drinking until dawn and became very drunk. I wrote this poem, thinking of Tzŭ-yu)

'Bright moon, when wast thou made?'
Holding up my cup, I ask of the blue sky.
I know not in heaven's palaces
What year it is this night.
I long to ride the wind and return;
Yet fear that marble towers and jade houses,
So high, are over-cold.
I rise and dance and sport with limpid shades;
Better far to be among mankind.

Around the vermilion chamber,
Down in the silken windows,
She shines on the sleepless,
Surely with no ill-will.
Why then is the time of parting always at full moon?
Man has grief and joy, parting and reunion;
The moon has foul weather and fair, waxing and waning.
In this since ever there has been no perfection.

All I can wish is that we may have long life,
That a thousand miles apart we may share her beauty.

(9) Cyril Birch 译

Tune: "Water Music Prelude" (*Shui-tiao ko-t'ou*) ①

When did the moon begin to shine?
Lifting my cup I ask of Heaven.
I wonder in the heavenly palaces and castles
What season it is tonight.
I wish to go up there on the wind
But am afraid the crystal domes and jade halls
Would be too cold on high.
So I dance with my limpid shadow
As if I were no longer on earth.

Around rich bowers,
Into sweet boudoirs,
Shining upon the inmates still awake
The moon should have no regrets.
Why is she always at the full when men are separated?
Men have their woe and joy, parting and meeting;
The moon has her dimness and brightness, waxing and waning.
Never from of old has been lasting perfection.
I only wish that you and I may be ever well and hale,
That both of us may watch the fair moon, even a thousand
miles apart.

① Written while thinking of his younger brother, Tzu-yu.

2.49 念奴娇(苏轼)

大江东去,
浪淘尽,
千古风流人物。
故垒西边,

人道是，
三国周郎赤壁。
乱石穿空，
惊涛拍岸，
卷起千堆雪。
江山如画，
一时多少豪杰。

遥想公瑾当年，
小乔初嫁了，
雄姿英发。
羽扇纶巾，
谈笑间，
樯橹灰飞烟灭。
故国神游，
多情应笑我，
早生华发。
人生如梦，
一尊还酹江月。

〖作品简介〗

此词通过对月夜江上壮美景色的描绘，借对古代战场的凭吊和对风流人物才略、气度、功业的追念，曲折地表达了作者怀才不遇、功业未就、老大未成的忧愤之情，同时表现了作者关注历史和人生的旷达之心。全词借古抒怀，雄浑苍凉，大气磅礴，境界宏阔，将写景、咏史、抒情融为一体，给人以撼魂荡魄的艺术力量，曾被誉为“古今绝唱”。

〖注　释〗

念奴娇：词牌名。又名《百字令》《酹江月》等。**赤壁**：此指黄州赤壁，一名“赤鼻矶”，在今湖北黄冈西。而三国古战场的赤壁，文化界认为在今湖北赤壁市蒲圻县西北。**大江**：指长江。**淘**：冲洗，冲刷。**风流人物**：指杰出的历史名人。**故垒**：过去遗留下来的营垒。**周郎**：指三国时吴国名将周瑜，字公瑾，少年得志，二十四为中郎将，掌管东吴重兵，吴中皆呼为“周郎”。下文中的“公瑾”，亦指周瑜。雪：比喻浪花。**遥想**：形容想得很远；回忆。**小乔初嫁了**[liǎo]：《三国志·吴志·周瑜传》载，周瑜从孙策攻皖，“得桥公两女，皆国色也。策自纳大桥，瑜纳小桥”。乔，本作“桥”。其时距赤壁之战已经十年，此处言“初嫁”，是言其少年得意、倜傥风流。**雄姿英发**[fā]：谓周瑜体貌不凡，言谈卓绝。**英发**：谈吐不凡，见识卓越。**羽扇纶[guān]巾**：古代儒将的便装打扮。**羽扇**：羽毛制成的扇子。**纶巾**：青丝制成的头巾。**樯橹**[qiáng lǔ]：这里代指曹操的水军战船。**樯**：挂帆的桅杆。**橹**：一种摇船的桨。“樯橹”一作“强虏”，又作“樯虏”或“狂虏”。《宋集珍本丛刊》之《东坡乐府》，元延祐刻本，作“强虏”。延祐本原藏杨氏海源阁，历经季振宜、顾广圻、黄丕烈等名家收藏，卷首有黄丕烈题辞，述其源流甚详，实今传各版之祖。**故国神游**：“神游故国”的倒文。**故国**：这里指旧地，当年的赤壁战场。**神游**：于想象、梦境中游历。**“多情”**二句：“应笑我多情，早生华发”的倒文。**华发**[fà]：花白的头发。**一尊还**[huán]**酹**[lèi]**江月**：古人以酒浇在地上祭奠。这里指洒酒酬月，寄托自己的感情。**尊**：通“樽”，酒杯。**强虏**：强大之敌，指曹军。**虏**：对敌人的蔑称。

〖译 文〗

(1) Wai-lim Yip 译

“Charming nien-nu”

Eastward goes the Yangtze!
Waves scour all
Free-soaring worthies of all years.
West of the ancient fortress,
They say:
Three Kingdoms, Master Chou, Red Cliffs,
Thrown-out rocks breaking clouds.
Startling surges tear at banks,
Roll up a thousand heaps of snow.
Mountains rivers-all picture!
One historic moment: how many heroes!

Think of Kung-chin back in those years-
Little Ch'iao newly married-
Heroic gait in full swing:
Feathered fan, silk scarf.
Between talks and laughs
The chief enemy ashes in winds, gone in smoke.
Spiritual tour of the ancient kingdom...
Sentimental! Yes, flout at me

At my early white hair
Life is dream!
A bottle to offer to the river-moon.

(2) Zong-qi Cai 译

To the Tune of "The Charm of Niannu": Meditation on the Past at Red Cliff

The Great Yangtze runs east,
Its waves have swept away heroes of past ages.
Lying to the west of the old fort, it is said.
Is the Red Cliff, known because of Zhou Yu of the Three Kingdoms.
Rugged stone wall pierce the sky.
Angry waves beat the banks,
Churning up water like piles of frosty snow.
The mountains and the River look like a painting,
And how many heroes were once here!

Thinking far back, I see Zhou Gongjin,
With Little Qiao as his new bride,
Beaming with valor.
He has feather fan in hand and is in silk headdress, and while chatting merrily,
The powerful enemy vanishes in flying ash and smoke.
My mind wandering over the old kingdom,
I become so sentimental that one may well laugh at me:
Too early have gray hairs crept onto my head.
Life is like a dream,
So let me offer this cup to the moon over the river.

(3) Stephen Owen 译

Tune: "The Charms of Nian-nu" (*Nian-nü jiao*): Meditation on the Past at Red Cliff by Su Shi

Eastward goes the great river,
its waves have swept away

a thousand years of gallant men.
And they say
    that west of the ancient castle here
is that Red Cliff
    of Zhou Yu and the Three Kingdoms.
A rocky tangle pierces sky,
leaping waves smash the shore,
surging snow in a thousand drifts.
Like a painting, these rivers and hills
where once so many bold men were.

I envision Zhou Yu back then,
just wedded to the younger Qiao,
his manly manner striking.
With black turban and feather fan
    laughing in conversation
as embers flew from mast and prow
    and the smoke was sinking away.
The spirit roams that long-ago land—
you will laugh at this sentimental me,
hair streaked with white before my time.
Yet this human world is like a dream
and I pour out my winecup as offering
    into the river's moonbeams.

(4) Alan Ayling and Duncan Mackintosh 译

The Red Cliff by Su Shih

    The great river surges east.
    Its waves have scoured away
    Since time began all traces of heroic man.
    To the west of the old fort,
    So people say,
Stands the Red Cliff of Chou of the Three Kingdoms.
    With piled up rocks to stab the sky
    And waves to shake them thunderously

Churning the frothy mass to mounds of snow,
It's like a masterpiece in paint.
Those ages hide how many a hero!

Think back to those old days; that first year when Chou Yu
Had just been married to the Little Ch'iao.
Then, what a hero he became!
With waving fan and silken cap
He talked and laughed at ease
While masts and oars were blotted out in smoke and flame.
My wits that stray to realms of old
Deserve the scorn of all who feel;
Years pass, and hair grows white so soon.
Though a man's life is like a dream
One toast continues still—the River and the Moon!

(5) Kenneth Rexroth 译

The Red Cliff by Su Shih

The River flows to the East.
Its waves have washed away all
The heroes of history.
To the West of the ancient
Wall you enter the Red Gorge
Of Chu Ko Liang of the
Days of the Three Kingdoms. The
Jagged peaks pierce the heavens.
The furious rapids beat
At the boat, and dash up in
A thousand clouds of spray like
Snow. Mountain and river have
Often been painted, in the
Memory of the heroes

Of those days. I remember
Long ago, Kung Ch'in newly

Married to the beautiful
Chiao-siao, shining in splendor,
A young warrior, and the other
Chu Ko Liang, in his blue cap,
Waving his horsetail duster,
Smiling and chatting as he
Burned the navy of Ts'ao Ts'ao.
Their ashes were scattered to
The four winds. They vanished away
In smoke. I like to dream of
Those dead kingdoms. Let people
Laugh at my prematurely
Grey hair. My answer is
A wine cup, full of the
Moon drowned in the River.

(6) Ch'u Ta-kao 译

Tune: "The Charms of Nien-nu" [*Nien-nu chiao*] by Su Shih

The waves of the mighty river flowing eastward
Have swept away the brilliant figures of a thousand generations.
West of the old fortress,
So people say, is Lord Chou's Red Cliff of the time of the
Three Kingdoms.
The tumbling rocks thrust into the air;
The roaring surges dash upon the shore,
Rolling into a thousand drifts of snow.
The River and the mountains make a vivid picture—
What a host of heroes once were!

And I recall the young Lord then,
Newly married to the fair Younger Ch'iao,
His valorous features shown forth;
With a feather fan and silken cap
Amid talking and laughing he put his enemy's ships to
ashes and smoke.
While my thoughts wander in the country of old,

Romantic persons might smile at my early grey hair.
Ah! Life is but like a dream;
With a cup of wine, let me yet pour a libation to the moon
on the River.

2.50 临江仙(苏轼)

夜饮东坡醒复醉，归来仿佛三更。家童鼻息已雷鸣。敲门都不应，倚杖听江声。

长恨此身非我有，何时忘却营营。夜阑风静縠纹平。小舟从此逝，江海寄余生。

【作品简介】

此词作于神宗元丰五年，即东坡黄州之贬的第三年。全词风格清旷而飘逸，写作者深秋之夜在东坡雪堂开怀畅饮，醉后返归临皋住所的情景，表现了词人退避社会、厌弃世间的人生理想、生活态度和要求彻底解脱的出世意念，展现了作者旷达而又伤感的心境。

【注　释】

临江仙：唐教坊曲名，后用作词牌名。此词双调六十字，平韵格。**东坡**：在湖北黄冈县东。苏轼贬谪黄州时，友人马正卿助其垦辟的游息之所，筑雪堂五间。**听江声**：苏轼寓居临皋，在湖北黄冈县南长江边，故能听长江涛声。**“长恨”句**：引用庄子典。《庄子·知北游》云：“舜问乎丞曰：‘道何得而有乎?’”曰：“汝身非汝有也，汝何得有夫道?”舜曰：“吾身非吾有也，孰有之哉?”曰：“是天地之委形也。”**营营**：周旋、忙碌，内心躁急之状，形容奔走钻营，追逐名利。《庄子·庚桑楚》云：“全汝形，抱汝生，无使汝思虑营营。”**夜阑**：夜尽。司马迁《史记·高祖本纪》有“酒阑”，裴骃集解曰：“阑，言希也。谓饮酒者半罢半在，谓之阑。”文选·谢庄《宋孝武宣贵妃诔》有“白露凝兮岁将阑”，李善注曰：“阑，犹晚也”。**縠(hú)纹**：比喻水波微细。**縠**：绉纱类丝织品。

【译　文】

(1) Wai-lim Yip 译

Tune: “Immortal by the River”

Drinking into deep night at East Slope, sober then drunk.

I return home perhaps at small hours,
My page-boy's snoring already like thunder.
No answer to my knocking at the door,
I lean on my staff to listen to the river rushing.

I grieve forever that this body, no body of mine.
When can I forget this buzzing life?
Night now still, wind quiet, waves calm and smooth,
A little boat to drift from here.
On the river, on the sea, my remaining years.

(2) James Robert Hightower 译

Tune: "Immortal by the River"

I drank at night on East Slope, sobered up, got drunk again.
When I came home it was sometime past midnight,
The houseboy was already snoring like thunder.
I pounded on the gate and got no response,
Then leaned on my staff and listened to the river noises.

I have long deplored that this body is not one's own.
When can I forget the restless striving?
The night is late, the wind still, the ripples smooth.
In a little boat I shall put out from here,
Entrusting my remaining days to river and sea.

(3) Burton Watson 译

Tune: "Immortal at the River"

Drank tonight at Eastern Slope, sobered up, drank again;
got home somewhere around third watch.
The houseboy by now is snoring like thunder:
I bang the gate but nobody answers.
Leaning on my stick, I listen to river sounds.

Always it irks me—this body not my own.
When can I forget the world's business?
Night far gone, wind calm, the river's crepe of ripples stilled:
I'll leave here in a little boat,
on far waters spend the years remaining.

(4) Stephen Owen 译

Tune: "Immortal by the River" (*Lin-jiang xian*) by Su Shi (1037-1101)

I was drinking that night on Eastern Slope,
    I sobered and got drunk again,
and when I went back it seemed about midnight.
My servant boy was snoring,
    it sounded like the thunder,
When I knocked at the gate, no one answered,
then I leaned on my staff
    and listened to the river.

I've always resented how this body
    has never been my own,
will the time ever come when I can forget
    being always busy?
The night ended, the winds calmed,
    the wrinkled waves grew flat,
I'll set off from here in my small boat,
on river and lakes lodge the rest of my days.

(5) Lin Yutang 译

Returning to Linkao at Night, to the Tune of "Linchainghsien"

After a drink at night, Tungpo wakes up and gets drunk again.
By the time I come home it seems to be midnight.
The boy servant is asleep snoring like thunder
And does not answer the door.
Resting on a cane I listen to the murmur of the river

And feel with a pang that I am not master of my own life.
When can I stop this hustling about?
The night is late, the air is calm,
And the water a sheen of unruffled light.
Let me take a small boat down the river hence
To spend beyond the seas the remainder of my days.

2.51 浣溪沙(苏轼)

【其一】

(略)

【其二】

旋抹红妆看使君，三三五五棘篱门。相挨踏破茜罗裙。
老幼扶携收麦社，乌鸢翔舞赛神村。道逢醉叟卧黄昏。

【其三】

麻叶层层檾叶光，谁家煮茧一村香。隔篱娇语络丝娘。
垂白杖藜抬醉眼，捋青捣麨软饥肠。问言豆叶几时黄。

【其四】

簌簌衣巾落枣花，村南村北响缫车。牛衣古柳卖黄瓜。
酒困路长惟欲睡，日高人渴漫思茶。敲门试问野人家。

【其五】

软草平莎过雨新，轻沙走马路无尘。何时收拾耦耕身。
日暖桑麻光似泼，风来蒿艾气如薰。使君元是此中人。

『作品简介』

此词乃宋代文学家苏轼的组词作品，为作者43岁任徐州太守时率众赴徐门(徐州)石潭谢雨路上所作，主要写作者途中的所见、所闻及所感，其文风朴实、格调清新，不取艳辞，不采僻典，语言清丽自然，洗尽华靡见真淳。其主要艺术特色是以诗的句法入词，完全突破了“词为艳科”的藩篱。此外，该词作还以农村题材入词，给词坛带来了朴素清新的乡土气息，对后来词作的题材选择具有开拓意义。

『注 释』

浣溪沙：词牌名。**旋**：立即；**使君**：词人自称。**棘篱**：以荆棘围成的篱笆。**茜**：茜草，此处指代红色。**罗裙**：丝绸裙子。**收麦社**：麦子收过之后举行的祭神谢恩的活动。**乌鸢**：乌鸦，老鹰。**赛神**：用仪仗鼓乐迎神、周游街巷等活动。**檾**[qǐng]：同“苘”。**络丝**

娘：本为虫名，此处代指缫丝的妇女。**垂白**：鬓发将白的老人；**杖藜**：倚仗藜茎制成的手杖。**捋青**：从未全熟的麦穗上捋下麦粒：用麦子制成的干粮；**软**：“饱”之意。**簌**[sù]**簌**：花落貌，意即纷纷下落的样子，一作“蔌蔌”，音义皆同。**缫**[sāo]**车**：纺车。**缫**：一作“缲”，把蚕茧浸在热水里，抽出蚕丝。**牛衣**：蓑衣之类。这里泛指用粗麻织成的衣服。《汉书·王章传》：“章疾病，无被，卧牛衣中。”宋程大昌《演繁露》卷二《牛衣》条：“案《食货志》，董仲舒曰：‘贫民常衣牛马之衣，而食犬彘之食。’然则牛衣者，编草使暖，以被牛体，盖蓑衣之类也。”此处指卖瓜者衣着粗劣。或谓本作“半依”，如曾季貍《艇斋诗话》：“予尝见东坡墨迹作‘半依’，乃知‘牛’字误也。”**漫思茶**：想随便去哪里找点茶喝。**漫**：随意，一作“谩”。**野人**：农夫。**平莎**[suō]：莎草，多年生草本植物。**耦耕**[ǒu gēng]：两个人各拿一耜并肩耕作，此处泛指耕作。**蒿艾**：即艾蒿，多年生草本植物。**薰**：一种香草。**使君**：词人自称。**元**：“原”之意。

【译 文】

(1) Burton Watson 译

Tune: “Sand of Silk-washing Stream”

Five poems written along the road to Stone Lake at Hsü-chou, where I went to give thanks for rain. The lake is 20 li east of the city. Though separated from the Ssu River, its water level is always the same as that of the river and its water of the same degree of learness or muddiness.

(*Written in 1078, when the poet was governor of Hsü-chou in Kiangsu. There was a drought this year and Su had gone to Stone Lake, said by local lore to be the home of a rain-making dragon, to pray for rain. When rain fell, he made a second trip to give thanks. The first of the five poems is omitted.*)

1.

2.

Throw on rouge and powder, watch the governor pass!
In threes and fives by thorn hedge gates
they push and trample each other's red silk skirts.

Lead the old, bring the children! Like a harvest festival,
crows and hawks wheeling above the village shrine—
At dust I met an old man lying drunk beside the road.

3.

Layer on layer of hemp leaves, jute leaves shining:
some family is boiling cocoons—the whole village smells good.
Beyond the hedge, spinning girls[①] call invitingly.

White-haired, with goosefoot staff, he raises drunken eyes—
Pick greens, grind parched grain, ease an empty belly!
Tell me, when will bean leaves turn yellow here?

4.

Flutter flutter on clothes and cap, jujube flowers fall;
village south, village north echo to spinning reels.
Half leaning on the old willow, they peddle yellow melons.

Wine-drowsy, a long road, I'm getting sleepier;
sun high, throat parched, thinking only of tea—
I'll knock on a gate and see what the villagers 'll give me.

5.

Soft grasses, a plain of sedge fresh with passing rain;
horses race the light sand road but raise no dust.
When can I quit and take up plowing and planting?

Sun warm on mulberry and hemp glints like water;
wind over mugwort and moxa comes perfumed.
Your governor, long ago, lived in a place like this.

① "Spinning girls" is probably the name of a singing insect, though the term may mean real girls working at their spinning.

(2) 许渊冲 译

Tune: "Sand of Silk-washing Stream" by Su Shi

2.

Maidens make up in haste to see the magistrate;

By threes and fives they come out at their hedgerow gate.
They push and tweeze and trample each other's skirt red.

Villagers old and young to celebration are led;
With crows and kites they dance thanksgiving in array.
At dusk I see an old man lie drunk on my way.

3.

The leaves of jute and hemp are thick and lush in this land;
The scent of boiling cocoons in the village spreads.
Across the fence young maidens prate while spinning threads.

An old man raises dim-sighted eyes, cane in hand;
He picks new wheat so that his hunger he may ease.
I wonder when will yellow the leaves of green peas.

4.

Date-flowers fall in showers on my hooded head,
At both ends of the village wheels are spinning thread,
A straw-cloak'd man sells cucumber beneath a willow tree.

Wine-drowsy when the road is long, I yawn for bed;
Throat parched when sun is high, I long for tea,
I'll knock at this door. What have they for me?

5.

After rain the paddy fields look fresh as soft grass;
No dust is raised on sandy roads where horses pass.
When can I come to till the ground with household mine?

Hemp and mulberry glint as if steeped in sunshine;
Mugwort and moxa spread a sweet scent in the breeze.
I remember I was companion of all these.

2.52 鹧鸪天(苏轼)

林断山明竹隐墙，乱蝉衰草小池塘。翻空白鸟时时见，照水红蕖细细香。
村舍外，古城旁，杖藜徐步转斜阳。殷勤昨夜三更雨，又得浮生一日凉。

【作品简介】

此词作于作者贬谪黄州时期，表现作者雨后游赏的欢快闲适心境，也是其当时乡间幽居生活的自我写照。全词上片写景，下片刻画人物形象，描绘了一幅夏日雨后的农村小景。其描写全无平铺直叙之俗套，读来婉转蕴藉，令人回味无穷。

【注 释】

鹧鸪天：词牌名。**林断山明**：树林断绝处，山峰显现出来。**翻空**：飞翔在空中。**红蕖**（qú）：荷花。**古城**：当指黄州古城。**杖藜**：拄着藜杖。杜甫《漫兴九首》其五："杖藜徐步立芳洲。"**藜**：一种草本植物，这里指藜木拐杖。**殷勤**：劳驾，有劳。**浮生**：意为世事不定，人生短促。李涉《题鹤林寺僧舍》："偶经竹院逢僧话，又得浮生半日闲。"

【译 文】

(1) Burton Watson 译

Tune："Partridge Sky"

Mountains shine through forest breaks, bamboo hides the wall;
withered grass by small ponds, jumbled cicada cries.
White birds again and gain cut across the sky;
fain scent of lotus shining pink on the water.

Beyond the village,
by old town walls,
with goosefoot cane I stroll where late sunlight turns.
Thanks to rain that fell at the third watch last night
I get another cool day in this floating life.

(2) 许渊冲 译

Tune："Partridges in the Sky" by Su Shi

Through forest breaks appear hills and bamboo-screened wall,
Cicadas shrill o'er withered grass near a pool small.

White birds are seen now and then looping in the air;
Pink lotus blooms on lake-side exude fragrance spare.

Beyond the cots,
Near the old town,
Cane in hand, I stroll round while the sun's slanting down.
Thanks to the welcome rain which fell when night was deep,
Now in my floating life one more-fresh day I reap.

(3) Jiaosheng Wang 译

Tune: "Partridge Sky"
Written While Banished to Huang-chou by Su Shih

Where the forest breaks,
Hills emerge into view;
Where the walled courtyard is hidden in bamboo,
Obstreperous cicadas riot over a small pond o'ergrown with withered grass.
Frequent is the appearance of white birds looping in the air,
Delicate fragrance of pink lotus blooms mirrored in water.

Beyond the village houses,
Beside the ancient town,
Cane in hand, a leisurely stroll I take
In the wake of the slanting sun.
Thanks to last midnight's bounteous rain,
My floating life[①] now enjoys one more day of delicious cool.

① An expression meaning "precarious life" which originates from the Chuang Tzu.

2.53 定风波(苏轼)

(三月七日，沙湖道中遇雨。雨具先去，同行皆狼狈，余独不觉，已而遂晴，故作此词。)

莫听穿林打叶声，何妨吟啸且徐行。竹杖芒鞋轻胜马，谁怕？一蓑烟雨任平生。

料峭春风吹酒醒，微冷，山头斜照却相迎。回首向来萧瑟处，归去，也无风雨也无晴。

〖作品简介〗

此词描写的是作者在野外途中偶遇风雨这一生活中的小事，于简朴中见深意，于寻常处生奇景，表现出旷达超脱的胸襟，饱含道家旷达豪放的精神，寄寓着超凡脱俗的人生理想。上片聚焦于雨中，下片着眼于雨后，篇幅虽短，但意境深邃、内蕴丰富，诠释着作者的人生信念，体现出一个正直文人在坎坷人生中力求解脱之道，也展现了作者的精神追求。

〖注 释〗

定风波：词牌名。**沙湖**：在今湖北黄冈东南三十里，又名螺丝店。**狼狈**：进退皆难的困顿窘迫之状。**已而**：过了一会儿。**穿林打叶声**：指大雨点透过树林打在树叶上的声音。**吟啸**：放声吟咏。**芒鞋**：草鞋。**一蓑烟雨任平生**：披着蓑衣在风雨里过一辈子也处之泰然。**一蓑**[suō]：蓑衣，用棕制成的雨披。**料峭**：微寒的样子。**斜照**：偏西的阳光。**向来**：方才。**萧瑟**：风雨吹打树叶声。**也无风雨也无晴**：意谓既不怕雨，也不喜晴。

〖译 文〗

(1) Stephen Owen 译

Tune："Settling Wind and Waves"(*Ding-feng-bo*) by Su Shi (1037-1101)

(*On May 7 I ran into a rainstorm on the Sand Lake Road. The raincoats had all been sent on ahead, and the people traveling with me were all thrown into confusion. I didn't even notice. Soon it cleared up, and I wrote this.*)

Pay no heed to those sounds,
    piercing the woods, hitting leaves—
why should it stop me from whistling or chanting
    and walking slowly along?
With my bamboo cane and sandals of straw
    I move more free than on horse.
Who's afraid?
Let my life be spent with a raincoat
    in the misty rain.

A biting chill in the spring breeze
blows me sober from wine.
A bit cold,
but the sunshine that sinks on the hilltop
comes back to welcome me.
Turn your head to where you just were,
where the winds were howling,
go back—
on the one hand, it's not a storm;
on the other, not clear skies.

(2) 许渊冲 译

Tune: "Calming the Waves" by Su Shi

(On the 7th day of the 3rd month we were caught in rain on our way to the Sandy Lake. The umbrellas had gone ahead, my companions were quite downhearted, but I took no notice. It soon cleared, and I wrote this.)

Listen not to the rain beating against the trees.
Why don't you slowly walk and chant at ease?
Better than a saddle I like sandals and cane.
I'd fain,
In a straw cloak, spend my life in mist and rain.

Drunken, I am sobered by the vernal wind shrill
And rather chill.
In front, I see the slanting sun atop the hill;
Turning my head, I see the dreary beaten track.
Let me go back!
Impervious to rain or shine, I'll have my own will.

2.54 卜算子(李之仪)

我住长江头，君住长江尾。日日思君不见君，共饮长江水。
此水几时休，此恨何时已。只愿君心似我心，定不负相思意。

【作品简介】

此词深得民歌的神情风味，明白如话，复叠回环，同时又具有文人词构思新巧的特点，写出了隔绝中的永恒之爱，给人以江水长流情亦长的感受。

【注 释】

休：停止。已：完结，停止。定：此处为衬字。在词规定的字数外适当地增添一二不太关键的字词，以更好地表情达意，谓之衬字，亦称“添声”。思：想念，思念。

【译 文】

(1) Victor H. Mair 译

Tune: "The Diviner" by Li Chih-yi (fl. 1071)

I live at the head of the Long River, ①
You live along its lower reaches;
Day after day I think of you but cannot see you,
Yet we both drink the waters of the Long River.

When will these waters ever cease?
When will this yearning ever end?
I wish only that your heart will be like my heart,
And that you will never repudiate our mutual affection.

① The Yangtze.

(2) 许渊冲 译

Tune: "Song of Divination" by Li Zhi-yi

I live upstream and you
Downstream by River Blue.
    Day after day of you I think,
But you are not in view,

Although as one we drink
The water clear of River Blue.

When will the water no more flow?
When will my grief no longer grow?
I wish your heart be but like mine,
Then not in vain for you I pine.

(3) 龚景浩 译

"Bu Suan Zi (Song)"
Li Zhi Yi

I live by the head of the Long River.
You, my love, at its end.
I think of you day and night but cannot see you,
Yet on the same drinking source we depend.

When will the water stop flowing?
When will I cease to be longing?
I only wish your heart would be like mine:
Returning all my loving thoughts with thine.

2.55 千秋岁(黄庭坚)

世间好事。恰恁厮当对。乍夜永，凉天气。雨稀帘外滴，香篆盘中字。长入梦，如今见也分明是。

欢极娇无力，玉软花欹坠。钗罥袖，云堆臂。灯斜明媚眼，汗浃瞢腾醉。奴奴睡，奴奴睡也奴奴睡。

『作品简介』

此词描写男女之情。

『注　释』

香篆[zhuàn]盘：焚香用的器皿及用具。**欹[qī]坠**：向一边坠下。**欹**：倾斜，歪向一边。**罥[Juàn]**：缠绕。这里是指女方发卡紧挨着男方的衣袖。**汗浃瞢腾醉**：这里是指男女双方因汗多而朦朦，宛如喝醉了酒一般。瞢[méng]：混沌不清的样子。

【译 文】

(1) James Robert Hightower 译

Tune: "A Thousand Autumns"
By Huang T'ing-chien

The best thing in the world
Is precisely being together like this;
The nights getting longer,
The weather cool,
The rain dripping a bit outside the curtain,
The molded incense in the burner—
I've long dreamed about it
And now it's really happening.

Our joy reached its peak and she turned lovely limp;
The jade was soft, the flower drooped and fell,
Her hairpin dangling on my sleeve,
Her hair piled on my arm.
The lamp lights her ravishing eyes,
Wet with perspiration, intoxicated—
Sleep, sweetheart, sleep;
Sweetheart, sleep.

(2) Ronald C. Egan 译

To the Tune of "Thousand Year Longevity"

One of life's greatest joys,
Being together here with you.
Just when nights are long.
The air cool.
Light rain drips outside the curtain.
Incense words lie in the dish.
I often dream of you,

But tonight it's really you.

The pleasure over, lovely and listless
Jade turns soft, flowers droop to fall.
The hairpin dangles on my sleeve,
Cloud locks pile on my arm.
The lamp shines on her lovely eyes,
Perspiration-soaked, intoxicated.
'Go to sleep darling,
Sleep darling, go to sleep.'

2. 56 清平乐(黄庭坚)

春归何处。寂寞无行路。若有人知春去处。唤取归来同住。
春无踪迹谁知。除非问取黄鹂。百啭无人能解,因风飞过蔷薇。

〖作品简介〗

此词为惜春之作。词中以清新细腻的语言,表现了词人对美好春光的珍惜与热爱,抒写了作者对美好事物的执著追求。

〖注　释〗

“春归”两句:化用白居易《落花》“留春春不住,春归人寂寞”诗句。**唤取**:呼唤。**取**:语气词。**黄鹂**:黄莺。**百啭**:形容黄鹂婉转的鸣声。**因风飞**:顺着风逝,“飞”一作“吹”。

〖译　文〗

(1) Wai-lim Yip 译

Tune:“CH'ING-P'ING SONG” by Huang T'ing-chien (1045-1105)

Where does Spring return?
All solitary: no road.
If someone knows where Spring goes,
Call Spring back to stay.

Spring leaves no trace. Who knows?

But to ask the yellow orioles.
A hundred songs: no one understands—
With the winds, fly over the roses.

(2) Weng Xianliang 译

Spring Is Gone

Spring is gone. Which way, which way? Whoever knows, let her forward this message: come back, come back and stay.

Spring is gone. Which way, which way? Who would know, if not you, Oriole? She answers in song, trills and twitters that nothing tell. Then she takes wing and, mounting with the wind, sweeps over the rose bush and—she too is gone.

(3) 许渊冲 译

Tune: "Pure Serene Music"
Late Spring by Huang Ting-jian

Away Spring goes!
Which way, which way?
Whoever knows,
Please call her back to stay!

Spring's gone. Towards which land?
Ask orioles, who sing
A hundred tunes none understand.
Riding the wind, they're on the wing.

(4) 许渊冲 译

Tune: "Pure Serene Music"
Late Spring by Huang Ting-jian

Where has Spring gone?
No trace is left on pathway lone.

If you know where she is today,
Please call her back to stay.

Who can find traceless Spring?
Unless you ask the orioles which sing
A hundred tunes none understand.
Riding the wind, they fly past rose-grown land.

2.57 满庭芳(黄庭坚)

北苑春风，方圭圆璧，万里名动京关。
碎身粉骨、功合上凌烟。
尊俎风流战胜，降春睡、开拓愁边。
纤纤捧，研膏溅乳，金缕鹧鸪斑。

相如虽病渴，一觞一咏，宾有群贤。
为扶起灯前，醉玉颓山。
搜搅胸中万卷，还倾动、三峡词源。
归来晚，文君未寝，相对小窗前。

〖作品简介〗

此词以茶为中心，纵横于名物之中，出入于典故之间，写尽古今风流。其上片极言茶之风神，下片写邀朋呼侣集茶盛会。实乃咏茶之佳作。

〖注　释〗

北苑：即今福建建瓯，是贡茶的主要产地。**春风**：意指社前之茶。**方圭圆璧**：以喻茶饼形状。建瓯贡茶讲究产地节令，且“日费数千工”，制成的方圆茶饼，蔡絛《铁围山丛谈》卷六且云“岁但可十百饼”，故无怪要声传万里、名动汴京了。“**碎身粉骨**”二句：以研磨制茶之法攀合将相报国之事，以贡茶之贵比之开业之功，着意联想生发，避实就虚。**凌烟**：凌烟阁的省称，是唐朝为表彰功臣而建筑的绘有功臣图像的高阁，因“凌烟阁二十四功臣”而闻名于世，可惜毁于战乱。“**尊俎风流战胜**”：此句是“战胜风流尊俎”的倒装，意指茶能解酒驱睡、清神醒脑、排忧解愁。**鹧鸪斑**：代指茶盏，极珍贵。

〖译 文〗

James Robert Hightower 译

Tune: "The Courtyard Full of Fragrance"
Tea by Huang T'ing-chien (1045-1105)

Spring wind in North Park—
Square tablet, round disk of jade,
Fame that stirs capital and frontier a myriad miles away;
Shattered body, powdered bones—
Achievements worthy of the Ling-ye Hall of Heroes.
At the banquet it wins the palm of refinement.
Downs spring sleep,
Pushes back the boundary of grief.
Offered by slender hands,
Rubbed to paste and whipped to milky froth.
Golden thread, partridge-stripped.

Ssu-ma Hsiang-ju, though sick of thirst,
Produced a song for every flask—
We have poets here,
And it will support them by the lamp—
Drunken jade, toppling mountain.
Rummage through your memory of a thousand volumes,
And pour forth your inexhaustible spring of poetry;
When I go home at last,
Wen-chün is waiting up
By the little window, to sit with me.

2.58 品令(二之二)(秦观)

掉又惧。天然个品格。于中压一。帘儿下时把鞋儿踢。语低低、笑咭咭。
每每秦楼相见，见了无限怜惜。人前强不欲相沾识。把不定、脸儿赤。

【作品简介】

此词用质朴流畅的白话描写了一位天真可爱的少女，字里行间透露出作者的怜爱之情。

【注 释】

掉又惧：既喜欢露脸又有点害羞。**掉**：卖弄，这里引申为喜欢人前作秀。**惧**：恐惧，这里引申为害羞。**帘**：眼帘。**秦楼**：传说中秦穆公为其女弄玉所建之楼，据张岱《西湖梦寻》所记也可指苏轼所建水月楼；这里是指女子的闺楼。**沾识**[zhān shí]：犹言结识亲近。

【译 文】

Ronald C. Egan 译

To the Tune of "Flute Song"

Naughty but timid,
Her natural manner
Makes her best of the lot.
When the blind is lowered she kicks off her slippers
Whispering,
Giggling.

Whenever we tryst in her boudoir
She reveals boundless love.
In front of others she pretends not to know me.
But despite herself,
Her face turns red.

2.59 鹊桥仙(秦观)

纤云弄巧，飞星传恨，银汉迢迢暗度。金风玉露一相逢，便胜却人间无数。
柔情似水，佳期如梦，忍顾鹊桥归路。两情若是久长时，又岂在朝朝暮暮。

〖作品简介〗

此词是一曲纯情的爱情颂歌。其上片写牛郎织女聚会，下片写他们的离别。全词哀乐交织，熔抒情与议论于一炉，融天上人间为一体，优美的形象与深沉的感情结合起来，起伏跌宕地讴歌了美好的爱情。此词议论自由流畅、通俗易懂，却又显得婉约蕴藉，余味无穷，尤其是末二句，使词的思想境界升华到一个崭新的高度，成为词中警句。

〖注 释〗

纤云：轻盈的云彩。**弄巧**：指云彩在空中幻化成各种巧妙的花样。**飞星**：流星。一说指牵牛、织女二星。**银汉**：银河。**迢迢**：遥远的样子。**暗度**：悄悄渡过。**金风玉露**：指秋风白露。李商隐《辛未七夕》："恐是仙家好别离，故教迢递作佳期。由来碧落银河畔，可要金风玉露时。"**忍顾**：怎忍回视。**朝朝暮暮**：指朝夕相聚。语出宋玉《高唐赋》。

〖译 文〗

(1) 许渊冲 译

Tune: "Immortal at the Magpie Bridge" by Qin Guan

Clouds float like works of art;
Stars shoot with grief at heart.
Across the Milky Way the Cowherd meets the Maid.
When autumn's Golden Wind embraces Dew of Jade,
All the love scenes on earth, however many, fade.

Their tender love flows like a stream;
This happy date seems but a dream.
Can they bear a separate homeward way?:
If love between both sides can last for aye,
Why need they stay together night and day?

(2) Stephen Owen 译

To "Gods on the Magpie Bridge"

Fine wisps of cloud sport their craft,
shooting stars bear word of the lovers' pain,
and now far off in the River of Stars

they are making the crossing unseen.
To meet just once in fall's metal wind
and in the jade white dew
turns out to be better by far
than the countless meetings of mortals.

Their tender feelings seem like water,
this sweet moment is as in dream—
how can they bear to turn their heads
to the path leading back over Magpie Bridge?
But so long as both of them love
and so long as their love lasts on,
it does not need to be done
every night and every morning at dawn.

2.60 行香子(秦观)

树绕村庄，水满陂塘。倚东风、豪兴徜徉。小园几许，收尽春光。有桃花红，李花白，菜花黄。

远远围墙，隐隐茅堂。飏青旗、流水桥旁。偶然乘兴、步过东冈。正莺儿啼，燕儿舞，蝶儿忙。

【作品简介】

此词以白描的手法、浅近的语言，勾勒出一幅春光明媚、万物竞发的田园风光图。

【注　释】

陂塘：池塘。**徜徉**：闲游，安闲自在地步行。**“小园”二句**：是说小园不大，却仿佛将外面的春光尽数收揽入内。形容小园中春意盎然，非园外可比。

【译　文】

龚景浩 译

“Xing Xiang Zi (Song)”
Qin Guan

A tree-encircled village,
A swollen pond.

Against the east wind,
I strolled blithely along.
The little garden isn't much,
But it has on display every bit of spring:
With the peach blossoms red, the plums white,
And the rape flowers yellow.

Afar, an enclosing wall;
Half-hidden from view, the sight of a thatched hut.
The blue flags of a wine-shop flapping
By the bridge over the creek.
In a sudden whim
I walked round East Mound:
The orioles were singing, the swallows dancing,
And the butterflies bustling around.

2.61 浣溪沙(秦观)

漠漠轻寒上小楼，晓阴无赖似穷秋。淡烟流水画屏幽。
自在飞花轻似梦，无边丝雨细如愁。宝帘闲挂小银钩。

〖作品简介〗

此词描绘了一个女子春日里的闲愁和寂寞。上阕写阴冷的春天早晨，独上小楼，空房内画屏竖立，显得格外清幽；下阕所写眼前景物，待慢慢挂起窗帘，观落花轻飘、细雨蒙蒙，触目伤情。作者用“轻描淡写”的笔法，融情入景，明写景，实写人的闲愁，其构思之精巧、意境之优美，犹如一件精致小巧的艺术品。

〖注　释〗

漠漠：像清寒一样的冷漠。**清寒**：阴天，有些冷。**晓阴**：早晨天阴着。**无赖**：词人厌恶之语。**穷秋**：秋天走到了尽头。**淡烟流水**：画屏上轻烟淡淡，流水潺潺。**幽**：意境悠远。**自在**：自由自在。**丝雨**：细雨。**宝帘**：缀着珠宝的帘子。**闲挂**：很随意地挂着。

【译 文】

Jiaosheng Wang 译

Tune: "Sand of Silk-Washing Brook"
A Spring Morning by Ch'in Kuan(1049-1100)

A suggestion of chill pervades the little bower,
The haze of dawn sulky as though it were deep autumn.
On the painted screen, thin mist hovering over a running brook—
A scene tranquil and serene.

Fallen petals flying at ease—ethereal like dreams;
Mizzling rain in an endless stream—fine as sorrow.
The jeweled curtain hung up idly on a little hook of silver.

2.62 满庭芳(秦观)

山抹微云，天连衰草，画角声断谯门。暂停征棹，聊共引离尊。多少蓬莱旧事，空回首、烟霭纷纷。斜阳外，寒鸦万点，流水绕孤村。

消魂当此际，香囊暗解，罗带轻分。谩赢得青楼薄幸名存。此去何时见也？襟袖上、空惹啼痕。伤情处，高城望断，灯火已黄昏。

【作品简介】

此词描写了词人与他所眷恋的一个女子的离别情景。上片描写别时的景色及对往事的回忆；下片抒写离别时的留恋、惆怅之情。全词把凄凉秋色、伤别之情融为一体，通过对凄凉景色的描写，用婉转语调表达伤感的情绪，致使作品充满了低沉婉转的感伤情调。

【注 释】

满庭芳：词牌名。双调九十五字，前片四平韵，后片五平韵。**连**：一作"黏"。**谯门**：城门。**引**：举。**尊**：酒杯。**蓬莱旧事**：男女爱情的往事。**烟霭**[ǎi]：指云雾。**消魂**：形容因悲伤或快乐到极点而心神恍惚、不知所以的样子。**谩**[màn]：徒然。**薄幸**：薄情。

【译　文】

(1) Jiaosheng Wang 译

Tune: "Perfumed Garden"
Bidding Adieu by Ch'in Kuan

Mountains wreathed in wisps of light cloud;
Withered grass stretches to meet the far horizon.①
Muted the sound of bugles on the gate tower;
Ready to depart, a boat moored at the river's edge.
How many things bygone at the Fairy Pavilion
Return to mind in a misty haze,
As listlessly we drain our cups to bid adieu!
Beyond the setting sun, a scattering of crows in the cold air
Are winging above a stream.
That winds round a solitary village.②

Heart-rending this moment of separation
When the scented bag is tenderly given away as a memento,
And the silk girdle untied in token of farewell.③
All this, however, has but earned me the name of a fickle lover,
A drifter in the Green Mansions.④
Once parted, who can say when we'll meet again?
On my coat and sleeves are stains of tears shed in vain.
It grieves me to see the lofty city-walls
Receding from view in the lurid lights of evening.

①② These lines in the original Chinese are widely recited.

③ The scented bag was worn at his waist by a man as a mark of affection for the girl he loved, and silk girdle worn by the girl had a knot which she would cut should mean the romantic relation come to an end.

④ A euphemism for brothels.

(2) 张炳星 译

The Sorrow of Parting

Qin Guan

A few strands of light clouds spread over the mountain pass.
In the distance the sky touches the withered grass.
The bugle call on the city tower ceased at last.
You, sailing boat, please wait for a moment.
Let us raise wine cups at the farewell dinner party.
At the Peng Lai Pavilion, have happened so many romantic
events of the past!
Now when I vainly recall them, they vanish like smoke and dust.
Beyond the setting sun, a few jackdaws adorn the sky,
and a stream surrounding the lonely village flows murmuring by.

How grieved we were at that moment,
when we had secretly untied our perfumed sachets and silk
belts as souvenirs at parting!
What I have got since our parting?
I've won the name of a fickle lover in the courtesans' quarters.
When shall we meet again after this parting?
My garment and sleeves are all stained with tears.
What a pity!
I can't see her in the city,
even the tall tower disappeared in the evening heat!

2.63 鹧鸪天(贺铸)

重过阊门万事非，同来何事不同归？梧桐半死清霜后，头白鸳鸯失伴飞。
原上草，露初晞。旧栖新垅两依依。空床卧听南窗雨，谁复挑灯夜补衣！

〖作品简介〗

这是一首情真意切、语深辞美、哀伤动人的悼亡词，表现了词人对亡妻患难与共、相濡以沫之情的深切怀念。

【注 释】

鹧鸪天：词牌名。因此词有"梧桐半死清霜后"句，贺铸又名之为"半死桐"。**阊[chāng]门**：苏州城西门，此处代指苏州。**何事**：为什么。**梧桐半死**：枚乘《七发》中说，龙门有桐，其根半生半死(一说此桐为连理枝，其中一枝已亡，一枝犹在)，斫以制琴，声音为天下之至悲，这里用来比拟丧偶之痛。**清霜后**：秋天，此指年老。**"原上草"二句**：形容人生短促，如草上露水易干。语出《薤露》："露晞明朝更复落，人死一去何时归。"**晞**：[xī]干。**旧栖**：旧居，指生者所居处。**新垅**：新坟，指死者葬所。

【译 文】

(1) 许渊冲 译

Tune: "The Partridge Sky" by He Zhu

All things have changed. Once more I pass the Gate.
We came together, I go back without my mate.
Bitten by hoary frost, half the parasol dies;
Life-long companion lost, one lonely love-bird flies.

Grass wet with dew
Dries on the plain.
How can I leave our old abode and her grave new!
Lying in half empty bed, I hear the pelting rain.
Who will turn up the wick to mend my coat again?

(2) 龚景浩 译

"Zhe Gu Tian (Song)"

He Zhu

Passing through Changmen Gate① a second time,
Everything is gone wrong.
You came with me on this trip,

Why do you not return with me too?②
Half of the Wutong is now dead,③
After crystalline frost descends.
The white-headed mandarin duck, losing his mate,
Now singly flies.

Grass on the plain,
The dews first evaporate.
A new grave now stands close to the old house.
In my empty bed I lie
Listening to raindrops beating on the south window.
Who will now trim the wicks and mend my clothes?

① Changmen Gate—in the old days a city gate leading out of Suzhou; the area was, and still is, a busy part of the city.
② The poet's wife died on this trip.
③ In Chinese folk legend it was possible for half of a Wutong tree to be dead while the remaining half stayed alive.

2.64 风流子(周邦彦)

新绿小池塘，风帘动、碎影舞斜阳。羡金屋去来，旧时巢燕；土花缭绕，前度莓墙。绣阁、凤帏深几许？听得理丝簧。欲说又休，虑乖芳信；未歌先咽，愁近清觞。

遥知新妆了，开朱户、应自待月西厢。最苦梦魂，今宵不到伊行。问甚时说与，佳音密耗；寄将秦镜，偷换韩香。天便教人，霎时厮见何妨！

〖作品简介〗

此词描述一位男子对所爱女子的渴念之情。写作手法极为别致独特，除上片起首三句写景外，以下全是想象，写来灵活多变，又极有层次；感情随着想象而逐渐加强，最后达到几乎控制不住的境地。全词巧用比喻，刻画细腻，用典贴切，所写虽全是想象，却形象极其鲜明，富于感染力。整首词至真之情由性灵肺腑中流出，读来既明快又饶有情致，具有动人的艺术魅力。

〖注 释〗

风流子：唐教坊曲名。**金屋**：美人住的地方。《汉武故事》曰："(胶东王)数岁，长公主嫖抱置膝上，问曰：'儿欲得妇否？'胶东王曰：'欲得妇。'长公主指左右长御百余人，皆云不用，末指其女问曰：'阿娇好否？'于是乃笑对曰：'好！若得阿娇作妇，当作金屋贮之也。'"此处金屋犹言'金闺'，系闺阁的美称。**土花**：此指贴墙而生的苔藓类植物。**莓墙**：长满苔藓之墙。**莓**：莓苔，青苔。**丝簧**：管弦乐器。**乖**：错过。**清觞**[shāng]：洁净的酒杯。**待月**：元稹《会真记》莺莺与张生诗："待月西厢下，迎风户半开。"**不到伊行**[háng]：不到她身边。**行**：那边，旁边。**秦镜**：汉徐淑赠给丈夫秦嘉的明镜，此处喻作情物。**韩香**：《晋书·贾充传》载，贾充女午，与韩寿私通，窃武帝赐其父西域所进异香以赠寿。充发觉后，以女稼寿。乐府诗云："盘龙明镜饷秦嘉，辟恶生香寄韩寿。"后以此指男女暗中通情。

『译 文』

Stephen Owen 译

Tune:"Gallant"(Feng-liu-zi) by Zhou Bang-yan(1056-1121)

A new green in the tiny pond,
breeze stirs curtains, dancing
    shattered shadows in setting sun.
How I envy their passage
    in and out of her gilded rooms—swallows, the same
    that nested there before—
    and the flowering vines that twine
    on mossy walls
    as in a previous time.
From within her splendid chambers
    deep behind figured veils
    I hear the harps and oboes play.
There is something she would say, then refrains,
    and her troubled thoughts fail
    their sweet communication.
Before she can sing, her voice chokes in sobs
    and , dejected, she has someone bring
    a cup of clear wine.

Though far from her, I know

Her make-up has just been done,
and opening her vermilion door,
I am sure she waits alone for the moon
in the western corridor.
Most bitter of all for the dreaming soul
that tonight I will not reach her side.
And I wonder when she will tell to me
sweet words and secrets of her heart.
She sends me Qin Jia's mirror①,
and Han Shou's perfume in furtive exchange.
What's to keep Heaven
from letting us meet just a little while!

① Qin Jia's mirror (received from his wife) and the incense given to Han Shou by the daughter of superior official (who fell in love with Han at first sight) are both figures for love tokens.

2.65 玉楼春(周邦彦)

桃溪不作从容住，秋藕绝来无续处。当时相候赤阑桥，今日独寻黄叶路。
烟中列岫青无数，雁背夕阳红欲暮。人如风后入江云，情似雨馀粘地絮。

【作品简介】

此词是作者于元祐四年(1089年)自庐州府教授离任时所作。作者将别桃溪，回想起从前的旖旎生活，内心无限惆怅，颇是难舍，于是作此首《玉楼春》。词作以一个仙凡恋爱的故事起头，写词人与情人分别之后，旧地重游而引起的怅惘之情。整首词通篇对偶，凝重而流丽，情深而意长。全词句句含情，字字含情，前后照应，累累如贯珠。

【注　释】

玉楼春：词牌名。词谱谓五代后蜀顾夐词起句有“月照玉楼春漏促”“柳映玉楼春欲晚”句；欧阳炯起句有“日照玉楼花似锦”“春早玉楼烟雨夜”句，因取以调名(或加字令)亦称《木兰花》《春晓曲》《西湖曲》《惜春容》《归朝欢令》《呈纤手》《归风便》《东邻妙》《梦乡亲》《续渔歌》等。双调五十六字，前后阕格式相同，各三仄韵，一韵到底。**桃溪**：虽说在宜兴有这地名，这里不作地名用。周济《宋四家词选》所谓“只赋天台事，态浓意远”是也。刘晨阮肇天台山故事，本云山上有桃树，山下有一大溪，见《幽明录》《续齐谐记》。韩愈《梨花发赠刘师命》：“桃溪惆怅不能过。”魏承班《黄钟乐》词：“遥想玉人情事远，音容浑似隔桃溪。”用法均相同。**秋藕绝来无续处**：“秋藕”与“桃溪”，约略相对，不必工稳。俗语所谓“藕断丝连”，这里说藕断而丝不连。**赤阑桥**：此处似不作地名用。顾况《题叶道士山房》：“水边垂柳赤栏桥。”温庭筠《杨柳枝》词：“一渠春水赤栏桥。”韩偓《重过李氏园亭有怀》：“往年同在弯桥上，见倚朱栏咏柳绵，今日独来春径里，更无人迹有苔钱。”诗虽把“朱栏”“弯桥”分开，而本词这两句正与诗意相合，不仅关合字面。黄叶路点名秋景，赤阑桥未言杨柳，是春景却不说破。**列岫**：陈元龙注引《文选》“窗中列远岫”，乃谢朓《郡内高斋闲望》诗。全篇细腻，这里宕开，远景如画，亦对偶，却为流水句法。类似这两句意境的，唐人诗中多有，如刘长卿、李商隐、马戴、温庭筠。李商隐《与赵氏昆季燕集》“虹收青嶂雨，鸟没夕阳天”，与此更相近。**情似雨馀粘地絮**：晏几道《玉楼春》词：“便教春思乱如云，莫管世情轻似絮。”本词上句意略异，取譬同，下句所比亦同，而意却相反，疑周词从晏句变化。

【译 文】

Stephen Owen 译

Tune：“Spring in the Mansion of Jade”（*Yu-lou chun*）by Zhou Bang-yan（1056-1121）

At Peach Creek I did not stay
　　enjoying myself at leisure；
once lotus roots break in fall，
　　they never can be rejoined.
I waited for her back then
　　on the bridge with red rails，
and today I follow all alone
　　a path of yellowed leaves.

Lines of hilltops in the mist
　　green beyond counting，
geese turn their backs to evening sun
　　toward dusk growing redder.
The person，like clouds coming after the wind
　　and moving onto the river；
the passion，like floss that sticks to the ground
　　in the aftermath of rain.

2.66 关河令(周邦彦)

秋阴时晴渐向暝，变一庭凄冷。伫听寒声，云深无雁影。
更深人去寂静，但照壁孤灯相映。酒已都醒，如何消夜永！

〖作品简介〗

此词描写羁旅孤栖之情景。全词以时光的转换为线索，表现了在深秋萧瑟清寒中作者因人去屋空而生的凄切孤独感。

〖注　释〗

关河令：词牌名，为作者首创。古乐府有《清商曲辞》，其音多哀怨，欧阳修曾以此曲填写思乡之作，首句是“关河愁思望处满”。作者遂取其中“关河”二字，命名为“关河令”来作词牌，隐寓着羁旅思家之意。**时**：片时、偶尔的意思。**晴**：一作“作”。**伫听**：久久地站着倾听。**伫**：久立而等待。**寒声**：即秋声，指秋天的风声、雨声、虫鸟哀鸣声等。此处是指雁的鸣叫声。**照壁**：古时筑于寺庙、广宅前的墙屏。与正门相对，作遮蔽、装饰之用，多饰有图案、文字。亦谓影壁，指大门内或屏门内做屏蔽的墙壁。也有木制的，下有底座，可以移动，又称照壁、照墙。**消夜永**：度过漫漫长夜。**夜永**：犹言长夜。

〖译　文〗

龚景浩 译

“Guan He Ling (Song)”
Zhou Bang Yan

Overcast is the autumn sky,
Sunlight shining through from time to time,
While evening draws near—
This brings a courtyard steeped in chilling sadness.
I stand listening to the voices of autumn coolness.
The clouds are thick
And no swan goose is seen in the sky.

The hours late,
The guests gone,
Leaving a blank stillness to me alone.
A single lamp shines—on empty walls.
My drunkenness is now gone.
How am I to while away the long night?

2.67 兰陵王(周邦彦)

柳阴直,
烟里丝丝弄碧。
隋堤上、
曾见几番,
拂水飘绵送行色。
登临望故国,
谁识、
京华倦客。
长亭路、
年去岁来,
应折柔条过千尺。

闲寻旧踪迹,
又酒趁哀弦,
灯照离席,
梨花榆火催寒食。

愁一箭风快,
半篙波暖,
回头迢递便数驿,
望人在天北。
凄恻,
恨堆积。
渐别浦萦回,
津堠岑寂,

斜阳冉冉春无极。
念月榭携手，
露桥闻笛。
沉思前事，
似梦里、
泪暗滴。

〖作品简介〗

此词描写作者离去之愁，通篇充满别离伤感之情。词中有生活细节，有人物活动，有抒情主体的心理意绪，构成词作较为鲜明的叙事性和戏剧性特色。全词构思萦回曲折，似浅实深，有吐不尽的心事流荡其中，无论景语、情语，都很耐人寻味。

〖注　释〗

兰陵王：词牌名，首见于周邦彦词。一百三十字，分三段。**柳阴直**：长堤之柳，排列整齐，其阴影连缀成直线。**烟**：薄雾。**丝丝弄碧**：细长轻柔的柳条随风飞舞，舞弄其嫩绿的姿色。**弄**：飘拂。**隋堤**：汴京附近汴河之堤，隋炀帝时所建，故称。是北宋时来往京城的必经之路。**拂水飘绵**：柳枝轻拂水面，柳絮在空中飞扬。**行色**：行人出发前的景象、情状。**故国**：指故乡。**京华倦客**：作者自谓。**京华**：指京城，作者久客京师，有厌倦之感，故云。**长亭**：古时驿路上十里一长亭，五里一短亭，供人休息，又是送别的地方。**“应折”句**：古人有折柳送别之习。**柔条**：柳枝。**过千尺**：极言折柳之多。**旧踪迹**：指过去登堤饯别的地方。**又**：又逢。**酒趁哀弦**：饮酒时奏着离别的乐曲。**趁**：逐，追随。**哀弦**：哀怨的乐声。**离席**：饯别的宴会。**“梨花”句**：饯别时正值梨花盛开的寒食时节。唐宋时期朝廷在清明日取榆柳之火以赐百官，故有“榆火”之说。**寒食**：清明前一天为寒食。**一箭风快**：指正当顺风，船驶如箭。**半篙波暖**：指撑船的竹篙没入水中，时令已近暮春，故曰波暖。**迢递**：遥远。**驿**：驿站。**“望人”句**：因被送者离汴京南去，回望送行人，故曰天北。**望人**：送行人。**凄恻**：悲伤。**恨**：这里是遗憾的意思。**渐**：正当。**别浦**：送行的水边。**萦回**：水波回旋。**津堠**：渡口附近供瞭望歇宿的守望所。**津**：渡口。**堠**：哨所。**岑寂**：冷清寂寞。**冉冉**：慢慢移动的样子。**春无极**：春色一望无边。**念**：想到。**月榭**：月光下的亭榭。**榭**：建在高台上的敞屋。**露桥**：布满露珠的桥梁。

〖译　文〗

Wai-lim Yip 译

Tune: "PRINCE LAN-LING"

Willows shadows hang straight
In the smoke, lines of silk, in green sheen,
Upon the dam
How many times
Fluttering water, floating catkins, sending off friends?
I ascend to view my home country.
Who knows
This tired traveler of the Capital
Tall Pavilion Road:
Years come years go,
They must have broken off soft branches a thousand feet!

I sometimes look for all the footprints.
Again wine to whining strings.
Lamps brightening farewell tables.
Pear blossoms flaming elms quicken the Cold Food Day

Sorrow, one shaft, faster than wind.
Punting half way of warming waves,
I look back into the distance to count the mail-posts,
Longing for friends at sky's north end.
Stricken
Grief teeming up.
Separation: water twists and turns.
Garrisoned fords all quiet.
Sun slants slowly: spring, no end.
Under the moon, hand in hand.
Dew-dappled bridge: to listen to flutes.
Think of thing past:
Like dream,
Tears darkly drip.

2.68 夜游宫(周邦彦)

叶下斜阳照水,卷轻浪、沈沈千里。

桥上酸风射眸子。立多时，看黄昏，灯火市。

古屋寒窗底，听几片、井桐飞坠。
不恋单衾再三起。有谁知？为萧娘，书一纸。

〖作品简介〗

此词乃作者伤离怀旧之作。其结构采用新巧的“悬念法”，先层层加重读者的疑惑，最后一语道破意蕴，读来跌宕顿挫、波澜起伏、委婉凄绝。其上下两片描写由傍晚斜阳到黄昏灯火，由桥上酸风到古屋寒窗的情景，时空依次推移，景物随时变换，感情随之深化，最后揭出“为萧娘，书一纸”的底蕴，写来层层深入、环环相扣、跌宕起伏、引人入胜。

〖注 释〗

萧娘：唐杨巨源《崔娘》诗：“风流才子多春思，肠断萧娘一纸书。”唐人每以“萧娘”作为女子的泛称。

〖译 文〗

Burton Watson 译

Tune: “Palace of Night Revels”

Leaves fall, slanting sun lights the river
that rolls its gentle ripples
on and on for a thousand miles.
On the bridge, an acid wind strikes my eyes,
I stand a long while
watching the twilight,
the lamp-lit town.

In my old house, under the cold window,
I hear countless leaves
flutter and fall from the parasol tree by the well.
I've no love for this lonely quilt, get up again and again.
Who knows that

it's for her sake
I cover this sheet with words?

2.69 苏幕遮(周邦彦)

燎沈香，消溽暑。鸟雀呼晴，侵晓窥檐语。叶上初阳干宿雨，水面清圆，一一风荷举。

故乡遥，何日去？家住吴门，久作长安旅。五月渔郎相忆否？小楫轻舟，梦入芙蓉浦。

〖作品简介〗

此词主要表达词人的思乡之情。作品由眼前的荷花想到故乡的荷花，游子浓浓的思乡情，向荷花娓娓道来，构思尤为巧妙别致。上片主要描绘荷花姿态，下片由荷花梦回故乡。全词写景、写人、写情、写梦皆语出天然，不加雕饰而风情万种，通过对清圆的荷叶、五月的江南、渔郎的轻舟这些情景进行虚实变幻的描写，将思乡之苦表达得淋漓尽致。

〖注 释〗

燎[liáo]：细焚。**沈香**：沈，现写作沉。沈(沉)香，一种名贵香料，置水中则下沉，故又名沉水香，其香味可辟恶气。**溽**[rù]**暑**：夏天闷热潮湿的暑气。沈约《休沐寄怀》诗："临池清溽暑，开幌望高秋。"**溽**：湿润潮湿。**呼晴**：唤晴。旧有鸟鸣可占晴雨之说。**侵晓**：拂晓。**侵**：渐近。**宿雨**：隔夜的雨。**清圆**：清润圆正。**一一风荷举**：意为荷叶迎着晨风，每一片荷叶都挺出水面。**举**：擎起。司空图《王官二首》诗："风荷似醉和花舞，沙鸟无情伴客闲。"**吴门**：古吴县城亦称吴门，即今之江苏苏州，此处以吴门泛指吴越一带。作者是钱塘人，钱塘古属吴郡，故称之。**久作长安旅**：长年旅居在京城。**长安**：借指北宋的都城汴京(今河南开封)。**旅**：客居。**楫**[jí]：划船用具，短桨。**芙蓉浦**：有荷花的水边。有溪涧可通的荷花塘。词中指杭州西湖。唐张宗昌《太平公主山亭侍宴》诗："折桂芙蓉浦，吹萧明月湾。"**浦**：水湾，河流。**芙蓉**：又叫"芙蕖"，荷花的别称。

〖译 文〗

许渊冲 译

Tune："Screened by Southern Curtain" by Zhou Bang-yan

I burn an incense sweet

To temper steamy heat.
Birds chirp at dawn beneath the eaves,
Announcing a fine day. The rising sun
Has dried last night's raindrops on lotus leaves
Which, clear and round, dot water surface. One by one
The lotus blooms stand up with ease
And swing in morning breeze.

My homeland is far away,
When may I return to stay?
My kinsfolk live in South by city wall.
Why should I stay long in the capital?
Will not my fishing friends remember me in May?
In a short-oared light boat, it seems,
I'm back 'mid lotus blooms in dreams.

2.70 伤情怨（周邦彦）

枝头风势渐小。看暮鸦飞了。又是黄昏，闭门收返照。江南人去路缈。信未通、愁已先到。怕见孤灯，霜寒催睡早。

【作品简介】

此词又曰《清商怨》，描写词人触情伤情、思亲怀愁的心境。

【注　释】

暮鸦：暮色中的老鸦。

【译　文】

Robert Kotewall and Norman L. Smith 译

To "Wounded Feelings"

At the top branch tops the faithful breeze abates;
I see the evening crows in flight.

Once more it is twilight;
I close the door and catch the afterglow.

South of the River my man has gone on a road
　　unknown.
His letters come not;
Only sadness is his harbinger.
I dread to see the solitary lamp,
As frosty cold urges me to an early bed.

2.71　长相思(万俟咏)

一声声。一更更。窗外芭蕉窗里灯。此时无限情。梦难成。恨难平。不道愁人不喜听。空阶滴到明。

〖作品简介〗

这首《长相思·雨》是写景遣怀，讲述一个相思之人整夜难眠，在雨夜中听着雨打芭蕉，触景生情，词人心中有无限的情怀，孤灯照人难入梦，表达了客居异乡的羁旅愁思。

〖注　释〗

万俟咏(“万俟”是复姓，读作 mò qí)：北宋末南宋初词人。**长相思**：词牌名，唐教坊曲名。**一更更**：一遍遍报时的更鼓声。**恨**：遗撼。**道**：知。**阶**：台阶。

〖译　文〗

Robert Kotewall and Norman L. Smith 译

Rain
To “Enduring love”

The rain drips and drips!
The hour strikes and strikes!
Outside the window the plantain, inside the window the lamp,
At such a time the feelings are unbounded.

Dreams hard to fashion!
Regrets hard to smooth out!
No wonder a sorrower mislikes to hear:
In the empty courtyard the dripping lasts till dawn.

2.72 如梦令(李祁)

不见玉人清晓，长啸一声云杪。
碧水满阑塘，竹外一枝风袅。
奇妙，奇妙，半夜山空月皎。

【作品简介】

此词描写了词人清晨起来不见佳人，于是长啸一声，音入云霄，但见屋外池塘、竹林及皓月美景。

【注　释】

玉人：佳人。**云杪**：云霄。**阑塘**：环状的池塘。**风袅**：摇曳；飘动的样子。

【译　文】

许渊冲 译

Tune: "Dreaminglike Song" by Li Qi

At early dawn no jade-white beauty is in sight. Long, long I sigh to clouds on high. Green water brims over the rail-girt pool; beyond bamboos I find mume branch with ease sway in the breeze. How wonderful! How wonderful to see the beauty steeped in moonlight at dead of night!

第三章
南宋

3.1 鹧鸪天(朱敦儒)

我是清都山水郎，天教懒慢带疏狂。曾批给露支风敕，累奏留云借月章。诗万首，酒千觞，几曾着眼看侯王？玉楼金阙慵归去，且插梅花醉洛阳。

〖作品简介〗

此词体现了词人鄙夷权贵、傲视王侯的风骨，读来令人感佩。

〖注　释〗

清都山水郎：在天上掌管山水的官员。**清都**：指与红尘相对的仙境。**疏狂**：狂放，不受礼法约束。**玉楼金阙慵归去**：不愿到那琼楼玉宇之中，表示作者不愿到朝廷里做官。

〖译　文〗

(1) 龚景浩 译

"Zhe Gu Tian (Song)"

Zhu Dun Ru

Placed in charge of creeks and hills by orders of Heaven,
I'm by nature feisty and carefree.
Vouchers for dews and soft breezes have been writ for me;
I've been granted the power to detain clouds
And borrow the moon.

Ten thousand poems,
A thousand jugs of wine—
When have I ever eyed those earls and princes sublime?
To jade houses and golden facades I won't return.
Sticking my hair with flowers
I prefer to stay drunk in Luoyang①.

① Luoyang in Henan Province—the west capital of the Northern Song Period (960-1127A. D.)

(2) 许渊冲 译

"Partridge Sky"
Written at the West Capital

I am in charge of mountains and rivers divine,
Heaven tells me to be free to give orders mine.
I have commanded rain to fall and wind to blow
And asked the cloud to stay and the moon not to go.

Thousands of verses fine,
Hundreds of cups of wine,
I've only looked down upon the lords in power,
I would never go back high in my golden tower.
But drunk in the west capital with the mume flower.

3.2　念奴娇(朱敦儒)

老来可喜，是历遍人间，谙知物外。看透虚空，将恨海愁山，一时挼碎。免被花迷，不为酒困，到处惺惺地。饱来觅睡，睡起逢场作戏。

休说古往今来，乃翁心里，没许多般事。也不蕲仙不佞佛，不学栖栖孔子。懒共贤争，从教他笑，如此只如此。杂剧打了，戏衫脱与呆底。

〖作品简介〗

此词抒发了作者年老时对人生的体悟和感怀。

【注 释】

历：经历。**物外**：外界各种环境事物。**虚空**：虚荣权力等。**惺惺**：清醒。**休说**：别再跟我提。“**也不蕲仙不佞佛**”句：我既不去求仙，也学不来佛，更不想去学到处周游讲学的孔子。“**懒共贤争**”句：我已经懒得与那些贤能们去争论辩解了，任他们去嘲讽讥笑吧，这样就这样了。“**杂剧打了**”句：与上片结尾句“睡起逢场作戏”相对应，喻还原本色后，今后不论什么人，男女老少，能笨智愚，忠奸良莠，谁演都行，与我已经无关了。

【译 文】

James Robert Hightower 译

Tune: “Nien-nu Is Charming”
By Chu Tun-ju (1081-1159)

Old age has come and I am glad;
I've experienced what the world holds
And know too well the way things are,
Have seen through the shams.
The sea of sorrow, the mount of pain,
All shattered in a trice.
No longer misled by flowers
Or led into trouble by wine,
I know all the scores now.
When full I look to take a nap;
Awake again, I play the role called for.

Don't talk of time a-passing!
In this old man's heart
Is no wish to meddle much in affairs.
I don't try to become a Taoist immortal
Or flatter the Buddha
Or imitate the busy Confucius.
I have no wish to compete with worthy men;
Let them laugh—

This is just the way I am.
When the play is over,
I will leave my costume for the dumb actors.

3.3 卜算子(朱敦儒)

古涧一枝梅，免被园林锁。路远山深不怕寒，似共春相趓。
幽思有谁知，托契都难可。独自风流独自香，明月来寻我。

〖作品简介〗

此词乃朱敦儒代表作之一。作者富有文才，但不喜仕途，虽曾入仕途，却一心向往自在的生活，作者对梅花格外喜爱，多用梅花自喻——这首词便为其真实写照：作者无意高官厚禄，无意显达世间，单求如一孤梅独立深山，自由成长。

〖注 释〗

涧：两山间之水沟也。趓[duǒ]：同“躲”，躲避；避开；作者的幽思不知寄托在谁的身上，因此才独自风流独自香。

〖译 文〗

(1) Robert Kotewall and Norman L. Smith 译

To “The Fortune-teller”

By the ancient rill there is a single plum-tree
That refuses to be imprisoned in garden or park.
Far away in the mountain depth it fears not the cold,
As though at hide-and-seek with Spring.

My inmost thoughts, who can know them?
Ties of friendship are hard to make.
Alone in my romance, alone in my fragrance,
The moon comes to look for me.

(2) 许渊冲 译

"Song of Division"

A mume tree grows by creekside old;
It won't be locked in garden small.
In deep mountains so far away it fears no cold;
It seems to shun spring's call.

Who knows its lovely heart?
From friendship it will part.
It shows its beauty and fragrance alone,
Sought after by the moon.

3.4 诉衷情(李清照)

夜来沉醉卸妆迟，梅萼插残枝。酒醒熏破春睡，梦远不成归。
人悄悄，月依依，翠帘垂。更挼残蕊，更捻余香，更得些时。

〖作品简介〗

此词乃一首咏梅之作。其笔墨没有集中在写梅的姿容、特质上，而是缘梅抒情，以残梅的幽香为引线，串联全篇。全词以写头戴残梅沉醉入睡开始，继由梅香"熏破春睡"使"梦远不成归"，引起词人心情的怅惘；甜美的梦境与凄苦的现实互为映衬，深刻地表达了理想与现实之间的矛盾。全词虽不着一个"愁"字，却处处含愁。

〖注 释〗

"夜来"二句：此二句中的"沉醉"云云，当系化用《诗·邶风·柏舟》的"微我无酒，以敖以游"二句。**梅萼**：梅的萼片，此处代指梅。**"人悄悄"**三句：既是化用《诗·邶风·柏舟》的"忧心悄悄"等的句意，亦可能同时对顾夐《献衷心》一词(其词云："绣鸳鸯帐暖，画孔雀屏欹。人悄悄，月明时。想昔年欢笑，恨今日分离。银缸背，铜漏永，阻佳期。小炉烟细，虚阁帘垂。几多心事，暗地思维。被娇娥牵役，梦魂如痴。金闺里，山枕上，始应知。")有所取意。**挼**：揉搓。**捻**：用手搓转，如捻麻绳，其揉搓程度比"挼"更进一层。

〖译 文〗

Burton Watson 译

Tune: "Telling of Innermost Feelings"

Night comes and, drowsy with drink, I'm slow to shed my
ornaments,
these plum petals stuck on a withered twig.
I wake from wine, its aroma scattering my spring sleep,
the dream grown distant—no returning there now.

No sound from anyone,
the moon still lingering,
kingfisher blinds lowered,
and once more I crush the withered stamens,
once more finger the fragrance left in them,
once more possess that time.

3.5 点绛唇(李清照)

蹴罢秋千，起来慵整纤纤手。露浓花瘦，薄汗轻衣透。
见客入来，袜刬金钗溜。和羞走，倚门回首，却把青梅嗅。

〖作品简介〗

此词描述了少女的天真情态。上片写主人公下了秋千以后的情景，下片写主人公在来客忽至时的羞赧情状，形象生动地刻画了一个天真纯洁、感情丰富却又矜持的少女形象。

〖注 释〗

点绛唇：词牌名。**蹴**：踏。此处指打秋千。**慵**：懒，倦怠的样子。**袜刬**：这里指跑掉鞋子以袜着地。**金钗溜**：意谓快跑时首饰从头上掉下来。**倚门回首**：这里是靠着门回头看的意思。“倚门”语出《史记·货殖列传》的“刺绣文不如倚市门”。司马迁以此说明“农不如工，工不如商”的道理。而“倚门卖笑”是后人的演绎，以之形容妓女生涯是晚至元代和清代的事：“你看人似桃李春风墙外枝，卖俏倚门儿”(王实甫《西厢记》三本一折)、“婉変倚门之笑，绸缪鼓瑟之娱，谅非得已”（汪中《经旧苑吊马守真文》）。

〖译 文〗

（1）Jiaosheng Wang 译

Stepping down from the swing,
Languidly she smooths her soft, slender hands,
Her flimsy dress wet with light perspiration—
A slim flower trembling with heavy dew.

Spying a stranger, she walks hastily away in shyness:
Her feet in bare socks,
Her gold hairpin fallen.
Then she stops to lean against a gate,
And looking back,
Makes as if sniffing a green plum.

（2）C. H. Kwôck and Vincent McHugh 译

Tune: "Crimson Lips Adorned" [*Tien chiang chu'un*]

Ride in the swing
    over
she stands up
    languid
    flexing delicate hands
Multitudinous dew
    on thin flower
a mist of sweat
    dampens
    her light dress through

She looks
    A stranger coming
Her stockings down
    Gold hairpin slipped

Shyly
　　she runs
and
　　leaning against the door jamb
looks back
lingering
　　to sniff at a green plum

(3) 徐忠杰 译

"Dianjiangchun"

I left off playing on the swing, rather tired.
My clothes are soaked through; enough I had perspired.
On my face was sweat like dew; my figure—lean.
After I wrung my hand, I considered them clean.

When I saw people come, my socks off my feet—
My hair-pin missing, I beat a shy retreat.
Leaning on a door, I looked to see who comes.
In less than no time, I sniffed at the green plums.

3.6 如梦令(李清照)

昨夜雨疏风骤，浓睡不消残酒。试问卷帘人，却道海棠依旧。知否？知否？应是绿肥红瘦。

〖作品简介〗

这首小令通过对人物、场景和对白的描写，充分显示了作者的语言才华。小词借宿酒醒后询问花事的描写，曲折委婉地表达了词人的惜花伤春之情，语言清新，词意隽永。

〖注　释〗

雨疏风骤：雨点稀疏，晚风急猛。**疏**：指稀疏。**浓睡不消残酒**：虽然睡了一夜，仍有余醉未消。**浓睡**：酣睡。**残酒**：尚未消散的醉意。**卷帘人**：有学者认为此指侍女。**绿肥红**

瘦：绿叶繁茂，红花凋零。

〖译 文〗

(1) Wai-lim Yip 译

"DREAM SONG"

Last night, scattering rains, sudden winds,
Deep sleep abates not the remaining wine.
Try ask he who rolls up the blind:
Thinking the begonia blooming as before.
Know it?
Know it?
Fattening leaves' green, thinning petals' red.

(2) 许渊冲 译

Tune: "Like A Dream" by Li Qing-zhao

Last night the wind was strong and rain was fine,
Sound sleep did not dispel the taste of wine.
I ask the maid who's rolling up the screen.
"The same crab-apple tree," she says, "is seen."
　　"Don't you know,
　　Don't you know
The red should languish and the green must grow?"

(3) 杨宪益、戴乃迭 译

To the Tune of "Ru Meng Ling"

Last night the rain was light, the wind fierce,
And deep sleep did not dispel the effects of wine.
When I ask the maid rolling up the curtains,
She answers, "the crab-apple blossoms look the same."
I cry, "Can't you see? Can't you see?

The green leaves are fresh but the red flowers are fading!”

3.7 如梦令(李清照)

常记溪亭日暮，沉醉不知归路。兴尽晚回舟，误入藕花深处。争渡，争渡，惊起一滩鸥鹭。

【作品简介】

此词乃小令，用词简练，只选取了几个片断，把移动着的风景和作者怡然的心情融合在一起，写出了作者青春年少时的好心情，让人不禁想随她一道荷丛荡舟，沉醉不归。

【注　释】

常记：时常记起，“难忘”之意。**溪亭**：临水的亭台。**日暮**：黄昏时候。**沉醉**：大醉。**兴尽**：尽了兴致。**晚**：此处的意思是天黑路暗了。**回舟**：乘船而回。**误入**：不小心进入。**藕花**：荷花。**争渡**：怎渡，怎么才能划出去。**惊**：惊动。**起**：飞起来。**一滩**：一群。**鸥鹭**：这里泛指水鸟。

【译　文】

(1) Burton Watson 译

Tune: “As in a Dream: Song”

Always I recall the river arbor at twilight,
so muddled with wine we didn’t know the way back,
excitement over, heading home by evening boat,
a wrong turn taking us deep into lotus blossoms,
and struggling to push through,
    struggling to push through,
    we’d startle into flight a whole sandbar full of herons.

(2) Stephen Owen 译

“Like a Dream”

I will always recall that day at dusk,

the pavilion by the creek,
and I was so drunk I couldn't tell
the way home. My mood left me,
it was late when I turned back in my boat
and I strayed deep among lotuses —
how to get through?
how to get through?
and I startled to flight a whole shoal
of egrets and gulls.

3.8 渔家傲(李清照)

天接云涛连晓雾，星河欲转千帆舞。仿佛梦魂归帝所。闻天语，殷勤问我归何处。

我报路长嗟日暮，学诗谩有惊人句。九万里风鹏正举。风休住，蓬舟吹取三山去！

〖作品简介〗

此词描写了梦中海天溟蒙的景象及与天帝的问答，隐寓对社会现实的不满与失望、对理想境界的追求和向往。作者把真实的生活感受融入梦境，以浪漫主义的艺术构思、梦游的方式、奇妙的设想，倾述隐衷，寄托情思。全词打破了上片写景下片抒情或情景交错的惯常格局，以故事性情节为主干，以人神对话为内容，实现了梦幻与生活、历史与现实的有机结合，用典巧妙，景象壮阔，气势磅礴，音调豪迈，充分显示了作者性情中豪放不羁的一面。

〖注 释〗

渔家傲：词牌名。**星河**：银河。**转**：《历代诗余》作“曙”。**帝所**：天帝居住的地方。**天语**：天帝的话语。**殷勤**：关心地。**我报路长嗟(jiē)日暮**：**路长**：隐括屈原《离骚》“路曼曼其修远兮，吾将上下而求索”之意。**嗟**：慨叹。**日暮**：隐括屈原《离骚》“欲少留此灵琐兮，日忽忽其将暮”之意。**学诗谩有惊人句**：隐括杜甫句“语不惊人死不休”。**谩有**：空有。**九万里**：《庄子·逍遥游》中说大鹏乘风飞上九万里高空。**鹏**：古代神话传说中的大鸟。**蓬舟**：像蓬蒿被风吹转的船。古人以蓬根被风吹飞，喻飞动。**吹取**：吹得。**三山**：《史记·封禅书》记载：渤海中有蓬莱、方丈、瀛洲三座仙山，相传为仙人所居住，可以望见，但乘船前往，临近时就被风吹开，终无人能到。蓬莱，又称蓬壶。

【译 文】

(1) Jiaosheng Wang 译

Tune: "Fisherman's Pride"
A Dream by Li Ch'ing-chao

Billowing clouds surging across the heavens
Merge into dawn's hazy mist.
Sails in their thousands toss and dance
As the Milky Way recedes.
In a vision I find myself before the Heavenly Ruler,
Who asks solicitously
Where I wish to be off to.

"My journey is a long one," I reply.
"The sun is setting all too soon.
And my brilliant poetic attempts, alas!
Have come to no purpose."
Presently a whirlwind rises, and lo!
The Mighty Roc① is winging to the Empyrean
On a flight of ninety thousand tricents.
Blow, O Whirlwind! Blow on without cease.
Blow my tiny craft to the three far-off isles②
Where the Immortals dwell.

① A fabulous bird first described in the works of Chuang Tzu. When migrating to the South Seas, it is said to strike the waters for three thousand tricents before soaring to a height of ninety thousand tricents on a whirlwind. Hence the popular saying "Roc's Journey" used by Chinese to this day to congratulate some one embarking on a career of lofty aspirations.

② The three legendary isles, P'eng-lai, Fang-chang, and Ying-chou in the Po-hai Sea.

(2) Stephen Owen 译

Tune: "Free-Spirited Fisherman" (*Yu-jia ao*)

Billowing clouds touch sky and reach

the early morning fog,
the river of stars is ready to set,
a thousand sails dance.
My dreaming soul moves in a daze
to where the high god dwells—
I hear Heaven speak,
asking me with urgent concern
where I am going now.

And I reply that my road is long,
And, alas, twilight draws on;
I worked at my poems and for nothing have
bold lines that cause surprise.①
Into strong winds ninety thousand miles
upward the Peng now flies.②
Let that wind never stop,
let it blow this tiny boat away
to the Three Immortal Isles.

① The first line of the second stanza recalls Wu Zi-xu's response after flogging the corpse of the King of Chu, declaring his indomitable will. The line that follows echoes Du Fu, speaking with pride of his own poetry.

② The Peng was a huge mythical bird described in the *Zhuang-zi*. Li Qing-zhao uses it as a figure of such greatness that smaller creatures cannot comprehend its magnitude.

(3) 许渊冲 译

Tune: "Pride of Fishermen" by Li Qing-zhao

Morning mist and surging clouds spread to join the sky,
The Milky Way fades, a thousand sails dance on high.
It seems as if my soul to God's abode would fly,
And I
Be kindly asked where I'm going. I reply:

"The road is long, alas! The sun on the decline,
In vain I'm famed for clever poetical line.
The roc soars up to ninety thousand miles and nine.
O wind mine!

Don't stop but carry my boat to three isles divine!"

(4) Kenneth Rexroth 译

TO THE TUNE OF "THE HONOR OF A FISHERMAN"

The heavens join with the clouds.
The great waves merge with the fog.
The Milky Way appears
Turning overheard.
A thousand sails dance.
I am rapt away to the place of the Supreme,
And hear the words of Heaven,
Asking me where I am going.

I answer, "It is a long road, alas,
Far beyond the sunset."
I try to put it into verse
But my words amaze me.
The huge roc bird is flying
On a ninety thousand mile wind.
O wind, do not stop
Until my little boat has been blown
To the Immortal Islands
In the Eastern Sea.

3.9 声声慢(李清照)

寻寻觅觅，冷冷清清，凄凄惨惨戚戚。乍暖还寒时候，最难将息。三杯两盏淡酒，怎敌他、晚来风急！雁过也，正伤心，却是旧时相识。

满地黄花堆积，憔悴损，如今有谁堪摘？守着窗儿，独自怎生得黑！梧桐更兼细雨，到黄昏、点点滴滴。这次第，怎一个愁字了得！

〖作品简介〗

此词是作者晚年流落江南为抒发家国身世之愁而作。该词妙用叠字，借物抒情，大气包举，别无枝蔓，相关情事逐一说来，却始终紧扣悲秋之意。该作品深得六朝抒情小赋之神髓，而以接近口语的朴素清新的语言谱入新声，运用凄清的音乐性语言进行抒情，却又体现了倚声家不假雕饰的本色。

〖注 释〗

寻寻觅觅：若有所失、彷徨不安的样子。**冷冷清清**：指环境的空寂无人。**戚戚**：忧愁、悲伤。**乍暖还寒时候**：指深秋季节天气变化无常，忽而暖和，忽又转冷。**将息**：将养，调养休息。**敌**：挡，对付。**“雁过也”**三句：是说正伤心时，有旧曾相识的雁行飞过。**黄花**：菊花。**损**：凋零，零落。**谁**：何，什么。**堪**：可，能。**怎生**：怎样。**生**：语气助词，无义。**次第**：情况，光景。**了得**：了却，总括，包含。

〖译 文〗

(1) Stephen Owen 译

Tune: “Note After Note” (*Sheng-sheng man*) by Li Qing-zhao (1084-ca. 1151)

Searching and searching, seeking and seeking,
so chill, so clear,
dreary,
    and dismal,
    and forlorn.
That time of year
    when it’s suddenly warm,
    then cold again,
now it’s hardest of all to take care.
Two or three cups of weak wine—
how can they resist the biting wind
    that comes with evening?
The wild geese pass by—
that’s what hurts the most—
and yet they’re old acquaintances.

In piles chrysanthemums fill the ground,
looking all wasted, damaged—
who could pick them, as they are now?
I stay by the window,
how can I wait alone until blackness comes?

The beech tree,
　　on top of that
　　the fine rain,
on until dusk,
the dripping drop after drop.
In a situation like this
How can that one word "sorrow" grasp it?

(2) Zong-qi Cai 译

To the Tune of "One Beat Followed by Another, a Long Tune"

Searching and searching, seeking and seeking,
Chilly and cold, quiet and desolate,
Sad, sorrowful, miserable.
This time of year when it's warm now, soon cold again,
I just cannot take care of myself.
Two or three cups of bland wine
Are not enough to resist the rushing evening wind.
The wild geese passing by
Break my heart,
And they are none other than my old acquaintances!

In piles chrysanthemums are everywhere.
Withered and damaged;
Now who will pick them?
I cling to the window;
All alone, what am I going to do before it gets dark?
The drizzle on the wutong leaves
Drips and drops, drops and drips into evening.
How can all this
Be summed up by one word, "sorrow"?

(3) Kenneth Rexroth 译

A Weary Song to a Slow Sad Tune

Search. Search. Seek. Seek.

Cold. Cold. Clear. Clear.
Sorrow. Sorrow. Pain. Pain.
Hot flashes. Sudden chills.
Stabbing pains. Slow agonies.
I drink two cups, then three bowls,
Of clear wine until I can't
Stand up against a gust of wind.
Wild geese fly over head.
They wrench my heart.
They were our friends in the old days.

Gold chrysanthemums litter
The ground, pile up, faded, dead.
This season I could not bear
To pick them. All alone,
Motionless at my window,
I watch the gathering shadows.
Fine rain sifts through the wu t'ung trees,
And drips, drop by drop, through the dusk.
What can I ever do now?
How can I drive off this word—
Hopelessness?

(4) John A. Turner 译

Sorrow

I pine and peak
And questless seek
Groping and moping to linger and languish
Anon to wander and wonder, glare, stare and start
Flesh chill'd
Ghost thrilled
With grim dart
And keen canker or rankling anguish.

Sudden a gleam

Of fair weather felt
But fled as fast—
And the ice-cold season stays.
How hard to have these days
In rest or respite, peace or truce.
Sip upon sip of tasteless wine
Is of slight use
To counter or quell
The fierce lash of the evening blast.

The wild geese—see—
Fly overhead
Ah, there's the grief
That's chief—
Grief beyond bearing,
Wild fowl far faring
In days of old you sped
Bearing my true love's tender thoughts to me.

Lo, how my lawn is rife with golden blooms
Of bunched chrysanthemums—
Weary their heads they bow.
Who cares to pluck them now?
While I the casement keep
Lone, waiting, waiting for night
And, as the shades fall
Upon broad leaves, sparse rain-drops drip.
Ah, such a plight
Of grief—grief unbearable, unthinkable.

(5) 许渊冲 译

Tune: "Slow, Slow Tune"

I look for what I miss;
I know not what it is.
I feel so sad, so drear,

So lonely, without cheer.
How hard is it
To keep me fit
In this lingering cold!
Hardly warmed up
By cup on cup
Of wine so dry,
Oh, how could I
Endure at dusk the drift
Of wind so swift?
It breaks my heart, alas,
To see the wild geese pass,
For they are my acquaintances of old.

The ground is covered with yellow flowers,
Faded and fallen in showers.
Who will pick them up now?
Sitting alone at the window, how
Could I but quicken
The pace of darkness that won't thicken?
Upon the plane-trees a fine train drizzles
As twilight grizzles.
Oh, what can I do with a grief
Beyond belief?

(6) 林语堂 译

So dim, so dark,
So dense, so dull,
　　So damp, so dank,
　　So dead!
The weather, now warm, now cold,
　　Makes it harder
　　Than ever to forget!
How can a few cups of thin wine
Bring warmth against
　　The chilly winds of sunset?
I recognize the geese flying overhead:

My old friends,
Bring not the old memories back!
Let fallen flowers lie where they fall.
To what purpose
And for whom should I decorate?
By the window shut,
Guarding it along,
To see the sky has turned so black!
And the drizzle on the kola nut
Keeps on droning:
Pit-a-pat, pit-a-pat!
Is this the kind of mood and moment
To be expressed
By one word "sad"?

(7) Jiaosheng Wang 译

A Long Melancholy Tune (Autumn Sorrow)[1]
Despair by Li Ch'ing-chao

Searching, seeking,[2]
Seeking, searching,
What comes of it but
Coldness and desolation,
A word of dreariness and misery
And stabbing pain!
As soon as one feels a bit of warmth
A sense of chill returns:
A time so hard to have a quiet rest.
What avail two or three cups of tasteless wine
Against a violent evening wind?
Wild geese wing past at this of all hours,
And it suddenly dawns on me
That I've met them before.

Golden chrysanthemums in drifts—
How I'd have loved to pick them,
But now, for whom? On the ground they lie strewn,

Faded, neglected.③
There's nothing for it but to stay at the window,
Motionless, alone.
How the day drags before dusk descends!
Fine rain falling on the leaves of parasol-trees—
Drip, drip, drop, drop, in the deepening twilight.
To convey all the melancholy feelings
Born of these scenes
Can the one word "sorrow" suffice?④

① In this poem, Li Ch'ing-chao expresses her sentiments with rapidity and abandon but none of the characteristics of the elegant, restrained style in which most of her lyrics are written. The poem is in fact rather like a rhapsody that recalls to mind Ou-yang Hsiu's famous prose-poem "Autumn Sounds".

② This masterpiece of Li Ch'ing-chao's is admired, among other things, for the three groups of reiterated characters at the beginning of the poem. The three groups are ingeniously interrelated, with the second group being the result of the first, and the third the result of the second. This arrangement heightens the pathos.

③ Some commentators interpret the above lines as follows:
"Golden chrysanthemums in full bloom,
Their fallen petals in drifts—
Who would pick them
Now I'm withered and worn?
On the ground they lie strewn, neglected."

④ Instead of using hyperboles in the conventional way, Li Ch'ing-chao shows great creativity in saying that the word "sorrow" is inadequate to convey a multitude of melancholy feelings.

3.10 醉花阴(李清照)

薄雾浓云愁永昼，瑞脑消金兽。佳节又重阳，玉枕纱橱，半夜凉初透。
东篱把酒黄昏后，有暗香盈袖。莫道不销魂，帘卷西风，人比黄花瘦。

〖作品简介〗

此词是作者婚后所创，抒发的是重阳佳节思念丈夫的心情。

〖注 释〗

云：《古今词统》等作“雰”，《全芳备祖》作“阴”。**永昼**：漫长的白天。**瑞脑**：一种薰香名，又称龙脑，即冰片。**消**：一本作“销”，《花草粹编》等作“喷”。**金兽**：兽形的铜香炉。**重阳**：农历九月九日为重阳节。《周易》以“九”为阳数，日月皆值阳数，并且相重，故名。这是个古老的节日。南梁庾肩吾《九日侍宴乐游苑应令诗》：“朔气绕相风，献寿重阳节。”**纱橱**：即防蚊蝇的纱帐。宋周邦彦《浣溪沙》：“薄薄纱橱望似空，簟纹如水浸芙蓉。”**橱**：《彤管遗篇》等作“窗”。**凉**：《全芳备祖》等作“秋”。**东篱**：泛指采菊之地。陶渊明《饮酒诗》：“采菊东篱下，悠然见南山。”为古今艳称之名句，故“东篱”亦成为诗人惯用之咏菊典故。唐无可《菊》：“东篱摇落后，密艳被寒吹。夹雨惊新拆，经霜忽尽开。”**暗香**：这里指菊花的幽香。《古诗十九首·庭中有奇树》：“攀条折其荣，将以遗所思。馨香盈怀袖，路远莫致之。”这里用其意。**销魂**：形容极度忧愁、悲伤。**西风**：秋风。**比**：《花草粹编》等作“似”。**黄花**：指菊花。《礼记·月令》：“鞠有黄华。”鞠，本用菊。唐王绩《九月九日》：“忽见黄花吐，方知素节回。”

〖译　文〗

(1) 许渊冲 译

Tune: “Tipsy in the Flower’s Shade” by Li Qing-zhao

In the thin mist and thick cloud of incense, sad I stay.
The animal-shaped censer I see all day.
The Double Ninth Festival comes again.
　　Still alone I remain
In the curtain of gauze, on a pillow of jade,
Which the midnight chill begins to invade.

After dusk I drink wine by East Hedge in full bloom,
My sleeves filled with fragrance and gloom.
　　Say not my soul
Is not consumed! Should the west wind uproll
　　The curtain of my bower,
’T would show a thinner face than yellow flower.

(2) 龚景浩 译

“Zui Hua Yin (Song)”

Li Qing Zhao

Light mists, thick clouds, and the long day is sad.
Winter-daphne incense smoke spouts from metal animals.

'Tis Double Ninth Day[①] again, when
The midnight chill first invaded
The green muslin summer bed.

By the east fence
Holding a cup of wine after dusk fell,
A darkened fragrance filled my sleeve bell.
Do not say one is not thrilled:
With the door-curtains flapping in the west wind,
One is thinner than the yellow flowers[②].

① The ninth day of the ninth lunar month, a day to climb a hill.
② Chrysanthemums.

3.11 武陵春(李清照)

风住尘香花已尽，日晚倦梳头。物是人非事事休，欲语泪先流。
闻说双溪春尚好，也拟泛轻舟。只恐双溪舴艋舟，载不动许多愁。

作品简介

此词乃宋高宗绍兴五年(1135年)作者避难浙江金华时所作。其时金兵进犯，丈夫病故，家藏金石文物也散失殆尽，作者孑然一身，在连天烽火中飘泊流寓，历尽世路崎岖和人生坎坷，处境凄惨，内心极其悲痛。这首词借暮春之景，写出了词人内心深处的苦闷和忧愁。全词语言优美、意境深远，有言尽而意不尽之美。

注 释

武陵春：词牌名，又作《武林春》《花想容》，双调小令。双调四十八字，上下阕各四句三平韵。这首词为变格。**尘香**：落花触地，尘土也沾染上落花的香气。**花已尽**：《词谱》、清万树《词律》作"春已尽"。**日晚**：一作"日落"，一作"日晓"。**梳头**：古代的妇女习惯，起床后的第一件事是梳妆打扮。**物是人非**：事物依旧在，人不似往昔了。三国曹丕《与朝歌令吴质书》："节同时异，物是人非，我劳如何?"宋贺铸《雨中花》："人非物是，半晌鸾肠易断，宝勒空回。"**泪先**：《彤管遗编》《彤管摘奇》作"泪珠"，沈际飞《本草堂诗余》注："一作珠，误。"《崇祯历城县志》作"欲泪先流"，误删"语"字。**闻说**：清叶申芗辑《天籁轩词选》作"闻道"。**双溪**：水名，在浙江金华，是唐宋时有名的风光佳丽的游览胜地。**春尚好**：明程明善辑《啸余谱》作"春向好"。**拟**：准备，打算。宋姜夔《点绛唇》："第四桥边，拟共天随住。"辛弃疾《摸鱼儿》："长门事，准拟佳期又误。"**轻舟**：《汇选历代名贤词府》、清陆昶《历朝名媛诗词》作"扁舟"。**舴艋**[zé měng]**舟**：小船，两头尖如蚱蜢。唐张志和《渔父》词："钓台渔父褐为裘，两两三三舴艋舟。"

【译 文】

(1) Jiaosheng Wang 译

Tune: "Spring at Wu Ling"
Spring Ends by Li Ch'ing-chao

The wind has subsided.
Faded all the flowers:
In the muddy earth
A lingering fragrance of petals.
Dusk falls. I'm in no mood to comb my hair.
Things remain, but all is lost
Now he's no more.
Tears choke my words.

I hear Twin Brooks[①] is still sweet
With the breath of spring.
How I'd, too, love to go for a row,
On a light skiff.
I only fear at Twin Brooks my grasshopper of a boat
Wouldn't be able to bear
Such a load of grief.[②]

① A stream in the southeast of Chin-hua often visited by the poets in Tang and Sung times as a scenic resort.
② A line (three lines in the format presented here) famed for the beauty and freshness of its imagery.

(2) Robert Kotewall and Norman L. Smith 译

To "Spring at Wu-ling" by Li Ch'ing-chao (Li I-an)

The wind stops, earth is fragrant with fallen petals.
At the end of day I am weary to tend my hair;
Things remain, but he is not, and all is nothing.
I try to speak but the tears will flow.

I hear it said that at the Twin Brook the Spring is still
    fair,
And I, too, long to float in a light boat.
Only I fear that the 'locust boat' at the Twin Brook,
Cannot move with a freight
Of so much grief.

(3) C. H. Kwôck and Vincent McHugh 译

Tune: "Spring at Wu-ling" [*Wu-ling ch'un*]

Wind stopped
    earth
    smelling of fallen blossoms
Day almost over
    Too weary to comb my hair
His belongings here
    He here no longer
    Everything useless
Before I can say a word
    tears flow first

At Twin Stream
    they say
    the spring still beautiful
I too
    would like to go rowing in a light boat
but I'm afraid
    that little boat on Twin Stream
would not carry
    so much sorrow!

3.12 采桑子(李清照)

晚来一阵风兼雨，洗尽炎光。理罢笙簧，却对菱花淡淡妆。
绛绡缕薄冰肌莹，雪腻酥香。笑语檀郎，今夜纱厨枕簟凉。

【作品简介】

此词据说是在李清照新婚后的第二天所写。全词描述的是这番景象：向晚轻雨扫尽白日暑热之气，女子一支筝曲才罢，又在菱花镜前轻施淡妆；对镜卸去重纱，只著薄如蝉翼的轻衫，冰肌玉肤若隐若现。她皓腕凝脂，体香芬芳，眉目传情，嗔笑着对那良人说道：今晚的枕簟一定很凉爽。

【注　释】

炎光：夏天的酷热。**炎**：意为“热”。韩愈《南山》：“夏炎百木盛，阴郁增埋履。”**光**：借以指气。**笙簧**：通指乐器，这里是指琴。**理罢笙簧**：李清照在少女时代就善于弹琴。其《浣溪沙》中就有“重帘未卷影沉沉。倚楼无语理瑶琴”句。**菱花**：菱花铜镜 。“**绛绡缕薄冰肌莹**”句：穿上件粉红色的透明睡衣，雪白的肌肤若隐若现，一阵一阵的幽香散发出来。这里是作者形容自己雪白的肌肤、醉人的幽香。**檀郎**：出自成语“檀郎谢女”。檀郎指的是晋代潘岳(潘安，小名檀奴)，其人姿仪美好，人云“貌若潘安”。这里是对作者的丈夫赵明诚的爱称。“**今夜纱厨枕簟凉**”句：今晚的竹席应该很凉快！“纱橱”一般解作笼罩于床上的帏幛或隔开厅堂的纱屏。作者的《醉花阴》也有“佳节又重阳，玉枕纱厨，半夜凉初透”之句。**枕簟**：枕头和竹席。这两句是和夫君在一起时的缠绵。这里的“枕簟凉”是夏日里的清爽凉意，同时也是对夫君的暗示。

【译　文】

Burton Watson 译

Tune: “Song of Picking Mulberry”

Evening comes with an onslaught of wind and rain,
washing clean the heat and glare.
I put away my reed pipes,
face the flower-formed mirror, applying light makeup.

Red silk gauze so sheer my white skin shines through,
snowy-smooth, cream-fragrant:
I smile and say to my husband,
Tonight inside the light curtains, pillow and mat will be cool!

3.13 清平乐(李清照)

年年雪里，常插梅花醉。挼尽梅花无好意，赢得满衣清泪。
今年海角天涯，萧萧两鬓生华。看取晚来风势，故应难看梅花。

『作品简介』

此词是作者赏梅之作，也是她对自己一生早、中、晚三期带有总结性的追忆。全词借不同时期的赏梅感受写出了词人个人的心路历程：词人截取早年、中年、晚年三个不同时期赏梅的典型画面，深刻地表现了自己早年的欢乐、中年的悲戚、晚年的沦落，对自己一生的哀乐作了形象的概括与总结。作品词意含蓄蕴藉，感情悲切哀婉，以赏梅寄寓自己的今苦之感和咏国之忧，感慨深沉。

『注　释』

清平乐：词牌名，取汉乐府“清乐”和“平乐”两乐调命名。双调，四十六字，八句，上片四仄韵，下片三平韵。**挼**[ruó]：揉搓。**无好意**：心情不好。**赢得**：落得。**海角天涯**：犹天涯海角，本指僻远之地，这里当指临安。**萧萧两鬓生华**：形容鬓发花白稀疏的样子。**“看取”**二句：“看取”是观察之意，观察自然界的“风势”。虽然出于对“梅花”的关切和爱惜，但此处“晚来风势”的深层语义，当与《菩萨蛮·归鸿声断残云碧》和《忆秦娥·临高阁》的“西风”埒同，均当喻指金兵对南宋的进逼。因此，结尾的“梅花”除了上述作为头饰和遣愁之物外，尚含有一定的象征之意。**故应**：还应。

『译　文』

(1) Burton Watson 译

Tune：“Pure Serene Music”

Year after year in the snow
Always we'd pick plum blossoms，drunk as we were，
Shattering every cluster—what did we care？—
And their clear tears fell all over our clothes.

This year by sea's bed，sky's border，

Lonely, lonely, gray invading both temples,
I watch, as evening comes, the wind rising
And know that I'll be hard put to discover a single blossom.

(2) Kenneth Rexroth and Ling Chung 译

Year after year in the snow, intoxicated,
I have put the new plum blossoms
In my hair.
Now the fallen petals
Only depress me.
All I have gained is a dress
Wet with crystal tears.

This year I am at the corner
Of the sea and the edge of Heaven.
I am old and lonely.
My temples have turned white.
I realize that the evening wind
Is too strong for me.
It is no longer possible
For me to contemplate
The blossoming plums.

3.14 一剪梅(李清照)

红藕香残玉簟秋。轻解罗裳，独上兰舟。云中谁寄锦书来，雁字回时，月满西楼。

花自飘零水自流。一种相思，两处闲愁。此情无计可消除，才下眉头，却上心头。

【作品简介】

此词作于词人与丈夫赵明诚离别之后，寄寓着作者不忍离别的一腔深情，反映出初婚少妇沉溺于情海之中的纯洁情思。全词格调清新，以“不落俗套”的表现方式展现了女性特有的沉挚情感，给人以美的享受，实属工致精巧的别情词作。

【注 释】

玉簟[diàn]**秋**：意谓时至深秋，精美的竹席已嫌清冷。**兰舟**：《述异记》卷下谓：木质坚硬而有香味的木兰树是制作舟船的好材料，诗家遂以木兰舟或兰舟为舟之美称。一说“兰舟”特指睡眠的床榻。**锦书**：对书信的一种美称。《晋书·窦滔妻苏氏传》云：苏蕙织锦为回文旋图诗，以赠其被徙流沙的丈夫窦滔。这种用锦织成的字称锦字，又称锦书。

【译 文】

(1) 许渊冲 译

Tune: “A Twig of Mume Blossoms” by Li Qing-zhao①

The jade-like mat feels autumn’s cold, I change a coat
　　And ’mid the fading fragrance
　　Of lotus pink alone I boat.
Will wild returning geese bring letters through the cloud?
　　When they come, with moonbeams
　　My west chamber’s o’erflowed.

As water flows and flowers fall without leaving traces,
　　One and the same longing
　　O’erflows two lonely places.
I cannot get rid of this sorrow: kept apart
　　From my eyebrows,
　　It gnaws my heart.

① This lyric depicts the loneliness of the poetess longing for messages from her husband who was far away. The last three lines may be compared with Fan Zhong-yan’s verse:

　　Such sorrow as appears
　　On the brows or the heart
　　Cannot be put apart.

(2) Kenneth Rexroth 译

Tune: "Plum Blossoms Fall and Scatter"

The perfume of the red water lilies
Dies away. The Autumn air
Penetrates the pearl jade curtain.
Torches gleam on the orchid boats.
Who has sent me a message
Of love from the clouds? It is
The time when the wild swans
Return. The moonlight floods the women's
Quarters. Flowers, after their
Nature, whirl away in the wind.
Spilt water, after its nature,
Flows together at the lowest point.
Those who are one being
Can never stop thinking of each other.
But, ah, my dear, we are apart,
And I have become used to sorrow.
This love—nothing can ever
Make it fade or disappear.
For a moment it was on my eyebrows,
Now it is heavy in my heart.

(3) Kenneth Rexroth 译

Tune : "Cutting a Flowering Plum Branch"

Red lotus incense fades on
The jewelled curtain. Autumn
Comes again. Gently I open
My silk dress and float alone
On the orchid boat. Who can
Take a letter beyond the clouds?
Only the wild geese come back
And write their ideograms

On the sky under the full
Moon that floods the West Chamber.

Flowers, after their kind, flutter
And scatter. Water after
Its nature, when spilt, at last
Gathers again in one place.
Creatures of the same species
Long for each other. But we
Are far apart and I have
Grown learned in sorrow.
Nothing can make it dissolve
And go away. One moment,
It is on my eyebrows.
The next, it weighs on my heart.

(4) K. Y. Hsü 译

Tune: "One Sprig of Plum" [*Yi chien mei*]

The scent of red lotus fades, and the mat feels cool.
I loosen my robe
　　To board the boat alone.
Who sends a message through the clouds?
　　As the swan formation returns
　　Moonlight fills the western chamber.

The petals shall fall and the water shall flow:
　　One kind of longing,
　　Two victims of unnamed grief.
There is no way to be rid of this thought;
　　Just as it recedes from the eyebrows
　　In the heart it swells.

3.15 永遇乐(李清照)

落日熔金，暮云合璧，人在何处？

染柳烟浓，吹梅笛怨，春意知几许?
元宵佳节，融和天气，次第岂无风雨?
来相召，香车宝马，谢他酒朋诗侣。

中州盛日，闺门多暇，记得偏重三五，
铺翠冠儿，捻金雪柳，簇带争济楚，
如今憔悴，云鬟雪鬓，怕见夜间出去。
不如向，帘儿底下，听人笑语。

【作品简介】

此词乃作者流寓临安时所作，虽写元夕，却一反常调，以今昔元宵的不同情景作对比，抒发了深沉的盛衰之感和身世之悲。全词通过南渡前后过元宵节两种情景的对比，抒写离乱之后愁苦寂寞的情怀。上片从眼前景物抒写心境。下片从今昔对比中抒发国破家亡的感慨，表达沉痛悲苦的心情。全词情景交融、跌宕有致，由今而昔，又由昔而今，形成今昔盛衰的鲜明对比，感情深沉、真挚，语言于朴素中见清新、平淡中见工致。

【注　释】

落日熔金：落日的颜色好像熔化的黄金。**合璧**：像璧玉一样合成一块。**吹梅笛怨**：指笛子吹出《梅花落》曲幽怨的声音。**次第**：接着，转眼。**中州**：这里指北宋汴京。**三五**：指元宵节。**铺翠冠儿**：饰有翠羽的女式帽子。**捻金雪柳**：元宵节女子头上的装饰。**簇带**：装扮之意。

【译　文】

(1) Kenneth Rexroth 译

To the Tune of "Everlasting Joy"

LI CH'ING-CHAO

The sun sets in molten gold.
The evening clouds form a jade disk.
Where is he?
Dense white mist envelops the willows.
A sad flute plays "Falling Plum Blossoms."

How many Spring days are left now?
This Feast of Lanterns should be joyful.
The weather is calm and lovely.
But who can tell if it
Will be followed by wind and rain?
A friend sends her perfumed carriage
And high-bred horses to fetch me.
I decline the invitation of
My old poetry and wine companion.

I remember the happy days in the lost capital.
We took our ease in the women's quarters.
The Feast of Lanterns was elaborately celebrated —
Gold pendants, emerald hairpins, brocaded girdles,
New sashes — we competed
To see who was most smartly dressed.
Now I am withering away,
Wind-blown hair, frosty temples.
I am embarrassed to go out this evening
Among girls in the flower of youth.
I prefer to stay beyond the curtains,
And listen to talk and laughter
I can no longer share.

(2) 许渊冲 译

Tune: "Joy of Eternal Union" by Li Qing-zhao

The setting sun like molten gold,
Gathering clouds like marble cold,
    Where is my dear?
Willows take misty dye,
Flutes for mume blossoms sigh.
    Can you say spring is here?
On the Lantern Festival
The weather is agreeable.
    Will wind and rain not come again?

I think my friends in verse and wine,
With scented cabs and horses fine
    Coming to invite me in vain.

I remember the pleasure
Ladies enjoyed at leisure
    In the capital on this day:
Headdress with emerald
And filigree of gold
    Vied in fashion display.
Now with a languid air
And disheveled frosty hair,
    I dare not go out in the evening.
I'd rather forward lean
Behind the window screen
    To hear the others' laughing ring.

(3) C. H. Kwôck and Vincent McHugh 译

Tune: "Endless Union" [*Yung yu lo*]

Sunset
    molten bronze
evening clouds
    marbled white jade
    Where is he?
A mist of light
    stains the willows
Plum blowing
    A flute's wail
    Spring reveries
    how much you know!
New Year's Eve
    the merrymaking festival
Serene weather—
    wind

no in its wake?
rain
Friends come
to invite me out
horses
traveling carts
wine-drinking friends
I think these
poem-making companions
At the capital
joyful days
In my room
much
time to myself
I recall
another New Year's Eve
how I put on
the green-feather headdress
narrow snow-white sash
worked
with gold thread
Headdress and sash
to vie with any beauty
I
haggard now
wind-tangled locks
hair
frosted white
at the temple
Too diffident
to venture among flowers
I loiter
under the window screen
eavesdropping
on the talk
and laughter
of others

3.16 南歌子(李清照)

天上星河转，人间帘幕垂。凉生枕簟泪痕滋。起解罗衣聊问、夜何其。
翠贴莲蓬小，金销藕叶稀。旧时天气旧时衣。只有情怀不似、旧家时。

【作品简介】

此词描写闺怨。上片由景及事，下片睹物感怀，真切细致地表现了主人公对特定环境的感受、对生活变迁的痛切情绪。全词有锻炼精巧之语句，而以寻常言语入词则为其最感人之处。

【注 释】

南歌子：又名《断肠声》等。一说张衡《南都赋》的“坐南歌兮起郑舞”，当系此调名之来源。而李清照此词之立意，则与又名《肠断声》相合。**星河**：银河，到秋天转向东南。**枕簟**[diàn]：枕头和竹席。**滋**：增益，加多。**夜何其**：《诗经·小雅·庭燎》：“夜如何其？夜未央。”“其”，语气助词。**翠贴**、**金销**：即贴翠、销金，均为服饰工艺。**情怀**：心情。**旧家**：从前。《诗词曲语辞汇释》卷六：“旧家犹言从前，家为估量之辞。”其所引例中即有此句。

【译 文】

Stephen Owen 译

Poem to be Sung to the Tune of “Southern Song” (*Nan-ge-zi*)
By Li Qingzhao

Up in heaven the star-river turns,
in man’s world below
curtains are drawn.
A chill comes to pallet and pillow,
damp with tracks of tears.
I rise to take off my gossamer dress
and just happen to ask, “How late is it now?”

The tiny lotus pods,
kingfisher feathers sewn on;
as the gilt flecks away
the lotus leaves grow few.
The same weather as in times before,
the same old dress —
only the feelings in the heart
are not as they were before.

3.17 眼儿媚（林少瞻）

霁霞散晓月犹明，疏木挂残星。山径人稀，翠萝深处，啼鸟两三声。
霜华重逼云裘冷，心共马蹄轻。十里青山，一溪流水，都做许多情。

【作品简介】

此词描写了少年早行时的景象和心情。

【注 释】

霁霞[jì xiá]：雨后的彩霞。翠萝：绿色萝叶。云裘[yún qiú]：轻柔的皮衣。

【译 文】

Robert Kotewall and Norman L. Smith 译

Journey at Dawn
To "Eyes' Fascination"

A glow ushers in dawn while the moon is still bright;
Over the sparse trees hang some fading stars.
On the hill-paths men are few;
In the depth of the blue wistaria,
Singing birds make two or three notes.

Petals of frost, heavy on my fur coat, strike chill,
But my heart is light as my horse's hoofs.
Ten miles of green mountain,
One stream of flowing water—
All add to the inspiration.

3.18 临江仙(陈与义)

忆昔午桥桥上饮，坐中多是豪英。长沟流月去无声。杏花疏影里，吹笛到天明。

二十余年如一梦，此身虽在堪惊。闲登小阁看新晴。古今多少事，渔唱起三更。

〖作品简介〗

此词乃作者晚年为追忆洛中朋友和旧游所作。上片写对已经沦落敌国之手的家乡以及早年自在快乐生活的回顾，下片宕开笔墨回到现实，概括词人从踏上仕途所经历的颠沛流离和国破家亡的痛苦生活，结句将古今悲慨、国恨家愁，都融入“渔唱”之中，将沉挚的悲感化为旷达的襟怀。

〖注　释〗

临江仙：词牌名，又称《鸳鸯梦》《雁后归》《庭院深深》。双调，上片五句，押三平韵，三十字；下片同，共六十字。**午桥**：在洛阳南面。**坐中**：在一起喝酒的人。**豪英**：出色的人物。这两句说：想从前在午桥桥头饮宴，在一起喝酒的都是英雄好汉。**长沟流月**：月光随着流水悄悄地消逝。此句即杜甫《旅夜书怀》“月涌大江流”之意，谓时间如流水般逝去。**去无声**：表示月亮西沉，夜深了。**疏影**：稀疏的影子。这两句说，在杏花稀疏的影子里吹起短笛，一直欢乐到天明。**二十余年**：二十多年来的经历(包括北宋亡国的大变乱)。**堪惊**：总是心惊胆跳。这两句说，二十多年好像一场春梦，我亲身经历了亡国的变乱，自己虽然还活着，回想起来总是胆战心惊。**新晴**：新雨初晴。**晴**：这里指晴夜。**渔唱**：打渔人编的歌儿。**三更**：古代以更漏记时，自黄昏至指晓分为五刻，即五更，三更正是午夜。这三句说，百无聊赖地登上小楼，看看雨后初晴的月夜景色。古往今来多少大事，也不过让打鱼的人编作歌儿在三更半夜里唱唱罢了。

【译 文】

许渊冲 译

Tune: "Immortal at the River"
Mounting a Tower at Night and Recalling
The Old Friends Visiting Luoyang Together by Chen Yu-yi[①]

I still remember drinking on the Bridge of Noon
    With bright wits of the day.
    The silent moon
    On endless river rolled away.
In shadows sparse of apricot flowers
We played our flutes till morning hours.

O'er twenty years have passed like dreams,
    It is a wonder that I'm still alive.
Carefree, I mount the tower bathed in moonbeams.
    So many things passed long
    Ago survive
Only in fishermen's midnight song.

① Chen Yu-yi(1090-1138) was a native of Luoyang who fled to the South after the Jurchen invasion. The Bridge of Noon was scenic spot in the South of Luoyang where a villa was built by an official of the Tang Dynasty.

3.19 采桑子(吕本中)

恨君不似江楼月，南北东西，南北东西，只有相随无别离。
恨君却似江楼月，暂满还亏，暂满还亏，待得团圆是几时？

【作品简介】

此词从江楼月联想到人生的聚散离合。月有阴晴圆缺，却又不分南北东西，而与人相随。词人取喻新巧，正反成理。

〖注 释〗

采桑子：词牌名。又名《丑奴儿令》《罗敷艳歌》《罗敷媚》。**君**：这里指词人的妻子。一说此词为妻子思念丈夫。**江楼**：靠在江边的楼阁。**暂满还亏**：指月亮短暂的圆满之后又会有缺失。**满**：此指月圆。**亏**：此指月缺。

〖译 文〗

(1) 龚景浩 译

"Cai Sang Zi (Song)"

Lü Ben Zhong

I wish you were the moon,
Shining on the river from behind the waterside lodge.
North, South, East, West;
North, South, East, West,
You always follow and will never leave me.

But then, I wish you wouldn't be that moon:
Temporarily full but soon waning;
Temporarily full but soon waning,
How long have I got to wait
Before it is again full?

(2) Alan Ayling and Duncan Mackintosh 译

Why can't you be like the moon
over the house by the river?
South and North, East and West,
South and North, East and West,
While I can follow it we're together.

Why are you so like the moon
over the house by the river?

Full for a time then slipping away,
Full for a time then slipping away?
When can I be one with you for ever?

(3) Hans H. Frankel 译

Feelings at Separation
Tune Pattern: "The Mulberrypicker"

I wish you were like the moon on the river.
South, north, east or west,
South, north, east or west,
You'd always be near and never part.

I wish you weren't like the moon on the river.
Full for a time, it wanes again.
Full for a time, it wanes again.
How long for the wait for full reunion?

(4) Robert Kotewall and Norman L. Smith 译

To "Picking Mulberries"

I GRIEVE that my love is not like the moon over the
riverside tower:
South and North, East and West,
South and North, East and West,
Only constant companionship and no separation.

I grieve that my love is all too like the moon over the
riverside tower:
A brief waxing, and then a waning,
A brief waxing, and then a waning,
I wait for the full circle of union—but how short-lived!

(5) 许渊冲 译

A Free Translation

I regret you could not be like the full moon bright,
Shining all night.
Shining all night,
It is ever in view and never out of sight.

I regret that you are just like the fickle moon,
Waning so soon.
Waning so soon,
When will you wax again to turn my night into noon?

3.20 贺新郎（张元干）

梦绕神州路。
怅秋风、连营画角，故宫离黍。
底事昆仑倾砥柱，九地黄流乱注。
聚万落千村狐兔。
天意从来高难问，况人情老易悲难诉。
更南浦，送君去。

凉生岸柳催残暑。
耿斜河，疏星残月，断云微度。
万里江山知何处？回首对床夜语。
雁不到，书成谁与？
目尽青天怀今古，肯儿曹恩怨相尔汝！
举大白，听《金缕》。

【作品简介】

此词乃作者于绍兴八年为胡铨壮行所作。高宗绍兴十二年(1142 年)，胡铨因反对“和议”、请斩秦桧等三人而被贬为福州签判，后又再次遭遣，除名编管新州(今广东新兴)，作者作此词以相送，并因此获罪而被削职为民。作品上片感时，对中原故国横遭掳掠、南宋朝廷的昏庸腐败无能忧心忡忡，抒发了对金国统治者猖狂侵略、南宋统治者卖国投降的一腔悲愤；下片赠别，抒写离情，追忆往事，表现了朋友间的真挚友谊和共同的爱国情怀。全词采用虚实结合的表达手法，深刻表达了作者既悲国事，又悲远别的心情，体现了当时南宋仕者普遍的悲愤心情。

〖注 释〗

神州：一般指中国，这里专指被金兵占领的中原。**怅**：心里愁闷。**画角**：号角。**故宫**：北宋首都汴京(今河南开封市)。**离黍**：长满了庄稼。**底事**：何事。**昆仑**：昆仑山，喻北宋王朝。**砥柱**：砥柱山，在黄河中。**九地**：遍地。**黄流**：黄河水，这里指金兵。**乱注**：到处流。**狐兔**：指金兵。**天意从来高难问**：皇帝高高在上，他的意图没人了解。**况人情老易悲难诉**：更何况人们很快忘记了亡国之恨。**更**：再。**南浦**：送别的码头。**耿**：明亮。**斜河**：银河斜转(夜深了)。**断云微度**：一朵朵浮云缓慢飘过去。**万里江山知何处**：江山阻隔，相距万里，知道你在哪里呢？**回首**：回忆。**对床夜语**：对躺在床上的人谈话到深夜。**“雁不到”**二句：(你去的地方)大雁也飞不到，写好的信交给谁？**“目尽青天”**一句：远望天空，想到古今世态的变化。**肯儿曹恩怨相尔汝**：(我们谈的都是国家大事)怎么能像孩子那样只顾说个人恩怨呢？**大白**：酒杯。**金缕**：《金缕曲》就是《贺新郎》词牌的别名。

〖译 文〗

许渊冲 译

Tune: “Congratulating the Bridegroom”

Seeing His Excellency Hu Quan Banished to the South by Zhang Yuan-gan①

Haunted by dreams of the lost Central Plain,
I hear the autumn wind complain.
From tent to tent horns dreary blow;
In ancient palace weeds o'ergrow.
How could Mount Pillar suddenly fall down?
And Yellow River flow throughout the town?

A thousand villages o'errun with foxes and hares?
    We can't question the Heaven high,
The court will soon forget embarrassing affairs.
    'Tis sad and drear
    To say goodbye
    At Southern Pier!

Cold breath of river willows flies away
    The remnant of a summer day.
    The Milky Way slants low,
Past pale moon and sparse stars clouds slowly go.
Mountains and rivers stretch out of view.
    Oh! where shall I find you?
I still remember our talking at dead
Of night while we two lay in bed.
    But now wild geese can't go so far.
Who will send my letter there where you are?
    I gaze on the blue sky,
Thinking of the hard times gone by.
Can we have but personal love or hate
As beardless young men often state?
    Hold up a cup of wine
    And hear this song of mine!

① Zhang Yuan-gan (1091-1161) was a patriotic poet of the Southern Song Dynasty (1127-1279). This lyric was written for Hu Quan, a high official opposing the capitulationist Premier Qin Hui, who banished him in 1142 to the southernmost place where even the wild geese carrying messages were not supposed to go. In this lyric "Mount Pillar" alludes to the Royal Court, the "Heaven" to the emperor, and "foxes and hares" to the Jurchen aggressors.

3.21 满江红(岳飞)

怒发冲冠，凭栏处、潇潇雨歇。抬望眼，仰天长啸，壮怀激烈。三十功名尘与土，八千里路云和月。莫等闲、白了少年头，空悲切！

靖康耻，犹未雪。臣子恨，何时灭！驾长车，踏破贺兰山缺。壮志饥餐胡虏肉，笑谈渴饮匈奴血。待从头、收拾旧山河，朝天阙。

〖作品简介〗

此词表现了作者抗击金兵、收复故土、统一祖国的强烈的爱国精神。

〖注 释〗

怒发冲冠：气得头发竖起，以至于将帽子顶起。形容愤怒至极，冠是指帽子而不是头发竖起。**潇潇**：形容雨势急骤。**长啸**：大声呼叫。汉·司马相如《上林赋》："长啸哀鸣，翩幡互经。"**三十功名尘与土**：三十年来，建立了一些功名，如同尘土。**八千里路云和月**：形容南征北战、路途遥远、披星戴月。**等闲**：轻易，随便。**靖康耻**：宋钦宗靖康二年（1127年），金兵攻陷汴京，掳走徽、钦二帝。**贺兰山**：贺兰山脉位于宁夏回族自治区与内蒙古自治区交界处。一说是位于邯郸市磁县境内的贺兰山。**朝天阙**：朝见皇帝。**天阙**：本指宫殿前的楼观，此指皇帝生活的地方。明·王熙书《满江红》词碑作"朝金阙"。

〖译 文〗

(1) 许渊冲 译

Tune: "The River All Red" by Yue Fei

Wrath sets on end my hair,
I lean on railings where
I see the drizzling rain has ceased.
Raising my eyes
Towards the skies,
I heave long sighs,
My wrath not yet appeased.
To dust is gone the fame achieved in thirty years;
Like cloud-veiled moon and the thousand-mile land disappears.
Should youthful heads in vain turn gray,
We would regret for aye.

Our emperors captured,
It is a burning shame.
How could we generals
Quench our vengeful flame!
Driving our chariots of war, we'd go

To cut through our relentless foe.
Valiantly we'd cut off each head;
Laughing, we'd drink the blood they shed.
When we've reconquered our lost land,
In triumph would return our army grand.

(2) 张炳星 译

Avenging an Insult by Yue Fei

Angry hair shooting up my hat,
I climbed a height alone full of hate
and leaned on a balustrade to gaze into a distant land,
when a torrential rain just stopped.
I raised my head to look up into the sky
and heaved a deep sigh, while blood in my heart ran high.
Now I am over thirty years old,
but my merits are as trifling as dust cold,
although I've fought day and night, north and south,
for eight thousand miles all told.
Don't fritter away your precious time,
for when white hair creeps into your head,
you'll be vainly grieved.

The deep disgrace received in Jingkang age(1127)
by Emperors Wei and Qing has not been revenged.
When will the indignation of officials be subdued?
I must drive a chariot to He Lan Mountain Range
to crush our enemy's stronghold, for a long age.
With a noble aspiration, I'll eat the Tartar's meat
when I am hungry,
and merrily drink the Hun's blood when I am thirsty.
Let me from the start recapture our lost territory
and report victories to the Imperial Court.

3.22 西江月(张孝祥)

问讯湖边春色，重来又是三年。东风吹我过湖船。杨柳丝丝拂面。
世路如今已惯，此心到处悠然。寒光亭下水如天。飞起沙鸥一片。

〖作品简介〗

此词上片以作者自己与风物的互相映衬，表达了重访三塔湖离岸登船之际的快意感受；下片则以世路与湖亭的强烈对比，抒发了置身寒光亭时的悠然心情。

〖注　释〗

湖：指三塔湖。**寒光亭**：在三塔寺内。

〖译　文〗

(1) 许渊冲 译

Tune: "The Moon Over the West River" by Zhang Xiao-xiang

Does the lakeside spring scene the same remain?
Three years have passed now that I come again.
Across the surface of the lake the east wind blows my boat,
The willow branches wreath by wreath caress my face and coat.

I'm used to life both high and low,
My heart's at ease where'er I go.
Water looks like the sky below Bower Cold-Light,
It's ruffled only by the water birds in flight.

(2) 龚景浩 译

"Xi Jiang Yue (Song)"

Zhang Xiao Xiang

'Tis now three years
Since I visited spring at the lakeside,
And here I am again.
The east wind blows across my boat cruising,
The new willow twigs my face caressing.

I'm now well-traveled on the roads of this world,
My heart at ease wherever I go.
Down the Cool Bright Pavilion the water and sky merge.
A flock of seagulls skyward surge.

3. 23 好事近(杨万里)

月未到诚斋，先到万花川谷。不是诚斋无月，隔一林修竹。
如今才是十三夜，月色已如玉。未是秋光奇绝，看十五十六。

〖作品简介〗

这是一首咏月词，上阕是以物托月，下阕则以月自托。

〖注 释〗

诚斋：作者的书斋名，且因以之为号。**万花川谷**：作者故居的花园名。

〖译 文〗

龚景浩 译

"Hao Shi Jin (Song)"
Yang Wan Li

The moon has not come to my study;
It has reached the Creek Valley of Many Flowers.
Not that my study has no moon,
It is that in my courtyard stand groves of slender bamboo.

Tonight is only the thirteenth night,
The moonlight is already jade white.
To see the marvels of autumn brilliance,
Wait till the fifteenth and sixteenth.

3.24 卜算子(陆游)

驿外断桥边，寂寞开无主。已是黄昏独自愁，更著风和雨。
无意苦争春，一任群芳妒。零落成泥碾作尘，只有香如故。

〖作品简介〗

此词乃咏梅之作，也是作者自己的咏怀之作。作者巧借饱受摧残、花粉犹香的梅花，比喻自己虽终生坎坷，绝不媚俗的忠贞。

〖注　释〗

卜算子：为词牌名。《词律》以为调名取义于“卖卜算命之人”。又名《百尺楼》《眉峰碧》《楚天遥》《缺月挂疏桐》等。相传是借用唐代诗人骆宾王的绰号。骆宾王写诗好用数字取名，人称“卜算子”。山谷词“似扶著，卖卜算”，取卖卜算命的意思。**驿[yì]外**：指荒僻、冷清之地。**驿**：驿站，古代传递政府文书的人中途换马匹休息、住宿的地方。**断桥**：残破的桥。一说“断”通“簖”，簖桥乃古时在为拦河捕鱼蟹而设簖之处所建之桥。**寂寞**：孤单冷清。**无主**：无人过问，无人欣赏。**更著[zhuó]**：更加受到。**无意**：不想，没有心思。自己不想费尽心思去争芳斗艳。**苦**：尽力，竭力。**争春**：与百花争奇斗艳。此指争权。**一任**：任凭。**群芳**：群花，百花。隐指权臣、小人。**妒[dù]**：嫉妒。**零落**：凋谢。**碾[niǎn]**：轧碎。**作尘**：化作灰土。**香如故**：香气依旧存在。

〖译　文〗

(1) 许渊冲 译

Tune：“Song of Divination” by Lu You

Beside the broken bridge and outside the post-hall,
　　A flower is blooming forlorn.
Saddened by her solitude at night-fall,
　　By wind and rain she's further torn.

Let other flowers their envy pour.
　　To Spring she lays no claim.
Fallen in mud and ground to dust, she seems no more,

But her fragrance is still the same.

(2) 龚景浩 译

"Bu Suan Zi (Song)"

Lu You

By the broken-down bridge, outside the coach inn,
Belonging nowhere,
It blooms alone and thin.[①]
All by itself in the dusk—'Tis sad enough;
Add to that the rain and the wind.

Not deigning to compete in spring,
Let the beauties their envy fling.
Scattered and fallen,
It is ground into mud and turned to dust,
Only its fragrance persists.

① This poem was written in praise of the winter-plum. See Note to *Pu Sa Man* ("Foreign Girls") by Feng Yan Si.

(3) Alan Ayling and Duncan Mackintosh 译

In Praise of Plum Blossom

Outside the post-house by a broken bridge
Solitary and unremarked it flowers;
Melancholy, alone in the twilight
Or buffeted by squally showers;

Never presuming to rival spring's colours,
Unmoved when others mass round it enviously.
Its petals fall to earth, are trampled to dust;
A fragrant memory.

(4) 外文社 译

Ode to the Plum Blossom
To the Tune of "Pu Suan Tzu"

Outside the post-house, beside the broken bridge,
Alone, deserted, a flower blooms.
Saddened by her solitude in the falling dusk,
She is now assailed by wind and rain.

Let other flowers be envious!
She craves not Spring for herself alone.
Her petals may be ground in the mud,
But her fragrance will endure.

3.25 钗头凤(陆游)

红酥手。
黄縢酒。
满城春色宫墙柳。
东风恶。
欢情薄。
一怀愁绪,
几年离索。
错!错!错!

春如旧。
人空瘦。
泪痕红浥鲛绡透。
桃花落。
闲池阁。
山盟虽在,
锦书难托。
莫!莫!莫!

〖作品简介〗

此词描写了作者与原配唐氏(一说为唐婉)的爱情悲剧。全词记述了词人与唐氏被迫分开后，在禹迹寺南沈园的一次偶然相遇的情景，表达了他们眷恋之深和相思之切，抒发了作者怨恨愁苦而又难以言状的凄楚痴情，是一首别开生面、催人泪下的作品。

〖注　释〗

黄縢[téng]：此处指美酒。宋代官酒以黄纸为封，故以黄封代指美酒。**宫墙**：南宋以绍兴为陪都，故绍兴的某一段围墙，有宫墙之说。**东风**：喻指陆游的母亲。**离索**：离群索居的简括。**浥**[yì]：湿润。**鲛绡**[jiāo xiāo]：神话传说鲛人所织的绡，极薄，后用以泛指薄纱，这里指手帕。**绡**：生丝，生丝织物。**池阁**：池上的楼阁。**山盟**：旧时常用山盟海誓，指对山立盟、指海起誓。**锦书**：写在锦上的书信。**莫！莫！莫**：相当于今“罢了”之意。

〖译　文〗

(1) Wai-lim Yip 译

“HAIRPIN PHOENIX”

Rouged hands.
Yellow wine.
A city of spring, walls of willows.
The east wind is wicked,
Togetherness now dispersed.
A bosom of confused silk.
Many years of separation.
Wrong! Wrong! Wrong!

Spring as before.
You, thin for no end.
Tears streak pink soaking shagreen silk.
Peach blossoms fall.
Bower of Leisure Pond.
Vows are there;

A letter, no way to send:
No! No! No!

(2) Burton Watson 译

Tune: "Phoenix Hairpin"

(*Said to have been written in 1155, when the poet chanced to meet his first wife in the Shen family garden in Shao-hsing. They had been happily married, but the poet's mother forced them to divorce. At the time of the meeting here, both were remarried.*)

Pink tender hand,
yellow-corded wine,
city crammed with spring hues, willow by garden wall:
east winds hateful,
the one I loved, cold—
a heart all sadness,
parted how many years?
wrong! wrong! wrong!

Spring as always,
someone grown needlessly thin,
red tear stains wet the kerchief, soaking through mermaid gauze.
Peach petals falling,
stillness of a pond pavilion:
mountain-firm vows go on forever,
but a letter would be useless now—
don't! don't! don't!

(3) 许渊冲 译

Tune: "Phoenix Hairpin" by Lu You

Pink hands so fine,
Gold-branded wine,

Spring paints green willows palaces walls cannot confine.
East wind unfair,
Happy times rare.
In my heart sad thoughts throng:
We've severed for years long.
Wrong, wrong, wrong!

Spring is as green,
In vain she's lean,
Her silk scarf soak'd with tears and red with stains unclean.
Peach blossoms fall
Near desert'd hall.
Our oath is still there, lo!
No word to her can go.
No, no, no!

(4) Kenneth Rexroth 译

"Phoenix Hairpin"

Pink and white hands like roses and rice cake!
Cups full of golden pools of wine!
Today the willows are blooming
By the palace wall. The Spring wind
Brings me no pleasure and I
Hate it. My bowels are knotted
With bitterness. I cannot
Loosen the cord of the years
Which has bound us together.

The Spring is still the Spring
Of other days, but I am
Empty, withered with pain.
My rouge is streaked with tears, my
Dress is stained with tear drops.

The peach trees are in blossom
Over my room, here by the
Still lake that mirrors the hills.
I no longer have the strength
To finish this letter and
Wrap it in cloth gold. When
You receive it, everything
Will be over forever.

3.26 诉衷情(陆游)

当年万里觅封侯。匹马戍梁州。关河梦断何处，尘暗旧貂裘。
胡未灭，鬓先秋。泪空流。此生谁料，心在天山，身老沧洲。

〖作品简介〗

此词描写了作者一生中最值得怀念的一段岁月，通过今昔对比，反映了一位爱国志士的坎坷经历和不幸遭遇，表达了作者壮志未酬、报国无门的悲愤不平之情。上片开头追忆作者昔日戎马疆场的意气风发，接着写当年宏愿只能在梦中实现的失望；下片抒写敌人尚未消灭而英雄却已迟暮的感叹。全词格调苍凉悲壮，语言明白晓畅，用典自然，不着痕迹，不加雕饰，如叹如诉，有较强的艺术感染力。

〖注 释〗

诉衷情：词牌名。**万里觅封侯**：奔赴万里外的疆场，寻找建功立业的机会。《后汉书·班超传》载：班超少有大志，尝曰，大丈夫应当"立功异域，以取封侯，安能久事笔砚间乎？"**戍**[shù]：守边。**梁州**：《宋史·地理志》："兴元府，梁州汉中郡，山南西道节度。"治所在南郑。陆游著作中，称其参加四川宣抚使幕府所在地，常杂用以上地名。**关河**：关塞，河流。一说指潼关黄河之所在。此处泛指汉中前线险要的地方。**梦断**：梦醒。**尘暗旧貂裘**：貂皮裘上落满灰尘，颜色为之暗淡。这里借用苏秦典故，说自己不受重用，未能施展抱负。据《战国策·秦策》载，苏秦游说秦王："书十上而不行，黑貂之裘敝，黄金百斤尽，资用乏绝，去秦而归。"**胡**：古泛称西北各族为胡，亦指来自彼方之物。南宋词中多指金人。此处指金入侵者。**鬓**：鬓发。**秋**：秋霜，比喻年老鬓白。**天山**：在中国西北部，是汉唐时的边疆。这里代指南宋与金国相持的西北前线。**沧洲**：靠近水的地方，古时常用来泛指隐士居住之地。谢朓《之宣城郡出新林浦向板桥》诗有"既欢怀禄情，复协沧州趣"句。这里是指作者位于镜湖之滨的家乡。

【译 文】

许渊冲 译①

Tune: "Telling of Innermost Feelings" by Lu You

Alone I went a thousand miles long, long ago
　　To serve the army well at the frontier.
The fortress town in dreams I could not go,
　　Dusty and outworn my sable-coat of cavalier.

　　The foe not beaten back,
　　My hair no longer black,
　　My tears have flowed in vain.
Who could have thought that in this life I would remain
　　With a mountain-high aim
　　But an old mortal frame!

① In 1172 the patriotic poet served in the army stationed in Liangzhou (present-day Shaanxi Province) on the northwest frontier, with the high aim of repelling the Jurchen invasion and recovering the lost territory, but his dream was not realized even when he grew old.

3.27 鹧鸪天(陆游)

家住苍烟落照间，丝毫尘事不相关。斟残玉瀣行穿竹，卷罢《黄庭》卧看山。

贪啸傲，任衰残，不妨随处一开颜。元知造物心肠别，老却英雄似等闲！

【作品简介】

此词塑造了作者歌咏自得、旷放而不受拘束的形象，词中虽细写词人隐居之闲适，但其胸中抑郁不平之气仍然流露出来，难以隐藏。

【注 释】

玉瀣[xiè]：美酒。**《黄庭》**：道家经典著作，论养生之道。**啸傲**：放歌长啸，傲然自得。元：通假字，同“原”，本来。

【译 文】

Stephen Owen 译

Tune: "Partridge Weather" (*Zhe-hu tian*) by Lu You

My home is set in blue-gray mists,
    within the waning light;
the world's concerns concern me not
    a whit, nor a hair.
Misty fluids, marble white, poured to the last drop,
    I walk my way through bamboo;
tracts on extending my life rolled away,
    I lie here and look at the hills.

I yearn for carefree independence,
yet accept that my body grows frail—
but it won't stop me from cracking a smile
    no matter where I go.
At last I grasp the Creator's mind,
    So different from mortal man's:
he lets his heroes age away
    with utter unconcern.

3.28 菩萨蛮(辛弃疾)

郁孤台下清江水，中间多少行人泪。西北望长安，可怜无数山。
青山遮不住，毕竟东流去。江晚正愁余，山深闻鹧鸪。

【作品简介】

此词乃作者任江西提点刑狱驻节赣江途经造口时所作，描写作者登郁孤台(今江西省赣州市城区西北部贺兰山顶)远望，“借水怨山”，抒发国家兴亡的感慨。上片由眼前景物引出历史回忆，抒发家国沦亡之创痛和收复无望的悲愤；下片借景生情，抒愁苦与不满之情。全词对朝廷苟安江南的不满和自己一筹莫展的愁闷，却是淡淡叙来，不瘟不火，以极高明的比兴手法，表达了蕴藉深沉的爱国情思。

【注 释】

菩萨蛮：本唐教坊曲，后用为词牌。亦作《菩萨鬘》，又名《子夜歌》、《重叠金》《花溪碧》《晚云烘日》等。另有《菩萨蛮引》《菩萨蛮慢》。《菩萨蛮》也是曲牌名，属北曲正宫，字句格律与词牌前半阕同，用在套曲中。**郁孤台**：今江西省赣州市城区西北部贺兰山顶，又称望阙台，因"隆阜郁然，孤起平地数丈"得名。**清江**：赣江与袁江合流处旧称清江。**长安**：今陕西省西安市，为汉唐故都。此处代指宋都汴京。宋刘敞《九日》："可怜西北望，白日远长安。"**愁余**：使我发愁。《楚辞·九歌·湘夫人》："帝子降兮北渚，目眇眇兮愁予。"**鹧鸪**：鸟名。传说其叫声如云"行不得也哥哥"，啼声凄苦。

【译 文】

(1) 许渊冲 译

Tune: "Buddhist Dancers"
Written on the Wall at Zaokou, Jiangxi

Below the Gloomy Terrace flow two rivers clear,
The tears of refugees were shed when they were here!
I gaze afar on land long lost in the northwest,
Alas! I see but hill on hill and crest on crest.

But blue hills can't stop water flowing,
Eastward the river keeps on going.
At dusk the river grieves me still,
The partridges call in the hill.

(2) 张炳星 译

Recalling the Past and Regretting the Present

Under the Yugu Terrace there flows the QingJiang River.
How many tears have been shed by the refugees into the river!

In the northwest lies the Capital Chang-an.
What a pity!
So many mountains have blocked the view of my native land!

Green mountains can't block the River,
it'll flow to the east, however.
In the evening I stand alone much grieved by the river,
and hear cuckoos cry deep in the mountain, forever.

3.29 丑奴儿(辛弃疾)

少年不识愁滋味，爱上层楼。爱上层楼。为赋新词强说愁。
而今识尽愁滋味，欲说还休。欲说还休。却道天凉好个秋。

【作品简介】

此词通过回顾作者少年时不知愁苦，衬托"而今"深深领略了愁苦的滋味，却又说不出道不出，表现了作者受压抑排挤、报国无门的痛苦以及对南宋统治集团的讽刺和不满。

【注 释】

少年：指年轻的时候。**不识**：不懂，不知道什么是。**层楼**：高楼。**强说愁**：无愁而勉强说愁。**强**：勉强地，硬要。**识尽**：尝够，深深懂得。"尽"字有概括、包含着作者诸多复杂感受的意思，使整篇词作在思想感情上作了一大转折的表达效果。**欲说还休**：想要说还是没有说。**却道天凉好个秋**：却说好一个凉爽的秋天啊。意谓言不由衷地顾左右而言他。

【译 文】

(1) Stephen Owen 译

Tune: "Ugly Slave" (*Chou nu-er*) by Xin Qi-ji

When I was young, I didn't know
how sorrow tastes.
I loved to climb up high in a tower,

I loved to climb up high in a tower,
And writing new songs, I forced myself
to speak of sorrow.

But now I know the taste of sorrow all too well.
I'm ready to speak of it, then stop,
I'm ready to speak of it, then stop,
And say instead, "Cool weather—a nice autumn."

(2) Burton Watson 译

Tune: "Ugly Rogue" by HSIN CH'I-CHI (1140-1207)

When I was young, not knowing the taste of grief,
I loved to climb the storied tower,
loved to climb the storied tower,
and in my new songs I'd make it a point to speak of grief.

But now I know all about the taste of grief.
about to speak of it, I stop;
about to speak of it, I stop
and say instead, "Days so cool—what a lovely autumn!"

(3) Lin Yutang 译

In My Young Days

In my young days,
I had tasted only gladness,
But loved to mount the top floor,
But loved to mount the top floor,
To write a song pretending sadness.

And now I've tasted
Sorrow's flavors, bitter and sour,
And can't find a word,
And can't find a word,

But merely say, "What a golden autumn hour!"

(4) Chu Dagao 译

Now I Know

In my youth I had no idea of what sorrow was,
And loved to go up lofty buildings.
Upon the lofty buildings,
For composing new poems I was forced to talk of sorrow.

Now I know sorrow thoroughly well,
And am loath to talk of it.
Loath to talk of it,
I say instead: "What a chilly autumn day!"

(5) Lin Tongji 译

To the Tune of "Chou Nu Er" (*The Ugly Valet*)

(*Written on the Rocky Wall along the path in Bo Shan*)

When young, I knew not, ah, what Sorrow's taste be;
Fain would I climb the turret—
Fain would I climb the turret,
For new songs' sake, a-prattling loud on Sorrow's ways.

I've gone now through the numberless ways Sorrow be;
I'd tell the tale, but then—
I'd tell the tale, but then
I hail: These are jolly cool, bracing autumn days!

(6) John A. Turner 译

Enlightenment

In youth, ere Grief to me was known

I loved to climb on high, I loved to climb on high:
In many a laboured lay
Grief would I there portray.

But now, with Grief familiar grown,
Slower to speak am I, slower to speak am I.
At most, I pause and say,
"What a fine autumn day!"

(7) Hans H. Frankel 译

Tune Pattern: "The Ugly Slave"

When I was young I did not know the taste of grief.
I loved to climb tall buildings,
I loved to climb tall buildings,
Composing original poems that artificially spoke of grief.

Now I fully know the taste of grief.
I want to speak of it but don't,
I want to speak of it but don't,
I just say, "What a nice cool autumn day!"

(8) Dr. D. C. Lau 译

To the Tune of "Ch'ou Nu Erh"

In youth, not knowing what grief was about,
I loved to seek a melancholy spot,
I loved to seek a melancholy spot,
And for a new song I would pretend to speak of grief.

And now, knowing what grief is all about,
On the point of speaking, I hold back,
On the point of speaking, I hold back,
And say, instead, what a fine autumn, so very cool.

(9) Arthur Cooper 译

To the Tune of "Ch'ou Nu Erh"

When I was green and hadn't seen
    The bitterness of sorrows,
    And upper floors
    I loved to gain:
    And upper floors
    I loved to gain,
To put in odes, tres a la mode,
    My sorrows, I sought 'em!

Now all there's been, so that I've seen
    The bitterness of sorrows,
    I long to tell,
    But I refrain:
    I long to tell,
    But I refrain,
And only say: "Cooler today,
    Quite a nip of Autumn!"

(10) Siu-kit Wong 译

To the Tune of "Ch'ou Nu-Er"

In youth I knew not the taste of sorrow;
I loved going up the pavilion,
I loved going up the pavilion,
To make a new poem I made up sorrow.

Now that the taste of sorrow I have known,
I would rather become taciturn,
I would rather become taciturn,
Or say, autumn, rather cool it has grown.

(11) John Scott 译

Youth Does Not Know How Sorrow Tastes

Youth does not know how sorrow
tastes
But loves ‘to haunt autumnal glades
to haunt autumnal glades’
‘And pen new verses’
forcing out the melancholy.

But now I know all right how sorrow
tastes
And when about to mention it
I just say Steady
Steady that’s all I say
Or maybe Nice weather,
Cool autumn.

(12) Weng Xianliang 译

I’d Rather Not Tell

When I was young, to sorrow yet a stranger, I loved to go up the tallest towers, the tallest towers, to compose vapid verses simulating sorrow.

Now that I am to sorrow fallen prey, what ails me I’d rather not tell, rather not tell, only saying: It’s nice and cool and the autumn tints are mellow.

(13) Xu Zhongjie 译

“Caisangzi”

While young, I didn’t taste of sadness or despair.
That I must climb aloft is what I did care.
I strained too much after sorrow as the theme,
For a young poet to work out in his scheme.

Now, I have had my bitter cup to the brim.
The sorrow that I have tasted of is grim.
I was about to harp on gloom as a rule.
I veer and say, "Autumn has been fine and cool."

(14) 许渊冲 译

Tune: "Song of Picking Mulberries"
Written on My Way to Boshan

While young, I knew no grief I could not bear;
　　I'd like to go upstairs.
　　I'd like to go upstairs
To write new verses with a false despair.

I know what grief is now that I am old;
　　I would not have it told.
　　I would not have it told,
But only say I'm glad that autumn's cold.

(15) Robert Kotewall and Norman L. Smith 译

To "The Ugly Slave" by Hsin Ch'i-chi

In youth, not knowing the taste of sorrow,
I love to ascend the storeyed towers,
I love to ascend the storeyed towers,
And, to fashion new verses, I made myself speak of
　　sorrow.

But now, having known all the taste of sorrow,
I should speak of it but refrain,
I should speak of it but refrain,
Instead, I say: 'A cool day, a fine Autumn'.

3.30 青玉案(辛弃疾)

东风夜放花千树，更吹落、星如雨。宝马雕车香满路。凤箫声动，玉壶光转，一夜鱼龙舞。

蛾儿雪柳黄金缕，笑语盈盈暗香去。众里寻他千百度。蓦然回首，那人却在，灯火阑珊处。

作品简介

此词描绘了元宵佳节通宵灯火的热闹场景，上片写元夕之夜灯火辉煌、游人如云的热闹场面，下片写不慕荣华，甘守寂寞的一位美人形象。该美人形象实为作者所寄托的理想人格之化身。

注 释

花千树：花灯之多如千树开花。**星如雨**：指焰火纷纷，乱落如雨。**星**：指焰火。形容满天的烟花。**宝马雕车**：豪华的马车。**凤箫**：箫的名称。**玉壶**：比喻明月，故继以“光转”二字，亦或指灯。**鱼龙舞**：指舞动鱼形、龙形的彩灯。(即舞鱼舞龙。是元宵节的表演节目。)宋夏竦《奉和御制上元观灯》：“鱼龙漫衍六街呈，金锁通宵启玉京。”**蛾儿、雪柳、黄金缕**：皆指古代妇女元宵节时头上佩戴的各种装饰品。这里指盛装的妇女。**盈盈**：声音轻盈悦耳，亦指仪态娇美的样子。**暗香**：本指花香，此指女性们身上散发出来的香气。**他**：泛指，当时就包括了“她”。**千百度**：千百遍。**蓦然**：突然，猛然。**阑珊**：零落稀疏的样子。

译 文

(1) 许渊冲 译

Tune: “Green Jade Cup”
Lantern Festival by Xin Qi-ji

One night's east wind adorns a thousand trees with flowers
　　And blows down stars in showers.
Fine steeds and carved cabs spread fragrance en route,
　　Music vibrates from the flute,
　　The moon sheds its full light
While fish and dragon lanterns dance all night.

In gold-thread dress, with moth or willow ornaments,
Giggling, they melt into the throng with trails of scents.
　　But in the crowd once and again
　　I look for her in vain.

When all at once I turn my head,
I find her there where lantern light is dimly shed.

(2) 龚景浩 译

"Qing Yu An (Song)"

Xin Qi Ji

At night the east wind blew open a thousand flowering trees.
It blew down stars,
Falling like rain.①
Sleek horses and carved coaches lined the roads,
Sounds of the melodious vertical flute wafted in the air.
The bright orb shed its light, revolving;
A night of fish and dragons dancing.

Wearing exquisite ornaments and gold-laced willow twigs,
The ladies' giggles and whispers
Left a trail of dark fragrance.
Looking for that man in the crowds a thousand times—
Turning suddenly,
She saw the man standing where the lights were low.

① Display of fireworks on a festive night.

(3) 张炳星 译

The Lantern Festival

During the night the east wind blew open thousands of silver flowers,
and blew down fireworks like stars and raindrops on the floor.
Painted carriages and precious horses bustled to and fro,
while fragrance filled the road.
Sweet music was played high,
and a bright moon hang in the sky.
Fish-like and dragon-like lanterns danced merrily the whole night.

Pretty women wore ornaments on their heads of various kinds.
They chatted cheerfully and laughed heartily,

leaving secret fragrance behind.
In the crowd for a thousand times,
I failed to look for my love.
Suddenly she turned her head and appeared in the corner,
Where lights were sparse and somber.

3.31 清平乐(辛弃疾)

柳边飞鞚，露湿征衣重。宿鹭窥沙孤影动，应有鱼虾入梦。
一川明月疏星，浣纱人影娉婷。笑背行人归去，门前稚子啼声。

〖作品简介〗

此词描写了作者策马沿途的见闻：驱马从柳树旁边疾驰而过，柳枝上的露水拂落在行人身上，衣衫就沾湿变重了；行经河滩旁边时，看到一只白鹭栖宿在沙滩上，不时地眯着眼睛向沙面窥视，它映在沙上的身影也轻轻摇晃，准是在梦中见到鱼虾了吧！路经溪流附近的村庄时夜深人静，溪山沐浴在疏星明月的清光中，年轻的妇女在月光下于溪边浣纱，美丽轻盈的身影映在水中和沙上。宁静的村舍门前忽然响起孩子的哭声，正在溪边浣纱的母亲立即起身往家赶，路上遇见陌生的行人，只羞怯地低头一笑，随即背转身匆匆离去。全篇意境清新、语言淡朴，虽是写景，无一句抒情，却又处处融情于景中，寄意言外。

〖注 释〗

鞚[kòng]：马勒，“纵鞍则行，揽鞚则止”。**宿鹭**[sù lù]：是指栖息的鹭。**娉婷**[pīng tíng]：指女子姿态曼妙，亦借指美人。辛延年《羽林郎》：“不意金吾子，娉婷过我庐”，唐朝长孙无忌的杂言体歌行《新曲》：“婉约娉婷工语笑。”**稚子**[zhì zǐ]：幼子，小孩。

〖译 文〗

Stephen Owen 译

Tune: “Clear and Even Music” (*Qing-ping yue*)
An Account on the Censer Mountain Road by Xin Qi-ji

A harness goes flying beside the willows,
the weight of a travel coat soaked with dew.

A sleeping egret peers at the sand
　　its lonely reflection stirs;
and I am sure that its dreams
　　are filled with fish and shrimp.

Bright moonlight and the scattered stars
　　lie all along the stream,
the gorgeous outline of a woman
　　washing filmy gauze.
She laughs and turns from the traveler,
　　goes off back to her home
at the sound of a child crying in front of her gate.

3.32 清平乐(辛弃疾)

茅檐低小，溪上青青草。醉里吴音相媚好，白发谁家翁媪？
大儿锄豆溪东，中儿正织鸡笼。最喜小儿无赖，溪头卧剥莲蓬。

【作品简介】

此词描写农村清新秀丽和朴素雅静的环境，通过对翁媪及其三子形象的刻画，表现出词人对农村和平及宁静生活的喜爱。

【注　释】

茅檐：茅屋的屋檐。**吴音**：作者当时住在江西东部的上饶，这一带古时是吴国的领土，所以称这一带的方言为吴音，即吴地的方言。**相媚好**：这里指互相逗趣、取乐。**翁媪**：老翁，老太。**锄豆**：在豆地里锄草。**溪东**：小溪的东面。**织**：编织，文中指编织鸡笼。**卧剥**：趴着剥(莲蓬)。**莲蓬**：莲花开过后的花托，倒圆锥形，里面有莲子。

【译　文】

(1) 许渊冲 译[①]

Tune: "Pure Serene Music"
Rural Life by Xin Qi-ji

The thatched roof is slanting low,

Beside the brook green grasses grow.
Who talks with drunken Southern voice so sweet?
A white-haired man and wife in their retreat.

East of the brook their eldest son is hoeing weeds;
Their second son now makes a cage for hens he feeds.
I like their youngest son who, having nothing done,
Lies by the brook podding lotus seeds one by one.

① This lyric depicts a happy family of Southern villagers.

(2) Jiaosheng Wang 译

Tune: "Pure Serene Music"
Rural Life

Low hang the eaves of the thatched hut,
Green, green grows the grass beside the brook.
To whose family belongs that tipsy white-haired couple,
Chatting and merry-making in the dulcet accents of the south?

Their eldest son is hoeing the bean-field east of the brook,
The second is busy weaving a hen-coop;
But they one they think most lovable is the youngest, that scamp of a boy:
Lo! he is sprawled on the bank peeling lotus pods!

(3) 龚景浩 译

"Qing Ping Yue (Song)"
Xin Qi Ji

The straw hut has low eaves,
The banks of the small creek, grassy.
In their drunkenness
The Wu accents① sound exceedingly charming.
Who are the white-haired couple?

My eldest son is hoeing beans east of the creek;
My middle son is weaving chicken coops;
But I like my youngest son better, the rascal:
He is loitering by the creek
Gathering lotus seeds.

① *Wu* accents—A regional dialect spoken in parts of Jiangsu and Zhejiang provinces.

3.33 西江月(辛弃疾)

明月别枝惊鹊，清风半夜鸣蝉。稻花香里说丰年，听取蛙声一片。
七八个星天外，两三点雨山前。旧时茅店社林边，路转溪头忽见。

〖作品简介〗

此词描写田园风光，全词散发着浓郁的生活气息，表现了词人丰收之年的喜悦和对乡村生活的热爱之情。

〖注 释〗

别枝惊鹊：惊动喜鹊飞离树枝。**鸣蝉**：蝉叫声。**旧时**：往日。**茅店**：茅草盖的乡村客店。**社林**：土地庙附近的树林。**社**：土地神庙。古时，村有社树，为祀神处，故曰社林。**见**：通假字"见"通"现"，意为"发现，出现，显现"。

〖译 文〗

(1) 许渊冲译

Tune: "The Moon over the West River"

A Summer Night on My Way Home from the Yellow Sand Ridge by Xin Qi-ji

Startled by magpies leaving the branch in moonlight;
I hear cicadas shrill in the breeze at midnight.
The ricefields sweet smell promises a harvest great,

I listen to the frogs' croak when the night grows late.

Beyond the clouds seven or eight stars twinkle;
Before the hills two or three raindrops sprinkle.
There is an inn beside the Village Temple. Look!
The winding path leads to the hut beside the brook.

① The Yellow Sand Ridge was situated to the west of Shangrao, Jiangxi, where the poet lived when he could not fulfill his ambition to fight against the Jurchen aggressors. This lyric depicts a nocturnal journey of the poet who was startled and surprised to see magpies leaving the branch in moonlight and glad to smell the sweet smell of the ricefields and to hear the frogs croak which announced a good harvest, and then again surprised by the coming rain and glad to find an inn by the side of the brook.

(2) 龚景浩 译

"Xi Jiang Yue (Song)"
Xin Qi Ji

A bright moon shining on yonder bough
Alarmed the magpie;
A soft wind in the deep of the night
Made the cicadas sing.
Amid the fragrance of young rice shoot
There is talk of a bumper year.
I heard frogs croaking, here, there, everywhere.

Seven, eight stars shining in yonder sky;
A few drops of rain this side of the hill.
At the old straw-hut general store,
By the side of the communal woods,
The road turns, and suddenly the creek bridge comes into view.

3. 34　西江月(辛弃疾)

醉里且贪欢笑,
要愁那得工夫。

近来始觉古人书，
信著全无是处。

昨夜松边醉倒，
问松"我醉何如"。
只疑松动要来扶，
以手推松曰"去"。

『作品简介』

此词仅从字面来看好像是抒写词人喝酒贪笑的悠闲心情，但字里行间却透露出其不满现实的思想感情和倔强的生活态度。其上片前两句写饮酒，后两句写读书。酒可消愁，他生动地说是"要愁那得工夫"；书可识理，他说对于古人书"信著全无是处"。折射出词人无法排解的内心苦闷和忧愁。下片写词人醉酒的神态：有对话，有动作，有神情，又有性格的刻画，写出了词人惟妙惟肖的醉态，也写出了其倔强的性格。全词语言明白如话，文字生动活泼，表现手法新颖奇崛，体现了作者晚年清丽淡雅的词风。

『注　释』

"近来始觉古人书，信著全无是处"两句：不要相信古书中的一些话，现在是不可能实行的。此处乃作者翻用《孟子·尽心下》中"尽信书，则不如无书"。之词。原文的本意是说古书上的话难免有与事实不符的地方，未可全信，而作者此处翻用话中却含有另一层意思：古书上尽管有许多"至理名言"，现在却行不通，因此信它不如不信。"著"通"着"。**"以手推松曰'去'"**句：《汉书·二疏传》有疏广"以手推常曰：'去'!"的句子。此处乃词人采用散文句法来写，用经史典故入词，可谓手法新颖。

『译　文』

(1) Wai-lim Yip 译

"MOON OF THE WESTERN RIVER"

While drunk, I seek merriment.
To get sad—where is the time?
Recently, about ancient books I feel
To believe them—none of any use.

Last night I got drunk beside a pine.
I asked it: how is my drunken way?
Suspecting the pine would rise to hold me up,
I pushed it and said: GO!

(2) Stephen Owen 译

Tune: "West River Moon" (*Xi jiang yue*)
Expressing What Was on My Mind

I was drunk and craved some pleasure and fun—
no time for sorrow even had I wished.
Just lately I've grasped that in books of the past
there are really some points that are not at all true.

Last night I fell over drunk by a pine,
and asked that pine, "Just how drunk am I?"
It seemed the pine moved to give me a hand,
I shoved the pine and said to it, "Scram!"

(3) 许渊冲 译

Tune: "The Moon over the West River"
Written at Random by Xin Qi-ji

Drunken, I'll laugh my fill,
    Having no time to be grieved.
Books of the ancients may say what they will,
    They cannot be wholly believed.

Drunken last night beneath a pine-tree,
    I asked it if it like me so drunk.
Afraid it would bend to try to raise me,
    "Be off!" I said and pushed back its trunk.

3.35 沁园春(辛弃疾)

杯汝来前！老子今朝，点检形骸。甚长年抱渴，咽如焦釜；于今喜睡，气似奔雷。汝说“刘伶，古今达者，醉后何妨死便埋”。浑如此，叹汝于知己，真少恩哉！

更凭歌舞为媒。算合作人间鸩毒猜。况怨无小大，生于所爱；物无美恶，过则为灾。与汝成言，勿留亟退，吾力犹能肆汝杯。杯再拜，道“麾之即去，招则须来”。

『作品简介』

此词写于庆元二年(1196年)作者闲居瓢泉时。词作以戒酒为题，通过“我”与杯的问答，委婉地述说了作者自己长期壮志不展，积愤难平，故常借酒发泄，以至于拖垮了身体，而自己戒酒，实出于不得已这样一种复杂的心情，进而风趣而又委婉地表达了作者对南宋政权的失望与自己心中的苦闷。

『注　释』

汝：你，此指酒杯。**点检形骸**：检查身体。**甚**：说什么。**抱渴**：得了酒渴病，口渴即想饮酒。**焦釜**：烧煳的锅。**气似奔雷**：鼾声如雷。**“汝说‘刘伶’”句**：《晋书·刘伶传》载，刘伶纵酒放荡，经常乘一辆车，带一壶酒，令人带着锄头跟随，并说“死便掘地以埋”。**浑如此**：竟然如此。**为媒**：作为媒引，诱人饮酒。**算合作**：算起来应该看作。**鸩毒**：用鸩鸟羽毛制成的剧毒，溶入酒中，饮之立死。古时常以鸩酒杀人。**成言**：说定，约定。《离骚》：“初既与余成言兮，后悔遁而有他。”**亟**：快。**肆**：原指处死后陈尸示众。《论语·宪问》：“夫子固有惑志于公伯寮，吾力犹能肆诸于朝。”这里指打碎酒杯。**再拜**：古代一种隆重的礼节，先后拜两次。

『译　文』

James Robert Hightower 译

Tune：“Spring in the Ch’in Garden”

（About to Swear off Drinking, He Warns the Wine Cup to Go Away）by Hsin Ch’i-chi

Cup, you come here!
Your old man has been
Looking himself over today.
For years on end he’s had a thirst

With a throat like a scorched pot.
But now he's ready to go to sleep and snore like thunder.
You say, "Liu Ling[①]
Was the great philosopher of all time.
Once drunk, what did it matter if he died and was buried on the spot."
A shame you're so ruthless
With your very best friend.

Worse, you're in leaguer with song and dance.
I reckon you are man's worst poison.
What's more, the thing we hate, a lot or a little,
Is what we once loved.
Nothing itself is good or bad,
It's excess makes the trouble.
Here's my ultimatum:
Don't stay, go away fast.
I have the strength to dispose of you.
The cup bowed and said,
"If you say so, I'll leave;
I'll come again when you call me."

① Liu Ling (ca. 221-300) was one of the seven bohemian sages of the Bamboo Grove. A famous toper and author of "Hymn to the Virtue of Wine", Liu declared that he would not mind being buried so long as he died drunk. His abstinence-advocating wife once compelled him to renounce wine before the god, but he tricked her by persuading her to prepare an offering of meat and wine for the celestial spirits and then guzzling down the alcoholic beverage by himself.

3.36 贺新郎（辛弃疾）

（邑中园亭，仆皆为赋此词。一日，独坐停云，水声山色，竞来相娱。意溪山欲援例者，遂作数语，庶几仿佛渊明思亲友之意云。）

甚矣吾衰矣。怅平生、交游零落，只今馀几！白发空垂三千丈，一笑人间万事。问何物、能令公喜？我见青山多妩媚，料青山见我应如是。情与貌，略相似。

一尊搔首东窗里。想渊明《停云》诗就，此时风味。江左沉酣求名者，岂识浊醪妙理。回首叫、云飞风起。不恨古人吾不见，恨古人不见吾狂耳。知我者，二三子。

〖作品简介〗

此词的全名为《贺新郎 · 甚矣吾衰矣》，作于宋宁宗庆元四年(1198年)左右。此时作者被免官闲居已经四年。全词在一个个典故的层叠中抒发了词人昂扬激越的豪放情怀，表达了罢职闲居时的寂寞与苦闷的心情。

〖注 释〗

贺新郎：后人创调，又名《金缕曲》《乳燕飞》《貂裘换酒》。传作以《东坡乐府》所收为最早，唯句读平仄，与诸家颇多不合。因以《稼轩长短句》为准。一百一十六字，前后片各六仄韵。大抵用入声部韵者较激壮，用上、去声部韵者较凄郁，贵能各适物宜耳。**邑**：指铅山县。辛弃疾在江西铅山期思渡建有别墅，带湖居所失火后举家迁之。**仆**：自称。**停云**：停云堂，在瓢泉别墅。**甚矣吾衰矣**：源于《论语 · 述而》之句："甚矣吾衰也！久矣吾不复梦见周公。"这是孔丘慨叹自己"道不行"的话("梦见周公，欲行其道")。作者借此感叹自己的壮志难酬。**白发空垂三千丈，一笑人间万事**：这两句出典于李白的《秋浦歌》："白发三千丈，缘愁似个长。"**问何物、能令公喜**：源于《世说新语 · 宠礼篇》记郗超、王恂"能令公(指晋大司马桓温)喜"等典故。意为"还有什么东西能让我感到快乐"。**妩媚**：潇洒多姿。**搔首东窗**：借指陶潜《停云》诗就，自得之意。**江左**：原指江苏南部一带，此指南朝之东晋。**浊醪**(láo)：浊酒。**云飞风起**：化用刘邦《大风歌》之句"大风起兮云飞扬"。**不恨古人吾不见，恨古人不见吾狂耳**：引《南史 · 张融传》的典故："不恨我不见古人，所恨古人又不见我。"**知我者，二三子**：引《论语》的典故："二三子以我为隐乎。"

〖译 文〗

Zong-qi Cai 译

To the Tune of "Congratulating the Bridegroom"

(I have composed songs to the tune of "Hexinlang" for all the gardens and pavilions in my district. One day when I was sitting by myself at the Halting Cloud Pavilion, the gurgling streams and green mountains vied with one another to please me. Presuming that they also wanted me to write something for them, I put down a few lines. They might bear some resemblance to Tao Yuanming's poem "Halting Clouds," in which he expresses his longing for his friends.)

Too much I have decayed!

Alas, all my life I've seen friends and companions fade away,
And now how many of them are left?
With gray hair hanging in vain three thousand *zhang* long,
I laugh away all worldly things.
Is there anything left, you ask, that might cheer me up?
I see in green mountains such alluring charm;
I expect that they see the same in me,
For in heart and in appearance
We are a bit similar.

Goblet in hand, scratching my head by the east window,
I presume that Tao Yuanming, having finished his poem "Halting Clouds,"
Was in the same mood now I am.
Those on the south side of the Yangtze who got drunk only to seek fame,
How could they know the magic of the turbid wine?
Looking back, I conjure a gust of wind and send clouds flying.
I regret not that I can't meet the ancients.
But that the ancients had no chance to see my wildness.
The number of people who understand me
Is no more than two or three.

3.37 水调歌头(陈亮)

不见南师久,漫说北群空。当场只手,毕竟还我万夫雄。自笑堂堂汉使,得似洋洋河水,依旧只流东?且复穹庐拜,会向藁街逢!

尧之都,舜之壤,禹之封。于中应有,一个半个耻臣戎!万里腥膻如许,千古英灵安在,磅礴几时通?胡运何须问,赫日自当中!

〖作品简介〗

此词的全称是《水调歌头·送章德茂大卿使虏》。淳熙十二年(1185年)十二月,宋孝宗命章森(字德茂)以大理少卿试户部尚书衔为贺万春节(金世宗完颜雍生辰)正使,陈亮作此词为章德茂送行。对这种耻辱性的事件,一般很难写出振奋人心的作品,但陈亮由于有饱满的政治热情和对诗词创作的独特见解,敏感地从消极的事件中发现有积极意义的因素,开掘词意,深化主题,使作品显得气势磅礴。全词采用通篇议论的写法,言辞慷慨,充满激情,表达了不甘屈辱的正气与誓雪国耻的豪情。

〖注　释〗

水调歌头：词牌名，又名《元会曲》《台城游》《凯歌》《江南好》《花犯念奴》等。双调九十五字，平韵(宋代也有用仄声韵和平仄混用的)。相传隋炀帝开汴河自制《水调歌》，唐人演为大曲，“歌头”就是大曲中的开头部分。**北群空**：语出韩愈《送温处士赴河阳军序》“伯乐一过冀北之野而马群遂空”，指没有良马，借喻没有良才。**当场只手**：当场大事，只手可了。**毕竟还我万夫雄**：毕竟我还是万夫之雄。**我**：指章德茂。**自笑堂堂汉使，得似洋洋河水，依旧只流东**：我们汉使哪肯年年去朝见金廷。**得似**：哪得能像。**且复穹庐拜，会像藁街逢**：且去再拜你一拜，将来必将把你抓到我们的国家来。**穹庐**：北方少数民族居住的圆顶毡房，这里借指金廷。**藁街**：汉朝长安城南门内给少数民族居住的地方。汉将陈汤曾斩匈奴郅支单于首悬之藁街。《汉书 · 陈汤传》曾载陈汤斩郅支单于后奏请“悬头藁街蛮夷邸间，以示万里明犯强汉者，虽远必诛”。**尧之都，舜之壤，禹之封**：那本就是我汉族所有的国土，尧、舜、禹那些先祖都曾经生活在那片土地。**都**：定都。**壤**：土地。**封**：疆界。**于中应有，一个半个耻臣戎**：那里总有几个有骨气，以向异族俯首称臣为耻的！**耻臣戎**：指以投降敌人为耻辱的爱国志士。**戎**：指戎狄，这里就是指金人。**腥膻**：代指金人。因金人膻肉酪浆，以充饥渴。**如许**：如此的意思。**千古英灵安在，磅礴几时通**：千古以来，英雄们所发挥的浩然正气，几时才有人能和他们的精神相通呢？**磅礴**：这里指的是浩然的气势。**胡运**：金国的命运。**赫日自当中**：宋王朝的国运如赤日之在中天，前途光明。**赫**：光明的样子。

〖译　文〗

许渊冲 译

Tune：“Prelude to Water Melody”
Farewell to Zhang De-mao,
Envoy to Jurchen Aggressors by Chen Liang[1]

Not seeing Southern troops for long,
　　Don't say the Northern steeds can't run.
　　Single-handed, at once the thing is done,
After all, we are heroes millions strong.
　　His Majesty's Envoy—what fun! —
Should eastwards go like overbrimming River
　　Which east wards flows forever.

We bend to the Jurchen tents now,
Another day to us they'll bow.

In the capital of one emperor
And the land of another great, long
Empire built by our ancestor,
Is there none who thinks it wrong
To submit to the foe
Whose stink of mutton spreads for miles and miles?
Where's the spirit of heroes who died long ago?
When will our army beat the Jurchen ranks and files?
Why ask about the enemy's fate?
The sun will surely radiate.

① Chen Liang(1143-1194) was a patriotic poet and a friend of Xin Qi-ji's. Zhang De-mao was His Majesty's Envoy sent single-handed to bow to the Jurchen chieftain who was accustomed to mutton-eating. The Northern steeds refer to those of the Southern troops and the sun to the Song Empire.

3.38 蝶恋花(朱淑真)

楼外垂杨千万缕。欲系青春，少住春还去。犹自风前飘柳絮。随春且看归何处。

绿满山川闻杜宇。便做无情，莫也愁人苦。把酒送春春不语。黄昏却下潇潇雨。

〖作品简介〗

这是一首惜春词，词人通过丰富的想象力和贴切的拟人手法，将暮春景色表现得委婉多姿、细腻动人。

〖注　释〗

犹自：仍然。**“绿满”句**：在漫山遍野茂密的丛林中听见了杜鹃的叫声。**“莫也”句**：(鸟儿)莫非也因为人间的愁苦而忧愁吗？**苦**：又作“意”。**潇潇雨**：暴雨，急雨。潇潇是雨声。

【译 文】

龚景浩 译

"Die Lian Hua(Song)"

Zhu Shu Zhen

Outside the lodge the weeping willow twigs hang numerous,
To tie down tender spring.
But spring, briefly held, goes on its way.
The catkins float around on the wind
To follow in spring's footsteps to see where it may stay.

Green fills up the streams and hills
And one hears the cuckoo bird.
Even if unfeeling,
Is not one tormented by the sadness?
I hold up my wine cup to see off spring;
Spring nevertheless has no word for me.
By dusk time a silent rain is falling.

3.39 清平乐(朱淑真)

恼烟撩露。留我须臾住。
携手藕花湖上路。一霎黄梅细雨。
娇痴不怕人猜。随群暂遣愁怀。
最是分携时候，归来懒傍妆台。

【作品简介】

此词描写天真少女与恋人相会的喜悦和离别的惆怅。上片点明留住须臾，故当时携手情景，藕花细雨历历在目；下片追写依恋情态，表现出对爱情的大胆追求。歇拍二句，叙分别时难言的情景，只用“最是”两字，蕴涵无限眷恋之情，意为“归来后哪得不怅然若失”。词中点缀夏日风光，使形象更为饱满。

〖注　释〗

恼烟撩露：恼人的梅雨撩烟拨露。**留我须臾住**：似留人小住。**藕花**：即荷花。

〖译　文〗

许渊冲 译

Tune：“Pure Serene Music”
A Summer Day on the Lake by Zhu Shu-zhen

Annoying mist and enticing dew retain me for a while with puzzling view. Hand in hand, we stroll by the Lake of Lotus Flower；a sudden rain drizzles into a shower.

Fond to be silly, I care not for others, never. Undoffed, I lie down with my breast against his chest. What can I do when comes the time to sever? Indolent when back, by my dresser I won’t rest.

3. 40　玉楼春(刘克庄)

年年跃马长安市，客舍似家家似寄。青钱换酒日无何，红烛呼卢宵不寐。
易挑锦妇机中字；难得玉人心下事。男儿西北有神州，莫滴水西桥畔泪。

〖作品简介〗

此词乃一首规劝之作，题为“戏林推”，其口吻幽默、诙谐，但戏笔中寓托庄重之意，在委婉批评中进行劝勉，“戏”而厚重。末二句感慨深沉，惊顽起懦。“男儿西北有神州”，这句话是全词中心思想所在。作者慨然指出，大丈夫生当国家难之秋，应以收复中原为己任。全词章法亦甚精巧，上片写人，下片致意，既各有所重，又相得益彰。

〖注　释〗

玉楼春：词牌名。词谱谓五代后蜀顾敻词起句有“月照玉楼春漏促”“柳映玉楼春欲晚”句；欧阳炯起句有“日照玉楼花似锦”“春早玉楼烟雨夜”句，因取以调名(或加字令)。亦称《木兰花》《春晓曲》《西湖曲》《惜春容》《归朝欢令》《呈纤手》《归风便》《东邻妙》《梦乡亲》《续渔歌》等。双调五十六字，前后阕格式相同，各三仄韵，一韵到底。**长安**：借指南宋都城临安。**寄**：客居。此句说客居的日子多于家居的日子。**青钱**：古铜钱成色不同，分青钱、黄钱两种。**无何**：不过问其他的事情。**红烛呼卢**：晚上点烛赌博。**呼卢**：古时一种赌博，又叫樗蒲，削木为子，共五个，一子两面，一面涂黑，画牛犊，一面涂白，画雉。五子都黑，叫卢，得头彩。掷子时，高声大喊，希望得到全黑，所以叫呼卢。李白《少年行》："听卢百万终不惜，报仇千里如咫尺。"**锦妇机中字**：织锦中的文字。化用前秦窦滔妻苏惠织锦为回文诗以寄其夫的典故。晋窦滔妻苏惠字若兰，善属文。滔仕前秦符坚为秦州刺史，被徙流沙。苏氏在家织锦为回文璇玑图诗，用以赠滔。诗长八百四十字，可以宛转循环以读，词甚凄惋。玉人：美人，这里指妓女。这句说妓女的心事是不易捉摸的。**水西桥**：刘辰翁《须溪集·习溪桥记》载"闽水之西"(在福建建瓯县，为当时名桥之一，又《丹徒县志·关津》载："水西桥在水西门。"此处泛指妓女所居之处。

【译 文】

许渊冲 译

Tune: "Spring in Jade Pavilion"
Written in Jest for a Friend by Liu Ke-zhuang

You gallop in the capital year after year,
More than at home in brothels you appear.
You spend your coins on wine, washing your day;
By candlelight you gamble all the night away.

Why should you abandon your wife faithful to you?
Don't you know a fair mistress's heart won't be true?
A gallant man should not forget lost northwest lands.
Do not shed tears where your mistress's mansion stands!

3.41 卜算子(刘克庄)

片片蝶衣轻，点点猩红小。道是天公不惜花，百种千般巧。
朝见树头繁，暮见枝头少。道是天公果惜花，雨洗风吹了。

【作品简介】

此词用比兴手法，委婉含蓄地表达了词人才不见用的凄楚情怀。上片先写花的可爱，下片写花被"雨洗风吹了"的惋惜之情。

【注 释】

“片片蝶衣轻，点点猩红小”句：片片花瓣儿宛如蝴蝶轻盈的翅膀；点点花朵儿猩红如染，那么鲜艳娇美。**天公**：自然界的主宰。

【译 文】

Robert Kotewall and Norman L. Smith 译

To “The Fortune-teller”

Every petal is light as the butterfly's raiment;
Every speck is blood-red and tiny.
If you say that God cares not for the flowers,
Consider the hundred kinds and the thousand varieties,
  skillfully fashioned.

At morn you see the tree-tops luxuriant,
At eve you see the branch-tops denuded.
If you say that God, in truth, cares for the flowers,
Consider the rain's drenching, and the wind's blast.

3.42 风入松(吴文英)

听风听雨过清明，愁草瘗花铭。楼前绿暗分携路，一丝柳，一寸柔情。料峭春寒中酒，交加晓梦啼莺。

西园日日扫林亭，依旧赏新晴。黄蜂频扑秋千索，有当时、纤手香凝。惆怅双鸳不到，幽阶一夜苔生。

【作品简介】

此词表现了作者的暮春怀人之情，上片写伤春怀人的愁思，下片写伤春怀人的痴想。全词风格质朴淡雅，不事雕琢、不用典故，不论写景写情、写现实写回忆，都委婉细腻、情真意切。

【注 释】

风入松：词牌名。词调名出自古琴曲《风入松》(相传为晋代嵇康所作)。**愁草**：没有心情写。**草**：起草，拟写。**瘗**[yì]：埋葬。**铭**：文体的一种。庾信有《瘗花铭》。古代常把铭文刻在墓碑或者器物上，内容多为歌功颂德，表示哀悼，申述鉴戒。**绿暗**：形容绿柳成荫。**分携**：分手，分别。**料峭**：形容春天的寒冷。**中**[zhòng]**酒**：醉酒。"中酒"见《史记·樊哙传》，亦见《汉书》，意酒酣也。中，读仄声也。又如杜牧："残春杜陵客，中酒落花前。"(《睦州四韵》)**交加**：形容杂乱。**黄蜂**：这里指蜜蜂。**凝**：凝聚。**双鸳**：成对的鸳鸯，是指一双绣有鸳鸯的女鞋，这里兼指女子本人。

【译 文】

(1) Stephen Owen 译

Tune: "Wind Enters Pines" (*Feng ru song*) by Wu Wen-ying (ca. 1200-1260)

I listened to wind and listened to rain
    passing the Festival of Light,
too sad to draft a eulogy
    for funerals of flowers.
The green before my hall darkens
    the path where clasped hands parted,
every inch of those willow fronds
    is an inch of tender passion.
Then shivering at spring's chill,
    the wine hits me,
and warbling through my morning dream,
    orioles sing.

Day after day in the western park I sweep
    the pavilion in the grove
and enjoy as ever the newly cleared skies.
Orange bees often go batting against
    the rope of the swing

where is printed the scent of her tiny hand
from days gone by.
Despair that those paired duck slippers do not come,
and moss on the secret stairs grows all night long.

(2) 许渊冲 译

Tune: "Wind Through Pines" by Wu Wen-ying

Hearing the wind and rain while mourning for the dead,
Sadly I draft an elegy on flowers.
We parted on the dark-green road before these bowers,
Where willow branches hang like thread,
Each inch revealing
Our tender feeling.
I drown my grief in wine in chilly spring,
Drowsy, I wake again when orioles sing.

In Garden West I sweep the pathway
From day to day,
Enjoying the fine view
Still without you.
On the ropes of the swing the wasps often alight
For fragrance spread by fingers fair.
I'm grieved not to see your foot-traces: all night
The mossy steps are left untrodden there.

3.43 夜合花(吴文英)

柳暝河桥，莺晴台苑，短策频惹春香。当时夜泊，温柔便入深乡。词韵窄，酒杯长。翦蜡花、壶箭催忙。共追游处，凌波翠陌，连棹横塘。

十年一梦凄凉。似西湖燕去，吴馆巢荒。重来万感，依前唤酒银罂。溪雨急，岸花狂。趁残鸦、飞过苍茫。故人楼上，凭谁指与，芳草斜阳。

【作品简介】

此词是一首怀人之作。据杨铁夫《吴梦窗词笺释》记载，作者曾在苏州与一歌姬同居，此词为姬去后，作者重来苏州觅去不得，回杭州时所作。词的上阕写过去在苏州时的欢乐；下阕写重来苏州不见故人之凄凉。词韵响亮、飞扬，表现了作者急狂、苍茫的失落无依之情。

【注 释】

夜合花：词牌名，调见南宋福建书肆刻本《琴趣外篇》。夜合花，合欢树也，唐韦应物诗："夜合花开香满庭。"调名取此。**柳暝河桥**：日暮时停舟于杨柳掩映的河桥之下。**暝**：日落黄昏之时。**河桥**：苏州河上的小桥。**莺晴台苑**：晴日登上莺声婉转的苏州台苑。**台苑**：指苏州姑苏台的苑圃。**短策**：短的马鞭。《左传·襄公十七年》："左师为己短策，苟过华臣之门，必骋。"孔颖达疏："策，马捶也……必为短策者，私助御者，不欲使人知也。"**策**：马鞭。**词韵**：词致气韵。唐杨炯《〈王勃集〉序》："兄勉及勮，磊落词韵，铿鍧风骨，皆九变之雄律也。"**蜡花**：蜡烛燃点时，烛心结成的花状物。唐李商隐《独居有怀》诗："蜡花长递泪，筝柱镇移心。"**壶箭**：古代的计时仪器。铜壶装水滴漏，壶中有箭标识时辰。北齐邢邵《献武皇帝寺铭》："晓夜自分，不劳鸡鹤之助；六时靡惑，非待壶箭之功。"**凌波翠陌**：与美人在岸上遨游。**凌波**：女子步履轻盈貌。**翠陌**：长着青草的道路。**连棹[zhào]横塘**：与美人在水上遨游。**棹**：船桨，指船。**横塘**：一个连一个的池塘。**似西湖燕去，吴馆巢荒**：形容人去楼空如燕去巢荒。**吴馆**：原指春秋吴王夫差所筑的馆娃宫，遗址在今江苏吴县灵岩山，这里喻指苏姬住处。西湖吴馆是作者经常住宿的地方。此处指佳人离去。**万感**：种种感触。**银罂[yīng]**：银质或银饰的贮器，用以盛流质。唐杨巨源《石水词》之一："银罂深锁贮清光，无限来人不得尝。"**斜阳**：傍晚西斜的太阳，夕阳。唐赵嘏《东望》诗："斜阳映阁山当寺，微绿含风树满川。"

【译 文】

Stephen Owen 译

Tune: "Night-Closing Flowers" (*Ye he hua*) by Wu Wen-ying

Where willows darken the river bridge
and orioles stay sunlit in terraced parkes,
there my short walking cane is often lured
    by scents of spring.
Once before we moored here by night
when we voyaged deep into passion's land.
Hard rhymes were set for the lyrics,

wine-filled cups kept coming.
We trimmed waxen sparks of the candle
　　as the water-clock's arrow sped on.
Those spots where together we roamed:
wave-walking footsteps on azure paths,
　　lines of oars at Heng-tang.

Ten years spent in one long dream, now dreary.
And it seems that West Lake's swallows have gone
to nest in an unkempt inn in Wu.
Coming again I am moved in so many ways,
and shout, as before, for a pitcher of wine.
On the creek the rain drives hard,
flowers toss wildly on the shore.
I enjoy the last crows flying past
　　in this gray magnitude.
On this upper story once shared with my friend
for whom can I now point out
plants blooming here in the setting sun?

3.44 唐多令(吴文英)

何处合成愁?离人心上秋。纵芭蕉、不雨也飕飕。都道晚凉天气好,有明月,怕登楼。

年事梦中休,花空烟水流。燕辞归、客尚淹留。垂柳不萦裙带住,漫长是,系行舟。

〖作品简介〗

此词描写羁旅怀人,其字句不事雕琢,自然浑成,在吴词中为别调。

〖注　释〗

心上秋:"心"加"秋"字,即合成"愁"字。**飕(sōu)**:形容风雨的声音。这里指风吹蕉叶之声。**年事**:指岁月。**"燕辞归"句**:曹丕《燕歌行》:"群燕辞归鹄南翔,念君客游多思肠。慊慊思归恋故乡,君何淹留寄他方。"此用其意。**客**:作者自指。**淹留**:停留。**萦**:旋绕,系住。**裙带**:指燕,指别去的女子。**漫**:徒然,空费心思。**长是**:总是。

『译 文』

龚景浩 译

"Tang Duo Ling (Song)"

Wu Wen Ying

What makes up the word "sorrow"?
The autumn in the heart of one who's left you;
Even while there's no rain the plantain rustles.
In the evening coolness they say it's pleasant.
But there is the bright moon—
Oh, to mount the stairways I'll be reluctant.

My years have been wasted in dreams;
The flowers, in vain, on misty water flow.
The swallows are gone
But the guests still stay.
Instead of tangling up their skirts and belts,
The weeping willows, often as not,
Are tying up the departing boat.

3.45 点绛唇(吴文英)

卷尽愁云，素娥临夜新梳洗。暗尘不起，酥润凌波地。
辇路重来，仿佛灯前事。情如水。小楼熏被，春梦笙歌里。

『作品简介』

此词乃作者于元宵前夕正月十三观灯怀人所作。上片着意写试灯之夜的景色：愁云卷尽，月明如洗。作者以拟人手法，描摹精巧传神。下片写重游元宵灯会之感：重来身单影孤，情侣无踪，恍如梦境，无限感伤。

『注 释』

素娥：以月宫仙女"素娥"代指月亮。**凌波地**：靓装舞女经行的街道。凌波原本用来形容洛神亭亭玉立的姿态，后来借指步履轻盈的女子。**辇路**：帝王车驾经行之路，这里指京城繁华的大街。

『译 文』

Jiaosheng Wang 译

Tune:"Rouged Lips"
Rain Just over on the Night of the Lantern Preview by Wu Wen-ying (ca. 1200-1260)

Dark clouds have rolled clean away.
Goddess of the Moon looks down after her evening toilet,
Laying the dust andmoistening the ground
That Fairy Maidens tread.

Back again in the bustling thoroughfare,
I feel myself reliving
Scenes of jolly lantern shows of other days.
With nostalgic feelings tender as water,
What can I do but retrace my steps to the small chamber,
Where under heated quilts
I'm soon lost in spring dreams,
Still haunted by the din of music and song.

3.46 踏莎行(吴文英)

润玉笼绡，檀樱倚扇。绣圈犹带脂香浅。榴心空叠舞裙红，艾枝应压愁鬟乱。

午梦千山，窗阴一箭。香瘢新褪红丝腕。隔江人在雨声中，晚风菰叶生秋怨。

『作品简介』

此词是一首端午节怀人感梦之作。词的上片写梦境，句句写梦，却始终没有点破是梦。下片写醒后的情思和愁闷，前两句写午梦方醒，揭出上片全为梦境，片末两句词笔再转，由梦中回到眼前，借写所见夜雨景致，暗抒从午梦初醒至夜雨洒落、晚风吹拂这段时间内的幽思和哀愁。

【注 释】

踏莎[suō]**行**：调名从唐韩翃诗句“踏莎行草过春溪”而来。双调，五十八字，十句，上下片各五句三仄韵。起首四个四言句，前人多用对偶。**润玉**：指肌肤。**笼绡**：薄纱衣服。**檀樱**：浅红色的樱桃小口。檀，浅红色，唐罗隐《牡丹》诗：“艳多烟重欲开难，红蕊当心一抹檀。”**绣圈**：绣花圈饰。**榴心**：形容歌女红色舞裙上印着重叠的石榴子花纹。**艾枝**：端午节用艾叶做成虎形，或剪彩为小虎，粘艾叶以戴。见《荆札岁时记》。**一箭**：指刻漏。古代计时工具。**香瘢**[bān]：指手腕斑痕。**红丝腕**：民俗端午节以五色丝系在腕以驱鬼祛邪。一名长命缕，一名续命缕，一名辟兵缕。见《风俗通》。**菰**[gū]：水生植物，也称茭白，可作菜，子实可食。

【译 文】

Stephen Owen 译

Tune: “Treading the Sedge” (*Ta suo xing*) by Wu Wen-ying

Glossy marble swathed in lace,
lips’ cherry rests upon a fan,
braided bracelet still bearing
    lotion scent faint.
Pomegranate hearts in empty folds,
    the red of her dancing skirt;
tarragon twigs surely must weigh
    her sad hair-coils to tangles.

Noon dreams, thousands of hills,
through the window, an arrow of light,
wrist’s scented ringmark, removed just recently,
    the red threads.
She is there across the river
    inside the sound of the rain,
the evening wind in the kumi leaves

stirs sadness and reproach.

3.47　八声甘州(吴文英)

渺空烟、四远是何年，青天坠长星？幻苍崖云树，名娃金屋，残霸宫城。箭径酸风射眼，腻水染花腥。时靸双鸳响，廊叶秋声。

宫里吴王沉醉，倩五湖倦客，独钓醒醒。问苍波无语，华发奈山青。水涵空、阑干高处，送乱鸦斜日落渔汀。连呼酒、上琴台去，秋与云平。

〖作品简介〗

此词乃词人的怀古之作。全词通过凭吊吴宫古迹，叙述吴越争霸往事，叹古今兴亡之感和白发无成之恨。上片怀古，下片伤今。整首词意境悠远，气势雄浑，情景交融，清丽高雅。作者改变正常的思维方式，将常人眼中的实景化为虚幻，将常人眼中的虚幻化为实景，通过奇特的艺术想象和联想，创造出如梦如幻的艺术境界。虚实相衬，沉郁苍凉，体现了作者在雕镂组绣以外的奇特才气。

〖注　释〗

八声甘州：词牌名。唐教坊大曲有《甘州》，杂曲有《甘州子》，是唐边塞曲，因以边塞地甘州为名。《八声甘州》是从大曲《甘州》截取一段改制的。因全词前后片共八韵，故名八声。慢词，与《甘州遍》之曲破，《甘州子》之令词不同。《词语》以柳永词为正体。九十七字，前片四十六字，后片五十一字，前后片各九句四平韵。亦有在起句增一韵的。前片起句、第三句，后片第二句、第四句，多用领句字。另有九十五字、九十六字、九十八字体，是变格。又名《甘州》《潇潇雨》《宴瑶池》。**长星**：彗星。**苍崖云树**：青山丛林。**名娃金屋**：此指西施，为越王勾践献给吴王夫差的美女。**金屋**：用汉武帝金屋藏娇的故事。《汉武故事》载汉武帝为胶东王时，曾对其姑母说："若得阿娇，当作金屋贮之也。"借指吴王在灵岩山上为西施修建的馆娃宫。**残霸**：指吴王夫差，他曾先后破越败齐，争霸中原，后为越王勾践所败，身死国灭，霸业有始无终。**箭径**：即采香径。《苏州府志》："采香径在香山之旁，小溪也。吴王种香于香山，使美人泛舟于溪水采香。今自灵岩山望之，一水直如矢，故俗名箭径。"**酸风射眼**：寒风吹得眼睛发痛。化用李贺《金铜仙人辞汉歌》，"魏官牵牛指千里，东关酸风射眸子"句意。**酸风**：凉风。**腻水**：宫女濯妆的脂粉水。**靸**[sǎ]：一种草制的拖鞋。此作动词，指穿着拖鞋。**双鸳**：鸳鸯履，女鞋。**廊**：响屧廊。《吴郡志·古迹》：响屧廊在灵岩山寺，相传吴王令西施辈步屧。廊虚而响，故名。**五湖倦客**：指范蠡。范蠡辅佐越王勾践灭吴后，功成身退，泛舟五湖(太湖)。**醒醒**：清楚，清醒。**华发**：花白头发。**涵空**：指水映天空。**琴台**：在灵岩山上。

『译 文』

许渊冲 译

Tune: "Eight Beats of a Ganzhou Song"
Visiting the Star Cliff[①] with My Friends by Wu Wen-ying

Mist spreads as far as sees the eye.
When did this big star fall from the blue sky?
It changed to a green cliff with cloud-like trees,
　　With golden bowers built for lady fair
In Wu's great palace, now in sad debris.
　　On Arrow Lane the eyes were hurt in chilly air,
And rouged water stained with fallen flowers sweet.
　　Leaves fall on hollow ground,
　　'Tis Autumn's sound,
It seems as if I heard the lady's slippered feet.

In Wu's great palace, drunk the king did lie,
　　But the tired hermit on the lake
　　Fished all alone awake.
In vain I ask the silent sky,
My hair turns gray in face of mountains green.
The sky in water mirrored seen,
Leaning on railings high,
I see crows scatter on the beach in setting sun.
　　I ask for wine both long and loud,
And stand upon Lute Terrace where is none
　　But autumn high and lonely as the cloud.

① The Star Cliff is situated in the west of Suzhou, capital of the ancient Kingdom of Wu (c. 200 B. C.). The king of Wu built a palace on the Cliff with a golden bower for his favorite mistress Xi Shi and drank with her in the Gallery of Hollow Ground, beside the Arrow Lane or on the Lute Terrace. At last his kingdom was conquered by the king of Yue and General Fan Li who, after the conquest of Wu, retreated as a hermit to the lakeside and lived together with the beautiful lady Xi Shi.

3.48 一剪梅(蒋捷)

一片春愁待酒浇。江上舟摇，楼上帘招。秋娘渡与泰娘桥，风又飘飘，雨又萧萧。

何日归家洗客袍？银字笙调，心字香烧。流光容易把人抛，红了樱桃，绿了芭蕉。

【作品简介】

此词是作者乘船经过吴江县时所作的一首词。全词以首句的“春愁”为核心，用“点”“染”结合的手法，选取典型景物和情景层层渲染，写出了词人伤春的情绪及久客异乡思归的情绪。

【注 释】

浇：浸灌，消除。**帘招**：指酒旗。**秋娘渡**：指吴江渡。**秋娘**：唐代歌伎常用名，或有用以通称善歌貌美之歌伎者，又称杜仲阳，为唐德宗时镇海军节度史李锜侍女。**渡**：一本作“度”。**桥**：一本作“娇”。**萧萧**：象声词，雨声。**银字笙**：管乐器的一种。**调笙**：调弄有银字的笙。**心字香**：点熏炉里心字形的香。

【译 文】

许渊冲 译

Tune: “A Twig of Mume Blossoms”
My Boat Passing by Southern River by Jiang Jie

Can boundless vernal grief be drowned in vernal wine? My boat tossed by waves high, streamers of wineshop fly. The Farewell Ferry and the Beauty’s Bridge would pine: Wind blows from hour to hour; Rain falls shower by shower.

When may I go home to wash my old robe outworn, to play on silver lute and burn the incense mute? Oh, time and tide will not wait for a man forlorn: With cherry red spring dies, when green banana sighs.

3.49 虞美人(蒋捷)

少年听雨歌楼上。红烛昏罗帐。壮年听雨客舟中。江阔云低、断雁叫西风。

而今听雨僧庐下。鬓已星星也。悲欢离合总无情。一任阶前、点滴到天明。

〖作品简介〗

此词乃作者自己一生的写照，概括了从少到老在环境、生活、心情各方面所发生的巨大变化。

〖注 释〗

断雁：失群的孤雁。**僧庐**：佛舍，寺院中。**星星**：白发点点如星，形容白发很多。左思《白发赋》："星星白发，生于鬓垂。"**悲欢离合**：化用苏轼《水调歌头》"人有悲欢离合"句。**"一任"句**：**任**：听任。此句化用温庭筠《更漏子》"一叶叶、一声声，空阶滴到明"词句。

〖译 文〗

(1) 许渊冲 译

"The Beautiful Lady Yu"
Listening to Rain

While young, I listen to rain in the house of song,
Overjoyed in curtained bed
Beside a candle red.
In prime of life I heard rain on the river long,
In lonely boat, when wailed wild geese
Beneath low clouds in western breeze.

Now that I listen to rain under temple's eaves,
My hair turns grey
Like starry ray.
Who cares if men will meet or part, rejoice or
    grieve?
Can I feel joy or sorrow?
Let it rain till tomorrow!

(2) 龚景浩 译

"Yu Mei Ren (Song)"
Jiang Jie

When I was young,
I listened to the rain in sing-song girls' boudoirs,
The red candles on the brocade canopy casting a dim light.
When I was middle-aged,
I listened to the rain in travelers' boats:
The clouds low, the river wide,
In the west wind the stray geese cried.

Now I listen to the rain in monasteries,
My temples specked with grey.
Joy and sorrow, parting and re-union—
They do not touch me so much any more.
Let the raindrops drip, on the doorsteps till morn.

3.50 暗香(姜夔)

旧时月色。算几番照我，梅边吹笛。
唤起玉人，不管清寒与攀摘。
何逊而今渐老，都忘却、春风词笔。
但怪得、竹外疏花，香冷入瑶席。

江国。正寂寂。叹寄与路遥，夜雪初积。
翠尊易泣。红萼无言耿相忆。

长记曾携手处，千树压、西湖寒碧。
又片片、吹尽也，几时见得。

【作品简介】

此词是词人所作两首著名咏梅词之一。作者无句非梅，同时又借梅喻人。起句写旧时豪情，以月色、梅花勾连过去和现在，唤起与玉人月下摘梅的回忆；随即以“而今”转到当前，“长记”二字追忆赏梅雅事；末句又回到当下，惋惜片片落梅，暗含故人不知何日重逢之意。全词不断在过去和现在之间往复摇曳，结构空灵精致，意境清虚骚雅。

【注 释】

暗香：语出北宋诗人林逋《山园小梅》诗：“疏影横斜水清浅，暗香浮动月黄昏。”**唤起玉人**：写过去和美人冒着清寒、攀折梅花的韵事。贺铸《浣溪纱》词：“美人和月摘梅花。”**何逊**：南朝梁诗人，早年曾任南平王萧伟的记室。任扬州法曹时，廨舍有梅花。以何逊自比，说自己逐渐衰老，游赏的兴趣减退，对于所喜爱的梅花都忘掉为它而歌咏了。**但怪得**：惊异。**竹外疏花**：竹林外面几枝稀疏的梅花。**香冷**：寒梅的香气透进诗人的屋子里。**瑶席**：席座的美称。**江国**：江乡。**寄与路遥**：表示音讯隔绝。这里暗用陆凯寄给范晔的诗：“折梅逢驿使，寄与陇头人。”**翠尊**：翠绿的酒杯，这里指酒。**红萼**[è]：红色的花，这里指红梅。**耿**：耿然于心，不能忘怀。**千树**：写寒冬时千树红梅映在西湖碧水之中的美丽景色。宋时杭州西湖上的孤山梅树成林，所以有“千树”之说。

【译 文】

(1) Zong-qi Cai 译

“Secret Fragrance”

The moonlight of the old days,
How many times has it shone upon me
Playing the flute by the plum trees?
I called my jade lady to rise,
Ignoring the chill, to pick blossoms with me.
He Xun is now aging,
His pen, once spring wind, is wholly forgotten.
He’s only bemused by the few flowers past the bamboos,

Whose cold fragrance enters the banquet hall.

The River Country
Is just now lonely and still.
I sigh that the road is too long to send a blossom,
And the evening snow begins to pile up.
Tears fall freely before the green wine pot;
The red calyxes are speechless, disturbed by reminiscence.
Long shall I remember the places where we held hands:
A thousand trees press against West Lake's cold green.
Petal by petal, all blown away,
When shall I see them again?

(2) Stephen Owen 译

Tune: "Fragrance from Somewhere Unseen" (*An xiang*) by Jiang Kui

(In the winter of 1191, I went off in the snow to visit Fan Cheng-da at Stone Lake. When I had stayed with him a month, he handed me some paper and asked for some lines to appear in a new style song. I composed these two melodies. Fan Cheng-da couldn't get over his pleasure in them, and had a pair of singing girls practice them until the tones and the rhythms were sweet and smooth. Then I gave them the name "Fragrance from Somewhere Unseen" and "Broken Shadows".)

The moon's hue of days gone by—
I wonder how often it shone on me
playing my flute beside the plums?
It called awake that woman, white marble,
and heedless of cold,
    together we snapped off sprays.
But now this poet grows old,
and the pen that once wrote songs
    of the breeze in spring
    is utterly forgotten;
I'm just intrigued by those sparse blooms
    over beyond the bamboo,
how their chill scent
    seeps into party mats.

These river lands now
lie somber and still.
And I sigh
    to send them to someone traveling far,
as tonight their snow begins to heap high.
With kingfisher cups
    and easily brought to tears,
restive, I recall
    pink petals that never speak.
I always think back where we once held hands:
where the freight of a thousand trees weighed
    on West Lake's cold sapphire.
Now petal by petal once more
    they all blow away,
never again to be seen.

3.51 疏影(姜夔)

苔枝缀玉，有翠禽小小，枝上同宿。客里相逢，篱角黄昏，无言自倚修竹。昭君不惯胡沙远，但暗忆、江南江北。想佩环、月夜归来，化作此花幽独。

犹记深宫旧事，那人正睡里，飞近蛾绿。莫似春风，不管盈盈，早与安排金屋。还教一片随波去，又却怨、玉龙哀曲。等恁时、重觅幽香，已入小窗横幅。

【作品简介】

此词与作者的上一首词是姊妹篇，主题咏梅。全词表现梅的高洁、幽独，并借此咏叹作者自己的身世。上片先描写出梅花不同凡俗的形貌，又表现其孤芳自赏的清姿和高洁情怀，再化用杜甫、王建诗意，把远嫁异域不能生还汉邦的王昭君故事神话化，将眷恋故国的昭君之魂和寒梅的幽独之魂合而为一，带有极深的悲剧意味，境界又极凄美；下片则借眼前梅花盛开推想其飘落之时，用寿阳公主及陈阿娇典故，寓无限怜香惜玉之意，又借笛里梅花哀怨的乐曲，加深怅惋的感情，末二句想到梅花凋尽，唯余空枝幻影映上小窗，语意沉痛。全词熔铸绝妙，运气空灵，变化虚实，曲折动荡，摇曳多姿。

〖注　释〗

疏影：词牌名，词人的自度曲，语出北宋诗人林逋《山园小梅》诗："疏影横斜水清浅，暗香浮动月黄昏。"**苔枝缀玉**：范成大《梅谱》说绍兴、吴兴一带的古梅"苔须垂于枝间，或长数寸，风至，绿丝飘飘可玩"。周密《乾淳起居注》："苔梅有二种，宜兴张公洞者，苔藓甚厚，花极香。一种出越土，苔如绿丝，长尺余。"**苔枝**：长有苔藓的梅枝。**缀玉**：梅花像美玉一般缀满枝头。**"有翠禽"**二句：用罗浮之梦典故。旧题柳宗元《龙城录》载，隋代赵师雄游罗浮山，夜梦与一素妆女子共饭，女子芳香袭人。又有一绿衣童子，笑歌欢舞。赵醒来，发现自己躺在一株大梅树下，树上有翠鸟欢鸣，见"月落参横，但惆怅而已"。殷尧藩《友人山中梅花》诗："好风吹醒罗浮梦，莫听空林翠羽声。"吴潜《疏影》词："闲想罗浮旧恨，有人正醉里，姝翠蛾绿。"**翠禽**：翠鸟。晋郭璞《客傲》："夫攀骊龙之髯，抚翠禽之毛，而不得绝霞肆、跨天津者，未之前闻也。"**客里**：离乡在外期间。唐牟融《送范启东还京》诗："客里故人尊酒别，天涯游子弊裘寒。"**黄昏**：日已落而天色尚未黑的时候。《楚辞·离骚》："曰黄昏以为期兮，羌中道而改路。""**无言**"句：杜甫《佳人》诗："天寒翠袖薄，日暮倚修竹。""**昭君**"四句：杜甫《咏怀古迹五首》其三："一去紫台连朔漠，独留青冢向黄昏。画图省识春风面，环佩空归夜月魂。千载琵琶作胡语，分明怨恨曲中论。"王建《塞上咏梅》诗："天山路边在株梅，年年花发黄云下。昭君已没汉使回，前后征人谁系马？""**犹记**"三句：用寿阳公主事。**蛾**：形容眉毛的细长。**绿**：眉毛的青绿颜色。《太平御览》引《杂五行书》云："宋武帝女寿阳公主，人日卧于含章殿檐下，梅花落公主额上，成五出花，拂之不去。皇后留之，看得几时，经三日，洗之乃落。宫女奇其异，竞效之，今'梅花妆'是也。"**安排金屋**：《汉武故事》载，汉武帝刘彻幼时曾对姑母说："若得阿娇作妇，当作金屋贮之。"**盈盈**：仪态美好的样子，这里借指梅花。**玉龙哀曲**：马融《长笛赋》："龙鸣水中不见已，截竹吹之声相似。"**玉龙**：即玉笛。李白《与史郎中钦听黄鹤楼上吹笛》诗："黄鹤楼中吹玉笛，江城五月落梅花。"哀曲，指笛曲《梅花落》。此曲是古代流行的乐曲，听了使人悲伤。唐皮日休《夜会问答》说听《梅花落》曲"三奏未终头已白"，由此可见一斑。故曰"玉龙哀曲"。**恁[nèn]时**：那时候。南唐冯延巳《忆江南》词："东风次第有花开，恁时须约却重来。"**小窗横幅**：晚唐崔橹《梅花诗》："初开已入雕梁画，未落先愁玉笛吹。"陈与义《水墨梅》诗："睛窗画出横斜枝，绝胜前村夜雪时。"此翻用其意。

〖译　文〗

Zong-qi Cai 译

"Dappled Shadows"

Mossy branches decked with jade;

A pair of little bluebirds
Roost on them together.
When wandering we meet—
By the corner of the fence in the dusk,
Without a word she leans on slender bamboos.
Unaccustomed to the remote barbarian sands,
Zhaojun secretly longed for the Yangtze's climes.
Surely it is her jade waistband
That returns on moonlit nights,
Transformed into this blossom so solitary.

The old palace tale still comes to mind;
As the beauty slept,
One blossom fluttered to her black moth-eyebrows,
Don't be like the spring wind,
Careless of beauty,
But early prepare a gold chamber for it.
If one lets all the petals drift off with the current,
He will resent hearing the sad tune for the Jade Dragon.
If one waits till then to pursue that subtle fragrance,
It will have entered a horizontal scroll over some small window.

3.52 鹧鸪天（姜夔）

肥水东流无尽期，当初不合种相思。梦中未比丹青见，暗里忽惊山鸟啼。
春未绿，鬓先丝，人间别久不成悲。谁教岁岁红莲夜，两处沉吟各自知。

【作品简介】

此词的全称为《鹧鸪天·元夕有所梦》。作品的上片先写对昔日恋情的悔恨，再写梦中无法看清情人的怨恨，足见作者恋情之深炽；下片说久别伤悲以致愁白了鬓发，煞拍两句想象在元宵放灯之夜，对方也在悲苦相思，语极沉痛。全词意境空灵蕴藉，语言自然清劲，耐人咀嚼。

【注 释】

鹧鸪天：词牌名，据传词名取自郑隅诗"春游鸡鹿塞，家在鹧鸪天"，又称《思越人》《剪朝霞》《骊歌一叠》《醉梅花》《思佳客》。双调，上片四句，押三平韵，二十八字，下片五句，押三平韵，二十七字，共五十五字。上片第三、四句及下片两个三字句多用对仗，用“大石调”。**肥水**：即淝水。源出安徽合肥紫蓬山，东南流经将军岭，至施口入巢湖。**不合**：不应当，不该。**种相思**：留下相思之情，谓当初不应该动情，动情后尤不该分别。**丹青**：泛指图画，此处指画像。**红莲夜**：指元宵灯节。**红莲**：指灯节的花灯。周邦彦《解语花·上元》：“露浥红莲，灯市花相射。”

〖译　文〗

许渊冲 译

Tune: “The Partridge Sky”
A Dream on the Night of Lantern Festival by Jiang Kui

The long River Fei to the east keeps on flowing
The love-seeds we once sowed forever keep growing.
Your face I saw in dreams was not clear to my eyes
As in your portrait, soon I'm woke up by birds' cries.

　　Spring not yet green,
　　My gray hair seen,
Our separation has been too long to grieve the heart.
　　Who makes the past reappear
　　Before us from year to year
On Lantern Festival when we are far apart?

3. 53　满江红(姜夔)

仙姥来时，正一望、千顷翠澜。旌旗共、乱云俱下，依约前山。命驾群龙金作轭，相从诸娣玉为冠。向夜深、风定悄无人，闻佩环。

神奇处，君试看。奠淮右，阻江南。遣六丁雷电，别守东关。却笑英雄无好手，一篙春水走曹瞒。又怎知、人在小红楼，帘影间。

〖作品简介〗

此词乃一首恢宏奇丽的咏仙词。上片即揭开了一个神话世界的面纱：千顷绿波翻滚，旌旗扬卷，乱云堆积，闻声而不见人，形成极具动感的态势。下片写仙姥的神奇威力，笔调亦愈益雄奇豪放，与作者一贯的词风不同。夏承焘、吴无闻《姜白石词校注》云：此词为祭祀巢湖仙姥而作。姥，和曹子建笔下的洛神和屈原笔下的湘夫人一样，都是水神，也都是女性。然而白石(姜夔的号)不采用“凌波微步，罗袜生尘”一类的艺术表现手法，而是另辟蹊径，把仙姥和曹操联系起来写，这真是别开生面的联想。

【注 释】

满江红：词牌名，又名《上江虹》《念良游》《伤春曲》。唐人小说《冥音录》载曲名《上江虹》，后更名《满江红》。宋以来始填此词调。**仙姥**：神仙妇女。**依约**：隐隐约约。**轭**：驾车时套在马颈上的曲型器具，一般为木制。**相从诸娣**[dì]：随从神姥的诸位仙姑。此句下白石自注：“庙中列坐如夫人者十三人。”**娣**：古称同夫诸妾。**佩环**：指诸神身上的装饰品。**奠**[diàn]：镇守。**淮右**：宋时在淮扬一带设置淮南东路和淮南西路。淮南西路称淮右，湖属淮右地区。**阻**：拱卫。六丁：传说中的天神。韩愈诗：“仙宫敕六丁，雷电下取将。”**别守**：扼守。**一篙**：一竿。**篙**：撑船的竿。**曹瞒**：曹操小字阿瞒。**帘影间**：帘幕之内的(弱质女子)。

【译 文】

Stephen Owen 译

Tune：“Red Filling the River”(*Man jiang hong*) by Jiang Kui (ca. 1155-1221)

When the Old Lady came, the goddess undying,
her gaze took in these thousand acres
    of azure rippling.
Her pennons and banners descended together
    with seething clouds
that blurred the view of the mountains ahead.
She bade her dragon herds be hitched,
    golden were their yokes,
and all the handmaidens in her train
    wore crowns of jade.
As the night grew deep, the winds died down
    in the unpeopled stillness,
and the rings on her sash were heard.

This spot where the goddess worked wonders—

come have a look! —
She holds secure the Huai's right bank,
bulwark of the Southland;
She sent six stout angels in lightning and thunder
specially to hold East Pass.
And I laugh at those warrior heroes,
    that none were any good:
a boat-pole's depth of springtime floods
    sent little Cao Cao running—
but then how could he have known
    that She who did it all
    was in this small red chamber
in the shadows of the blinds?

3.54 卜算子(高观国)

屈指数春来，弹指惊春去。檐外蛛丝网落花，也要留春住。
几日喜春晴，几夜愁春雨。十二雕窗六曲屏，题遍伤春句。

〖作品简介〗

此词乃一首送春词，抒写了伤春惜春的情怀。上片言春之短暂。屈指迎春，弹指春去。画檐蛛网，也留春住；下片抒写伤春愁绪。几日春晴，几夜春雨，春将归去矣！伤春之句，题遍屏窗。全词曲折有致，思绪缠绵，工巧婉丽，饶有韵味。

〖注　释〗

弹指：比喻时间短暂。

〖译　文〗

Robert Kotewall and Norman L. Smith 译

To "The Fortune-teller" by Kao Kuan-kuo

With much crooking of the fingers I counted for
    Spring's coming;

A snap of the fingers, and lo! Spring departs.
Out on the eaves the gossamer entangles the fallen petals,
Wishing likewise to keep Spring here.

How many days did I exult in Spring's sunshine?
How many nights did I lament Spring's rain?
The twelve carven casements and the six folds of the screen
Are all indited with verses that mourn for Spring.

3.55 念奴娇(文天祥)

水天空阔，恨东风，不借世间英物。蜀鸟吴花残照里，忍见荒城颓壁。铜雀春情，金人秋泪，此恨凭谁雪？堂堂剑气，斗牛空认奇杰。

那信江海余生，南行万里，属扁舟齐发。正为鸥盟留醉眼，细看涛生云灭。睨柱吞嬴，回旗走懿，千古冲冠发。伴人无寐，秦淮应是孤月。

『作品简介』

此词抒发词人难酬报国之志的感叹。上阙表达了国破家亡的悲愤，恨自己未能杀敌立功；下阙写要学习古代英雄，坚持斗争到底，与友人共勉，表达了战事失败后的悲愤，也表达了作者坚决的斗志。全词善用典故，言简意深。

『注 释』

恨东风：三国时吴将周瑜联合刘备大战曹操于赤壁，因东风有利火攻，取得了完全胜利，后人于是有孔明借东风的传说。**蜀鸟吴花**：蜀鸟指杜鹃鸟，鸣声凄厉，能动旅客愁思。**吴花**：指江南的花。**铜雀**：台名，曹操所造，旧址在今河南临漳县西南；杜牧《赤壁》诗“东风不与周郎便，铜雀春深锁二乔”，说赤壁之战如果不是东风帮忙，曹操打了胜仗，就会把大乔、二乔姊妹俩掳往铜雀台了(大乔嫁孙策，小乔嫁周瑜)；这里指南宋亡后，皇后嫔妃都被元兵掳往北方。**金人**：铜人，传说东汉亡后，魏明帝把长安建章宫前的铜人运往洛阳，在迁运时，铜人眼里流出泪水，这里借比南宋亡国之惨。**剑气**：古代传说好的宝剑有剑气直冲斗、牛(星名)，观望斗、牛之间的剑气，能够根据方位推测宝剑的所在。**奇杰**：指宝剑。**南行**：指作者从元军手中逃脱乘海船去温州和福州的事。**鸥盟**：隐居水乡，像和鸥鸟结盟做朋友，这里指战友。**睨[nì]柱**：睨柱吞嬴，指蔺相如完璧归赵的故事。睨是斜视。嬴即秦昭王嬴稷。**回旗走懿[yì]**：指蜀汉诸葛亮死后，当地百姓见蜀国退兵就告诉司马懿，司马懿断定诸葛亮已经死了，便率兵追杀蜀军，但魏延擅自据南谷口逆击杨仪。断后任务落到姜维手上，姜维令杨仪返旗鸣鼓，做出回击的样子，司马懿以为中计，急忙收军退回，不敢逼近。

〖译　文〗

(1) Alan Ayling and Duncan Mackintosh 译

Vast water, sky spread wide;
But no east wind as when
It saved the heroes of our country.
Birds and wild flowers of the south
In the evening light
Are hard to bear by crumbling walls, forsaken city.
The Palace women seized for pleasure;
The golden idols wrecked with grief;
Our shame! Who can be found to wipe it clean?
My precious sword, flashing light to the stars,
Looks for a hero's grip—in vain.

Who would have thought we could ever survive
That escape by sea,
Those endless miles we travelled south?
Putting faith in our fragile craft we sailed together.
Like true sea-gulls, bound by an oath
Till our eyes should dim,
We kept the watch through mist and stormy weather.
Lin out-faced a grasping ruler,
Chu non-plussed his enemy;
Such was the prick of courage in days gone by.
Haunted, I cannot sleep
For the solitary moon on the Ch'in Huai.

(2) 许渊冲 译

Tune: "Charm of a Maiden Singer"
Farewell to a Friend at Post House by Wen Tian-xiang[①]

The water's boundless like the skies,

But favorable wind won't rise,
To our regret, to help our heroes on the earth.
The cuckoo cries
'Mid Southern flowers in setting sun.
How could I bear to see the ruined town o'errun
By the Tartarian foe!
The captives have no mirth,
E'en golden statues that should hear
The story would drop tear on tear.
Who would not strike a vengeful blow?
The sword once shed a vengeful light,
But, swordsman beaten, when would it again shine bright?

Who would believe, confiding our lives to a boat,
Together we could keep afloat
On river and on sea,
Sailing southward for miles, then at last we were free!
We made our plan with our allies
To wait with drunken eyes
For waves and clouds dark to appear
And disappear.
Against the chieftain of the foe,
I would fight in weal and in woe.
Wrath sets my hair on end
And it will never die.
Sleepless at night, you would only have for friend
The lonely moon on the River Qinhuai.

① Wen Tian-xiang (1236-1283) passed the civil service examinations with the highest honor in 1256 and was appointed prime minister in the court of Song Dynasty. As a famous leader of anti-Tartarian forces, he was defeated in 1276 but by luck he and Liu Yan escaped in a boat sailing south on the sea, and they planned to reorganize loyal forces to turn the tide. Again beaten and captured in 1278, they were sent under escort to Yanjing (present-day Beijing). Passing by the River Qinhuai at Jinling (present-day Nanjing), Liu Yan should go no farther and Wen Tian-xiang wrote for him this lyric in which he regretted that the situation was not favorable for the anti-Tartarian forces. He could not bear the sight of ruined town of Jinling nor the cuckoo's song which seemed to say: "Better go home!" Having arrived at Yanjing, he would never yield to the chieftain of the Tartars and was imprisoned for three or four long years. At last he sacrificed his life heroically in a public place. The swordsman in this lyric refers to the poet himself.

3.56 满江红(文天祥)

试问琵琶，胡沙外、怎生风色。
最苦是、姚黄一朵，移根仙阙。
王母欢阑琼宴罢，仙人泪满金盘侧。
听行宫、半夜雨淋铃，声声歇。

彩云散，香尘灭。
铜驼恨，那堪说。
想男儿慷慨，嚼穿龈血。
回首昭阳离落日，伤心铜雀迎秋风。
算妾身、不愿似天家，金瓯缺。

〖作品简介〗

此词是词人应和王夫人词中的一首。作者通过翻作王夫人所写之词，寓自己的思想于其中，校正王夫人的原作在内容上的消极避祸的思想，强调身处逆境应洁身自爱，坚守操节。

〖注　释〗

姚黄：牡丹中名贵品种，暗指王夫人。**移根仙阙**：离开宋宫，被驱北行，较之公主远嫁，处境惨，悲愁深。“**王母**”句：西王母瑶池美宴的古代传说，用来指宫中的欢意已消失。“**仙人**”句：以铜仙坠泪的故事，感叹国土沦亡的惨痛。“**听行宫**”两句：这里借此典表述被迫北去途中的悲苦心境。唐代天宝年间，唐玄宗避乱入蜀，在马嵬坡军士哗变被迫缢死杨玉环，后来，在行宫内听到雨声和风吹檐铃声相应，引发心事，即《雨霖铃》曲 。**彩云散，香尘灭**：比喻美好生活的毁灭。**铜驼恨**：指南宋之覆亡。**那堪说**：悲痛之极，不能卒言。**想男儿慷慨，嚼穿龈血**：抗御元军、挽救宋室危亡之局的战场上，无数热血将士血战到底。“**回首昭阳离落日，伤心铜雀迎秋月**”句：“回首”“伤心”乃借王夫人口气，寓其自己的悲感中。“昭阳”“铜雀”均为古都城台殿名，这里用来借指南宋宫殿，落日和秋月将光辉洒在故国宫殿上，寄托一种思念的情感。“**算妾身、不愿似天家，金瓯缺**”句：点明文天祥代王清惠作此词的缘由。文天祥改变王清惠原作中消极避祸的思想，提出要洁身自爱，坚守操节，这实际上是词人借王夫人之口表达的自勉之词，并与王夫人和众宫娥共勉。

『译 文』

Alan Ayling and Duncan Mackintosh 译

Ask the lute-player
Beyond the Tartar sands
How harsh the winds of exile blew;
Most bitterly of all
On her, a pale gold peony
Snatched from the palace home she knew.
Even after the banquet of a goddess
Tears filled the golden bowl beside her place.
She listened in her tented palace
To mid-night eave-bells tinkling in the rain
Until all sound would cease.

Life's rainbow days were over,
Their scented pleasures dead.
What happened to our shrines
We cannot bear it said.
Think of the young men, brave, burning for justice;
Starved of revenge, teeth tasting blood, their own.
Turn in memory back to the old palaces at sunset
And feel the heart-break; empty buildings
Greet the autumn moon.
For my own part
I'll serve no other master
Now the gold cup's broken.

3.57 清平乐(张炎)

采芳人杳，顿觉游情少。客里看春多草草，总被诗愁分了。
去年燕子天涯，今年燕子谁家？三月休听夜雨，如今不是催花。

【作品简介】

此词乃"伤春"之佳作。作者借"燕子"比喻自己飘荡无依，借"夜雨"比喻摧花折绿的残暴的元兵。写作之中由景到人，由人到物，由物到情，层层深入，又层层翻新。抒发自己的国亡之伤情，感叹自己的家破之惨痛。

【注　释】

采芳人：指游春采花的女子。**杳**[yǎo]：没有踪迹。**顿觉**：顿时觉得。**游情**：游玩的心情。**草草**：草率。**燕子**：词人自喻。**天涯**：形容很远的地方。**谁家**：何处。

【译　文】

Jiaosheng Wang 译

Tune: "Pure Serene Music" by Chang Yen (1248-ca. 1320)

All of a sudden my delight in sightseeing wanes,
Now the maidens gathering flowers
Are nowhere to be found.
Away from home one cares little
For spring outings,
Distracted by composing mournful verses.

Under whose roof are the swallows
That last year were roaming the ends of the earth?
I'd rather not listen to the patter of evening rain:
Late spring is no time to speed
The blossoming of flowers.

3.58　眼儿媚(范成大)

酣酣日脚紫烟浮，妍暖破轻裘。困人天色，醉人花气，午梦扶头。
春慵恰似春塘水，一片縠纹愁。溶溶泄泄，东风无力，欲皱还休。

〖作品简介〗

此词作于作者调任静江府、广西经略安抚使赴桂林上任途中。据作者《骖鸾录》，乾道九年(1173年)闰正月路过萍乡(今江西萍乡市)，时雨方晴，乘轿困乏，歇息于柳塘畔。柳条新抽，春塘水满，这样的环境既便小憩，又易引发诗兴。作者在原序中这样写道："萍乡道中乍晴，卧舆中困甚，小憩柳塘"。

〖注 释〗

眼儿媚：词牌名，因张孝祥词"今宵眼底，明朝心上，后日眉头"句而得名。**酣酣**：指太阳如醉。艳盛貌。宋之问《寒食题黄梅临江驿》："遥思故园陌，桃李正酣酣。"**日脚**：穿过云隙下射的日光。**紫烟**：烟霞映日成紫色。**扶头**：扶头酒的省称，指易醉之酒。白居易《早饮湖州酒寄崔使君》诗："一榼扶头酒，泓澄泻玉壶。"此处指醉态。**慵**[yōng]：困倦，懒得动。**縠纹**[hú wén]：绉纱似的皱纹，常用以喻水的波纹。这里指有皱纹的纱类丝织品，如"绮罗绫縠"。**溶溶泄泄**：春水荡漾的样子。舒缓貌，弛缓之意也。"泄泄"亦写作"曳曳"[yè]。**东风无力**：李商隐《无题》诗："东风无力百花残。"**皱**：原本作"避"。

〖译 文〗

Robert Kotewall and Norman L. Smith 译

To "Eyes' Fascination"

Mellow, mellow at the sun's foot floats the purple mist;
The genial warmth dismisses my light fur.
Tired by the breath of heaven,
Drunk with the breath of flowers,
I dream at noontide with head on hands.

This lazy Spring is like the water of a pond in
 Springtime—
Wrinkled as by sorrow like a strip of crape.
Gently, gently, dragging and dragging,
The East Wind, strengthless,
Tries to make a ripple, but gives up.

3.59 鹧鸪天(无名氏)

镇日无心扫黛眉，临行愁见理征衣。尊前只恐伤郎意，阁泪汪汪不敢垂。
停宝马，捧瑶卮，相斟相劝忍分离？不如饮待奴先醉，图得不知郎去时。

〖作品简介〗

此词描写了妻子和丈夫别离时妻子的忧愁苦痛。有人认为作者乃夏竦，字子乔，北宋大臣，古文字学家，初谥“文正”，后改谥“文庄”。夏竦以文学起家，曾为国史编修官，也曾任多地官员，宋真宗时为襄州知州，宋仁宗时为洪州知州，后任陕西经略、安抚、招讨使等职。由于夏竦对文学的造诣很深，所以他的很多作品都流传于后世。

〖注 释〗

镇日：宋代口语，整日。**扫**：画。

〖译 文〗

Robert Kotewall and Norman L. Smith 译

Parting
To “Partridge Sky” by Author Unknown

All the day I have had no heart to tend my dark
    eyebrows;
As the parting approaches I sorrow to see his travelling
    clothes prepared.
Before the flagon I fear only to hurt my good man’s
    heart;
I restrain my tears that well up, and dare not let them
    drop.

I stay his noble steed;
I hold up the precious goblet.
We pour to each other, and exhort each other; but how

to endure this parting?
Better to drink until I am the first to be overcome,
Intent on knowing not when my good man departs.

第四章
元 代

4.1 喜春来(伯颜)

金鱼玉带罗襕扣，皂盖朱幡列五侯，山河判断在俺笔尖头。得意秋，分破帝王忧。

〖作品简介〗

此曲为作者兵会临安占领南宋都城庆祝宴上所作，表现了作者洋洋得意的愉快心情。按《元史》伯颜、弘范两传，至元十一年(1274 年)，左丞相伯颜领行中书省总兵攻宋。十二年十一月，元兵分三路攻临安(今浙江杭州)，伯颜率中军从建康(今江苏南京)进发。十三年正月，三路元兵会师于临安，二月，南宋幼主出降。细玩伯颜曲意，伯颜、弘范席上作曲之事，当在至元十三年元兵会师于临安之后。

〖注 释〗

金鱼：形状如鲤鱼的金符，标志官阶的一种佩饰。**玉带**：用玉装饰的官服腰带。**罗襕**：绮罗袍，元朝以丝罗制的官服。**皂盖朱幡**：黑色车盖红色旗帜，高官出行的仪仗。**列五侯**：位与五侯同列。“五侯”指公、侯、伯、子、男五等诸侯爵位。**得意秋**：称心得意的岁月。**分破**：分减，减少。元人口语。

〖译 文〗

许渊冲 译

Tune: “Welcome to Spring” by Bo Yan

Adorned with gold fish and belt of jade,

I button my robe of brocade,
Under black canopy and banners red,
Of the five highest lords I'm at the head.
The land is ruled at the tip of my pen.
What pride over all men!
I bear my share of the imperial care.

4.2　醉中天(王和卿)

弹破庄周梦，两翅驾东风，三百座名园、一采一个空。
谁道风流种，唬杀寻芳的蜜蜂。
轻轻飞动，把卖花人搧过桥东。

【作品简介】

此曲是作者所作的一首充满谑浪诙谐、戏谑调笑的散曲小令。相传中统(1260—1264)年初，燕市(北京)有一只蝴蝶，巨大异常，王和卿于是作此曲。该作品以一种放荡不羁、玩世不恭的情调，嬉笑怒骂间一针见血地对现实社会给予无情的批判。

【注　释】

醉中天：元曲的曲牌名。七句，句式为五五七五六四四，每句入韵，平仄混押。“**弹破**”句：意为蝴蝶大得竟然把庄周的蝶梦给弹破了。**庄周梦**：庄周，战国时宋国蒙人，曾为漆园吏，有《庄子》一书。据说他曾梦见自己化为大蝴蝶，醒来后仍是庄周，弄不清到底是蝴蝶变成了庄周，还是庄周变成了蝴蝶。**一采一个空**：一作“一采个空”。**谁道**：一作“难道”，意为“谁料”。**风流种**：一作“风流孽种”，风流才子，名士。**唬杀**：犹言“吓死”。唬，一作“謼[huò]”。**謼**：吓唬。**杀**：用在动词后，表程度深。**轻轻飞动**：一作“轻轻搧动”。一本“轻轻”后还有“的”字。

【译　文】

(1) James I. Crump 译

Tune: “Tsui-chung T'ien”
To the Giant Butterfly by Wang Ho-ch'ing

This butterfly escaped, it seems,

From the chrysalis of Chuang Tzu's dreams,[①]
Spread two great wings upon the spring air,
Then sucked three hundred gardens bare!
Might not elegant creatures such as these
Shame to death our simple honeybees?
Or, giving their wings a tiny shake,
Blow our flower vendors in the lake?!

① The wag of his times, Wang Ho-ch'ing composed occasional—and probably impromptu—pieces. This song is said to have been written in response to the sudden appearance of a species of large butterfly in the environs of the capital.

(2) 许渊冲 译

Tune: "A Drinker's Sky"
Song of a Huge Butterfly

Breaking a philosopher's dream,
He flaps his wings and rides on the
east wind in flight.
He gathers all the honey from the
flowers
In three hundred well-known gardens
and bowers.
Don't say the lover of beauty and
breeze
Has scared away all honey-seeking
bees!
Flapping his fan-like wings so light,
He blows the flower-seller off across
the stream.

(3) Zong-qi Cai 译

To the Tune of "Heaven in a Drunkard's Eye" [xianlü key]:
On the Big Butterfly

Having emerged from Zhuangzi's dream.

With its two wings mounting on the spring wind,
It empties three hundred gardens in one gulp.
Can this be the gallant breed?
How it scares away the flower-chaser bees!
With a gentle flap of its wings
It blows the flower vendors to the east side of the bridge.

4.3　胖妻夫(王和卿)

一个胖双郎，就了个胖苏娘，两口儿便似熊模样。成就了风流喘豫章，绣帏中一对儿鸳鸯象，交肚皮厮撞。

〖作品简介〗

这首小令用俚语俗言描写了一对胖夫妻，以他人生理上一残缺或特征为嘲谑对象，仅供一笑付之。

〖注　释〗

绣帏：绣帐，可以理解为四面带有绣帐的床。

〖译　文〗

Zong-qi Cai 译

To the Tune of "The Unbreakable String" [shuandiao key]: Fat Couple

A rather obese Master Shuang
Bore off an overweight Miss Su-niang
(Each one of that pair
Was the size of a bear!)
On the wings of romance, off they sped,
But paused a while at Yü-chang to pant—
These lovebirds the size of an eleophant—
And bang their bellyskins in bed!

4.4 人月圆(元好问)

重冈已隔红尘断，村落更年丰。移居要就，窗中远岫，舍后长松。十年种木，一年种谷，都付儿童。老夫惟有，醒来明月，醉后清风。

玄都观里桃千树，花落水空流。凭君莫问，清泾浊渭，去马来牛。谢公扶病，羊昙挥涕，一醉都休。古今几度，生存华屋，零落山丘。

【作品简介】

这首小令典重蕴深，带有较重的词味。一来是因为“人月圆”本属词牌，后因合于北曲宫调的缘故才转为小曲；二来是由于散曲初创时期，词、曲界限并无明显分野。日后的散曲也用典故或引前人诗句，但援例和用意都要显豁得多。全曲通过一系列典故和前人成句的化用，表现了国破家亡的沧桑巨痛，及“卜居外家东园”而苟延残生的沉重心情。

【注 释】

人月圆：黄钟调曲牌名。**重冈**：重重叠叠的山冈。**红尘**：这里指繁华的社会。**要就**：要去的地方。**远岫**[xiù]：远山。“**玄都**”句：唐刘禹锡《戏赠看花诸君子》：“玄都观里桃千树，尽是刘郎去后栽。”玄都观，唐代长安城郊的一所道观。**凭**：请。“**清泾**”二句：语本杜甫《秋雨叹》：“去马来牛不复辨，浊泾清渭何当分。”清泾浊渭，泾、渭皆水名，在陕西高陵县境汇合，泾流清而渭流浊。**谢公**：谢安(320—385年)，东晋政治家。在桓温谋篡及苻坚南侵的历史关头制乱御侮，成为保全东晋王朝的柱石。孝武帝太元年间，琅琊王司马道子擅政，谢安因抑郁成疾，不久病故。**羊昙**：谢安之甥，东晋名士。“**生存**”二句：三国魏曹植《箜篌引》：“生存华屋处，零落归山丘。”言人寿有限，虽富贵者也不免归于死亡。

【译 文】

许渊冲 译

Tune: “Man and Moon”
Moving to My Mother’s East Garden by Yuan Haowen (1190-1257)

I

Hill on hill keeps apart the vanity fair
From this village of bumper year.

I move house to come near
The window-enframed distant hill
And the pine-trees behind the windowsill.

I'll leave the woods and the fields to the care
Of my children dear
So that I may do what I will.
Awake, I'll enjoy the moon so bright;
Drunk, the refreshing breeze so light.

II

In Royal Temple there are thousands of
　　peach trees,
Whence fallen blooms in vain with water
　　flow.
Do not ask, please,
If water is not clear,
Or cows will come or horses go.

What matters if the minister was ill,
And his friend shed tear on tear!
What can I do but drink my fill?
How many splendid houses of olden
　　days appear
Fallen to ruins in the hill!

4.5　小圣乐(元好问)

绿叶阴浓，遍池亭水阁，偏趁凉多。海榴初绽，朵朵蹙红罗。乳燕雏莺弄语，有高柳鸣蝉相和。骤雨过，珍珠乱撒，打遍新荷。

人生百年有几，念良辰美景，休放虚过。穷通前定，何用苦张罗。命友邀宾玩赏，对芳樽浅酌低歌。且酩酊，任他两轮日月，来往如梭。

〖作品简介〗

此曲抒发了作者面对时世感发的及时行乐的思想。其上片写盛夏纳凉，流连光景的赏心乐事，主写景；下曲即景抒怀，宣扬浅斟低唱、及时行乐的思想。全曲写法与词相近，这是因为在宋元之交，词、曲均称乐府，都是被诸管弦，传于歌筵的，所以早期的词曲分疆并不甚严。《莲子居词话》认为此曲作词调，具有词味，也可算是此曲的一个特点。

〖注 释〗

小圣乐：据《九宫大成谱 · 总论》引《宋史 · 燕乐志》，双调、小石调，俱属商声七调。因此《太平乐府》以此曲入双调。小圣乐，是双调中一曲调(又称曲牌)名。从格调看，此即词里之慢词。**海榴**：即石榴。**蹙**[cù]：聚拢，皱缩。**罗**：即纱罗。**几**：几许，此处指多长时间。**穷通前定**：乃一种唯心的迷信说法，言个人命运之好坏系前世注定。**张罗**：料理与筹划。**芳樽**：精美的酒杯，此处指代美酒。**酩酊**：酒醉状。

〖译 文〗

许渊冲 译

Tune: "Minor Sacred Music"
Sudden Shower Beating on New Lotus Leaves by Yuan Haowen

I

Green leaves casting deep shade
Over pavilions and bowers by the pool
Bring a delightful cool.
The pomegranates in early flower
Look like frowning red brocade.
Young swallows chirp and orioles warble their song
While cicadas on high willow trees trill along.
A sudden shower
With raindrops like pearls or dew
Beats on lotus leaves new.

II

How many people can live to a hundred years?
Do not let golden hours and fine scenery
Slip away!
Our poor destiny
Cannot be turned another way,
It's better to invite friends and enjoy with peers
Good wine and songs we sing low.

Be tipsy while we may,
And let the sun and moon come and go
　　Like shuttles to and fro!

4.6　满江红(萨都剌)

六代繁华，春去也，更无消息。空怅望，山川形胜，已非畴昔。王谢堂前双燕子，乌衣巷口曾相识。听夜深、寂寞打孤城，春潮急。

思往事，愁如织；怀故国，空陈迹。但荒烟衰草，乱鸦斜日。《玉树》歌残秋露冷，胭脂井坏寒螀泣。到如今，唯有蒋山青，秦淮碧。

【作品简介】

此词的作者是萨都剌，元代诗人，公元1332年任职江南，移居金陵。其全名为《满江红·金陵怀古》，全词将山川风物依旧和六朝繁华不再进行对比，抒发了作者深沉而强烈的怀古感慨之情。

【注　释】

畴昔：从前。**胭脂井**：在今南京城内。隋兵攻打金陵，陈后主与妃子避入此井，终被擒。**寒螀**[jiāng]：寒蝉。**蒋山**：钟山。

【译　文】

(1) 丁祖馨 译

To the Tune of "Manjianghong"
Remembering the Ancient City of Jinling[①] by Sadula

The capital of the Six Dynasties: glorious
And vanished, like springtime
Sweeping suddenly away.
The earth looks just as it did,
Its rulers have changed.
Oh how life swings
First this way, then that!
Could swallows, my old acquaintances

That used to nest, once,
In old noblemen's houses
Tell what happened to them?
The city has been silenced by darkness.
Nothing moans but rushing spring rivers.

Recall the past events.
Grief grows deep.
Only ruins still stand,
Still remind you of the old states:
Useless to stare, to think.
Only flying crows ever turn their heads and look
Over withered grass and faint smoke,
And the sun sinking into the west.
The Song of *The Jade Trees*
Is heard no more.
And no more is the broken well
Where the Chen Emperor hid,
The old lesson of his downfall
Is forgotten, all forgotten.
Only the sad crickets.
Sing now.
What remains
Is wooded Jiang Mountain
And the green Qinhuai River.

① Jinling: present-day Nanjing.

(2) 徐忠杰 译

"Manjianghong"—Nanjing: a Reminiscence

The Six Dynasties have gone, as spring has.
Their pomp and glory are a passing scene.
No news of any kind could come from them.
Our disappointment! How vain it has been!
Hills and streams; scenic spots; historic sites —

Are not what they were in their former days.
The swallows in the Wang and Xie's① mansions —
Have preferred the commoners with their ways.
Deep night hears the Yangzi beating its banks.
Spring tide rises, bringing the past to mind.

It is grievous to think of past regimes —
Not leaving anything worthwhile behind.
Before me is drear mist and withered grass.
The sight of flying crows is quickly lost.
I seem to hear the echoes of the song,
"Backyard Flowers" amidst autumnal frost.
In ruin is the well where Chen and Zhang② plunged,
To them, chilled cicadas alone are true.
Until now, only the Jiangshan③ is green.
As before, the Qinhuaihe④ remains blue.

① Wang and Xie: two noble families of the Eastern Jin Dynasty (317-420)。
② Chen and Zhang: Emperor Chen of the late Chen Dynasty (557-589) and Zhang Lihua, the emperor's concubine
③ Jiangshan: today's Zijin in Nanjing, Jiangsu Province.
④ Qinghuaihe: a river that runs through Nanjing.

(3) 杨宪益、戴乃迭 译

To the Tune of "Man Jiang Hong" by Sadula

The splendor of the Six Dynasties①
Gone with the passing of spring,
And no more heard of again.
In vain I look with regret at the mountains and rivers
And all the well-known places,
But they are no longer as in the past.
Two swallows play before the former houses of Wang and Xie,②
In the Lane of Black Uniformed Guardsmen,③
And look familiar.
Late at night I hear the rising tide
Surging still against the lonely citadel.

When I think of the past
My mind is beset by many sorrows.
Only traces left of those former kingdoms
In ruins amid the mist and withered grass.
The sun sets and crows fly in confusion;
No more the song about jade trees and flowers in the back court.④
Only the autumn dew grow chill,
Only the ruins of the Rouge Well,⑤
As the cold insects chirp and weep.
But the Jiang Mountain remains green,
The Qinhuai River remains azure and serene.

① Between the third and the sixth centuries, the Wu, Eastern Jin, Song, Qi, Liang and Chen Kingdoms made Nanjing their capital.

② Two powerful families, that of Wang Dao and Xie An, had their houses in Nanjing.

③ The Lane of Black Uniformed Guardsmen was where these two powerful houses of Wang and Xie were situated.

④ The king of Chen had a favourite song sung by his favourite concubine Zhang Lihua.

⑤ When the Kingdom of Chen fell, the king and his concubine hid themselves in this well, but were discovered.

4.7 小桃红(杨果)

满城烟水月微茫，人倚兰舟唱。常记相逢若耶上，隔三湘，碧云望断空惆怅。美人笑道：莲花相似，情短藕丝长。

采莲湖上棹船回，风约湘裙翠，一曲琵琶数行泪。望君归，芙蓉开尽无消息。晚凉多少，红鸳白鹭，何处不双飞。

〖作品简介〗

此二曲的全名分别为《小桃红·满城烟水月微茫》和《小桃红·采莲湖上棹船回》。前一首主要描写的是作者感叹与佳人相处时间短暂，但两人的感情却深厚无比，表达了对于美好生活的期望之情。该曲写采莲女对爱情的思念。后一首是一支写少妇忆远的抒情小曲，既显示出文人高雅典丽的艺术修养，又体现了民歌自然清新的艺术特色。

【注 释】

烟水：氤氲迷蒙的水面。**兰舟**：兰木做的船，兰树坚硬有香味，是做船的上好的材料，这里是指华美的小船。**若耶**：溪水名，传说是西施浣纱的地方。范蠡就是在这条溪上遇见西施的。**三湘**：漓湘、潇湘、蒸湘。**碧云**：碧空中的云。**望断**：极目远望，直到看不见。**惆怅**：伤感。隔着漓江、潇水和蒸水，我极目远望，只看到碧天中的云，只能空自感伤惆怅。**丝**：谐音为"思"。**棹**：桨，作动词用，犹"划"。**约**：束，裹。**湘裙翠**：用湘地丝织品制成的翠绿色的裙子。**芙蓉**：荷花的别名。谐音为"夫容"，一语双关。

【译 文】

(1) 许渊冲 译

Tune: "Red Peach Blossoms"
The Lotus Gatherer by Yang Guo(1195-1269)

I.

The dimming moon o'er mist-veiled town and water looms.
The beauty in orchid boat sings her dream.
I oft remember our meeting on silk-washing stream.
Now severed by three rivers long,
In vain through clouds into the azure sky I gaze.
Smiling, the beauty says,
"Our hearts are like the lotus blooms:
Their root may snap, their fibres join like my song."

II.

Having gathered the lotus on the lake, she rows
On homeward way, her green skirt ripples when wind blows.
A song of pipa brings down tear on tear;
In vain she waits for her lord to appear.
Now lotus blooms all faded, he is not in sight.
How many lovebirds red and egrets white
She sees in the cool evening sky!
Nowhere but in pairs will they fly.

(2) 辜正坤 译

The Lotus-picking Girl(1)
To the Tune of "Light Pink"

Vapor and mist shroud the town, the moon is filmily seen.
Against a painted boat girls sing and careen,
Remember still on the Ruoye River we met,
Separated by three Xiang Rivers like a net,
Helplessly I sign looking at the blue and distant cloud,
Remember again, she once smiled and said aloud:
Our meeting is short, but our love is long to spend.
Just like the lotus's sap without an end.

The Lotus-picking Girl(2)
To the Tune of "Light Pink"

Back is a boat from plucking lotus on the lake,
The wind caressing her green skirt opaque,
At the music of a lute she sheds tears, silent and wan,
Longing for the return of her man.
Now all lotuses wither again, yet no word from him.
Cooler and cooler in the evening dim,
Looking afar, she sees everywhere
Red ducks and white egrets always fly in pair.

4.8 小桃红(王恽)

采菱人语隔秋烟，波静如横练。入手风光莫流传。共留连，画船一笑春风面。江山信美，终非吾土，何日是归年?

【作品简介】

此作"小桃红"又名"平湖乐"，是一首感情浓郁的乡思曲，为作者客居他乡秋日江游时所写。作者名王恽(1227—1304年)，字仲谋，号秋涧，卫州辉汲(今河南汲县)人。大德年间，累官至翰林学士、知制诰。工诗善文，词曲以小令见长。著有《秋涧先生大全集》。现存小令四十一首。

『注 释』

横练：横铺着的白绢。用以形容湖水的平静澄清。**入手风光**：映入眼帘的风景。入手：到手。

『译 文』

辜正坤 译

Lotus-pickers
To the Tune of "Enjoyment on the Peaceful Lake"

Amid the autumn smoke are heard the lotus-
plucking girls, charm,
Like a white ribbon the water looks calm.
Be careful not to this beautiful scene destroy,
Together we stay and ourselves enjoy,
In painted boats are smiling faces like spring so
fair,
Indeed, this land is beautiful beyond compare.
Alas, it's not my native place I roam
And wonder when I can be back at my home?

4.9 人月圆(倪瓒)

惊回一枕当年梦，渔唱起南津。画屏云嶂，池塘春草，无限销魂，旧家应在，梧桐覆井，杨柳藏门。闲身空老，孤篷听雨，灯火江村。

『作品简介』

此作品以孤舟、渔火和雨为主体，勾勒出诗人船中夜听江雨的画面，营造了一种孤寂、苍凉的意境，写出了诗人漂泊江中的凄苦情状。其作者生活在元末明初，始终难忘元兵南下、宋朝灭亡那段悲惨的历史。因此，他一生都没有在元政权下做官，隐逸山林，在他晚年时常追忆旧事，缅怀故国，抒写愁思。此曲即作者重登绍兴越王台时所作，包括江浙广大地区在内的"越地"，既有越王勾践报仇雪耻的历史传统，又是南宋政治经济的中心，人到这里尤其容易激发起亡国的惨痛和恢复河山的愿望，今天作者重游前朝重地，登上当年勾践点兵复仇的越王台，情不自禁地挥笔写下此曲。

〖注 释〗

南津：南面的渡口。**画屏**：形容远山。**池塘春草**：谢灵运曾梦得"池塘后春草"句(见《南史·谢灵运传》)。**孤篷**：孤舟。

〖译 文〗

(1) 许渊冲 译

Tune: "Man and Moon"

Startled on my pillow from my dream
Of bygone years by fishing song at southern
stream,
I see peak on peak veiled in clouds like a
screen,
And pool on pool seem overgrown with
grass green.
How much it grieves
My heart to think of my house of yore
Overshadowed by plane leaves.
With doors hidden amid willow trees.
At ease,
I am oldened in vain.
What can I do but listen to the rain
Or see flickering lights on river shore?

(2) 辜正坤 译

Title Lost(2)
To the Tune of "The Full Moon and Human Reunion"

Dream of the past is suddenly broken and gone,
There from the southern ferret comes the fisher-
man's song.

Around picture-like mountains the distant
clouds look like shawl,
The spring grass grows tender in the pond
small.
Oh, how these scenes my soul enthral!
My old home should have been safe and sound,
Where Chinese parasol branches wind the well
round.
Where the willows my home's door surround.
Look now, this idle body of mine gets so
gaunt,
In the lonely boat listening to pattering rain sit-
ting still,
Far and wide lamps are seen scattering the river
village chill.

4.10　人月圆(倪瓒)

伤心莫问前朝事，重上越王台。鹧鸪啼处，东风草绿，残照花开。
怅然孤啸，青山故国，乔木苍苔。当时明月，依依素影，何处飞来?

【作品简介】

此小令乃一首怀古之作，开篇即已忧思满腹、感慨万千。作品回顾了历史，从勾践卧薪尝胆，夫差昏庸亡国，直至赵宗王朝偏安一隅最后分崩离析；以及当朝(元朝)的由盛而衰。作者面对此情此景，不堪回首往事，却又无法回避。

【注　释】

前朝：此指宋朝。**越王台**：春秋时期越王勾践所建，为驻兵处。**鹧鸪啼处**：朱白《越中览古》："宫女如花满春殿，只今惟有鹧鸪飞。"这里用其意，而以"东风草绿，残照花开"烘托其荒凉的景象。**怅然**：惆怅失意的样子。**孤啸**：独自长叹啸歌。**啸**：放开嗓子拖长声音喊叫。**"青山故国"二句**：故国已成青山，乔木已长苍苔，极力形容其荒凉寂寞的景象。**依依**：眷恋不舍的样子。**素影**：月影。张若虚《春江花月夜》："人生代代无穷已，江月年年望相似。"刘禹锡《金陵》诗："淮水东边旧时月，夜深还过女墙来。"

【译　文】

辜正坤 译

Title Lost(1)
To the Tune of the "Full Moon and Human Reunion"

Never ask about past dynasties when one is
　　seized with pain,
Now I ascend the platform of King Yue again,
Partridges call everywhere,
The east wind greens grasses glare.
In the setting sun flowers are in bloom,
I sing alone over me falling a gloom,
Looking at the native palace where mountains
　　are green.
Woods and mosses are lushly seen.
From where flies in sight
That old moon at night
So shadowy and white?

4.11 水仙子(倪瓒)

东风花外小红楼，南浦山横眉黛愁。春寒不管花枝瘦，无情水自流。檐间燕语娇柔，惊回幽梦，难寻旧游，落日帘钩。

【作品简介】

此小令被认为是作者的早年之作，抒写了自己的离愁别绪，蕴藉婉约，情致绵远。前四句写景，景中有人；后四句直接描绘红楼主人。此曲的妙处在于处处似未从正面落笔，然处处又无不环绕着这离愁别绪。作者本人精于绘画，其曲精于写景，而其景物初看若"纯景"，细品则景中无不含情，深邃含蓄，正显示出其"诗中有画，画中有诗"的创作特色。

【注　释】

红楼：古代一般女子的住处。**南浦**：《楚辞九歌》有："送美人兮南浦。"南浦因此被后人用来指代送别之地。

【译 文】

许渊冲 译

Tune: "Song of Daffodils"

The east wind can't bring flower to
her small red bower;
The mountains bar the sky like eye-
brows in green dye.
The cold spring cares not of the slend-
er blooming tree,
The heartless water flows away, care-
free.
A pair of tender swallows whisper on
the beam,
Awaking her from her sweet dream.
Where can she find her lover? Look!
The setting sun seems to hang on the
curtain's hook.

4.12 殿前欢(阿里西瑛)

懒云窝，醒时诗酒醉时歌。瑶琴不理抛书卧，无梦南柯。得清闲尽快活，日月似撺梭过，富贵比花开落。青春去也，不乐如何？

【作品简介】

作者作《殿前欢》共三首，此曲为第一首。作者借此曲自述心志，表现了沉迷于琴书的快乐心境和对功名富贵的鄙弃。全曲直抒胸臆，朴素自然，活脱潇洒。

【注 释】

懒云窝：曲前自序云："西瑛有居号'懒云窝'，以《殿前欢》调歌此以自述。"

〖译 文〗

(1) Jerome P. Seaton 译

Lazy Cloud's Nest 1 by Ali Hsiying (Late Yuan)

Write poems when I'm sober, and sing when I'm drunk
I leave my fancy lute untuned,
Throw down my book, and sleep.
I don't dream dreams of empire
To have a little idle time is good enough
The sun and moon race like the weaver's shuttle
Wealth and rank are blossoms, bloom and fall
Spring goes
Why not enjoy it?

(2) 许渊冲 译

Tune: "Joy Before Palace" by Ali Xiying
My Nest for Idle Cloud

In my Nest for Idle Cloud,
Sober, I drink and write; while drunk, I
　　croon aloud.
I will not read nor on lute will I play,
Nor dream to climb up high.
I will make merry at leisure,
And let sun and moon like shuttles pass by.
Wealth and rank, after all,
Like flowers, will bloom and fall.
The prime of youth has passed away.
What should I do if not seek pleasure?

4.13 普天乐(张鸣善)

洛阳花，梁园月，好花须买，皓月须赊。花倚栏干看烂熳开，月曾把酒问团圆夜。月有盈亏花有开谢，想人生最苦离别。花谢了三春近也，月缺了中秋到也，人去了何日来也？

『作品简介』

此曲的全称为《普天乐·咏世》，其要表达的思想是：月有盈亏花有开谢，想人生最苦离别。全曲的前六句写洛阳牡丹盛开和梁园赏月的胜景，以欢乐场面为下曲曲情做形象化的铺垫；到七、八句笔锋一转，抒发感慨："想人生最苦离别"。最后三句是进一层补充说明七、八两句的意思，用花落会再开，月缺有重圆来对比、衬托"人去了何日来也"。此曲前面六句以对偶形式分咏花月，中间两句和后面三句则以花、月和人作对比，不但文字新巧，而且蕴涵哲理意味，耐人咀嚼。

『注　释』

洛阳花：即洛阳的牡丹花。欧阳修《洛阳牡丹记》称洛阳牡丹天下第一。**梁园月**：即梁园的月色。梁园，西汉梁孝王所建。孝王曾邀请司马相如、枚乘等辞赋家在园中看花赏月吟诗。**赊**：借钱买。**月曾把酒问团圆夜**：化用苏轼《水调歌头》词："明月几时有，把酒问青天。"**三春**：孟春、仲春、季春。

『译　文』

许渊冲 译

Tune: "Universal Joy"
Apart in the World

Zhang Mingshan

O peony flowers!
O moonlit bowers!
Bright flowers can be bought when
　　they are desired;
Bright moon cannot be brought down
　　when admired.
You may see full-blown flowers from
　　the balustrade,
And drink to the full moon when you
　　gather round.

The moon may wax and wane, flowers may bloom or fade.
What gnaws our heart is to be torn apart.
Faded flowers may blow again when spring comes around;
The waning moon may wax full on Mid-Autumn Day.
O When will you come back now you are far away?

4.14 大德歌·春(关汉卿)

子规啼，不如归。道是春归人未归。几日添憔悴，虚飘飘柳絮飞。一春鱼雁无消息，则见双燕斗衔泥。

〖作品简介〗

此曲表现了闺中少妇(少女)在丈夫(恋人)“道是春归人未归”时，对丈夫(恋人)的期盼、思念之情。其末句“则见双燕斗衔泥”起到了反衬作用。一对春燕比翼双飞，为筑爱巢而忙碌着，比赛着衔泥，这令孤居独处、郁郁寡欢的少妇(少女)无比羡慕，更增添了她对丈夫(恋人)的期盼、思念之情。

〖注　释〗

大德歌：曲牌名。**子规啼，不如归**：子规啼声很像人说“不如归”，容易引起离人的乡愁。**憔悴**：疲惫，没有精神。**鱼雁**：书信的代称。**则见双燕斗衔泥**：只见一对对燕子争相衔泥筑巢。**斗**：竞相，争着。

〖译　文〗

辜正坤 译

Spring
To the Tune of “Great Virtue”

The cuckoo calls: better, better to go home,

Now spring's back yet he did far away roam.
I am pining away.
Willow fluff comes fluttering on the way.
Throughout the spring no signs of message occur,
Only swallows vie with each other in pair,
Mud in their breaks, building their nest so fair.

4.15　大德歌·夏（关汉卿）

俏冤家，在天涯。偏那里绿杨堪系马。困坐南窗下，数对清风想念他。蛾眉淡了教谁画，瘦岩岩羞带石榴花。

〖作品简介〗

这首小令刻画了一位独守闺中而思念情人，爱怨交加、面容憔悴的女子形象。她因情人远在天涯而孤独寂寞，思念之情难以排遣，因相思而心生猜疑抱怨，以致身体瘦弱。

〖注　释〗

"偏那"句：偏偏只有那里留得住。张耒《风流子》："遇有系马，垂杨影下。"**数对**：屡次对着，频频地对着。**蛾眉**：指女子弯弯的长眉毛。**瘦岩岩**：瘦削的样子。**石榴花**：泛指红色的花。苏轼《贺新郎》"石榴半吐红巾蹙"，则借作石榴花了。

〖译　文〗

幸正坤 译

Summer
To the Tune of "Great Virtue"

My good-looking foeman, where
Are you, in the remotest region,
Tying your horse to green willows here and there?
Often I think of you by the southern window,
Sitting wearily in the cooling air.
Who could now paint my faded curved brows?
I have no heart to wear flower, thin and lonely standing in my house.

4.16　大德歌·秋(关汉卿)

风飘飘，雨潇潇，便做陈抟睡不着。懊恼伤怀抱，扑簌簌泪点抛。秋蝉儿噪罢寒蛩儿叫，淅零零细雨打芭蕉。

〖作品简介〗

这首小令以大自然的秋声来描写人物心灵的感受，声情并茂，直率中见委婉，委婉中情更真，再现了少妇因为“人未归”而引发的烦恼。此曲起头三句写风、写雨、写长夜不眠，由景入情，直入怀抱。风雨交加，突然而至，声势咄咄逼人，这就给脆弱的少妇带来很大压力。四、五句写女主人公愁苦情状——“扑簌簌泪点抛”，并在准确地捕捉这一典型细节以后留下空间，让读者想象补充，其闺房幽情在充实中越发空灵。最后二句继续写景，景语皆情语，蝉噪蛩鸣，雨打芭蕉。这些外界景物强烈地衬托出女主人公的孤独、寂寞和难以言喻的久别之苦，进一步凸显女主人公愁苦的心境。

〖注　释〗

便做陈抟睡不着：思人心切，即使做了陈抟也难以入睡。**便做**：就算，即使。**陈抟**：五代宋初著名道士，字图南，自号扶摇子，宋太宗赐名“希夷先生”，曾修道于华山，常一睡百天不醒。**扑簌簌**：流泪的样子。**秋蝉儿噪罢寒蛩儿叫**：白天秋蝉不断地鸣叫刚罢，蟋蟀接着在夜间又叫个不停。**蛩**：蟋蟀，又名促织。**淅零零**：形容雨声。

〖译　文〗

(1) Wai-lim Yip 译

“VAST VIRTUE”

Winds whistle.
Rains drizzle.
Even the Sleep Immortal cannot go to sleep.
Sorrow meshed on heart’s tip.
Downpour, downpour, tears drop.
Chilling cicadas stop, crickets creak.
Drip, drip, fine rains on banana-leaves beat.

(2) 许渊冲 译

Tune: "Song of Great Virtue"

The wind soughs hour after hour;
The rain falls shower by shower.
Even the Sleeping God cannot fall asleep.
Regret and sorrow hurt me deep,
My tears drip drop by drop,
After cicadas trill crickets chirp without stop.
It further grieves
To hear rain drizzle on banana leaves.

(3) 辜正坤 译

Autumn
To the Tune of "Great Virtue"

The wind forcibly blows,
The rain down in showers goes.
There's no way to fall asleep.
Worries hurt my heart deep,
Tears in flood I weep.
The autumn cicada echoes cricket here and there,
Drinks softly bent banana leaves fair.

4.17 大德歌·冬(关汉卿)

雪粉华，舞梨花，再不见烟村四五家。密洒堪图画，看疏林噪晚鸦。黄芦掩映清江下，斜缆着钓鱼艖。

〖作品简介〗

这首小令，作者通过对“冬景”的描绘，曲折地表现了元朝文人儒士无限的历世感叹和兴亡之感。

〖注 释〗

华：光彩，光辉。**黄芦**：枯黄的芦苇。**艖**[chā]：小船。

〖译 文〗

辜正坤 译

Winter
To the Tune of "Great Virtue"

Snow powders in the sky,
Pear blossoms dance on high.
Misty are villages out of sight.
What a beautiful picture white!
Evening ravens caw in the ragged wood near,
Yellow rushes reflect themselves in the river clear.
Tied in tangled halyards fishing boats appear.

4.18 四块玉·闲适(关汉卿)

其三

意马收，心猿锁，跳出红尘恶风波，槐阴午梦谁惊破？离了利名场，钻入安乐窝，闲快活！

其四

南亩耕，东山卧，世态人情经历多，闲将往事思量过。贤的是他，愚的是我，争甚么？

〖作品简介〗

这是关汉卿所作《四块玉·闲适》四首小令中的后两首。该曲创作于元代初期，具体创作年代不详。这四首曲子抒写了作者的闲适生活，表达了作者看破红尘、放下名利、参透荣辱、与世无争的思想，也反映出作者对黑暗官场的不满情绪，表现出作者傲岸的气骨和倔强的个性。全曲语言朴实自然，毫无雕琢痕迹，形象鲜明生动、传神感人。

【注 释】

意马、心猿：是来自佛教经典中的典故。把人的名利心比作奔腾的马、烦躁的猿，必须拴住、锁着才能静得下来。**槐阴午梦**：即南柯梦。据唐人传奇《南柯太守传》，书生淳于棼醉卧槐荫下，梦为大槐安国附马，任南柯郡太守荣华富贵显赫一时；醒来发现大槐安国就是槐树上的大蚂蚁洞，南柯郡就是槐树最南枝上的小蚂蚁洞。**南亩耕**：典出《诗经·豳风·七月》："同我妇子，馈彼南亩，田唆至喜。"**东山卧**：用东晋谢安的典故。谢安曾隐居在东山(今浙江上虞县西南)，后入朝为相。后来人们常用"东山高卧"形容那些高洁之士的隐居生活。**甚么**：即"什么"。

【译 文】

(1) 许渊冲 译

Tune: "Four Pieces of Jade"
Life of Easy Leisure by Guan Hanqing

(I)
Halt running horse and bind
Ape-like whimsical mind!
Leap out of a world which raves with dust and waves!
Wake up from noonday dream of glory vain!
Get rid of fame and gain!
Take a rest in your nest of pleasure
And enjoy your leisure!
(II)
Having tilled the southern field, I
At the foot of eastern hill lie.
I've known the world and its ways,
And ponder at leisure the past days.
O wise is he
And foolish me!
What should I contend to be?

(2) 辜正坤 译

Leisure
To the Tune of "Four Pieces of Jade"

(**I**)
Repressing my wish for fame,
Locking up my desire for game,
Out of this secular world I drop now,
To break those fond dreams I vow.
No longer in that vanity fair,
I worm into a cosy and peaceful nest with care.
Oh, this life of leisure is happy beyond compare.
(**II**)
Tao the poet once plows the southern drills,
Xie the scholar once dwells among the eastern hills.
Too many to narrate the things of worldly kind,
Calmly I try to measure them in my mind.
O. K. Let's believe he is the saint,
And I am the fool, so our life
Is prevented from a competitive strife.

4.19 沉醉东风·送别(关汉卿)

咫尺的天南地北，霎时间月缺花飞。手执着饯行杯，眼阁着别离泪。刚道得声保重将息，痛煞煞教人舍不得，好去者前程万里。

【作品简介】

这首小令是关汉卿写爱情的一首名作，描写女子在为情人饯别时的离愁别绪。整个曲子真切、恰如其分地描写了主人公在话别饯行之际时而含蓄时而坦率的情感，深挚真切，哀婉动人。刻画出了一个情感极为深挚凄婉，但毫不低沉感伤的痴情主人公形象，给人以积极向上的美感。

【注　释】

沉醉东风：是这个“双调”的曲牌。**霎时间**：一会儿。黄庭坚《两同心》：“霎时间，雨散云归，无处追雪。”**花飞**：花飘，花落。晁补之《行香子·梅》：“向未开时，愁花放，恐花飞。”**阁着**：噙着，含着，**阁**：同“搁”。**将息**：调养、休息的意思。李清照《声声慢》：“乍暖还寒时候，最难将息。”**痛煞煞**：表示痛苦的样子。亦作“痛设设”。**好去者**：安慰行者的套语，犹言“好走着”。马致远《要孩儿·借马》套：“道一声好去，早两泪双垂。”

【译　文】

(1) 许渊冲 译

Tune: "Intoxicated in East Wind"
Farewell Song
Guan Hanqing

We stand so near yet we'll be
　　poles apart soon;
In a moment flowers will fall and
　　wane the moon.
We hold in hand the farewell cup,
In our eyes tears well up.
I have just said, "Take care to
　　keep fit!"
How painful is it
To tear myself away!
I can only say, "Go your way for
　　the bright day!"

(2) 辜正坤 译

Untitled
To the Tune of "Heart-inebriating East Wind"

Close to me now the next minute you'll be far
　　away,
And in an instant the moon wanes and flowers
　　fade and decay.
With the cup in my shaking hand,
Tearfully I send you off to a distant land.

Waving goodbye I say "Take care,"
Oh, This leave-taking sorrow I cannot bear.
Now gradually you are out of sight,
I can only wish you a future so gloriously
bright.

4. 20 碧玉箫(关汉卿)

膝上琴横，哀愁动离情；指下风生，潇洒弄清声。锁窗前月色明，雕阑外夜气清。指法，助起骚人兴。听，正漏断人初静。

〖作品简介〗

这支小令写离别，是抒发主人公的离情之作。

〖注　释〗

风生：即生风，这里形容抚琴指法之快。**锁窗**：雕刻或绘有连环形花饰的窗子，与下句“雕阑”相对。**漏断**：即尽，指夜已深。**漏**：即漏壶，是古代滴水计时的一种仪器。

〖译　文〗

(1) 许渊冲 译

Tune: "Green Jade Flute"

With zither on my knees,
I'm moved to think of my far-off dear.
My fingers play with ease
On zither strings a music clear.
Before my window screen the moon is
bright;
Beyond the balustrade fresh is the night.
My touches light
Would make the poets' verve freer.
O Hear!
From water clock there comes no sound;

Silence begins to reign all around.

(2) 辜正坤 译

Untitled
To the Tune of "Green Jade Flute"

A zither on my laps overflows
With separation touches of woes.
The wind under my fingers resounds
So gracefully that the zither gives clear sounds.
Over the locked window hanging the moon
    bright,
Outside the engraved balustrade the night air is
    light.
Gently I finger with the strings,
Making the poet's feelings on wings.
Listen!
Night watch sound is heard to stop
When peace and quiet finally drop.

4.21 一枝花 ·不伏老(关汉卿)

攀出墙朵朵花，折临路枝枝柳；花攀红蕊嫩，柳折翠条柔。浪子风流。凭着我折柳攀花手，直煞得花残柳败休。半生来折柳攀花，一世里眠花卧柳。

〔尾〕我是个蒸不烂、煮不熟、捶不匾、炒不爆、响珰珰一粒铜豌豆；恁子弟每谁教你钻入他锄不断、斫不下、解不开、顿不脱、慢腾腾千层锦套头。我玩的是梁园月，饮的是东京酒，赏的是洛阳花，攀的是章台柳。我也会围棋、会蹴鞠、会打围、会插科、会歌舞、会吹弹、会咽作、会吟诗、会双陆，你便是落了我牙，歪了我嘴，瘸了我腿，折了我手，天赐与我这几般儿歹症候，尚兀自不肯休！则除是阎王亲自唤、神鬼自来勾，三魂归地府，七魄丧冥幽，天哪，那其间才不向烟花路儿上走！

『作品简介』

此曲乃一首带有自述心志性质的套曲作品的首尾部分。该套曲子用本色、生动、诙谐、夸张的语言，以大胆而又夸张的笔调，熟练地发挥了散曲形式的特点，描写了作者的浪漫生活和多才多艺，倾诉了一泻无余的感情，显示了作者狂放高傲的个性，表现了他顽强、乐观、热爱生活的性格。表明了他决不向黑暗现实妥协的决心。全曲气韵深沉、语势狂放，历来为人传颂，被视为关汉卿散曲的代表作。

〖注 释〗

煞：俗“杀”字，这里指摧残。**休**：语气助词。**匾**：同“扁”。**铜豌豆**：妓院中对老狎客的称呼。**恁**[nèn]：通“那”。如“我从来斩钉截铁常居一，不似恁惹草拈花没掂三”(元王实甫《西厢记》)。又有“恁每”一词，即“你们”的意思，所以“恁子弟每”就是“您子弟们”的意思。**斫**[zhuó]：用刀、斧头砍。**锦套头**：锦绳结成的套头，比喻圈套、陷阱。此两句连起来的意思是：那些浮浪子弟们每陷入风月场所、温柔之乡不能自拔，而自己却见多识广练就一身功夫，不把这些套数放在眼里，反而正好能够大展身手。**梁园**：又名“梁苑”。汉代梁孝王的园子，在今河南开封府附近，园内有池馆林木，梁王日与宾客游乐，因此后来以之泛指名胜游玩之所。**东京**：汉代以洛阳为东京，宋代以汴州(今开封市)为东京，辽时改南京(今辽阳)为东京。此处不必实指，元曲往往混用历史地名故事。总之这几句的意思是说自己行走的都是名胜之地。**洛阳花**：指牡丹。古时洛阳以产牡丹花著名。**章台柳**：代指妓女。**章台**：汉长安街名，娼妓所居。《太平广记·柳氏传》载，唐韩翃与妓女柳氏有婚约，安史之乱，两人分离，韩赋诗以表思念：“章台柳，章台柳，昔日青青今在否？纵使长条似旧垂，也应攀折他人手。”**蹴踘**[cù jū]：中国古代的一种足球运动，《汉书》中已有记载。唐宋时盛行(《水浒传》中的高俅即以此技得宠于皇帝)，至清代渐衰。这种球外面是皮革，里面实以物，所以又写成“蹴鞠”。**打围**：即打猎，相对于围场之说。**插科**：戏曲演员在表演中穿插的引人发笑的动作。常同“打诨”合用，称“插科打诨”。**咽作**：不详。可能是一种表演性的游戏。**双陆**[liù]：又名“双六”，古代一种博戏。据说为三国魏曹植所创，至唐代演变为叶子戏(纸牌)。**歹症候**：本是指病，借指脾性。**歹**：不好。**尚兀自**：仍然还。**兀自**：仍旧，还是。**则除是**：除非是。**则**：同“只”。**冥幽**：与前文“地府”同义，指传说中的阴间。**烟花**：原指妓院，亦指妓女。古代胭脂又写成烟肢、烟支等，烟花之意或由此引申。

〖译 文〗

(1) Wayne Schlepp 译

In the Southern Mode, to the Tune of “Sprig of Flowers”
The Refusal to Get Old by Kuan Han-ch’ing(ca. 1220-ca. 1300)

I’ve plucked every flower that grows over the wall,

And gathered every willow overhanging the road;[①]
The tenderest buds were the flowers I picked,
And the willows I gathered, of the supplest green fronds;
A wastrel, gay and dashing,
Trusting to my willow gathering, flower plucking hand,
I kept at it till the flowers fell and the willows withered;
Half my life I've been willow gathering and flower plucking
And for a whole generation slept with flowers and lain among the willows.

Yellow Bell Coda

But I am an
Un-steam-soft-able, un-boil-through-able,
Un-pound-flat-able, un-bake-dry-able
Rattling plunkety-plunk coppery old bean.[②]
Who said you young gentlemen could intrude upon her
Un-hoe-up-able, un-cut-down-able,
Un-disentwine-able, un-cast-off-able,
Intricate, thousand-fold brocade snare?[③]
As for me, I can take pleasure in the Liang-yüan[④] moon,
Drink no less than East Capital[⑤] wine,
Enjoy the flowers of Loyang,
And pluck the willow of Chang-t'ai.[⑥]
Besides, I can compose poems, write ancient script,
Play the lute and play the flute;
I know how to sing the Che-ku, dance the Ch'ui-shou,[⑦]
Drive game for the hunt, kick the football,
Play chess and roll dice;
Even if you knock out my teeth, stretch mouth out of shape,
Lame my legs, break my arms,
Even if heaven afflicted me with these several ills and disabilities,
I'd still not give up;
Not unless Yama[⑧] himself gives the order
And the evil spirits themselves come to hook out
My three souls and return them to hell,
My seven shades and consign them to oblivion,[⑨]
Only then
Will I retire from the path of mist and flowers.[⑩]

① Throughout the poem flowers and willows refer to courtesans.

② Literally, "coppery old bean"—Yüan slang for a libertine who is somewhat past his prime.

③ A courtesan's methods of getting a man into her clutches.

④ Liang-yüan was vast park built in Han times by Prince Hsiao of Liang, here suggesting sophisticated tastes.

⑤ The Eastern Capital, i. e., Loyang, was noted for its luxuriance and beauty.

⑥ A district of Ch'ang-an, the Western Capital, where a famous T'ang courtesan named Liu (i. e. "willow") lived. *Chang-t'ai liu* is often used in reference to courtesans generally.

⑦ *Che-ku* ("Partridge") or *Che-ku t'ien* ("Partridge Sky") is the name of a lyric verse form. *Ch'ui-shou* (Hanging Hands) is the name of a song to which one danced, hands hanging down the while.

⑧ King of the underworld.

⑨ The belief that one dies only after the evil spirits have hooked out of one's body all ten of its souls.

⑩ The gay life among courtesans.

(2) 许渊冲 译

Tune: "A Spring of Flowers"

(1) Don't Say I'm Old

I pluck flower on flower over the wall,
And break off branch on branch of willow
　　tree.
The red pistil of the flower is tender;
The green twigs of the willow are slender.
A gallant like me
Will gather flowers and break off
　　branches till I see
Withered leaves and flowers fall.
I have been picking them half my life;
I'll love and sleep with them as with a
　　wife.

(IV) Tune: "Epilogue"

I'm a resounding copper pea
Which could not be
Hammered out, cooked, fried or stewed.
How can you young gallants penetrate into me

Like a manifold harness which cannot be
Hoed up or cut down,

Slowly rid of or quickly hewed?
I have enjoyed in royal garden the moonshine
In the east capital good wine,
And peony flowers in the west,
And plucked a twig from my lover's breast.
I'm good at poetry
And at calligraphy;
I can play on the string
And draw a picture of bamboo,
I can also sing
The songs of partridge too.
With hands hanging down I can dance,
In hunting I can advance,
I know how to play football and chess,
And! gamble by chance.
You may knock my teeth down
Or my mouth wry,
Even if you break
My leg and hand,
Though disabled am I,
Still firm I'll stand,
Unless
The Satanic Majesty
Or the demons come to summon me.
Even one-third of my soul goes to the
    hell
And two-thirds sink into the internal
    well,
O Heaven, only then
Will I got go on the dark willowy lane.

4.22 一半儿·题情(关汉卿)

碧纱窗外静无人，跪在床前忙要亲。骂了个负心回转身。虽是我话儿嗔，一半儿推辞一半儿肯。

〖作品简介〗

该作是作者所作《一半儿·题情》四首小令中的第二首。描绘一对青年男女的爱情，描写大胆泼辣，略无顾忌，有审美情感浓烈的一面，而无审美情感隐秘的一面，体现了关曲雅俗共赏、本色当行的特色。

〖注　释〗

一半儿：曲牌名。碧纱：指碧绿的纱帘。

〖译　文〗

(1) Zong-qi Cai 译

To the Tune of "A Half"[xianlü key]: On Love

All was quiet outside the green-gauze window curtain;
He knelt down in front of my bed and wanted to get intimate.
I just called him an ingrate and turned my back on him.
Though there was annoyance in what I said,
Half of it meant to reject; the other half, consent.

(2) 辜正坤 译

Untitled
To the Tune of "Half"

Outside curtained window no one is in sight,
He kneels before my bed attempting a kiss with
　　might.
I chide him "a heartless man" and then turn to
　　the wall,
Though I make angry remarks so tart,
I half refuse and half wish for the kiss at heart.

4.23 阳春曲·题情(1)(白朴)

轻拈斑管书心事。细析银笺写恨词，可怜不惯害相思。则被个肯字儿，迤逗我许多时。

〖作品简介〗

此作品乃作者一组六首曲子的第一首，名曰“题情”，写的是男女之间的相思之情。

〖注 释〗

斑管：有斑纹的竹子做成的毛笔。**银笺**：洁白的信笺。**恨词**：抒写离愁别恨的话。**迤(yí)逗**：勾引，挑逗。《秋胡戏妻》四：“谁着你戏弄人家妻儿，迤逗人家婆娘。”

〖译 文〗

(1) 许渊冲 译

Tune: “Song of Spring”
For My Love

I take up my pen light stained with tears to write
My heart-felt grief and then I fold the paper white.
Alas! unused to lasting longing for a mate,
It takes me such a long, long time to wait
For your vain promise of a date.

(2) 辜正坤 译

Ode on Love (1)
To the Tune of “Young Spring”

Gently I use a bamboo pen to write down what I
    have in mind,
This white piece of paper is full of complaint
    and grief,

How can I bear the lovesickness' weight of this
kind!
Your promise "Yes" giving me relief
Has long kept me in a bind.

4.24 阳春曲·题情(3)(白朴)

笑将红袖遮银烛，不放才郎夜看书，相偎相抱取欢娱。止不过迭应举，及第待何如?

『作品简介』

此作品乃作者一组六首曲子的第三首，写的是男女之间的相思之情。

『注 释』

红袖：红色的衣袖。**银烛**：雪亮的蜡烛。温庭筠《七夕》："银烛有光妨宿燕，画屏无睡待牵牛。"**迭应举**：屡次参加科举考试。**及第**：科举应试后中选。

『译 文』

(1) Zong-qi Cai 译

To the Tune of "Spring Song" [zhonglu key]: On Love

Laughing, I block out the silver candlelight with a red sleeve,
And forbid my erudite dear one to read books.
Nestling together, we have such fun.
Isn't that only about exams?
Who cares even if you pass?

(2) 辜正坤 译

Ode on Love(3)
To the Tune of "Young Spring"

Laughing, with red sleeve, I cover up the silvery

candle light,
Not to let you, my talented man, read at
night.
Please embrace me and kiss me as you choose,
For the official entrance exam you doggedly
fight,
But even if you have succeeded, what's the
use?

4.25　天净沙·春(白朴)

春山暖日和风，阑干楼阁帘栊，杨柳秋千院中。啼莺舞燕，小桥流水飞红。

〖作品简介〗

白朴作《天净沙·春、夏、秋、冬》共四首，分写四时景色。这首《天净沙·春》描写春景，给人一种和煦明丽的感觉。全曲运用绘画技法，从不同空间层次描写春天的景物，具体来说，第一句是整个画面的背景，是远景，第二句是人物的立足点，是近景，第三句庭院中喧闹的景象，展示了一幅充满生机、春意盎然的画面，是景中景，最能够体现春天特征的两个形容词是"暖"与"和"，而最能体现庭院中生机的景物是舞燕和飞红。曲中人物应是一位女子，她站在栏杆之旁、帘栊之下，窥探着春天的景致，她眼中的春天要更加细腻、更加秀美。此曲全由当代修辞学家谭永祥命名的列锦组成。所谓列锦乃古典诗歌作品中一种奇特的句式，即全句以名词或名词短语组成，里面没有动词或形容词谓语，却同样能起到写景抒情、叙事述怀的效果。(见谭永祥著《修辞新格》，福建教育出版社，1996年出版。)

〖注　释〗

飞红：指落花。

〖译　文〗

(1) 许渊冲 译

Tune: "Sunny Sand"
(1) Spring

The sun and gentle breeze warm hills in spring,

The curtained bower girt with balustrade.
Among the willows in the garden hangs the
swing.
The swallows dance and orioles sing
On running stream under the bridge fallen
reds fade.

(2) 辜正坤 译

Spring
To the Tune of "Sky Scouring Sand"

The temperate sun, the verdant hills and the
vernal breeze;
Towers, balustrades and curtained windows;
There in the yard are swings and willows at
their ease;
Orioles chirping and swallows dancing in the
sky,
The wooden bridge, the flowing water pink
with flowers that fly.

4.26 沉醉东风(卢挚)

恰离了绿水青山那答,
早来到竹篱茅舍人家。
野花路畔开,
村酒槽头榨。
直吃的欠欠答答。
醉了山童不劝咱,
白发上乱插黄花。

〖作品简介〗

这首小令是《双调·沉醉东风·闲居》中的第二首。全曲描写饮酒的意趣,全篇语言皆为口语。从绿水青山、竹篱茅舍的景色,到使人赏心悦目、野花路开、村酒槽榨的画面,再到主人公的酩酊醉态,形象生动,甚是传神。

『注 释』

恰：刚才。**那答**：那块，那边。**早来**：已经。**槽头**：酿酒的器具。**欠欠答答**：疯疯癫癫，痴痴呆呆，形容醉态。

『译 文』

(1) Wai-lim Yip 译

"DRUNK IN THE EAST WIND"

(Soon after)
　　The blue-water, green-mountain shore,
(We came to)
　　Bamboo-fenced homes of straw.
(Wild flowers)
　　Blooming by the road.
(Village wine)
　　To the wine-press.
　　Drink to a dead dull daze.
　　Flustered, mountain boys leave all advice behind.
　　Upon our white heads, plant yellow flowers, any kind.

(2) 许渊冲 译

Tune: "Intoxicated in East Wind"
(II) Rural Life

Having just left green hills and water
　　blue,
I come to thatched cots with fence
　　of bamboo.
By the roadside wild flowers blow;
In the trough I see home brew flow.
I eat till drunk I stagger along.
The lad won't care if I am wrong,

To wear yellow flowers on my white
    hair.

(3) 辜正坤 译

Stay at Home Idle
To the Tune of "Heart-inebriating East Wind"

Taking leave of blue waters and mountains
    whence,
Now I've come to this thatched house with a
    bamboo fence.
On either way wild flowers in bloom grow,
In village wine is being made to flow.
I drink to my heart's content, dizzy with intoxi-
    cation.
Drunkard I am, the village boy does not stop
    me drinking again,
My white hair is dotted with yellow flowers
    plain.

4.27 夜行船·落梅风(马致远)

天教富，莫太奢。无多时好天良夜。看钱奴硬将心似铁，空辜负锦堂风月。

【作品简介】

此曲是马致远的《双调·夜行船·秋思》组曲中的第四支。全组散曲虽凝聚着作者思索自然之秋和人生之秋的丰富内涵，然而更是包孕弘深、独具一格，因为它将作者参透名利、离绝是非的处世哲学寄托在叹古讽今、嘲风弄月的牢骚里，浓缩了他的剧目和其他散曲中反复宣泄的内心苦闷，表现了他因半世蹉跎、饱谙世情而形成的纵酒肆志、超然尘外的人生态度。该词曲由叹古转为讽今，意思更深一层：帝王豪杰的功业尚且化为乌有，更何况看钱奴的万贯家财？可笑这些人心硬似铁，一味地爱钱如命，看不透人生好景不常，为欢几何，空使锦堂风月虚设，哪里懂得什么赏心乐事？全曲分两层递进，看钱奴的庸俗愚蠢和昼锦堂的良辰美景两相对照，俚俗的白话和清雅的词藻各得其所。

〖注　释〗

好天良夜：好日子，好光景。**看钱奴**：元代杂剧家郑廷玉根据神怪小说《搜神记》，关于一个姓周的贫民在天帝的恩赐下，以极其悭吝、极其刻薄的手段，变为百万富翁的故事，塑造了一个为富不仁、爱财如命的悭吝形象——看钱奴。**锦堂风月**：富贵人家的美好景色。此句嘲讽守财奴情趣卑下，无福消受荣华。“锦堂”这里暗喻宋韩琦在相州故乡筑昼锦堂的故事，泛指富贵人家的宅第。

〖译　文〗

(1) 许渊冲 译

Tune: “Falling Mume Blossoms”

No matter how rich you may be,
Don’t live in luxury!
O happy days and nights cannot forever last.
No matter how hard a miser’s heart may be,
The breezy moonlit days will soon be past.

(2) 辜正坤 译

Untitled
To the Tune of “Sailing at Night”

Heaven favors you with riches and a fortunate
　　lot,
But be careful to be extravagant not.
Good days and fortunes do not last long,
You, sons of wealthy families, with hearts hard
　　and strong,
Are good-for-nothing in the pompous homes
　　with good time gone.

4.28 夜行船·风入松(马致远)

眼前红日又西斜，疾似下坡车。晓来清镜添白雪，上床与鞋履相别。莫笑鸠巢计拙，葫芦提一向装呆。

作品简介

此曲是马致远的《双调·夜行船·秋思》组曲中的第五支。该曲陈述了自己的人生哲学。“眼前红日又西斜”写一日之内光阴的流逝，遥承“百岁光阴”而来，“疾似下坡车”的比喻从羲和驾日车的常用典故脱出，化雅为俗，生动有趣。“晓来清镜添白雪”反用李白“君不见高堂明镜悲白发，朝成青丝暮成雪”的意思，引出“上床与鞋履相别”这句玩笑，好像把俗话说的“今晚脱下鞋和袜，不知明天穿不穿”稍加提炼发挥，便成了至理名言。不过这句貌似参透生死的俏皮话里隐藏着愤世嫉俗的深意，所以紧接着劝人莫笑自己像不会筑巢的斑鸠那样拙笨，这不过是糊里糊涂地装傻而已。自称不善营生之计，其实倒是离绝名利是非的上计，明说一向装呆，又点出浑浑噩噩混世的不得已。

注　释

添白雪：添白发。**鸠巢计拙**：指不善于经营生计。《经·召南·鹊巢》：“维鹊有巢，维鸠居之。”朱熹注：“鸠性拙不能为巢，或有居鹊之成巢者。”**葫芦提**：糊里糊涂。

译　文

(1) 许渊冲 译

Tune：“The Wind Through Pines”

The setting sun goes west before the eye
As quickly as the carriage rolling down
the height.
Don't let your hair in the mirror turn
snow-white!
Go to bed and say to your shoes goodbye!
Don't laugh at the cuckoo occupying the
magpie's nest!
Play the fool like a gourd and take your

rest!

(2) 辜正坤 译

Untitled
To the Tune of "Sailing at Night"

The red sun is setting in the west before my
　　eyes,
Fast as a carriage going downhill flies.
Indifferent to, in the mirror, my snow-white
　　hair on head,
I part with my shoes when going to bed,
Like the pigeon playing the fool,
That is often mocked for its lack of school.

4.29　寿阳曲·山市晴岚(马致远)

花村外，草店西，晚霞明雨收天霁。四围山一竿残照里，锦屏风又添铺翠。

『作品简介』

这支曲子写傍晚小山村雨过天晴的秀美景色。仰望天空，天空明净如洗，晚霞又照得满天光华绚艳，景色极为迷人。山村小镇四周的山峦，笼罩在夕阳的光辉里，给人一种柔和而明丽的感觉。本来就很美的像是小镇屏风的山峦，经过雨水的洗濯，又在夕阳的映照之下，还飘散着薄纱似的水汽，显得格外青翠，像是在原来的绿色上添上一层绿色。天上的晚霞和四周的山色，给这个山村小市增添了静谧气氛和美丽景色。该曲的一个突出特点是：层层描景，使山市晴岚景象鲜明突出。"花村外，草店西"首先展现的是"山市"，是鲜花盛放的村庄与商业性的草店。第三句"晚霞明雨收天霁"所写的是视觉中的山市景象。其中虽有雨过天晴的描写，但尚未直接写晴岚，只是为晴岚的描写作铺垫。第四句写残照中的四围山色，其中虽有晴岚在，但未直接写出。直至第五句"又添铺翠"出现，作者才把晴岚及其造成的景致和盘托出。以"又添铺翠"这样的点睛般句子煞尾，使"山市"与"晴岚"的意象都鲜明地呈现了出来。

『注　释』

寿阳曲：曲牌名，又名《落梅风》。**山市**：山区小市镇。**晴岚**：雨过天晴，山间散发的水汽。**天霁(jì)**：雨过天晴。**一竿残照里**：太阳西下，离山只有一竿子高。**屏风**：指像屏风一样的山峦。

〖译 文〗

(1) 许渊冲 译

Tune: "Song of Long-lived Sun"
The Sun-lit Mist-veiled Mountain

By blooming village-side,
West of the shop of wine,
Rainbow clouds after rain brighten the
　　sky far and wide.
The surrounding hills steeped in sinking
　　sunshine,
The embroidered screen is again paved
　　with emerald green.

(2) 辜正坤 译

Fine Clouds over the Mountain
To the Tune of "Life-giving Sun"

Beyond the village of flower,
West of the thatched shops,
Evening glow in the sky is washed by a recent
　　shower.
Around, the setting sun licks hill tops,
Like a brocade screen added to more green
　　props.

4.30 寿阳曲·潇湘夜雨(马致远)

渔灯暗，客梦回。一声声滴人心碎。孤舟五更家万里，是离人几行清泪。

〖作品简介〗

这支小令的全名为《双调 · 寿阳曲 · 潇湘夜雨》，写的是作者由江西至湖南的亲身感受，表达身处天涯、心系故园的“断肠人”的羁旅乡愁，与《天净沙 · 秋思》有异曲同工之妙。该曲将诗词中常有的意境和手法引入曲中，然又自出机杼地描写了特有景色中的特定氛围：雨夜、孤舟、渔灯中离家万里的旅人在点点滴滴的雨声里情不自禁流下“几行清泪”，这使读者也不由得产生强烈的共鸣，情景交融，言简意深，堪称佳作。

〖注　释〗

潇湘夜雨：曲题。“潇湘夜雨”是宋元人所称“潇湘八景”之一。**潇湘**：原指湘水与潇水在零陵的汇合处，后用以指湖南。**梦回**：梦醒。

〖译　文〗

(1) 许渊冲 译

Night Rain on the River

Dim fishers' lantern light,
I wake up from my dream.
The rain drips drop by drop to break my
　　heart.
My lonely boat is far from home deep
　　in the night.
It rains as tears which stream
Down from the eyes of those who
　　part.

(2) 辜正坤 译

The Night Rain on the Xiaoxiang River
To the Tune of "Life-giving Sun"

The lamplight is dim;
Broken is the stranger's dream

By drops of heart-rending rain
Like a traveler's passion-ridden tear in vain,
At dawn in the lonely fishing boat I roam,
Thousands of miles away from my home.

4.31 天净沙·秋思（马致远）

枯藤老树昏鸦，
小桥流水人家，
古道西风瘦马。
夕阳西下，
断肠人在天涯。

〖作品简介〗

此小令是一首著名的散曲作品，以多种景物并置，组合成一幅秋郊夕照图，让天涯游子骑一匹瘦马出现在一派凄凉的背景上，从中透出令人哀愁的情调，抒发了一个飘零天涯的游子在秋天思念故乡、倦于漂泊的凄苦愁楚之情。

〖注　释〗

枯藤：枯萎的枝蔓。**昏鸦**：黄昏时的乌鸦。**人家**：农家。此句写出了诗人对温馨的家庭的渴望。**古道**：古老荒凉的道路。**西风**：寒冷、萧瑟的秋风。**瘦马**：骨瘦如柴的马。**断肠人**：形容伤心悲痛到极点的人，此处指漂泊天涯、极度忧伤的旅人。**天涯**：远离家乡的地方。

〖译　文〗

(1) W. Schlepp 译

Tune to "Sand and Sky"
—Autumn Thoughts by Ma Zhiyuan

Dry vine, old tree, crows at dusk,
Low bridge, stream running, cottages,
Ancient road, west wind, lean nag,

The sun westering
And one with breaking heart at the sky's edge.

(2) Victor H. Mair 译

Tune: "Heaven-Cleansed Sands"
Autumn Thoughts by Ma Chih-yuan (ca. 1250-1323)

Withered wisteria, old tree, darkling crows—
Little bridge over flowing water by someone's house—
Emaciated horse on an ancient road in the western wind—
Evening sun setting in the west—
Broken-hearted man on the horizon.

(3) Wang Shi-jie 译

Autumn Meditation

Crows resting on the old tree's withered vines, send out fitful sad cries at the evening dusk. Across a foot bridge on the stream of running water, a solitary household stands. How lonely! How sad! Leading a scraggy horse, walk slowly along the ancient path against the west wind. The sun is going down in the west. At the remotest corner of the world, I, a heartbroken tramp, am thinking of my past.

(4) 许渊冲 译

AUTUMN THOUGHTS

Over old trees
Wreathed with rotten vines fly evening crows;
Under a small bridge near a cottage a stream flows;
On ancient road in the west wind a lean horse goes.
Westward declines the sun;
Far, far from home is the heartbroken one.

(5) 丁祖馨、Burton Raffel 译

Tune: "*Tian Jing Sha*"

Withered vines hanging on old branches,
    Returning crows croaking at dusk.
A few houses hidden past a narrow bridge,
And below the bridge quiet creek running.
    Down a worn path, in the west wind,
    A lean horse comes plodding.
    The sun dips down in the west,
And the lovesick traveler is still at the end of the world.

(6) Wai-lim Yip 译

SKY-PURE SAND

Dried vines, an old tree, evening crows;
A small bridge, flowing water, men's homes;
An ancient road, west winds, a lean horse;
Sun slants west;
The heart-torn man at sky's end.

(7) James Liu 译

Withered vines, aged trees, twilight crows.
Beneath the little bridge by the cottage the river flows.
On the ancient road and lean horse the west wind blows.
The evening sun westward goes.
As a broken-hearted man stands at heaven's close.

(8) Zong-qi Cai 译

To the Tune of "Sky-Clear Sand" [yuediao key]: Autumn Thoughts

Withered vines, old trees, crows at dusk,

A small bridge, flowing water, people's homes,
An ancient road, the west wind, a lean horse.
The evening sun goes down in the west.
One heartbroken man at the end of the earth.

(9) Stephen Owen 译

Autumn

Withered vines, old trees, twilight crows.
Small bridge, flowing water, people's homes.
Ancient road, the west wind, gaunt horse.
The evening sun sinks westward.
A man, broken-hearted, on a far horizon.

(10) 翁显良 译

Crows hovering over rugged old trees wreathed with rotten vine—the day is about done. Yonder is a tiny bridge over a sparkling stream, and on the far bank, a pretty little village. But the traveler has to go on down this ancient road, the west wind moaning, his bony horse groaning, trudging towards the sinking sun, farther and farther away from home.

(11) Cyril Birch 译

Autumn Thoughs

Dry vine, old tree, crows at dusk.
Low bridge, stream running, cottages,
Ancient road, west wind, lean nag,
The sun westering
And one with breaking heart at the sky' s edge.

4.32 清江引(马致远)

樵夫觉来山月底,

钓叟来寻觅。
你把柴斧抛，
我把鱼船弃。
寻取个稳便处闲坐地。

【作品简介】

这是作者所作《野兴》组曲（共八首）之一，它们并非写于一时一地，但表现忘情物外、避祸全身的思想和抒发恬适的隐居情怀却完全一致，乃作者归隐山林后所作。

【注 释】

觉来：一觉醒来。**山月底**：月亮已经落下去了。**钓叟来寻觅**：渔翁登上山来找他。**柴斧**：砍柴的斧子。"**你把柴斧抛**……"三句：你把砍柴的斧子扔了，我好把那渔船丢弃，一起去找个安安静静、没人打扰的地方闲坐着。

【译 文】

Wai-lim Yip 译

"SONG OF CLEAR RIVER"

Woodcutter wakes up：mountain moon is low.
Fisherman comes to visit.
You throw away firewoods and ax,
I throw away my fishing boat,
To find a neat little corner to sit and relax.

4.33 醉高歌·感怀（姚燧）

十年燕月歌声，几点吴霜鬓影。西风吹起鲈鱼兴，已在桑榆暮景。
十年书剑长吁，一曲琵琶暗许。月明江上别湓浦，愁听兰舟夜雨。

【作品简介】

这首曲子上半部分描写作者经历多年的仕宦生活，辗转北方、南方，如今上了年纪，有些厌倦，西风吹起，颇有思乡之感。“西风吹起鲈鱼兴”，用的是晋代张翰的故事。张翰是吴郡人，曾在洛阳做官，一日见秋风吹起，就想到家乡的莼菜和鲈鱼，便弃官回乡，并说：“人生贵得适志，何能羁宦数千里，以要名爵乎？”曲子使用这个典故，抒发了作者厌官思归的情怀。下半部分借咏白居易的故事来抒发自我的失意与郁闷。书剑飘零寄此生，恰逢浔阳江上，想起江州司马泪湿青衫，如为我作，如为我歌，不由得愁如夜雨，绵绵不绝。

【注 释】

醉高歌：一名《最高楼》。**“十年燕月”二句**：这是作者对自己大半生宦场生涯的概括。“燕月歌声”指在大都(今北京)任翰林学士期间一段清闲高雅的生活(北京为古燕国地)。“吴霜鬓影”，指出任江东廉访使的一段生活，江东(今江苏一带)为古吴国地，此时作者已渐近晚年，所以他说自己的双鬓已渐渐被吴霜染白了。**“西风”句**：意谓自己已有弃官还乡的想法。晋代吴地人张翰到洛阳做官，有一天刮起了秋风，他忽然想起了菰菜、莼羹、鲈鱼脍等家乡味，于是立即备车回家(见《晋书·张翰传》)。**桑榆暮景**：落日余晖返照在桑榆树梢上，比喻人的一生已到晚年。**“十年书剑”句**：想起十年来的宦游生活，不禁感慨万端。**书剑**：携书带剑，指在外宦游。**长吁**：长叹。**一曲琵琶暗许**：白居易贬官到江州，一次去江边送客，碰到一位琵琶女。听了她绝妙的演奏以后，很有感慨，于是写了一首《琵琶行》送给她，中有“同是天涯沦落人，相逢何必曾相识”之句。**许**：称许，称赞。**湓[pén]浦**：在今江西九江市西湓水入江处，白居易《琵琶行》序中称其为“湓浦口”。

【译 文】

(1) 许渊冲 译

Tune: “Drinking Song”

Reflection

Yao Sui (1238-1313)

Part I (Omitted)

Part II

I sigh after ten years with books and sword.
The lutist’s song is a promise without word.
I leave the river town when the moon shines bright,

Afraid to hear rain in orchid boat at night.

(2) 辜正坤 译

Reflections upon the Past
To the Tune of "Singing Loud in Tipsiness"

Part I

For ten years I lived in the north with its music grace,
The life in the south has left me some white hair.
In the west wind I think of fish in my native place,
Suddenly conscious of my advanced age in despair.

Part II (Omitted)

4.34 满庭芳(姚燧)

帆收钓浦，烟笼浅沙，水满平湖。晚来尽滩头聚，笑语相呼。鱼有剩和烟旋煮，酒无多带月须沽。盘中物，山肴野蔌，且尽葫芦。

〖作品简介〗

此作为姚遂所作"中吕·满庭芳"二首中的后一首(有人认为乃张弘范所作)。本曲写渔民的生活和乐观情绪，色彩鲜明，笔墨酣畅，给读者以无限的遐思和艺术享受。

〖注　释〗

钓浦：垂钓的港湾。**浦**：表示水边或河流入海的地区。本为入江支流之称，如"南有大浦一十八条"。

【译　文】

Wai-lim Yip 译

"FULL COURT OF FRAGRANCE"

Furl sails into fishermen's cove.
Smoke shrouds the shallow sand.
Water brims the Smooth Lake.
Evening comes: every step shoreward bend,
Laughing, talking, calling each other.
Leftover fish: cook in a smoke-swirling pan.
Not enough wine: go buy, through miles of moonlight.
For food now:
Mountain dishes, wild vegetables.
Let's empty all the gourd-bottles.

4.35　十二月过尧民歌·别情(王实甫)

自别后遥山隐隐，更那堪远山粼粼。见杨柳飞绵滚滚，对桃花醉脸醺醺。透内阁香风阵阵，掩重门暮雨纷纷。

怕黄昏忽地又黄昏，不销魂怎地不销魂？新啼痕压旧啼痕，断肠人忆断肠人。今春，香肌瘦几分，缕带宽三寸。

【作品简介】

这首曲描写了闺中女子思念远离家乡的心上人的情形。作品借境抒情，山、水、桃、柳、内阁、重门无不紧系思念之情，最后描写伤心的泪痕重重，以致身躯瘦损、衣带宽松。一种哀婉动人、不容易捉摸的感情，经过作者具体的景物描写和形象的描述，将它表露无遗。

【注　释】

粼粼：水波清澈的样子。**飞绵**：指飘飞的杨花柳絮。**"对桃花"**句：这是暗用崔护的"去年今日此门中，人面桃花相映红"的语义。**醺醺**[xūn xūn]，形容醉态很浓。**内阁**：深闺，内室。**重门**：庭院深处的门。**怕黄昏**：黄昏容易引起人们寂寞孤独之感。李清照《声声慢》:“梧桐更兼细雨,到黄昏点点滴滴,这次第,怎一个愁字了得。”**销魂**:神思茫然,仿佛魂消魄散的样子。江淹《别赋》:“黯然销魂者,唯别而已矣。”**断肠人**:悲愁到了极点的人。“**香肌瘦**”二句:形容为离愁而憔悴、消瘦。柳永《蝶恋花》:“衣带渐宽终不悔,为伊消得人憔悴。”**缕带**:用丝纺织的衣带。

〖译 文〗

许渊冲 译

Tune:“A Year's End”

Part I

Since we parted, far-flung hills disappear with you.
How can I bear to see the rippling stream anew,
And wave on wave of willow catkin's wafting trace.
And peach blossom's drunken face before my face?
The fragrant breeze invades my bower now and then;
Evening rain falls on my closed door again and again.

Part II (**Omitted**)

4.36 干荷叶(刘秉忠)

干荷叶,色苍苍,老柄风摇荡。减清香,越添黄,都因昨夜一场霜。寂寞在秋江上。

〖作品简介〗

此作品是全部三曲中的一首。全曲是作者因题起意、即物取喻之作。干荷叶又名《翠盘秋》,为作者自度曲。就作者的人生经历来看,该曲所表露的并非一位金遗民或宋遗民悼伤亡国、眷念前朝之情,而是在更广泛的意义上对生命的短促、人事的无常、朝代的更迭所怀的梦幻泡影之感。这是一位参与缔造王朝、饱历世事沧桑而又曾皈依空门、深受佛家洗礼者对自然界和人世间的观照和感慨。

〖注　释〗

苍苍：深青色。**老柄**：干枯的叶柄。

〖译　文〗

(1) 许渊冲 译

"Dried Lotus Leaves"

Lotus leaves dried
In color turned from green to grey,
Old stems in the wind sway.
With fragrance lost, they are in yellow
　　dyed.
Last night frost chilled their dream.
They look now lonely on the autumn
　　stream.

(2) 辜正坤 译

Untitled
To the Tune of "Dry Lotus Leaves"

Dry lotus leaves,
Dark and brown,
Shaking in the wind its bony stalk long,
Her color is deepened and balm gone.
The cause?
Last night by frost bound,
She lonely shivers in the autumn pond.

4.37　山坡羊(陈草庵)

晨鸡初叫，昏鸦争噪。那个不去红尘闹？路遥遥，水迢迢，功名尽在长安道。今日少年明日老。山，依旧好；人，憔悴了。

【作品简介】

元代士人求仁，本来就难于唐宋。自延祐年间正式设科取士，直到元末，开科十六次，取士人数仅占文官总人数的百分之四。南人要想入仁，尤其困难。何况即使做了官，还要受到歧视与猜忌，地位随时岌岌可危。政治社会如此黑暗，仍然有人热衷于功名，这岂不是深可嗟叹的吗？唐宋两代诗词中习见讽刺追逐功名者的作品，而陈草庵这首小令除了传统的主题意义外，还应包含着上述时代的特殊意义。短短40多字，用了比喻、对偶、反问、对比等修辞手法，把追逐功名人的一生说了个透。

【注　释】

红尘：佛家称人世间为红尘。此指纷扬的尘土，喻世俗热闹繁华之地，亦比喻名利场。长安：今陕西西安，汉唐京都，此泛指京城。

【译　文】

(1) 许渊冲 译

Tune: "Sheep on the Slope"
O World

At dawn cock crows;
At dusk caw crows.
Who to vanity fair is not eager to go?
Long long the way;
Far far the stream.
Only in the capital can you fulfill your
　　dream.
Tomorrow old will grow the youth of to-
　　day.
The hills are as green as before,
But the prime of youth is no more.

(2) 辜正坤 译

Lament on the World
To the Tune of "Sheep on the Hillside"

The cock begins crowing in the morning,
The ravens vie with each other calling in the
　　evening,
All worldly people want to find their fortune
star,
The road is long,
The river stretches far,
On the way to Chang'an① success and fame
　　throng.
The young today will be tomorrow old,
Mountains
Are as good as they were foretold,
Yet men
All pine away in cold.

① The then capital.

4.38　醉高歌过喜春来·题情(贯云石)

自然体态温柔，可意庞儿奈羞。看时节偷眼将人溜，送与人些风流证候。

蜂媒蝶使空迤逗，燕子莺儿不自由。恰便似一枝红杏出墙头，不能够折入手，空教人风雨替花羞。

〖作品简介〗

这支曲子乃作者描写男女之间的火热爱情。上半段从外貌体态和行为神情入手，刻画出深闺的少女形象：美丽活泼，惹人喜爱；下半段写与之相交而不得，抒发的是惆怅失意。全曲运用蜂蝶莺燕、墙头红杏、“风雨替花羞”等言辞，将主人公“不能够折入手”的处境映衬出来，既有嘲讽意味，又显得比较委婉。

〖注　释〗

庞儿：指脸庞。**迤逗**[yǐ dòu]：挑逗，引诱。

【译 文】

(1) Richard John Lynn 译

Tune: "Rapt with Wine, Loudly Singing—Joy in Spring's Coming"
My Love

Natural demeanor warm and soft,
Winsome face demure.
When we chance to meet, her sidelong glances encourage me,
Kindling the pangs of my lovesickness.

Matchmaker bees and go-between butterflies fail to coax her:
Swallows or orioles can't do as they please.
Just like a sprig of red almond blossoms peeping over a wall
She lies beyond the reach of plucking hand.
How I feel, in vain, that for those blossoms' sake the wind
　　and rain bear shame!

(2) 辜正坤 译

Ode on Love
To the Tune of "Sing Aloud in Tipsiness and Joy in the Coming of Spring"

So graceful is her demeanor and pace,
So pretty and demure is her face,
Now and then she gives her glances sidelong,
Those symbols of love weak or strong,
About match making, nothing can be done by
　　butterflies and bees,
Neither swallows and orioles can her coax or
　　please.
Like a sprig of red almond blossoms peeping over
　　the wall,
Just beyond the reach of a plucking hand

grease,
Shine or rain one can only to distress be in thrall.

4.39 清江引·咏梅(贯云石)

其一

南枝夜来先破蕊，泄露春消息。偏宜雪月交，不惹蜂蝶戏。有时节暗香来梦里。

其二

芳心对人娇欲说，不忍轻轻折，溪桥淡淡烟，茅舍澄澄月，包藏几多春意也。

〖作品简介〗

这支小曲通过描写梅花展露了作者的人生轨迹及人格品行。

〖注 释〗

破蕊：开花。**蕊**：这里指花蕾。**偏宜**：偏偏喜欢。**交**：交结，交朋友。**暗香**：清香，幽香。**芳心**：即芳情，优美的情怀。

〖译 文〗

许渊冲 译

Tune: "Song of Clear River"
The Mume Blossoms

Part Ⅰ
The southern branches of mume trees
At night are the first to blow,
Revealing vernal beams.
They love the company of moon and snow,
But will not play with butterflies or bees.
Sometimes their gloomy fragrance steals into our dreams.
Part Ⅱ (Omitted)

4.40 清江引·惜别(贯云石)

若还与他相见时，道个真传示：不是不修书，不是无才思，绕清江买不得天样纸!

〖作品简介〗

该小曲描写男子叹惜与情人离别之苦。其妙在不是直抒别怀的苦味，而是采用"节制"的笔法来表达这种郁结的情感。整支小曲句短情长，曲折深妙，似抑还扬，韵味无穷。

〖注　释〗

传示：消息，音信。**清江**：水名，一在湖北，即古夷水；一在江西，即流经新干、清江等地的那段赣江。也可泛指清澈的河流。

〖译　文〗

Zong-qi Cai 译

To the Tune of "Clear River, a Prelude" [shuandiao key]: On Separation, No. 4

If I meet him again,
This live message I will deliver to him:
Not that I didn't want to write,
Nor that I ain't talented and bright—
I circled along the Clear River, but could not find a piece of sky-size paper.

4.41　蟾宫曲·送春(贯云石)

问东君何处天涯。落日啼鹃，流水桃花。淡淡遥山，萋萋芳草，隐隐残霞。随柳絮吹归那答，趁游丝惹在谁家。倦理琵琶，人倚秋千，月照窗纱。

〖作品简介〗

这支小曲描绘了春天大自然绚丽的景色和春日里人间万象。

〖注　释〗

"**问东君**"句：问春之神到遥远的何处去了。东君，春之神。"**随柳絮**"二句：这是化用秦观《望海潮》"正絮翻蝶舞，芳思交加，柳下桃蹊，乱分春色到人家"的意境。**琵琶**：我国民族乐器。**秋千**：我国古代贵族妇女的体育游戏。相传春秋时齐桓公由北方的山戎所传入。

〖译　文〗

(1) 许渊冲 译

Tune: "Song of Moon Palace"
Parting Spring

I ask the Eastern God where's the end of the sky.
At sunset cuckoos cry,
On running water fall peach blooms,
Dim, dim distant hills loom,
Sweet grass seems filled with gloom,
Rainbow clouds thick with fumes.
Where is the willow down blown away
　　by the breeze?
In whose house floats gossamer over
　　the trees?
Tired of playing on the lute's string,
I lean against the swing.
The moon shines on my window
　　screen.

(2) 辜正坤 译

Sending off Spring
To the Tune of "Lunar Palace"

Oh, god of spring, where are the earth's ends?
In the calls of cuckoos, to the west the sun
wends.
Water flowing with blossoms of peach,
Dimly visible mountains are far to reach.
And fragrant grasses are lush in sight,

And evening clouds are fringed with sunlight.
Where do the willow catkins carry you away?
In which house with the wafting spider silk[①]
  will you stay?
Now a lute she languidly stops to play.
Leaning on the swing at pause,
While the moon shines on the window gauze.

① Willow catkins and wafting spider silk, both imply other women or prostitutes.

4.42 普天乐(张养浩)

楚《离骚》，谁能解？就中之意，日月明白。恨尚存，人何在？

空快活了湘江鱼虾蟹，这先生畅好是胡来。怎如向青山影里，狂歌痛饮，其乐无涯。

〖作品简介〗

这首曲子通过对屈原的独特议论，表现了作者政治失意后的放达与淡泊情怀以及享乐自为的人生思想；同时也表露出对封建社会黑暗的政治统治的激愤之情。

〖注 释〗

离骚：《楚辞》篇名，战国时期楚国屈原所作，表达美好的政治理想和强烈的爱国情感以及理想不能实现的悲伤、痛苦。**“这先生”句**：意谓实在没用、没价值的意思。曲意为，《离骚》饱含你(屈原)理想与抱负、深深的爱与恨，但又有谁能理解你的一片苦心呢？你投江而死，白白地去喂鱼。

〖译 文〗

Jerome P. Seaton 译

[Untitled]

Chang Yang-hao

Ch'ü Yüan's "sorrow"[①]

none can explain
yet its meaning is
clear as the sun and the moon.
the sorrow remains
the man is gone
to feed
    the shrimp and crabs of the river Hsiang.
that gentleman was silly
I'll stay in this green mountain shade
singing wild
    and drinking till it hurts
here's joy
    that's boundless.

① A native of Tsinan, Shantung, Chang Yang-hao was an official who held several important positions. He wrote most of his arias after retirement.

4.43 山坡羊·潼关怀古(张养浩)

峰峦如聚，
波涛如怒，
山河表里潼关路。
望西都，
意踌躇。
伤心秦汉经行处，
宫阙万间都做了土。
兴，
百姓苦。
亡，
百姓苦。

〖作品简介〗

此曲是张养浩晚年的代表作，也是元散曲中思想性、艺术性完美结合的名作。为其赴陕西救灾途经潼关所作。该曲从儒家经世济民的思想出发，抚今追昔，从历代王朝的兴衰更替，想到人民的苦难，一针见血地点出了封建统治与人民的对立，表现了作者对历史的思索和对人民的同情。

【注 释】

山坡羊：曲牌名，乃该散曲之格式；“潼关怀古”是标题。**峰峦如聚**：形容群峰攒集，层峦叠嶂。**聚**：聚拢，包围。**波涛如怒**：形容黄河波涛的汹涌澎湃。**“山河”句**：外面是山，里面是河，形容潼关一带地势险要。具体指潼关外有黄河，内有华山。**表里**：即内外。《左传·僖公二十八年》：“表里山河，必无害也。”注：“晋国外河而内山。”**潼关**：古关口名，在今陕西省临潼县，关城建在华山山腰，下临黄河，扼秦、晋、豫三省要冲，非常险要，为古代入陕门户，是历代的军事重地。**西都**：指长安(今陕西西安)。这是泛指秦汉以来在长安附近所建的都城。秦、西汉建都长安，东汉建都洛阳，因此称洛阳为东都，长安为西都。**踌躇**：犹豫，徘徊不定，心事重重，此处形容思潮起伏，感慨万端，陷入沉思，表示心里不平静。一作“踟蹰(chí chú)”。**“伤心”二句**：谓目睹秦汉遗迹，旧日宫殿尽成废墟，内心伤感。**伤心**：对……感到伤心，形容词作动词。**秦汉经行处**：秦朝(前221—前206年)都城咸阳和西汉(前206—25年)都城长安都在陕西省境内潼关的西面。**经行处**：经过的地方。指秦汉故都遗址。**宫阙**：**宫**：宫殿。**阙**：皇宫门前两边的楼观。兴、亡：指朝代的盛衰更替。

【译 文】

(1) Wai-lim Yip 译

“SHEEP ON THE MOUNTAIN SLOPE”

Peeks gather,
Waves in anger.
Between mountains and rivers, the T’ung Pass coils.
Looking toward the West Capital-
My thoughts all in turmoil.
Where the Ch’in and Han armies passed,
my heart is sorrow-filled.
A million palaces built and rebuilt.
Kingdoms rise,
The commonfolks suffer.
Kingdoms fall,
The commonfolks suffer.

(2) 许渊冲 译

Tune: "Sheep on the Slope"
Thinking of the Past on My Way to Tong Pass

Peaks like brows knit,
Angry waves spit.
With mountain and river far and near,
On the road to Tong Pass I appear.
Gazing on Western Capital,
I hesitate, alas!
To see the place where ancient warriors did pass.
The ancient palaces, hall on hall,
Are turned to dust, one and all.
Before my eyes,
The empire's rise
Is people's woe;
The empire's fall
Is also people's woe.

(3) Wayne Schlepp 译

Tune: "Sheep on the Hillside"
— Tong Pass

Zhang Yanghao

Peaks as if massed,
Waves that look angry,
Along the mountains and the river lies the road to Tong Pass.
I look to the West Capital
My thoughts unsettled.
Here, where the Qin and Han armies passed, I lament
The ten thousand palaces, all turned to dust.
Kingdoms rise,

The people suffer;
Kingdoms fall,
The people suffer.

(4) Zong-qi Cai 译

Tune: "Sheep on Mountain Slope"[zhonglü key]:
Meditation on the Past at Tong Pass

Peaks and ridges press together,
Waves and torrents rage,
Zigzagging between the mountains and the river runs the road through Tong Pass.
I look to the Western Capital,
My thoughts linger.
It breaks my heart to come to the old place of the Qin and the Han.
Now palaces and terraces have all turned to dust.
Dynasties rise,
The common folk suffer;
Dynasties fall,
The common folk suffer.

4.44 雁儿落带得胜令·无题(张养浩)

云来山更佳,云去山如画,山因云晦明,云共山高下。
倚仗立云沙,回首见山家,野鹿眠山草,山猿戏野花。
云霞,我爱山无价,看时,行踏,云山也爱咱。

〖作品简介〗

这首小曲子勾画出作者心中的山中行乐图,由此可以看到诗人相机而退、隐居山野的恬淡自适心情,以及静穆自守、自由自在、轻舒飘逸的气度。

〖注 释〗

晦[huì]:昏暗不明。

【译　文】

辜正坤 译

Untitled
To the Tune of "Wild Geese Coming Down and Song of Victory"

More beautiful are the mountains where clouds throng;
But they are still pictures when clouds are gone.
The mountains are dimly visible because of the veil-like cloud.
Against mountains high or low clouds complacently crowd.
I stand amid the clouds, on a crutch leaning.
I see homes on hills, my head turning.
Sleeping among wild grass are wild deers,
Playing with the wild flowers are monkeys with cheers.
Clouds are gilded with the red sun fair,
To me the value of the mountains is beyond compare,
Take a walk around the mountain at a good time,
The cloudy mountain's love of me is also sublime.

4.45　胡十八·无题(张养浩)

正妙年，
不觉的老来到。
思往常，
似昨朝，
好光阴流水不相饶。
都不如醉了，
睡着。
任金乌搬废兴，
我只推不知道。

【作品简介】

该小曲抒发了作者对人生之短暂、命运之多舛的感叹。

〖注 释〗

金乌：太阳的别名，也称为“赤乌”。如唐朝韩愈诗：“金乌海底初飞来”(太阳刚从海底冲出来)；白居易诗：“白兔赤乌相趁走”(月亮和太阳互相追赶)。

〖译 文〗

辜正坤 译

Untitled
To the Tune of “Eighteen Beats”

When of youthful years I got hold,
I was unaware that I became old.
To me, all that happened in the past
Seems to have happened only night last.
Like flowing water good time flies,
I'd better get drunk in sighs,
And fall asleep.
Let the golden sun take care of the empire's fall and rise.
I just pretend to know nothing either shallow or deep.

4.46 清江引·咏秋日海棠(张养浩)

睡起不禁霜月苦，
篱菊休相妒。
恰与东君别，
又被西风误，
教他这粉蝶儿无是处。

〖作品简介〗

本曲借物传情，用海棠的口吻倾诉了海棠粉蝶的坎坷命运。

【注 释】

东君：春之神。

【译 文】

幸正坤 译

Ode on Chinese Flowering Crabapple
To the Tune of "Prelude to the Limpid River"

Awake from dream she bears not the attack from frost and moon chill.
Chrysanthemum around the bamboo fence need not jealous feel.
She just sees off spring out of sight,
And again by the west wind is thrown into a sorry plight,
Making her always in the wrong and affright.

4.47 天净沙·闲居（张养浩）

休言咱是谁非，
只宜似醉如痴。
便得功名待怎的？
无穷天地，
那驼儿用你精细。

【作品简介】

这支小曲抒发了作者面对不公的社会所展露出的处世态度。

【注 释】

“无穷天地”句：意思是天地无穷大，有什么具体的地方需要你精打细算呢？**那驼儿**：犹言何处。

【译 文】

辜正坤 译

Stay at Home Idle
To the Tune of "Sky Scouring Sand"

Don't say we are right or someone is of wrong school,
The best policy is to play a drunkard or a fool.
What's the point after all of getting success and fame?
In this boundless world out of frame,
Where can your talent be employed as a useful tool?

4.48 水仙子·咏江南(张养浩)

一江烟水照晴岚，两岸人家接画檐。芰荷丛一段秋光淡，看沙鸥舞再三，卷香风十里珠帘。画船儿天边至，酒旗儿风外飐，爱煞江南。

【作品简介】

此小令描写了烟水、晴岚、人家、画檐、芰荷、沙鸥、香风、珠帘这些富有江南水乡特色的意象，表达了作者闲适自得的心态和对江南美景的赞叹之情。

【注 释】

晴岚[qíng lán]：晴天空中仿佛有烟雾笼罩。芰：菱角。飐：因风而颤动、飘扬。

【译 文】

辜正坤 译

An Ode on Southern China
To the Tune of "Narcissus"

The fogy woods are reflected in the smoky river water,
Houses with painted eyes on the banks are adjacent to each other.

Gently on the patches of lotuses shines the autumnal light,
Up and down in the sky are dancing gulls white.
The pearl-woven curtains are bathed in the fragrant wind of ten miles,
Painted boats come from the distant horizon beyond isles.
In the wind flags of wine shops flutter and fly,
Oh, how lovely is the southern scenery to the eye!

4.49 小桃红·离情(张可久)

几场秋雨老黄花，不管离人怕。一曲哀弦泪双下，放琵琶，挑灯羞看围屏画，声悲玉马，愁新罗帕，恨不到天涯。

〖作品简介〗

这首小令写秋景也写思情，但并不是把情和景融合在一起，而是和身骨联系在一起，构思十分巧妙。

〖注　释〗

老：此处为使役动词，即“使得……老”。**怕**：忧愁。**“恨不到”句**：我恨不得追随你到天涯海角。

〖译　文〗

(1) 许渊冲 译

Tune: “Red Peach Blossoms”
Parting Grief by Zhang Kejiu

The autumn rains have oldened yellow
　　flowers,
Careless of those in lonely bowers.
My tears stream down to hear the song
　　played by sad strings,
Putting down the lute and turning on
　　lamplight, I feel shy
To see the picture on the screen

And hear the bell of jade rings.
My grief has wetted the silk handker-
chief green.
Why could I not go with you to the end
of the sky?

(2) 辜正坤 译

Sights over Separation
To the Tune of "Light Pink"

Chrysanthemums get old, after several gusts of autumn rain,
Despite worries on the part of those who are to leave in pain,
At a sad echo of the lute strings she would herself in tears drown,
With the lute being put down.
Under the lamp she demurely gazes at the painting on the screen,
Outside the door the Aeolian bells give sound so sad and keen,
On her new handkerchief fresh are traces of tears,
Alas, to the earth's end she sends not her griefs and fears.

4.50 人月圆·春晚次韵(张可久)

萋萋芳草春云乱,
愁在夕阳中,
短亭别酒,
平湖画舫,
垂柳骄骢。
一声啼鸟,
一番夜雨,
一阵东风。
桃花吹尽,
佳人何在,
门掩残红。

【作品简介】

该曲以写景见长,景语又是情语,而所写的眼前景物,多与故事相关而显得典雅工丽，倍能体现缠绵委婉的情味。《词征》评此曲“丰约中度，旋复回环”，此论颇是。在表达情感时注意分寸，描写景色时又注意前后映照，属散曲中的精品。

〖注　释〗

人月圆：曲牌名，属黄钟调。黄钟宫的调性，比较适合表现雍容而缠绵的感情。《人月圆》的曲牌来自词牌。北宋王诜的词中有“人月圆时”，故名。句式为七五、四四四、四四四、四四四。十一句四韵。三组四字句，多用鼎足对。**次韵**：唱和诗词并依原诗用韵次序。**短亭**：旧时城外于五里处设短亭，十里处设长亭，是送行饯别的地方。

〖译　文〗

(1) 许渊冲 译

Tune: “Men and Moon”
Rhyming with Friend in Late Spring
Zhang Kejiu

Lush, lush sweet grass and spring clouds spread
　　pell-mell;
Grief seems exhaled by setting sunlight.
In the pavilion where we drank farewell,
I see no painted boat on the calm lake afloat,
Nor the proud steed neighing beneath willow trees.
I only hear the cry of birds in fright,
The dripping rain leftover last night,
And the sigh of the eastern breeze.
All the peach flowers are blown away.
Where is the beauty of the byone day?
Within the closed door only the fallen reds stay.

(2) 辜正坤 译

Spring Evening: Replying to a Song
To the Tune of “The Full Moon and Human Reunion”

Under riotous spring clouds is an expanse of

green grass,
In the setting sun sadness is felt to pass.
At a five-mile station we have farewell wine,
On a calm lake we row a painted boat so fine.
Under weeping willows our horses we tie.
There comes a bird's cry,
And a fall of rain at night,
Followed by the eastern wind light,
Blowing away all peach blossoms in the compound.
Where can the beauty be found?
Indoors, red petals fallen on the ground.

4.51 拨不断·会稽道中(张可久)

墓田鸦,
故宫花,
愁烟恨水丹青画。
峻宇雕墙宰相家,
夕阳芳草渔樵话,
百年之下。

【作品简介】

这首小令描写作者在旅途中的所见、所感,表达作者对历史和社会沧桑之变的感慨。

【注 释】

会稽:今浙江绍兴地区。**故宫**:会稽在春秋战国时期为越国都城,南宋高宗时亦一度作为行在所。

【译 文】

Wai-lim Yip 译

"UNBROKEN"

Graveyard crows.

Old palace flowers.
Smoke and water and ink-paintings filled with sorrow.
High halls, carved walls, premier's bowers.
Sunset, scented grasses, fishermen and woodcutters' hours.
A hundred years. O!

4.52　迎仙客·括山道中(张可久)

云冉冉，
草纤纤，
谁家隐居半山崦。
水烟寒，
溪路险。
半幅青帘，
五里桃花店。

【作品简介】

该作品描写了作者途经浙江东南部苍山时所见风景。天上的飘飞云彩，地上碧绿的细草，是谁家的房舍在半山崦里若隐若现？水上弥漫寒烟，溪边山路陡峭艰险，远处半幅青帘招展，那是五里外桃花路边的酒店。

【注　释】

迎仙客：中吕宫曲牌。句式：三三七、三三、四五。**括山**：指括苍山，在浙江省东南部。**纤纤**：草木茂盛的样子。**崦**[yān]：山坳。**青帘**：酒旗。

【译　文】

Wai-lim Yip 译

"TRAVELER WELCOMING THE IMMORTAL"

Clouds seen and unseen.
Grass thin and green.
Whose house hidden half up the hill?
Smoke-water's chill.

Path along the stream full of peril.
Half a curtain green.
Five-mile Peach Petal Inn.

4.53 殿前欢·客中(张可久)

望长安，前程渺渺鬓斑斑。
南来北往随征雁，行路艰难。
青泥小剑关，红叶湓江岸，白草连云栈。
功名半纸，风雪千山。

【作品简介】

这首小令描述了作者对人生的感受：处在元代统治者极端轻视知识分子的社会中，才华横溢的作者内心充满了矛盾。他曾反复讴歌归隐生活的乐趣，可是又摆脱不了名利的羁绊，以致长年累月淹留在外。他一生仕途蹭蹬，沉沦下僚，这其中有多少隐衷酸楚，有多少感慨不平，只有作者自己最清楚。

【注　释】

青泥：指青泥岭，又名泥功山。在今陕西略阳县西北，古为入蜀要道，道路崎岖，坎坷难行。**白草**：枯草。**连云栈**：栈道名，在陕西汉中地区，全长四百七十里，为古代川陕地区栈道。

【译　文】

Wai-lim Yip 译

Tune: "Merriment Before the Palace Hall" by Chang K'o-chiu

Toward Ch'ang-an—
Future course, all blurred; sideburns now white.
Go south go north following migrant geese's flight.
Traveling is a plight.
Up Green Mud Sword Pass.
Down Red Leaf River Pen.
White grass reaches the sky.

Name and rank：only half a sheet of paper.
Windblown snow，a thousand mountains，flies.

4.54　折桂令·湖山堂(赵善庆)

八窗开水月交光，
诗酒坛台，
莺燕排场。
歌扇摇风，
梨云飘雪，
粉黛生香。
红烛台已更旧邦，
白头民犹说新堂。
花妒幽芳，
人换宫妆，
惟有湖山，
不管兴亡。

【作品简介】

这是作者的一篇叹世之作。作者眼观现在，联想朝代的更迭，物转星移，唯有自然未变，不禁思绪万千。因其怀才不遇和一生飘泊，故其散曲于清新之中寓悲凉，于明丽之中寓感叹，比较抑郁、消沉。这在此小曲中也能窥见一斑。

【注　释】

湖山堂：即杭州有美堂。**梨云飘雪**：喻指歌舞宛如梨花飘洒、漫天扬花。**换宫妆**：指歌女们的打扮变成了正流行的宫妆，暗指社会动荡、朝代更迭。

【译　文】

许渊冲 译

Tune：“Plucking Laurel Branch”
Hall of Lake and Hill
Zhao Shanqing

Outside eight windows water dissolves in moonlight，

Orioles and swallows dance on the stage in a line
Before poets and drinkers of wine.
The dancers' fans bring a breeze light,
They dance like clouds or pear blossoms white,
With fragrance sweet their powdered faces spread.
The old state replaced by the new with candles red,
The white-haired still remember its newly built hall.
Dancers in their changed palace attire
Awaken envious flowers' desire,
But lakes and hills care not for the state's rise and fall.

4.55 凭栏人·春日怀古(赵善庆)

铜雀台空锁暮云,
金谷园荒成路尘。
转头千载春,
断肠几辈人。

〖作品简介〗

本曲抒写了作者面对铜雀台和金谷园,不禁触景生情,感叹古今变化的心境。

〖注　释〗

"铜雀台"句:言铜雀台已经荒废。**铜雀台**:在今河北省的漳县,由曹操所建。《三国志·魏武帝纪》:"建安十五年冬,作铜雀台。"**金谷园**:故址在今洛阳市西,由晋石崇所建。石崇以豪富著称,经常在金谷园中招待宾客。

〖译　文〗

辜正坤 译

Meditation on Antiquity on a Spring Day
To the Tune of "Person Leaning on the Railing"
Zhao Shanqing

Evening clouds stroll over the Brass Phoenix Tower,

Deserted Golden Valley Garden is buried in dust deep.
One thousand springs have passed like a sudden shower,
Generation after generation, heart-broken people are heard to weep.

4.56 醉太平·渔樵闲话(乔吉)

柳穿鱼旋煮，柴换酒新沽。斗牛儿乘兴老樵渔，论闲言怅语。燥头颅束云担雪耽辛苦，坐蒲团攀风咏月穷活路，按葫芦谈天说地醉模糊。入江山画图。

【作品简介】

这支曲描写了樵夫和渔夫二人一起吃鱼喝酒、谈天说地的自在生活。

【注 释】

束云担雪：形容渔夫、樵子在野外作业时的艰辛生活。

【译 文】

Zong-qi Cai 译

To the Tune of "Drunk in a Peaceful Time" [zhenggong key]: Idle Chats of the Woodcutter and the Fisherman

The fish, skewered on a willow twig, is cooked without delay.
The wine was newly obtained by bartering the firewood away.
Now the old woodcutter and the old fisherman have the leisure to watch fighting bulls,
And exchange gossip and idle hearsay.
The hardship of going through rain and snow troubles their heads,
Yet they make the best of their meager living by chanting of the moon and discussing the wind on a straw mat,
And with blurry eyes, they talk about heaven and earth over a wine gourd.
What a painting of mountains and rivers!

4.57 绿幺遍·自述(乔吉)

不占龙头选，不入名贤传。时时酒圣，处处诗禅，烟霞状元，江湖醉仙，笑谈便是编修院。留连，批风抹月四十年。

【作品简介】

这是作者客居江南时的一篇述志之作，让读者自然联想到这位闯荡江湖四十年文人的漂泊生涯。宋元以来，这些文人学士与伎艺人有着密切联系，其生活道路和思想情趣放射出一种特异的色彩。乔吉寄情山水，风月、诗酒、谈笑也颇放达，但与元初马致远的豪放派又有区别。其愤世之情更为隐秘，豪放之气则较为收敛。作品中更多的是随境自适的情调，然而却非浅薄轻狂。而他确实也是一位不遇于时，将一生才力倾注于曲的落魄文人。

【注 释】

龙头：头名状元。**名贤传**：登上名人贤者的册簿。**酒圣**：善饮酒的人。**诗禅**：以诗谈禅，以禅喻诗。即以禅语、禅趣入诗。**编修院**：即翰林院，编修国史的机关。**批风抹月**：犹言吟风弄月。

【译 文】

(1) Zong-qi Cai 译

To the Tune of "Luyobian"[zhenggong key]: Of Myself

I was not chosen to head the dragon list,
Nor was my name entered into the biography of worthies
From time to time I'm a sage of wine,
Finding everywhere the Zen of poetry—
Highest graduate of the college of clouds and mists,
Drunken angel of rivers and lakes,
My talks and jokes are fit for the Imperial Academy of Compilation.
Loitering,
I've been writing commentaries on the wind and the moon for forty years.

(2) 辜正坤 译

On Myself
To the Tune of "Overtures"

On the list of Imperial Scholars I am not found.

With who's who of worthies nor do I enter into
 a bond.
I am a great drunkard now and then,
Finding everywhere poetry with Zen.
About mists and clouds I am Scholar No. One.
Of rivers and lakes I am a drunkard living long.
My talks and jokes in the Imperial Compilation
 Academy belong,
Here and there I wonder and croon,
For forty years I've just made commentaries on
 winds and the moon.

4.58 折桂令·登姑苏台(乔吉)

百花洲上新台，檐吻云平，图画天开。鹏俯沧溟，蜃横城市，鳌驾蓬莱，学捧心山颦翠色，怅悬头土湿腥苔。悼古兴怀，休近阑干，万丈尘埃。

〖作品简介〗

这首小令描写的是姑苏台的宏丽建筑以及登台远眺时的感受，吊古感今。作者根据文献记载，驰骋想象，置身于千载之上的姑苏宫中，对它作形象的描写，而造语沉着，气势宏放，但又不发泄无余，有沉郁顿挫之妙。

〖注 释〗

檐吻云平：言飞檐画栋，高与云平。**图画天开**：言风景如画，自然展现在人们的面前。**鹏俯沧溟**：像大鹏之俯瞰海洋。**沧溟**：海水弥漫的样子。**蜃[shèn]横城市**：像“蜃景”横理成城市一样。“蜃景”是光线经过不同的密度层，把远处的景物折射在空中或地面所成的奇异幻景。《史记·天官书》：“海旁蜃气象楼台，广野气成宫阙然；云气各象其山川人民所聚积。”**鳌驾蓬莱**：《列子·汤问》：渤海中有五山：岱舆、员峤、方壶瀛洲、蓬莱。“巨鳌十五，举首而戴之，六万岁一交焉。”**“学捧心”**句：《庄子·天运》：“故西施病心而膑其里，其里之丑人见之而美，归而捧心而膑其里。其里之富人见之，坚闭门而不出；贫人见之，挈妻子而去之走。”这是把山拟人化，言山之苍翠是在学习美人的眉黛。**“怅悬头”**句：《史记·伍子胥列传》：“(吴王)乃使使赐伍子胥属镂之剑，曰：‘子以此死。’……(伍子胥)乃告其舍人曰：‘必树吾墓上以梓，令可以为器；而抉吾眼悬吴东门之上，以观越寇之入灭吴也。’”这里是下文所说的“悼古伤怀”的主要内容。

〖译 文〗

幸正坤 译

Ascend the Gusu Tower
To the Tune of "Plucking Cassia"

On the Hundred Flowers Islet is built up a new tower
With its eaves kissing the cloud,
What a beautiful picture of natural power!
Overlooking the great sea like a roc so proud,
Or a mirage forming a great town,
Or a fairy land on the back of a huge turtle adown.
Hills imitate a beauty by frowning their brows green,
Here, a loyal subject out of favour died for his Highness Serene,
For the ancient my sadness is keen.
Over the balustrades I dare not go and peep,
Where dust lies ten thousand feet deep.

4.59 三番玉楼人(无名氏)

风摆檐间马，雨打响碧窗纱。枕剩衾寒没乱煞，不着我题名儿骂，暗想他，暗想他，忒情杂。等来家，好生的歹斗咱。我将那厮脸儿上不抓，耳轮儿揪罢，我问你昨夜宿谁家。

〖作品简介〗

通俗、鲜明的民歌色彩，生动泼辣的语言风格，是这首小令的艺术特色。塑造了一个大胆、泼辣的女子形象。这首小令可分三部分，前三句是第一部分。“风摆檐间马，雨打响碧窗纱”两句点明这是一个风雨之夜。“没乱煞”的意思是急煞人，“枕剩衾寒”而又着急，是一副等人心焦的样子。中间五句是第二部分，她等得不耐烦了，准备回家时大吵一场。后四句是第三部分，设想，明天怎样对付他。

〖注 释〗

檐间马：元代挂在屋檐下的风铃。

【译 文】

(1) James I. Crump 译

Tune:"San-fan Yu-lou Jen"

Anonymous

Wind disturbing the eave-chimes again.
Cloth at the window rustles with rain.
That empty pillow,
Cold counterpane
All tangled up with me,
I curse with fine particularity.
My emotions are confused and dim
But the darker thoughts are reserved for him!
Oh, wait until he comes back here,
Then won't I pick a fight!
And scratch his face!
And twist his ear!
"And where did you sleep all last night!"

(2) 许渊冲 译

Tune:"Thrice in Jade Pavilion"

Anonymous

Bells hanging on the eaves ring in
 the breeze;
Rain beats loud on the green window
 without cease.
How can I bear alone the quilt and
 pillow cold!
How can I not blame the ungrateful
 gallant bold!
I can't keep him apart
With his divided heart.

Should he come to my place,
I would scold him without giving
　　him grace,
Scratch him on the face.
And pinch his ears tight.
I'd ask him, "With whom did you
　　pass the night?"

4.60 梧叶儿·嘲谎人(无名氏)

东村里鸡生凤，南庄上马变牛。六月里裹皮裘。瓦垄上宜栽树，阳沟里好驾舟。瓮来大肉馒头，俺家的茄子大如斗。

【作品简介】

此散曲的全称是《商调·梧叶儿·嘲谎人》，作者是元代人，姓名不详。这支小令题材与内容都很通俗，它对吹牛撒谎者进行了嘲讽，用归谬的手法，让说谎者自我独白，自我暴露，惟妙惟肖，使人忍俊不禁。曲辞朴素，幽默诙谐，颇具特色。

【注　释】

皮裘：皮衣。**瓦垄**：房上瓦脊。**阳沟**：屋檐下流水的明沟。

【译　文】

(1) James I. Crump 译

Tune: "Wu Yeh-erh"
Twitting the Teller of Tall Tales
Anonymous

In Easton a certain citizen
Had a Phoenix born to his hen!
In Southville there was a paradox,
Someone's horse turned into an ox!
August is the month for fur coats,
On a pile of tile you can plant a tree,

A dry-gulch[①] is good for sailing boat.
Our dumplings are bigger than soup-tureens;
We grow barrel-sized aubergines.

① *Yan-kou* (open ditch) was also the name of a famous fighting cock.

(2) 许渊冲 译

Tune: "Plane Leaves"
Satire on Liars
Anonymous

In eastern village phoenixes are born of
　　cocks;
In southern farm a horse changes into an
　　ox.
In summer we wear furs lest we should
　　freeze;
The roof is a good place to plant trees.
In a dry moat we may sail a boat;
In a jar we may bake bread and cook
　　meat.
My egg plant is as big as melon sweet.

4.61　水仙子（无名氏）

青山隐隐水茫茫，时节登高却异乡。孤城孤客孤舟上，铁石人也断肠，泪涟涟断送了秋光。黄花梦，一夜香，过了重阳。

〖作品简介〗

这支曲子描写了一个思乡游子的形象。作品通过“登高”“孤客”“泪涟涟”“黄花梦”展现了一个远在异乡为异客的游子浓厚的思乡之情。

〖注　释〗

涟涟[lián lián]：泪流不止貌。《诗·卫风·氓》：“不见復关，泣涕涟涟。”《汉书·

韦贤传》:“我既此登,望我旧阶,先后兹度,涟涟孔怀。”

『译 文』

(1) 许渊冲 译

Tune: “Song of Daffodils”

Anonymous

(I)

Green hills are veiled in mist along
the far-flung stream,
On Mountain-climbing Day I stand
in foreign land.
A lonely man in lonely boat by lone-
ly town,
However hard, can my heart not
break down?
Two streams of tears have blurred
out autumn light.
The golden dream
Is sweet but for one night.
This Mountain-climbing Day is
passed just as the last.

(2) 辜正坤 译

Untitled
To the Tune of “Narcissus”

Beyond the vast waters green mountains are
vaguely in sight,
On this double ninth day in the strange land I
ascend the height.
In this lonely coenue facing a lonely city is a
traveler alone,
Making even a man of an iron-heart bitterly

groan.
In tears he signs over the loss of this fiery au-
tumn time,
In dream are yellow flowers in their prime,
All over the night, their fragrance is strong,
Alas, now the Double Ninth Day is gone.

4.62　折桂令·微雪(无名氏)

朔风寒吹下银沙，蠹砌穿帘，拂柳惊鸦，轻若鹅毛，娇如柳絮，瘦似梨花。多应是怜贫困天教少洒，止不过庆丰年众与农家。数片琼葩，点缀槎丫。孟浩然容易寻梅，陶学士不彀烹茶。

『作品简介』

这支曲子描写生动、细腻，表现了作者宁静闲适的情趣，也表现了对贫苦百姓的怜悯和农家丰收的喜悦的赞美之情。作品描写道：寒冷的北风把雪花隔着屋帘吹进屋子。雪花飘过柳枝惊动了树上的乌鸦。雪花就像柳絮和梨花一样娇媚。可怜的是下得太少，就是来庆祝一下农家的丰收。

『注　释』

朔风：北风。**槎丫**：树木枝杈歧出貌。**陶学士**：即陶谷，五代时名士。性好茶事，曾得党太尉(党进)姬，命掬雪水烹茶，并戏之曰："党家应不识此？"姬曰："彼粗人，安知此，但能于销金帐中，浅斟低唱，饮羊羔酒耳。哪有这种风味。"后"陶学士"遂为风雅之士的代名词。

『译　文』

许渊冲 译

Tune: "Plucking Laurel Branch"
Slight Snow
Anonymous

The northern wind blows snow down
like silver sand,

It erodes the steps where I stand,
Passes through the screen, caresses
willow trees,
And startles crows. It's light as
feather of geese,
As willow down it's tender,
And as pear flower it's slender.
Heaven pities the poor and sheds
only snow slight,
To announce a bumper year to the
farmers' delight.
A few jade petals in full bloom
Adorn the branches of a tree.
It would be easier for the poet to
seek mume;
It's not enough for a scholar to brew
his tea.

4. 63 上小楼 · 杜鹃(无名氏)

堪恨无情杜宇,
你怎么伤人心绪:
啼的花残,
叫的愁来,
唤将春去。
索甚不把离人叮咛嘱咐,
我也道在天涯不如归去。

〖作品简介〗

这支带过曲,以闺中女子自诉心声的形式,淋漓尽致地表现了思妇的情怨。

〖注　释〗

杜宇:杜鹃鸟。其鸣声如“不如归去”。**索甚**:为什么。

【译　文】

(1) 许渊冲 译

Tune: "Ascending the Attic"
The Cuckoo
Anonymous

I do not like to hear pitiless
　　cuckoo cry,
Its home-going song breaks my
　　heart.
It cries till no flowers bloom,
Till grief comes with gloom,
Till spring from earth will part.
"Why don't you tell my love at
　　the end of the sky,
To come home lest I should die?"

(2) 辜正坤 译

Cuckoo Bird
To the Tune of "Ascending the Little Tower"
Anonymous

How annoying you are, the cuckoo bird,
How cruelly wounds my heart your singing word;
Your calling makes flowers fade,
And evokes grief in the blade,
And sends spring away.
Why don't you tell the traveling man today,
Saying "better be back, not at the earth's end stay!"

第五章
明至清

5.1　念奴娇(高启)

策勋万里，笑书生骨相，有谁曾许。壮志平生还自负，羞比纷纷儿女。

酒发雄谈，剑增奇气，诗吐惊人语。风云无便，未容黄鹄轻举。

何事匹马尘埃，东西南北，十载犹羁旅。只恐陈登容易笑，负却故园鸡黍。

笛里关山，樽前日月，回首空凝伫。吾今未老，不须清泪如雨。

〖作品简介〗

此词乃作者所作的一首抒怀词，真实地表现了封建社会里知识分子的不幸遭遇，抨击了封建社会统治者对人才的扼杀。词作者高启(1336—1374年)，汉族，江苏苏州人，元末明初著名诗人，在文学史上，与刘基、宋濂并称“明初诗文三大家”，又与杨基、张羽、徐贲并称“吴中四杰”。

〖注　释〗

“策勋”三句：词中指薛相士相面事。**策勋万里**：立功万里外而记功于策。**骨相**：骨骼相貌。古人以此推测人的命和性。**纷纷**：众多。**酒发雄谈**：雄辩的言论。**奇气**：不平凡的志气。**“诗吐”句**：杜甫《江上值水如海势聊短述》：“语不惊人死不休。”高启《赠薛相士》诗中有“我少言功名，轻事勇且狂”的豪壮之语。**风云无便**：言时局不给予施展抱负的机会。词人所居的苏州是张士诚的辖区，张士诚政权混乱，故言。**风云**：局势。**黄鹄轻举**：谓远走高飞，建立功业。**“何事”三句**：言词人16岁作诗至《赠薛相士》诗已有十年时间，其间曾游历于北郭、青丘、越中一带，尚未安身立命。**“只恐”句**：陈登，三国人，字元龙，多豪气，身处江湖却有救世之意。此处言自己的退世之思怕为陈登笑话。此处反用其意。**故园鸡黍**：家乡丰盛的饭菜。喻乡人深厚的情谊。**关山**：泛指各种关隘。或言有《关山月》横吹曲名，多表现边塞士兵久戍不归和家人互伤离别的情感。

〖译　文〗

F. W. MOTE 译

"About Myself" by Gao Qi

Boundless ambition for fame! Scorn for bookish men[such as I am]!
What physiognomer ever predicted success for me?
But all my life my fierce will has driven me on; I blush to be compared with those ordinary persons.
The wine takes hold; heroic the talk,
My sword bolsters my proud spirit;
I compose a poem, in lines that startle the hearer.
But the winds are adverse; they still do not permit the great bird to soar aloft.
For what have I wondered alone through this dusty sphere?
North, South, East, West-ten years I've been a traveller.
I've feared only that the likes of Ch'en Teng would scorn me; therefore have I ignored my own chickens and millet patch.
The flute recalls distant mountains and passes; the wine brings back those days and months.
I turn aside, transfixed by thought.
I'm not yet old; why should my gleaming tears fall like rain?

5.2　眼儿媚(刘基)

萋萋芳草小楼西，云压雁声低。两行疏柳，一丝残照，万点鸦栖。
春山碧树秋重绿，人在武陵溪。无情明月，有情归梦，同到幽闺。

〖作品简介〗

此词咏闺中秋思。上片写楼头秋色。草绿原野，念游人之不归；雁唳长空，盼音书之莫至。依依衰柳，一抹斜阳，万点寒鸦，千山栖宿。下片写秋闺念远。秋日风物，凄凉萧瑟，况树又重绿，而游人滞留不归。绵绵相思，何时能已。眼前明月照空，魂梦遥牵。有情无情，并到幽闺。岑寂之感，更复何如。全词绵丽清雅，委婉多姿。

〖注 释〗

武陵溪：此用陶渊明《桃花源记》故事，借指爱人在远方。**归梦**：指远游人惦念家里的魂梦。

〖译 文〗

Robert Kotewall and Norman L. Smith 译

To "Eyes' Fascination" by Liu Chi

Lush is the misty grass to the west of the little tower;
Clouds are low, and the wild geese cry softly;
Two rows of wide-spaced willows,
One streak of fading sunlight,
A few specks of perching crows.

Vernal hills and green trees renew their Autumn
    verdure,
But he is at the Wu-ling Brook.
Loveless is the bright moon,
But loving is the dream that comes,
Together they enter my solitary chamber.

5.3 长相思(李攀龙)

秋风清，秋月明。叶叶梧桐槛外声。难教归梦成。砌蛩鸣，树鸟惊。塞雁行行天际横。偏伤旅客情。

〖作品简介〗

此词是一首抒写思乡的小令。上片起首三句，月明风清，秋色宜人，栏杆外梧桐叶被秋风吹动，发出阵阵轻响。下片为户外近景，传入耳中的是台阶旁蟋蟀的悲鸣，夜间寂静，树上栖息的鸟儿见月光而惊飞。仰首望天，映入眼帘的是大雁成行，横于天际。全词把极寻常的思乡之情，写得含蓄蕴藉、曲折动人，移情于景，借各种具体可感的意象把无形的思乡曲传出，文心细密，动人心弦。

〖注　释〗

槛：栏杆。砌蛩：台阶旁的蟋蟀。蛩：蟋蟀。塞雁：秋天雁从塞上飞回，故称。

〖译　文〗

Robert Kotewall and Norman L. Smith 译

To "Enduring Love" by Li P'an-lung

Autumn's wind is pure,
Autumn's moon is bright,
Leaf on leaf the Wu-t'ung tree rustles outside the
　　balcony;
Hard it is to build the dream of home.

On the steps the crickets chirp,
On the trees the birds flutter,
The frontier wild-geese, line upon line, breast the
　　horizon,
Set upon wounding the exile's heart.

5.4　临江仙(杨慎)

滚滚长江东逝水，浪花淘尽英雄。是非成败转头空。青山依旧在，几度夕阳红。

白发渔樵江渚上，惯看秋月春风。一壶浊酒喜相逢。古今多少事，都付笑谈中。

〖作品简介〗

此作乃一首咏史词，借叙述历史兴亡抒发人生感慨，豪放中有含蓄，高亢中有深沉。全词基调慷慨悲壮、意味无穷，但又有一种淡泊宁静的气氛，折射出高远的意境和深邃的人生哲理。本词作者杨慎(1488—1559年)，字用修，初号月溪、升庵，又号逸史氏，明代著名文学家，明代三才子之首，东阁大学士杨廷和之子。

【注　释】

淘尽：荡涤一空。**渔樵**：此处并非指渔翁、樵夫，联系前后文的语境应为动词：隐居。此处作名词，指隐居、不问世事的人。**渚(zhǔ)**：原意为水中的小块陆地，此处意为江岸边。**都付笑谈中**：在一些古典文学及音乐作品中，也有作"尽付笑谈中"。

【译　文】

(1) 黄新渠 译

To the Tune "Lin Jiang Xian"
(Tune: "Riverside Immortal") by Yang Shen (1488-1559)

East flows the mighty Yangtze River,
Its rolling waves have washed away all the heroes.
In a blink of an eye,
Our rights, wrongs, gains and loses are all in vain
However, green hills still remain as ever,
How often have we enjoyed the rosy setting sun?

A grey hair stands on this fishing bank alone,
He is so used to the spring wind and autumn moon,
It's a real joy of reunion over a pot of wine.
All things past and present,
Are retold with nothing but peals of laughter!

(2) 龚景浩 译

"Lin Jiang Xian (Ming)" by Yang Shen

The roaring Yangtze flows ever eastward,
Its waves scouring away all heroes.
Success or failure, right or wrong—
They do not seem to matter so much
Once your back is turned.
But the green mountains will be there still,

And how many sunsets will carry the glorious afterglow?

White-haired fishermen work the shoals;
They've seen so much of the spring breeze and autumn moon.
A jug of cheap wine to drink to our happy meeting:
So many momentous events, past and present,
Are bandied about with a laughter!

(3) 丰华瞻 译

"Linjiangxian"

The torrents of the Yangzi wash away heroes of yore,
Right or wrong, success or failure, all are no more.
Green hills and wide rivers remain the same,
How many times has the setting sun spread its flame!

Fishermen with white hair work along rivers and on isles,
Rowing their little boats leisurely for miles.
They carry bottles with liquor and drink at ease
Chatting about the past and smiling in the breeze.

(4) Moss Roberts 译

On and on the Great River rolls, racing east.
Of proud and gallant heroes its white-tops leave no trace,
As right and wrong, pride and fall turn all at once unreal.
Yet ever the green hills stay
To blaze in the west-waning day.

Fishers and woodmen comb the river isles.
White-crowned, they've seen enough of spring and autumn tide
To make good company over the wine jar,
Where many a famed event
Provides their merriment.

(5) 许渊冲 译

Wave on wave the long river eastward rolls away;
Gone are all heroes with its spray on spray.
Success or failure, right or wrong, all turn out vain;
Only green mountains still remain;
To see the setting sun's departing ray.

The white-haired fishermen sail on the stream with ease,
Accustomed to the autumn moon and vernal breeze.
A pot of wine in hand, they talk as they please.
How many things before and after
All melt into gossip and laughter!

5.5 梦江南(二十首)(柳如是)

一 人去也，人去凤城西。细雨湿将红袖意，新芜深与翠眉低，蝴蝶最迷离。

二 人去也，人去鹭鹚洲。菡萏结为翡翠恨，柳丝飞上钿筝愁。罗幕早惊秋。

三 人去也，人去画楼中。不是尾涎人散漫，何须红粉玉玲珑。端有夜来风。

四 人去也，人去小池台。道是情多还不是，若为恨少却教猜。一望损莓苔。

五 人去也，人去绿窗纱。赢得病愁输燕子，禁怜模样隔天涯。好处暗相遮。

六 人去也，人去玉笙寒。凤子啄残红豆小，雉媒骄拥亵香看。杏子是春衫。

七 人去也，人去碧梧阴。未信赚人肠断曲，却疑误我字同心。幽怨不须寻。

八 人去也，人去小棠梨。强起落花还瑟瑟，别时红泪有些些。门外柳相依。

九 人去也，人去梦偏多。忆昔见时多不语，而今偷悔更生疏。梦里自欢娱。

十 人去也，人去夜偏长。宝带乍温青骢意，罗衣轻试玉光凉。薇帐一条香。

十一　人何在，人在蓼花汀。炉鸭自沉香雾暖，春山争绕画屏深。金雀敛啼痕。

十二　人何在，人在小中亭。想得起来匀面后，知他和笑是无情。遮莫向谁生。

十三　人何在，人在月明中。半夜夺他金扼臂，殢人还复看芙蓉。心事好朦胧。

十四　人何在，人在木兰舟。总见客时常独语，更无知处在梳头。碧丽怨风流。

十五　人何在，人在绮筵时。香臂欲抬何处坠，片言吹去若为思。况是口微脂。

十六　人何在，人在石秋棠。好是捉人狂耍事，几回贪却不须长。多少又斜阳。

十七　人何在，人在雨烟湖。篙水月明春腻滑，舵楼风满睡香多。杨柳落微波。

十八　人何在，人在玉阶行。不是情痴还欲住，未曾怜处却多心。应是怕情深。

十九　人何在，人在画眉帘。鹦鹉梦回青獭尾，篆烟轻压绿螺尖。红玉自纤纤。

二十　人何在，人在枕函边。只有被头无限泪，一时偷拭又须牵。好否要他怜。

作品简介

此组小令是作者抒发自己回忆与心上人相依相恋的美好时光，表达了作者对往昔爱情生活的无限深情和眷恋。作者柳如是乃明清之际著名歌妓。陈寅恪先生曾撰巨著《柳如是别传》，对于其考核甚详，称其为“女侠，名姝，文宗，国士”。陈子龙在为她的《戊寅草》写的序中称她“灵娇绝世之人”。柳如是早期的词作长于抒写男女爱情，词意委婉曲折，感情深挚细腻，风格清丽婉约，有花间美人之态。这组《梦江南》词共二十首。前十首均以“人去也”起头，描写作者与陈子龙离别之苦，抒发别后的无限思念与孤寂；后十首均以“人何在”的疑问句开端，看似无奈的追问，实则是深情的回忆，并以此引发出作者对以往爱情生活点点滴滴的回忆。

注　释

红袖：原为女子所穿的红色衣袖，古人常用“红袖”代指美人，这里是指作者本人。
翠眉：用黛螺画的眉，色浅而艳。此处的“翠眉”令人联想到的不是欢笑舒展的双眉，而是因忧伤紧锁的起皱的眉头。**蝴蝶最迷离**：此句化用“庄周梦蝶”的典故和李商隐“庄生晓梦迷蝴蝶”诗句，表达出作者与陈子龙分别的无限伤痛与迷惘。**鹭鹚**[lù cí]**洲**：地名。**菡萏**[hàn dàn]：古人称未开的荷花为菡萏，即花苞。南唐李璟《摊破浣溪沙》：“菡萏香销翠叶残，西风愁起绿波间。”**何须红粉玉玲珑**：既然自己深爱的人不在身边，何必要打扮自己呢？**红粉**：古代女子化妆用的胭脂和白粉。**凤子啄残红豆小**：凤凰啄剩下的“红豆”是如此之小，而诗人的相思却无比之深远、广大。**红豆**：相思豆。王维诗《相思》：“红豆生南国，春来发几枝。”**红泪**：这里是指为爱情诗人流下的悲伤之泪。**炉鸭自沉香雾暖，春山争绕画屏深**：化用晏几道《浣溪沙》“床上银屏几点山。鸭炉香过琐窗寒”的词句。此二句的意思是：闺房香雾缭绕，温暖如春，美人黛眉，如画屏春山，妖娆妩媚。“**金雀敛啼痕**”句：女主人破涕为笑的欢娱情态。**金雀**：钗名，这里代指女性。白居易《长恨歌》：“花钿委地无人收，翠翘金雀玉搔头。”**敛啼痕**：化用元稹《瘴塞》“瘴塞巴山哭鸟悲，红妆少妇敛啼眉”的诗句。**红玉**：用红色宝石比喻美人。李贺诗《贵主征行乐》：“春营骑将如红玉。”**自纤纤**：形容诗人形单影只，顾影自怜，为爱情不堪憔悴。**枕函**：枕头。

〖译 文〗

Kang-i Sun Chang 译

Tune: “Dreaming of Southerland”
Thinking of Someone by Liu Shih(1618-1664)

1

He is gone,
Gone somewhere west of Feng Ch’eng.①
A thin rain dampens my red sleeves,
New weeds lie as deep as my jade brows are low,
The butterfly is most bewildered.②

2

He is gone,
Gone from the Isle of Egrets.
Lotus blossoms turn to emerald remorse,
Willow catkins rise to join the zither’s grief,
Behind the brocade curtain—the early autumn startles.

3

He is gone,

Gone from the painted chamber tower,
No longer lustrous and beautiful. I sit idle,
Why bother about rouge powder and jade hairpin?
Only the wind coming at night.③

4

He is gone,
Gone from the small water pavilion.
Would you say we "have not loved enough"?
Or that we "have little to regret"?
All I see is trodden moss.

5

He is gone,
Gone from the green window gauze.
All I gain is frail sickness. Lighter than a swallow,
Pitiful is my lone self, now that we are far apart.
Secretly we hide sweet memories in our hearts.

6

He is gone,
Gone, leaving the jade pipe cold.④
Phoenix pecked at the scattered tiny red beans,
Pheasants, joyfully embracing the censer, gazed at us,⑤
Apricot was the color of my spring dress.

7

He is gone,
Gone from the shadow of the green *wu-t'ung*⑥ tree.
I can't believe this has earned us a heartbreaking tune,
Still I wonder why our love has failed.
Whence this brooding grief? No need to look.

8

He is gone,
Gone from the small Crab-apple Hall.
I force myself to rise; the fallen petals are quivering,
A few red parting tears still remain,

Outside the door, willows leaning against one another.

9

He is gone,
Gone, yet dreams of him come even more often.
Recalling the past: our shared moments were mostly wordless,
But now I secretly regret the growing distance.
Only in dreams can I find self-indulgence.

10

He is gone,
Gone, and the nights are longer.
How can this jeweled belt warm my thoughts about the black steed?⑦
Gently putting on the silk robe in chill jade moonlight,
Behind the rosy curtain, a single wisp of incense.

11

Where was he?
On the Isle of Smartweed.
The duck-censer burning low, the fragrant smoke warm,
Spring mountains winding deeply in the painted screen,
The golden sparrow ceased to weep.

12

Where was he?
At the middle pavilion.
Recall once after washing his face,
His carefree laughter seemed so unconcerned—
Who knows for whom he smiled?

13

Where was he?
In the moonlight.
In the middle of the night, I clutched his priceless arm,
Lethargic, I looked at the lotus flowers again and again,
My inner sentiments, how hazy!

14

Where was he?
In the magnolia boat.
Often talking to herself when receiving guests,
Feeling more lost while combing her hair,
This beauty still broods over his charms.

15

Where was he?
At the magnificent banquet.
My perfumed arms fluttered up and down,
Words issued in song, like profound thoughts,
Chiefly from my faintly glossed lips.

16

Where was he?
At the Autumn Crab-apple Hall.
Fun was playing hide-and-seek,
Round after round, no need to linger for long.
Again, how many sunsets have gone by!

17

Where was he?
On the Lake of Misty Rain.
Water rippled by the bamboo oar, the moon shining bright in the lustrous and gentle spring,
Our storied boat filed with wind and daphne fragrance,
Willows caressing the delicate waves.

18

Where was he?
At the jade steps.
No fool for love, yet I wanted to stay,
Overly sensitive to any sign of indifference,
It must be that I feared love would run too deep.

19

Where was he?
Behind the curtain patterned with thrushes.
A parrot dream ends in a black otter's tail,
Incense smoke lingers on the tip of the green spiral censer,
Delicate were the pink jade fingers.

20

Where was he?
By my pillow side.
Nothing but endless tears at the quilt edge—
Wiping off secretly, but only inducing more,
How I yearn for his pity and love.

Liu Shih's beginnings are obscure. What we know for sure is that she became an accomplished courtesan and poet-painter while still in her teens, and many literati in the Chiang-nan area (south of the Yangtze) came to admire her literary achievements. That several portraits of her were made by Ming-Ch'ing literati painters is proof of her standing among her male contemporaries. She published her first collection of poems at the age twenty and enjoyed the reputation of being a courtesan of superb talent and beauty. Her intense love relationship with young poet Ch'en Tzu-lung (1608-1647) and her later marriage to the literary giant Ch'ien Ch'ien-yi (1582-1664) made her a legendary figure in the field of literature. Most important, her numerous love poems to Ch'en Tzu-lung—and for that matter, Ch'en's to her—engendered a whole new interest in the lyric, a genre characterized by the intensity of emotion. Since traditionally a proficiency in song lyrics was closely associated with the courtesan culture, Liu Shih, as might be expected, greatly influenced the late Ming revival of the lyric genre.

Liu Shih and Ch'en Tzu-lung's lyric poetics was clearly patterned on the late Ming notion of reciprocal love. Her numerous poetic exchanges with Ch'en—are framed as personal letters, telling the secrets of a passion felt by two equally talented poets. She was no longer a mere singer like the earlier courtesans, whose prime duty was song lyrics for men. As a poet herself, she has acquired a personal voice. In her perhaps most brilliant song-series, "Dreaming of Southland" (subtitle "Thinking of Soneone," twenty poems), she tells a moving story of her relationship with Ch'en, narrating her struggles with love's agonized passion.

① Most likely refers to the hometown of the late Ming scholar-official and loyalist Ch'en Tzu-lung, with whom the poet was closely associated over a long period of time.

② A reference to Chuang Tzu's famous dream experience.

③ This song alludes to one of Li Shang-yin's love poems: "Last night's stars, last night's winds/ By the wall of painted chamber tower, east of the hall of cassia."

④ This line alludes to Li Chin's(916-961) line: "In the small chamber the song of the jade flute has become cold." By this allusion, Liu Shih's line is a subtle reference to the chamber in the Southern Villa where she lived with Ch'en Tzu-lung during the spring and summer of 1635.

⑤ The pheasant designs of the incense-burner.

⑥ *Wu-t'ung*: we-together.

⑦ The "jeweled belt" might be gift from Ch'en Tzu-lung. The "black steed," a symbol of the male lover, is metaphorically connected with Ch'en here.

5.6 眼儿媚(梁清标)

日射晴窗静无哗。风袅柳枝斜。有人深院，凝妆独坐，门掩桃花。
追思往日重回首，心事付啼鸦。隔墙笑语，却疑春色，只在邻家。

〖作品简介〗

此词全名为《眼儿媚·春昼》，收录于作者的《棠村词》。作者梁清标(1620—1691年)，字玉立，号棠村、蕉林、苍岩，直隶真定(今河北省正定县)人，明崇祯十六年进士，清顺治元年补翰林院庶吉士，授编修。累迁至兵、刑、户各部尚书。晋保和殿大学士卒。著有《蕉林诗集》《棠村词》等。

〖注 释〗

哗：人多声杂，乱吵。凝妆[níng zhuāng]：盛装，华丽的妆扮。

〖译 文〗

Robert Kotewall and Norman L. Smith 译

Spring Day
To "Eye's Fascination"

The sun's rays shoot through the shining window;
　　there is peace and not a sound.
In the light breeze the willow-branches bend.

There is one in the seclusion of her chamber,
In all her finery sitting alone,
With the door closed against the peach-blossoms.

Her memory is of bygone days as she turns her mind back;
Her heart's secret has been given to the cawing rooks.
Beyond the wall there is laughter and chatter.
Can it be that Spring's colours are only for her neighbor?

5.7 生查子(彭孙遹)

薄醉不成乡，转觉春寒重。枕席有谁同？夜夜和愁共。
梦好恰如真，事往翻如梦。起立悄无言，残月生西弄。

〖作品简介〗

这首词自写欲求梦而先借酒力，但薄醉仍难入梦，一直写到梦中和梦醒，意境幽清，情致婉然。

〖注　释〗

乡：指醉乡。西弄：西巷。

〖译　文〗

龚景浩 译

"Sheng Zha Zi(Qing)"[①]
Peng Sun Yu

Light intoxication hath not its own domain.
Coming out, the chill of spring is all pervasive.
Nobody on my pillows has lain,
Each night I bed down with thoughts pensive.

Dreams, if they be good, are virtual reality;
Reality, once past, is but a vanishing dream.
I rise and stand alone silent,
As a waning moon shines on West Lane.

① Qing Dynasty—1644-1911 A. D.

5.8　蝶恋花（纳兰性德）

又到绿杨曾折处，
不语垂鞭，
踏遍清秋路。
衰草连天无意绪，
雁声远向萧关去。

不恨天涯行役苦，
只恨西风，
吹梦成今古。
明日客程还几许，
沾衣况是新寒雨。

【作品简介】

此词倾吐行役之苦的同时，也流露出怀古伤今的情怀，表达了作者的惆怅之情。全词凄凉惆怅，上片写“衰草连天”的清秋景，景中有词人的离愁别恨；下片抒发“天涯行役”的怨恨情，情中有凄凉的西风寒雨。

【注　释】

绿杨曾折：古人在送别时，有折柳枝相赠的习俗。**不语垂鞭**：引用唐温庭筠《晓别》诗：“上阳宫里钟初动，不语垂鞭上柳堤。”**垂鞭**：放马慢行。**衰**[shuāi]**草**：指秋天的草。**意绪**：心绪，心情。南齐王融《咏琵琶》：“丝中传意绪，花里寄春情。”**萧关**：关口名。在今甘肃平凉县，古为西北边地要塞。**行役**[yì]：指因公务而长期在外跋涉。**成今古**：谓今与古距离遥远，实为感叹光阴易逝。**几许**：多少。

【译 文】

John Turner 译

Tune："Butterflies in Love with Flowers"

Here where we parted and did break
Green poplar sprigs that each should take
For true love's sake,
—Wordless, riding-crop limp trailing,
Again those well-remembered ways
I tread, in the clear autumn rays;
Fronting a world of blear grass, feeling failing:
And far unto the Frontier Pass wild geese are wailing.

'Tis not the bitterness of ever wending
On pilgrimage unending:
No, 'tis the West Wind's moaning makes me sorrow,
Which all our dreams must blow
Into the nothingness of Evermore.
Yet farther, ever farther, on the morrow
The wanderer must go,
Dress drenched, afresh to face wet winter frore.

5.9 蝶恋花(纳兰性德)

今古河山无定据，画角声中，牧马频来去。满目荒凉谁可语？西风吹老丹枫树。

从前幽怨应无数。铁马金戈，青冢黄昏路。一往情深深几许？深山夕照深秋雨。

【作品简介】

这是一首出塞词，上片写眼前之景，景象广袤空阔、荒凉凄冷，情感凄婉哀怨，下片抒发了词人报国志向无法实现的幽怨，景象气势磅礴、纵横驰骋，情感婉约深沉。

〖注 释〗

无定据：无定，无准。意谓自古以来，权力纷争不止，江山变化无定。一作“无定数”。**从前幽怨应无数**：一作“幽怨从前何处诉”。**铁马金戈**：谓战争。《旧五代史·李袭吉传》李克用与朱温书云：“岂谓运由奇特，谤起奸邪，毒手尊拳，交相于暮夜；金戈铁马，蹂践于明时。”辛弃疾《永遇乐·京口北固亭怀古》：“想当年，金戈铁马，气吞万里如虎。”**青冢**：用汉代王昭君出塞之典事。《汉书·匈奴传下》：“元帝以后宫良家子王嫱，字昭君赐单于。”昭君死后葬于南匈奴之地(即今内蒙古呼和浩特)，人称“青冢”。

〖译 文〗

龚景浩 译

“Die Lian Hua (Qing)”

Nalan Xing De

From of old to the present
There are no certain boundaries:
Amid the sound of painted bugles,
The nomads' horses swept back and forth.
A wasteland as far as the eye can see—
Who can you talk to?
The west wind has aged the maple tree.

Cases of past suffering would be numerous:
Metal spears and iron horses;
New graves by dusky roads.
Loving-feelings running deep—how deep do they go?
Like the evening glow, deep in the mountains—
And like late, late autumn rain.

5.10 如梦令(纳兰性德)

万帐穹庐人醉，星影摇摇欲坠，归梦隔狼河，又被河声搅碎。还睡、还睡，解道醒来无味。

【作品简介】

此词乃作者于康熙二十一年(1682 年)春扈从圣驾东巡时所作，描写了千古壮丽的大境界，表现了深沉的思乡之情，以及作者对官场生活的厌烦。

【注　释】

如梦令：相传为后唐庄宗自制曲，中有“如梦，如梦，残月落花烟重”句，因改今名。**穹庐**：圆形的毡帐。**“归梦”**二句：言家乡远隔狼河，归梦不成。纵然做得归梦，河声彻夜，又把梦搅醒。**狼河**：白狼河，即今大凌河，在辽宁省西部。**解道**：知道。

【译　文】

(1) David McCraw 译

Tune: “As If in a Dream” by Nara Singde

In a myriad arched yurts, the men are drunk.
Stars' reflections quiver, about to drop.
　　My homing dream, sundered by Wolf River①,
Is then shaken to bits by the river's roar.
　　Back to sleep!
　　Back to sleep!
Well I know that in waking there's no savor.

① The White Wolf River flows east from White Mountain (near Ling-yuan, Liaoning) into the Pohai Sea.

(2) Alan Ayling and Duncan Mackintosh 译

To the Tune-title “As in a Dream, a Short Lyric” by Nalan Singde

Ten thousand felted tents filled with exhausted men;
Flicker and fade of stars about to set.
I was travelling home and trapped by the Wolf-River—that dream;
And again the river's clamour has broken it!

Let me sleep on,
Let me sleep on;
Awake, I know the savour of life will be gone.

(3) 杨宪益、戴乃迭 译

To the Tune of "Ru Meng Ling" by Nalan Xingde

The vast encampment is locked in drunken slumber.
The stars whirl and whirl, as if to crash to earth.
Dreams of return blocked and crashed by the Bailang River.
Sleep on! Sleep on!
To wake would be too doleful and too drear.

5.11　长相思(纳兰性德)

山一程，水一程，身向榆关那畔行，夜深千帐灯。
风一更，雪一更，聒碎乡心梦不成，故园无此声。

【作品简介】

这首词描写了将士在外对故乡的思念，抒露着情思深苦的绵长心境。全词采用自然真切、简朴清爽的白描语句，写得天然浑成，毫无雕琢之处，却格外真切感人。

【注　释】

长相思：唐教坊曲，双翅小令。又名《双红豆》。**程**：道路，路程，山一程，水一程，即山长水远。**榆关**：即今山海关，在今河北秦皇岛东北。**那畔**：即山海关的另一边，指身处关外。**千帐灯**：皇帝出巡临时住宿的行帐的灯火。千帐言军营之多。**更**：旧时一夜分五更，每更大约两小时。风一更，雪一更，即言整夜风雪交加。**聒**[guō]：声音嘈杂，这里指风雪声。**故园**：故乡，这里指北京。**此声**：指风雪交加的声音。

【译　文】

(1) Alan Ayling and Duncan Mackintosh 译

The mountain, a march;

The river, a march;
To the uplands and over the Yü-kuan pass I go.
Countless lamps in the tented darkness glow.

A night-watch of wind,
A night-watch of snow—
And a clamour that shatters my sleepless home-sick heart.
I know a garden where it is not so.

(2) 杨宪益、戴乃迭 译

To the Tune of "Chang Xiang Si" by Nalan Xingde

Over mountains, over rivers
We plod to the Shanhai Pass.
A myriad of fires light the night
From our camp on the river bank.
The shrieking snowstorm breaks my dream
Of my peaceful, tranquil home.

(3) Christopher Kelen and Han Lili 译

Marching

climbing a mountain
crossing water
i was marching for the Yu Guan frontier

midnight
in thousands of homes
lamps lighted

one night of wind
one night of snow

these things
mar my dream

of a homeland
where i knew
no such sounds

5.12　好了歌(曹雪芹)

世人都晓神仙好，只有功名忘不了！
古今将相在何方？荒冢一堆草没了！
世人都晓神仙好，只有金银忘不了！
终朝只恨聚无多，及到多时眼闭了！
世人都晓神仙好，只有娇妻忘不了！
君生日日说恩情，君死又随人去了！
世人都晓神仙好，只有儿孙忘不了！
痴心父母古来多，孝顺儿孙谁见了？

【作品简介】

该作品乃《红楼梦》中的经典诗词，为小说中的跛足道人所作，表现了作者现实主义和宗教思想。

【注　释】

荒冢[huāng zhǒng]：荒凉的坟墓。

【译　文】

(1) 杨宪益、戴乃迭 译

All Good Things Must End

All men long to be immortals
Yet to riches and rank each aspires;
The great ones of old, where are they now?
Their graves are a mass of briars.
All men long to be immortals
Yet silver and gold they prize

And grub for money all their lives
Till death seal up their eyes.
All men long to be immortals
Yet dote on the wives they've wed,
Who swear to love their husband evermore
But remarry as soon as he's dead.
All men long to be immortals
Yet with getting sons won't have done.
Although fond parents are legion,
Who ever saw a really filial son?

(2) David Hawkes 译

Won-Done Song

Men all know that salvation should be won,
But with ambition won't have done, have done.
Where are the famous ones of days gone by?
In grass graves they lie now, everyone.
Men all know that salvation should be won,
But with their riches won't have done, have done.
Each day they grumble they've not made enough.
When they've enough, it's goodnight everyone!
Men all know that salvation should be won,
But with their loving wives they won't have done.
The darlings every day protect their love:
But once your're dead, they are off with another one.
Men all know that salvation should be won,
But with children won't have done, have done.
Yet though of parents fond there is no lack.
Of grateful children saw I ne'er a one.

5.13 浣溪沙(王国维)

本事新词定有无。这般绮语太胡卢。灯前肠断为谁书。隐几窥君新制作,背灯数妾旧欢娱:区区情事总难符。

【作品简介】

此词是作者对自己无聊填词的一种深深的调侃，“区区情事总难符”是情感忱挚之人方有的感悟。

【注 释】

本事：原事，实事。**绮语**：佛家把藻饰不实之辞称为绮语。后来也称描摹男女私情的诗文文字为绮语。**胡卢**：“胡芦提”之省。这里有可笑、笑话之意。

【译 文】

Stephen Owen 译

Does something real lie behind
　　the words in your new songs?
Fancy phrases such as these
　　can make you want to laugh.
“Broken-hearted in lamplight”—
　　now who did you write that for?

I lean on the desk and peer around
　　at recent compositions,
then turn off the light and reckon up
　　joys known in the past—
trivial passions of the heart,
　　and nothing corresponds.

5.14 浣溪沙(王国维)

已落芙蓉并叶凋，半枯萧艾过墙高。
日斜孤馆易魂销。
坐觉清秋归荡荡，眼看白日去昭昭。
人间争度渐长宵。

【作品简介】

此词乃作者于1908年秋作于北京，所表述的情怀虽然悲秋然而却不落俗套。作品以诗法入词，骨格硬朗。上阕写景中有寓意，芙蓉萎谢，萧艾得时，正是时政变革的写照；下阕就展开对个人不遇为导向的主旋律，进而抒发对整个人间的感悲。

【注 释】

芙蓉：荷花的别名。**萧艾**：蒿类植物名。即艾蒿。《楚辞》中常以喻小人。如《离骚》："何昔日之芳草兮，今直为此萧艾也？"**孤馆**：孤寂的客舍。**清秋**：明净爽朗的秋天。**白日去昭昭**：白日指太阳、阳光。**昭昭**：指明亮。**去昭昭**：意谓公然地离去。**争度**：怎么度过。**渐长宵**：一天比一天长的夜晚。

【译 文】

Jiaosheng Wang 译

Tune："Sand of Silk-Washing Brook"

Faded hibiscus and its leaves
Wilt side by side
Artemisia that stood high above the wall
Now half-decayed
Under the slanting sun's gaze
Someone in a lonely lodge
Is prone to heart-rending sorrow.

Sit and you sense the broad sleep
Of clear returning autumn;
Watch and you are dazzled by
The brilliance of the departing sun
How can the human world ever
Live out these lengthening nocturnal hours?

5.15 点绛唇(王国维)

屏却相思，近来知道都无益。不成抛掷，梦里终相觅。

醒后楼台，与梦俱明灭。西窗白，纷纷凉月，一院丁香雪。

【作品简介】

此词抒写相思缠绕的惆怅心情，委婉曲折，新颖别致。

【注 释】

屏却：放弃。**"醒后楼台"**二句：谓梦中虚构的空中楼阁，醒后还若明若灭，隐约可见。**纷纷凉月**：形容丁香院落的月色。杜甫诗有："缔衣挂萝薜，凉月白纷纷。"

【译 文】

龚景浩 译

"Dian Jiang Chun (Qing)"

Wang Guo Wei

Suppressing my lovesick pining?
Lately I learnt 'tis no good.
Should I then cast it overboard?
But I would still be looking for it in my dreams.

The halls and terraces after I awake
Fade away and reappear with my dreams.
The west casement shines white,
Lit by a desolate cool moon.
Outside lies a yard full of white lilacs like snow.

参 考 文 献

龚景浩．英译中国古词精选[Z]．北京：商务印书馆，1999.

辜正坤．元曲一百五十首[Z]．北京：北京大学出版社，2004.

林语堂．林语堂英译诗文选：东坡笔意[M]．北京：外语教学与研究出版社，2015.

吕淑湘．中诗英译比录[Z]．上海：上海外语教育出版社，1980.

许渊冲．汉英对照唐宋词三百首[Z]．石家庄：河北人民出版社，2003.

许渊冲．精选宋词与宋画：英汉对照[Z]．北京：五洲传播出版社，2005.

许渊冲．苏轼诗词选 [Z]．长沙：湖南人民出版社，2007.

许渊冲．唐宋词一百首[Z]．北京：中国对外翻译出版公司，1991.

许渊冲．元曲三百首[Z]．北京：中国对外翻译出版公司，2009.

张炳星．英译中国古典诗词名篇[Z]．北京：中华书局，2010.

Bullett, Gerald. *Five Seasons of a Golden Year: A Chinese Pastoral*[M]. Cambridge & New York: Cambridge University Press, 1946.

Bynner, Witter. *The Jade Mountain: A Chinese Anthology*[M]. New York: Knopf, 1931.

Cao, Xueqing and Gao E. *A Dream of Red Mansions*[M]. Translated by Yang, Xianyi & Gladys Yang. Beijing: Foreign Language Press, 2015.

Cooper, Arthur R. V. *Li Po and Tu Fu*[M]. Harmondsworth, Eng.: Penguin Books, 1973.

Cranmer-Byng, L. *A Lute of Jade* <cranmer-byng. thefreelibrary. com/Lute-of-Jade>.

Davis, A. R., ed. *The Penguin Book of Chinese Verse*[M]. Harmondsworth: Penguin Books, 1962.

Egan, Ronald C. *The Literary Works of Ou-yang Hsiu (1007-72)* [M]. Cambridge: Cambridge University Press, 1984.

Fletcher, W. J. B. *Gems of Chinese Verse*[M]. Shanghai: Commercial Press Ltd., 1919. Internet Archive. 23 Nov. 2007 < www. archive. org/details/gemsofchineseever00fletiala>.

Fletcher, W. J. B. *More Gems of Chinese Poetry*. Shanghai: Commercial Press Ltd., 1919. Hong Kong University Libraries Electronic Resources. 23 Nov. 2007. <ebook.

lib. hku. hk/CADAL/B31396227/>.

Hart, Henry H. *The Charcoal Burner, and Other Poems; Original Translations from the Poetry of the Chinese.* Norman: University of Oklahoma Press, 1974.

Hawks, David. *The Story of the Stone: a Chinese Novel in Five Volumes.* Harmondsworth: Penguin Books, 1973-1986; Bloomington: Indiana University Press, 1979-1987.

Liu, James J. Y. *The Art of Chinese Poetry*[M]. Chicago: The University of Chicago Press, 1962.

Liu, James J. Y. *Essentials of Chinese Literary Art*[M]. North Scituate, Mass.: Duxbury Press, 1979.

Liu, Shih Shun. *One Hundred and One Chinese Poems*[M]. Hong Kong, China: *Hong Kong University Press*, 1967.

Liu, Wu-chi & Irving Yucheng Lo, eds. *Sunflower Splendor: Three Thousand Years of Chinese Poetry*[M]. Bloomington: Indiana University Press, 1975.

Mair, Victor H. *The Shorter Columbia Anthology of Traditional Chinese Literature*[Z]. New York: Columbia University press, 2000.

Mair, Victor H., ed. *The Columbia Anthology of Traditional Chinese Literature*[Z]. New York: Columbia University Press, 1994.

Owen, Stephen. *The Great Age of Chinese Poetry: The High T'ang*[M]. New Haven: Yale University Press, 1981.

Owen, Stephen, ed. *An Anthology of Chinese Literature: Beginnings to 1911*[M]. New York: W. W. Norton, 1996.

Rexroth, Kenneth. *One Hundred Poems from the Chinese*[M]. New York: New Directions, 1965.

Schmidt, J. D. *Stone Lake: The Poetry of Fan Chengda*[M]. Cambridge, U. K.: Cambridge University Press, 1992.

Watson, Burton. *The Columbia Book of Chinese Poetry—From Early Times to the Thirteenth Century*[M]. New York: Columbia University Press, 1984.

Watson, Burton. *The Columbia Book of Chinese Poetry*[M]. New York: Columbia University Press, 1984.

Watson, Burton. *The Selected Poems of Du Fu*[M]. New York: Columbia University Press, 2002.

Weinberger, Eliot, ed. *The New Directions Anthology of Classical Chinese Poetry*[M]. New York: New Directions Pub. Corp., 2003.

Yang, Xianyi & Gladys Yang. *Poetry and Prose of the Tang and Song*[M]. Beijing, China: Chinese Literature, 1984.

Yip, Wai-lim. *Chinese Poetry—Major Modes and Genres*[Z]. Bekerley, Los Angeles and London: University of California Press, 1976.